The Orb's Gift from Heaven

The Orb's Gift from Heaven

E.A. STARK

BURCH Publishing

Those we love, who have now passed on,
their spirit is here - they have not gone.
Still in our hearts, never far away,
keeping watch over every moment of every day.
Forever unseen, sadly not whispering a word,
but if you have faith and believe, their voice can be heard.
Ask a detailed question. Look for blessed signs.
Attached to nature is how their spirit binds.
When least expected, never knowing what you'll see,
what an unforgettable experience it will be.
Upon receiving a response, something you've longed to hear,
their message is followed by an abundance of tears.
With little doubt, certain they communicate too,
all at once, you'll know what to do.
Remember the love that each of you shared,
from that moment on; you'll never be scared.
For our loved ones, watch over us day and night.
Thankfully, we are never far from their sight.

- E.A.Stark -

Printed in the United States of America
First Printing: October 2022
Ingram Spark / Burch Publishing
ISBN-978-1-7771124-4-8

The Orb's Gift from Heaven
is dedicated to the spiritual orbs that watch over every one of us.
You never know who is hovering outside your front door.

January
Chicago, Illinois

Faith is to believe what you do not see; the reward of faith is to see what you believe.

—Saint Augustine

"What do you have for me today?" Evily Landy curiously whispered while sitting in her spacious study, all bundled up in layers.

Surrounded by three walls of shelves covered in books, with drapes drawn closed, she intentionally dimmed her monitor to darken the room. Just the flame from a single pillar candle provided the only light. Patiently waiting for her guests to arrive, she was disappointed at the lack of blessed signs. While scanning the space and praying for protection, the air was very still - almost eerie.

"Maybe my connection isn't strong enough?" she questioned with a hint of doubt.

Expelling a deep cleansing breath, she changed her mindset and thought positively. That is when the candle flickered. Her heart raced at the sight of it. They were close. Concentrating on the flame, moving about erratically, it suddenly stopped, stood as straight as a pin, and then extinguished.

"Well, this is new," she mumbled, unafraid to venture outside the norm, not knowing what to expect from them now.

Barely able to see a thing, her senses heightened. Out of the darkness, a tiny spark ignited. Mesmerized by its pure brilliance, hovering mid-air, it slowly got brighter. Within seconds, more followed, raining down in unison, causing a prickly sensation to cascade over her body and quickly spread into her hands and feet. One after another, a flood of faint translucent orbs arrived and took their places, floating inches from the coffered ceiling. The twinkling lights gravitated to them like stars orbiting a galaxy of planets. Shimmering, flowing like a river overhead, the presence of so many brought a deep chill to the air, making her shiver. Thankful to be dressed warmly, she smiled. Every time she witnessed this miracle, it never ceased to amaze her. There was an unsurpassed feeling of peace and love. It was absolutely beautiful and almost addictive.

The misty orbs darted chaotically from side to side, desperate to be heard. Their movements created a breeze that caressed the author's face. Listening to the voices of many souls, each had a story to tell. Their pleas resembled the sounds of a million radios playing simultaneously, causing an array of emotions to surface.

"How can I choose only one?" she said.

Her heart went out to every spiritual visitor. They always appeared for a reason. Some had unfinished business, while others had departed without warning. Either way, the families left behind were forced to mourn their passing. Most had questions that nobody could answer. That is why the orbs came in search of Evily. She created a conduit linking them to this world. It was the only way to forward messages to their loved ones and grant closure. In essence, she was their lifeline.

The confident woman sat in her chair, exhibiting perfect posture, prepared for anything. Used to writing blindly, her eyes fell shut when she established a solid connection with a particular spirit vying for attention. Her name was Janie. Zeroing in on the woman's heavenly voice, a series of fuzzy images followed. While their bond became stronger - the pictures crisper, she could not ignore the profound feeling of grief and loss. With fingers positioned on the keyboard, she started recording the visions presented like a movie in her mind. The tragic tale included not only the woman but also her baby girl. Both had passed within hours of each other. Understanding their complicated situation, Evily wept as she typed. Overwhelmed by what Janie conveyed, she felt every ounce of her pain.

Immersed in the words flowing freely without reservation, unable to control the emotions radiating from her body, she suddenly sensed a negative shift in the room. A bone-chilling shiver followed when the first evil entity made its presence known. Stopping, not moving a muscle, she knew it had pierced the veil - the thin layer that stands between us and the spiritual realm. Alert, closing her eyes tightly not to make visual contact, the unwelcome visitors infused the air with the scent of sulfur.

"They can't hurt you. They can't hurt you. They can't hurt you," Evily quietly repeated, immune to their presence.

Hell-bent on swaying her focus, the villainous creatures hissed horrific things in her right ear - words meant to enchant, tempt, and lure their prey, frightening them to the brink of absolute terror.

Heart beating uncontrollably, Evily continued to whisper, "They can't hurt you. You are protected. They can't hurt you."

Her hands shook while they hovered over the keyboard. Weighted down, needing to concentrate, Evily stayed very still, almost in a zombie-like state. Over the years, through trial and error, she discovered that these fiends were not only drawn to fear and suffering, sadness, and despair but also fed off it. Forced into a spiritual battle between good and evil, she sharpened her abilities to overpower the growling and gnashing of teeth. Courageously exuding unparalleled strength, the faithful mother of two persevered and remained fully engaged in what Janie was sharing from the afterlife. Ignoring the evil entities, she slowly continued to type the words told to her. Page after page, replacing grief and sadness with the feeling of joy and love, the emotions doused the creepy apparition's appetite enough for them to vanish. Aware of her triumph, she cautiously opened one eye for a brief moment to confirm they were gone, then concentrated on the task at hand.

Janie stayed by her side for several hours, relaying an abundance of information. Trying to keep up, Evily transcribed every word. But some details were withheld. The orb explained that she would reveal more in due time. For now, the rest spilled effortlessly onto the faint screen. In the coming weeks, the writer would infuse fictional elements into the existing chapters, and the messages Janie shared would be weaved in seamlessly. The process was long and tedious but always worth the trouble. Once published and released, fate would take over and find the one person meant to read it. In this case, that person was Janie's husband. The information it concealed would ultimately change his life forever.

By late afternoon, only a few souls lingered. They could see Evily was now mentally and physically drained. Each departed, bidding her a blessed evening. Janie was the last to leave, and I assured her that she would return soon. In an instant, everything went quiet. Alone, the writer sat back in her chair and appreciated the peacefulness until the Westminster chime bellowed from the adjacent living room's grand-father clock.

"Is it that time already?" she questioned, double-checking her phone.

The six low-toned bells echoed in succession. With a final click of the mouse, Evily activated the printer and quickly produced the new draft in an orderly manner. Tidying up the stack of paper, tapping its edge on the desk, she was confident about meeting the proposed publishing deadline. Janie's request required at least seven months of work. She wanted the book finished and on shelves by mid-July. No earlier. No later. That was made quite clear. Regardless of this stipulation, Evily was up to the challenge and agreed to help without question.

Removing the extra layers of clothing that kept her warm all day, she stood on her feet and walked over to the window. Flinging open the drapes, the pretty middle-aged woman reached her arms above her head. Bending from left to right, she stretched and looked outside. Darkness had engulfed the city. The cul-de-sac in front of their house looked cold and stark, devoid of people as a few lazy snowflakes caught the beams of light cascading from the street lamps along the curb.

"The calm before the storm," she intuitively muttered before leaving the study with a dainty teacup resting upon a matching saucer in one hand and her cell phone in the other.

Moving past the dining room, captivated by Janie's endearing story, she found it difficult not to dwell on some of the entrusted details. Most of which could never be unseen and unheard. It seemed the conversation today resonated more than usual. Strangely, in tune with the spirit's soul, Evily clutched her heart. She envied the orb's deeply rooted love for her husband. They were separated in death but remained very much connected. Janie was determined to save him from something, but it wasn't clear what that entailed or why.

"How very rare to witness such a bond between two people. This infinite devotion that transcends beyond the grave." Smiling tearfully, she repeated, "Beyond the Grave. Yes, that title is perfect."

Convinced what she wrote had intricately knitted into the fabric of her being, she moved through the hallowed halls of her large Forest Glen home. The house was quiet in the absence of her teenage children. Still reeling from the visitation, the author struggled to return to reality and leave her work behind. Sometimes, it took hours to disconnect from the imaginary world she'd been immersed in all day. It was a process that was easier said than done. For some reason, this time, every thought kept gravitating toward the woman's husband. Alive and well, having suffered so much, the man felt abandoned when his wife passed. Able to experience his pain, Evily started connecting the dots and stopped at the entrance to the great room. Things were beginning to make sense.

Is that why the little orb came in search of me? Are these stories connected? She silently questioned, drawing parallels between the two incidents.

Lost in thought, she broke from that analytic state, realizing how late it was. Needing to change gears from author to mother, she bypassed the kitchen island and contemplated what to make for dinner, knowing her children would be famished when they got home from their after-school activities. Short on time, she ordered a few of Graziano's wood-fired pizzas and salads. Upon pressing send, the restaurant confirmed delivery within the hour.

Reaching the beverage counter displaying a vast assortment of coffee and tea, the mother of two gathered her long, wavy, light-brown hair from her shoulders and neatly let it fall along her back. Wishing she had an elastic handy to secure it in a messy bun, Evily turned on the kettle to boil some water and peered out the window into the back garden. It seemed so lifeless in the dead of winter. A layer of snow had covered the beautiful pool, concealing its location. Saddened by the long, dark days, she wished she would have enjoyed the awe-inspiring sunset that evening. Briefly recalling a sliver of the orangey glow creeping through the gap in the drapes an hour before, she was sure she missed a pretty one.

While listening to the water boil, she received a sudden notification that disturbed the peaceful moment. The phone screen brightened, illuminating the space. Pulling the black-framed glasses down from the top of her head to read the weather bulletin, Evily perused the warning, updating Chicago residents of the incoming storm.

"Just as I predicted," she smiled.

The alert warned of a significant snowfall expected to inundate the city over the next several hours, a tell-tale sign of the harsh January weather on the way. With glasses perched on the end of her nose, still feeling chilly, she tugged on the cozy polar fleece wrap to tighten it around her shoulders. Desperate for a soothing cup of tea, Evily picked a new bag from the nearby canister when the kettle beeped. Upon closing the lid, she heard a faint noise in the foyer.

Assuming it was one of the children, she said, "Hello?"

Her voice traveled through the main floor. Not receiving a response, Evily stopped and listened. About to pour the boiling water into the cup, that familiar shiver rolled down her spine, causing her to pause. The hair stood on her neck when the room's temperature plummeted drastically. Soon, goosebumps spread into her arms and legs. Her breath was clearly visible, floating as in the dead of winter before the peculiar tingling reached her hands and feet. Drawn to the covered front porch again for the second time, she immediately dropped everything and hurried down the hallway to grab her coat and boots from the closet, quite fearful of what could be lurking outside in the darkness. Those who see beyond this world know what hides in the shadows.

As a child, she often caught sight of monstrous creatures prowling in the night. At times, black, white, or grey misty figures appeared in her peripheral vision, while other black-cloaked beings with crimson or amber eyes stoically stood at the foot of her bed to watch her sleep. Some patiently waited for her to fall into a moment of vulnerable weakness, especially on gloomy days. Aware of this, young Evily Landy knew she was different. Strong in her faith, it thankfully made her untouchable. But daily, these experiences strengthened her bond with the spiritual realm and earned a level of trust. Something very much expected for a soul more angelically heightened than demonically charged.

Ready to ward off the bitter cold, dressed warmly, with a hat and mittens in tow, anticipation took over when she walked out the door. Whoever it was, their presence was strong. Greeted by lazy snowflakes falling from the sky, the winds were calm. Nervous, she removed the winter cover from one of the chairs, angled stylishly on either side of a decorative table by the window. All alone, lighting the candle inside the black lantern, willing to wait unwearyingly, she had a seat while the sounds of the city cascaded over the house. Rhythmically bouncing her feet, trying to stay warm, it was hard to block out the constant hum of traffic and the odd emergency siren wailing in the distance. But the gifted woman remained quiet and closed her eyes. Clearing her mind, filtering out all the unwanted noise, and controlling her emotions, Evily created the peaceful environment she needed. In minutes, she knew the spirit was close. Her eyes drifted open upon hearing a child giggle with delight. Instinctively looking up, a small white misty orb approached, playfully bouncing about, unable to stay still. But this time, a larger, more stable orb followed right behind her.

Happy to see the tiny soul, Evily whispered, "Good evening, little one. So we meet again. Who did you bring with you?"

Easily connecting with the adult spirit accompanying the little girl, Evily smiled and said, "Welcome back, Janie."

1

Seven Months Later
Wednesday, July 24th
Bel Air, California

The highest form of love is to be the protector of another person's solitude. ~ Rainer Maria Rilke

"Isn't this being a tad impulsive? I mean, what are you going to say to her?" Sean Bradley's assistant, Max, asked while standing in his boss's bedroom doorway, watching him atrociously pack a suitcase on the end of the bed.

"Not sure. I'm just going to confront her and ask why she wrote it - who her sources were," Sean replied with uncertainty while dipping in and out of his custom closet at a frantic pace.

A list of repercussions flooded Max's mind. "You need to be careful. You don't want to cause a scene and bring about negative press. Especially now."

"I don't care. I need to know everything, and I intend to get answers." The actor was livid, his face red with anger and his expression quite stern.

"How do you think she will react?" Max asked, realizing the woman was about to meet the not-so-nice Sean Bradley. The man who tried so desperately to keep his private life out of the spotlight year after year. The protective man who would defend himself and his family at all costs. He wouldn't want to be in her shoes right now.

The Hollywood star fired some clothes into his suitcase. Appalled by the disarray, Max pulled each one out and folded them neatly.

"You know, I don't care what she thinks or how she'll react. The story she wrote is about my life. It wasn't her story to tell. Those were personal details I wanted to stay private. She had no right!" Sean bellowed, increasingly enraged with every word that escaped his mouth. "You've got me booked in at the Godfrey, correct?"

"Yes," Max replied studiously before passing along the updated information his boss requested. "In checking her social media pages, she and her children arrived in Boston yesterday. They also had dinner at the Artisan Bistro last night."

Sean paused in the middle of the room. "Wait? She has kids?"

"Yes. Two. It seems a teenage boy and girl," Max rattled off, uninterested, trying to recall his last train of thought. "Where was I? Oh, yes. The Artisan Bistro is in the Ritz Carlton. It's on the same street as your hotel. I assume that's where she's staying. Are you sure you don't want a driver while you're there?" Max posed, saying under his breath, "Like flying commercial isn't bad enough?" Believing his boss was ignoring him, not registering a word of warning, he exclaimed, "And no security? That's not the brightest idea, either, and you know it. What would Ms. Sheri say to that?"

Sean Bradley abruptly turned to Max and pointed a finger his way, staring him down. "Well, for starters, Sheri doesn't know I am going, nor are you going to tell her. And two, I am more than capable of driving myself. If you should know, I decided to fly commercial to help me blend. It's not like I'm flying coach. I'm still in first class. The sole purpose here is not to bring unwanted attention. Taking the jet would do that. Someone at the airfield would surely announce my arrival and spark a frenzy. Max, I just want to deal with this situation and be done with it. Maybe chill for a few days afterward. Life has been so crazy. Honestly, I need a minute to breathe."

"I understand. You're the boss." Max conceded before whispering, "Don't say I didn't warn you."

He knew it wouldn't take long for the Hollywood heartthrob to get noticed. In turn, the actor's agent, Sheri Reade, would have to burst into damage control mode to handle the press - something that has been a growing trend recently.

Sean zipped up his now neatly packed suitcase and set it on the floor, extending the handle upward. "If I need anything while I'm there, I'll text you."

As he left the room, his assistant followed, balancing a laptop in one hand. Opening it on the fly, he consulted the maps of Logan International Airport as they descended the glass-enclosed, floating staircase.

"Let me have your attention for one more minute. I realize you're anxious to get going."

His boss stopped midway on the landing and flashed a frustrated expression. Well aware of how particular Max was with every detail, the Hollywood actor offered a nod to appease him. "You have my attention for two minutes. Go."

"Okay, good. So, you'll have to get off the plane and find the shuttle bus that will take you to the rental terminal," the well-dressed young man pointed out on the screen.

Before he could elaborate further, the movie star interrupted by raising his right hand. "Max, I'll be fine. I'll figure it out." Continuing down the second flight of stairs, he added, "All I have to do is follow the signs like everyone else."

Being overly structured and predictable, Max was about to explode at the thought of Sean traveling across to the East Coast without a plan. Realizing his words were falling on deaf ears, he gave up and said, "Well, all I can say now is Good Luck."

"You worry too much, man. Sometimes, it's best to just go with the flow. I don't do that enough in my life."

Double-checking that he had everything, packing his passport, wallet, and phone from the front table in the modern marble foyer, Sean Bradley stashed his laptop and the author's tell-all hard-covered book into his brown leather satchel. Grabbing the hooded jacket that always came in handy at the airport, he slipped on a ball cap and sunglasses, ready to go out the door incognito.

"I'll be back in a few days. Maybe sooner."

Heading outside to meet the SUV that Max had buzzed through the gates thirty minutes before, Sean left the house without saying goodbye.

Following him down the long walkway lined by a tranquil waterfall wall, the smartly dressed assistant shouted, "Don't worry! I'll lock up! Make sure you're back before the premiere!"

"Yeah, I know!" Sean hollered from the vehicle's back seat, disappearing inside as the driver closed his door.

"Have a good......trip," Max mumbled, realizing the Hollywood star hadn't heard a word he just said.

When the driver slipped behind the wheel, he confirmed, "LAX, Mr. Bradley?"

"Yes, Geoffrey. Thanks."

Geoffrey silently watched his famous client pull his phone from his pocket. Uncharacteristically preoccupied, not saying another word, a scowl soon appeared on the actor's face. Realizing he was not in the best mood, the driver stayed quiet and gave him his space.

Sean's attention was affixed to one task now. While scanning the social media pages, scouted and bookmarked on his phone days prior, he tried to gather more information before being dropped off at the terminal. All he knew was that her name was Evily Landy, and he had a score to settle with her.

2

Wednesday, July 24th
City of Boston

You have to defend your honor. And your family. ~ Suzanne Vega

Approaching Boston, circling high above the stormy city, Sean stared at the clouds whizzing by the window. The gravity of the situation he had imposed upon himself began to settle in deeply. He'd rehearsed so many confrontational scenarios on the six-hour flight that his head hurt. Still scrutinizing the tell-all book for the one-hundredth time, highlighting specific sections in bright yellow, thoughts of his past and the striking similarity between it and the author's account conjured many questions, some of which were quite haunting.

"How dare she write a story about my family," he said quietly to himself.

His thoughts fueled anger and hatred as the plane descended below the cloud bank. Distracted by the rains pelting the window, creating patterned lines, the actor knew it would only be a matter of hours before he'd have the information he needed. In the end, he planned to have Evily Landy's book removed from shelves, and every news outlet afterward would know why. The final blow would be to launch a lawsuit that would ruin the woman's career. All of it would be punishment for infringing upon his private life.

The handsome, exhausted man was ready to disembark when the plane touched down at Logan International. Slipping on his jacket, he quickly fixed his baseball cap and sunglasses. Being one of the first passengers to exit the plane, he removed his carry-on from the upper compartment and proceeded out the door with it trailing behind. About to emerge from the aerobridge, he flipped the hood over his head before entering the busy terminal, intent on staying anonymous. Nervous energy flowed, knowing security wasn't waiting in the wings. Determined to adapt to his surroundings, Sean followed the crowd keeping his head down, only glancing up to read the signs guiding him to the ground transportation area. With the street becoming more visible through the windows at the end of the building, he moved through the sliding doors to the marked terminal transfers bus stop.

The rains were now light, and the air was quite humid. Reading the live message board, Sean learned that the Blue Line bus would take him where he needed to go. Out of his element, anxiety surfaced. It seemed that blending was much more challenging than expected. Impatiently waiting, he checked Evily Landy's social media pages for updates. Discovering a new post, only moments old, he found the woman sitting inside an ice arena, watching hockey.

Game on! The caption read.

"Huh. Her son must play junior," he said, recalling some of his fondest childhood memories.

Spotting the blue and white people mover rounding the corner, double-checking its number, Sean stood behind the crowd, waiting for Bus 22 to inch to a complete stop. The second the doors parted, a group jumped off one by one, many in quite a hurry. With the vehicle now partially empty, Sean naively stepped aboard when everyone piled in like cattle. Before grabbing a seat, he placed his suitcase on the rack, mimicking the passengers boarding ahead of him. Each person claimed a spot in less than sixty seconds.

"How do people deal with this?" he whispered under his breath, shocked by the density on the bus.

Departing in a timely fashion, scanning those sitting around him, he noticed a woman dressed in a charcoal grey pantsuit standing with her overstuffed laptop bag slung on one shoulder. Disheveled, she was the last to board and looked tired and stressed. Clinging to the vertical pole bolted to the floor, she tried to stabilize herself as the bus swayed from side to side. Without having to think twice, Sean Bradley's gentlemanly nature kicked in.

"Excuse me, Miss. Would you like to have a seat?"

The woman raised her head, unaware that he had spoken to her. Locking eyes with the stranger's sunglasses, she said, "Pardon me?"

"Would you like to sit down?" Sean asked, getting up from his seat.

"Really? You don't mind?" the woman confirmed, surprised by the rare gesture.

Motioning for her to take his spot, he said, "Please, I insist."

"Thank you, Sir. That's so nice of you," the woman replied with a smile, relieved to rest her sore, tired feet.

When they switched places, Sean Bradley said in passing, "No problem. Happy to help."

Taking her place, repositioning his brown leather satchel strap across his chest, he rested his back against the suitcase shelves and took hold of the vertical pole while the bus moved along. He hoped the situation had not brought about unwelcome attention in the process. Calmly keeping his eyes on the digital route map, the shuttle managed another sharp corner before screeching to a halt. Sean grabbed his luggage off the rack and stepped down to the sidewalk when the doors opened. On the move, he double-checked his travel itinerary to confirm which company Max had booked with. In the notes, he'd also reminded him of the alias assigned for this trip–a fond reminder of years past. A thought that made him stop and think of the friend he'd lost years ago.

"Okay. I'm looking for Enterprise," he mumbled, quickly spotting the black, green, and white sign.

Inching toward the check-in desk, a young man with a bright smile greeted him.

"Good afternoon, Sir. How may I help you?

"Yeah, Hi. Reservation under Waters."

The attendant picked up on his customer's bluntness, knowing he wouldn't be interested in any mundane conversation since Sean didn't make eye contact.

"Yes, Sir," he responded formally. "First name?"

Keeping his head down, he replied, "Mike."

"Perfect. We have your reservation right here: Land Rover Sport." After making Sean sign a few forms, the man added, "Everything is in order, so please proceed up the escalator to your left. There, you will find our luxury rental kiosk. An attendant will alert you that you are on your way. Enjoy your trip, Mr. Waters. Welcome to Boston."

"Thanks," Sean said, ready to move on, not wanting to stay there longer than he needed.

Following the guys' instructions, he proceeded up the escalator. It had been so long since he played hooky from Hollywood. He'd almost forgotten how nice freedom was.

A tall, athletic dude met him courteously upon reaching the second floor. "Mr. Waters?"

"Yes," Sean confirmed, trying to maintain a low profile.

"Pleased to meet you, Sir." The man held out his hand to offer a handshake.

Hoping the guy wouldn't recognize him, the actor obliged.

"My name is Curtis. Right this way. We have your truck waiting."

"Great. Thanks, Curtis."

Escorted to the black SUV, the man had the Land Rover prepped and ready with the back hatch raised. Commandeering his customer's suitcase, he slid it in gently and closed the tailgate. Sean had moved along to the driver's side and was about to reach for the door handle to open it.

"Here, Sir. Let me get that for you," he said, beating Sean to the punch.

Once his client had slipped in behind the wheel, Curtis presented the company's scripted departure instructions on how the EZ-Pass transponder system worked. Closing the door, with the window still down, the attendant finished his spiel, then asked, "Do you have any questions for me before you get moving?"

"No. Thanks, man. Think I'm good." He was anxious to leave.

"Very well, Sir. Enjoy your stay in Boston."

Familiarizing himself with the controls, Sean raised a steady hand to bid Curtis goodbye. Closing the window, he turned the air conditioning on high and quickly referred to Max's email. It did not take long to enter The Godfrey Hotel address into his GPS app. The route soon calibrated, helping him get his bearings. Taking a deep breath, he passed through the main gates. Never paying attention to anything when traveling with a security team, the responsibilities before him brought about a bit of unease. Merging onto the highway into a line of heavy traffic, he kept both hands on the wheel.

"Come on, Sean. You can do this," he reassured himself, knowing he hadn't gone soft. "It's like riding a bike."

Proceeding along the route, following the signs leading him to the Ted Williams Tunnel, the freeway descended below Boston's waterfront as the Land Rover disappeared underground on his way to the city center on the other side. Low on the horizon, the sun caused a dim light to appear at the tunnel's far end while the traffic briefly surfaced before emerging into the downtown core. The rain had stopped, making visibility better.

Surrounded by tall buildings in the heart of the city, tourists flooded the streets taking in the sights since the storm passed. Heading northeast along Washington Street, knowing he was close to his destination, Sean caught sight of the Godfrey Valet Parking sign along the curb. Thankful that he made it, the actor pulled in and parked. When he got out of the vehicle, a man smartly dressed in business casual was waiting in the wings to welcome him.

"Good evening, Sir," the hip gentleman said in an upbeat tone.

Sean replied quietly, "Good evening."

"Checking in?"

He handed over his keys and replied, "Yes, I am."

The Hollywood star moved to the rear of the vehicle. Lowering his head while removing his suitcase, he tried to remain nameless.

"Please, allow me, Sir," the gentleman insisted, reaching in to take the luggage.

Tired, Sean outwardly rejected his help. "No. No. That's quite alright. I've got it."

The valet immediately stepped back. "Certainly, Sir," he said, giving him his space. "Umm, right this way, then. The check-in desk is through the doors, straight ahead."

"Thanks," Sean uttered.

In light of the young man's reaction, Sean knew he was to blame. The tone he used came across rudely. Witnessing an immediate change in the man's demeanor, his voice now monotone, not as cheerful, Sean reevaluated his actions. He felt terrible. It annoyed him when others treated people that way. There was no excuse. Tired or stressed, it didn't matter. He needed to make things right with the man who was only doing his job.

Passing through the main doors, he thought, *What is it about this trip? It feels toxic.* A dark cloud seemed to hang over him.

The hotel lobby was sleek and modern. Walking toward the front desk, Sean noticed a few people scattered throughout the various seating areas. Accented by a stark white geometric focal wall, the woman behind the counter greeted him with a smile.

With hair pulled back into a sleek, tight bun, the sharp lines of her dark, tailored suit softened by the crisp white blouse beneath and a vibrant, multi-colored scarf draped elegantly around her neck, she said happily, "Welcome to the Godfrey, Sir."

"Thank you. Reservation for Mike Waters."

The woman brought up his information on the screen.

"Yes, Mr. Waters. We have you booked in one of our executive corner king lofts for four nights, correct?"

"Yes. That's right."

Giving Sean his access card minutes later, along with directions to the elevators, the woman turned to the valet and confirmed their guest's room number for the vehicle's key tag.

"He's in room #4002," she revealed.

Sad to see the gentleman had kept his distance while awaiting further instructions, the action star took out his wallet and grabbed a few large bills.

Before heading back outside to move the vehicle to the garage, Sean stopped him and said apologetically, "Thank you, man. Sorry for being so abrupt. Appreciate your help. Have a good night."

The man's face brightened. "Thank you very much, Sir." About to walk away, his sights locked on the ceiling above them. Turning to Sean, he said, "I believe your stay here will be enlightening."

Confused by the comment, Sean stood stoically. All he could do was watch the man peacefully walk away.

At the last second, glancing over his shoulder to see the look on the guest's face, the valet smiled before disappearing through the main doors.

Not sure how to react, Sean stayed silent. On his way to the elevators, stepping inside an empty one when the doors slid open, he thought to himself, *Enlightening? What did he mean by that? How weird.*

Exhausted from his trip, Sean Bradley made it to the fourth floor and opened the door to his suite, dragging his suitcase behind him. Rounding the corner to the left, he collapsed on the bed adjacent to the floor-to-ceiling windows as all the energy drained from his body.

"Remember, you brought this upon yourself," he mumbled.

A sense of accomplishment washed over him, knowing he'd gotten there on his own without the usual first-class movie star treatment - something he hadn't done much of in the past fifteen years. Allowing his eyes to shut, it almost felt like he was living a normal life for once.

Those thoughts were short-lived when the infamous author crossed his mind.

"So, Evily Landy, where are you now?" he asked, sitting up and re-checking her social media pages, disappointed not to find anything new.

Settling in and walking around the room, Sean pulled back the drapes to see the view. By this time, dusk had fallen upon the city. The street below was heavily tourist-laden. Captivated by all the activity, he happened to look down. There, he found a dime and a quarter on the window ledge, perfectly centered from left to right. Believing the maid service had missed the coins while cleaning, Sean chose to leave them be. Distracted, not giving it another thought, he obsessively refreshed the author's page, hoping to find something that would indicate her whereabouts. His mind reeled impatiently. He wanted this confrontation over with so he could return to LA as fast as possible. But now, the only thing he could do was wait.

While getting ready for bed, listening to the news bellowing from the television, a notification alerted him of a new picture the author had posted. Resting his back against the headboard, he read the caption aloud. "So happy the rains stopped. Heading back to the hotel after a nice dinner and a walk through Boston Common. Early game tomorrow."

Sean studied the photo in great detail. Using Google maps on his laptop, he matched the street location where she took it. Enhancing the sign in front of the building, he discovered that she was, in fact, staying at the Ritz.

"Well, I will see you bright and early, Ms. Landy," the Hollywood star mumbled, setting his alarm for 6:00 am. "We need to have a little chat."

3

Thursday, July 25th
Downtown Boston

Good things come when you least expect. ~ Unknown

Rising the following day, with the constant hum of traffic emanating from the street below, overly exhausted, with a hint of anxiety surfacing, Sean ran through the devised plan, knowing he was about to confront a total stranger. A woman at that. Aiming to stay calm and refrain from aggressive behavior, intent on not making a scene, he knew his agent, Sheri, was about to have a terrible day if things went south.

Within the hour, ready to walk over to the Ritz, he exited the lobby wearing his baseball cap and sunglasses, hoping his casual attire of jeans, a black t-shirt, and loafers would help him blend in and look like a tourist. The nervous energy was almost overwhelming. His hands trembled slightly. The confidence he exuded yesterday was slowly fading the closer he got to the impending encounter. Trying to shake it off, he continued along the calculated route, following the map on his phone, unable to turn back now.

Tall buildings lined both sides of the concrete jungle. There was barely any greenery in sight. Realizing the street was a small theatre district, he checked the signs to see what was playing at each location as he passed. A welcome distraction while it lasted.

Along the way, the aroma of freshly brewed coffee lingered in the air, stopping him in his tracks. In desperate need of something to sharpen his senses, the craving was too strong to ignore, so he veered toward Café Nero across the street.

Before swinging open the door, the Hollywood star paused. Uneasy about the risk of compromising himself, he hesitated again, then decided to take the gamble. Walking into the shop, designed with a blend of contemporary elements and old-world charm, Sean scanned the room from left to right, admiring the exposed brick and the floor-to-ceiling bookshelves on either side of an eclectic fireplace. It all seamlessly worked with the jet-black industrial pipes suspended overhead.

Having found his place in line with everyone else, surrounded mostly by people dressed in business attire, it felt strange to be alone. Usually having at least two men flanking his back, Sean felt like he could actually breathe today despite the impending doom. It had been so long since he felt a sense of freedom.

Happy to receive his bold, black coffee with an added double shot of espresso, the incognito star continued on his way out the door, worried about what would transpire.

How is she going to respond? He thought while crossing the street. *Will she fight back and call her lawyer?*

Sean reminded himself to remain calm and not lash out in anger. He needed to control the conversation.

"Keep it clear and concise - all business and not emotionally driven," he muttered.

At the corner of Washington and Avery, he finally saw Boston Common Park not far from him. He quickly pulled up her post, which perfectly matched his surroundings with the photo, confirming that she had taken it there.

"Well, this is it. Let's get this done so you can go home," Sean said, taking a deep breath.

Entering through the Ritz hotel's main doors, the staff at the front desk briefly acknowledged his presence before he moved to the lounge area and found a seat at a long table near the back with a bird's eye view of the elevators. Patiently waiting, checking the author's media pages, refreshing them often, not feeling guilty for stalking the woman who'd exposed private details of his past, his eyes took notice of every person exiting minute by minute. Trying to remember what she looked like, he brought up her photo and took a screenshot.

Time passed ever so slowly. Sipping his coffee, an attendant approached and offered him a newspaper from the newly arrived stack. Opening it fully and hiding behind the black-and-white pages, Sean tried to read a few articles but was too distracted. After waiting for almost an hour, he figured Evily Landy must have bypassed the lobby and gone straight to the parking garage below.

How am I ever going to find her now? He thought.

Defeated, needing to reevaluate his next move, he wondered if he could look up the tournament Landy's son was playing in and possibly check the arenas for her, maybe even wait at the Artisan Bistro for them to eat dinner that evening. For whatever reason, he felt compelled to continue the search. Believing all this was beginning to sound obsessive and a bit crazy, he heard the elevator chime as it echoed through the halls again. But this time, a woman's voice urged her kids along calmly.

"Come on, you two. Let's get moving. We're running late," the voice said behind the marble columns between them.

Tilting his head from left to right to get a better view, Sean saw a teenager toting a sizeable equipment bag and two hockey sticks. With his hat backward, the epitome of cool, the boy looked confident, leading the way in the black and red team warm-up suit. Walking alongside the woman, not far behind, was a girl maybe thirteen years of age. She was slugging a stuffed backpack and looked tired. Even though it was very early in the morning, that didn't stop her from sporting a set of rose gold Beats. Ears covered, she walked with her eyes locked to a device in hand.

"Is that them?" he whispered, staying hidden. They were the only guests he'd seen with hockey gear in tow all morning.

On his feet, casually folding the paper, Sean followed the family of three. The teenage boy slipped out the front doors and dropped his equipment bag on the sidewalk. The young girl remained close to the woman who was checking her phone. That is when Sean knew it was now or never.

"Evily Landy?" he called out to the villainous author.

The name left his lips louder than intended, cutting through the soft murmur of the hotel lobby. A ripple of attention followed, staff and guests alike turning their heads. With his feet seemingly falling through the floor, his body went numb after the bold attempt to grab her attention. Suddenly, the enormity of what he'd done hit hard, and instantly, it felt like he'd made a mistake.

Alarmed, the daughter had glanced at him sharply, a warning in her eyes, but it was her Mother's reaction that sent a jolt through him.

She'd stopped mid-step, her posture rigid upon hearing her name spoken so sternly. Not moving an inch, it seemed she had anchored in place. Then, ever so slowly, the woman swiveled around. Appearing almost to levitate, she soon turned to face him.

Thrown off guard, taken by her eyes, Sean thought they were the bluest he'd ever seen. Framed by quiet confidence, the world around her felt less significant as she stared his way and offered a blank expression. In disbelief, possibly starstruck, a normal reaction to anyone famous, she stood, lost for words.

To him, her presence was almost angelic. Her skin glowed, and her eyes twinkled.

Watching the woman's daughter leave the building, a warm gust of wind flowed through the main doors. Whimsically tossing about the author's long brown hair, a smile emerged upon her face, which charmed him instantaneously, softening the dreaded confrontation. All had rendered him speechless, a factor he neither anticipated nor expected. That is when he felt it. His heart was hammering inside his chest - a stir of emotions he hadn't encountered in years. Reminded of the main reason for being in Boston, Sean tried to stay on task but knew he had failed horribly.

Breaking the silence between them, the pretty woman, dressed in layers of yoga attire, clutched a bag with warm blankets and jackets. Staring him down, she spoke. Her voice was smooth, steady, and laced with a quiet authority that left no room for hesitation. "Well," she said, tilting her head slightly, "it's about time you showed up. Let's go— we're already late."

Slowly dying inside, unsure how to react to the Hollywood star, Evily Landy wondered about his next move. Casually walking out of the lobby to join her children, she found them waiting curbside for the valet to bring their SUV around.

Alone, frozen just inside the doors, stunned by her straightforward statement and his mortifying reaction, Sean Bradley watched the family hover about the vehicle when it pulled up, unfazed by what just happened. Oddly going about their business, the teenage boy lifted the rear hatch and swung his heavy bag and sticks in the back. The author tossed her tote on top of his equipment before proceeding to the driver's side.

Inching out of the hotel toward the family, Sean stood on the sidewalk. He stayed about eight feet from the truck as the author looked over from across the hood in his direction.

"So..." she said with a brilliant smile. "Are you going to join us?"

4

Thursday, July 25th
Boston / Canton Massachusetts

Confrontation simply means meeting the truth head-on. ~ Mike Krzyzewski.

The city's chaotic sounds soon reduced to a white noise. Amidst a state of confusion, Sean felt enormous pressure. What she had just asked seemed ludicrous, but he found himself considering it for some reason. Not knowing what to do, lost for words, he focused on the woman and watched her attention deviate from him and move to her daughter standing alongside the back door, entirely captivated by her device in hand, with headphones still covering her ears.

"Sweetie pie?" the author said. "Get in. We have to go." Not receiving a response, she said a bit louder. "Ella!"

The girl immediately looked up and casually slid one headphone off her right ear. "Huh?" she mumbled.

Sean's heart skipped a beat.

"Get in, please." Her Mother used a milder tone. "We need to leave."

The valet opened the back door to assist the young girl and did the same for Sean on the passenger side, assuming he was part of the family.

Returning her sights to the strikingly handsome Hollywood star, she confidently prompted a second time, "Well? What is it going to be, Mr. Bradley? Are you staying here, or are you going to join us?"

Stunned, he hesitated, heavily weighing his options. Hearing the daughter's name cast this unexplainable sense of calm and produced a gravitational force, seemingly drawing him closer to the vehicle. Within seconds, Sean slipped into the empty front seat, feeling unsettled. At the same time, the teenager jumped in behind his Mother after closing the back hatch.

Waving to the group, the valet smiled and closed the door. Sean knew there was no going back now. He began to fidget while sitting mere inches from the malicious Evily Landy as she got comfortable behind the wheel. Concentrating on keying in their destination, she reached for her seat belt and secured it with a click.

Out of the blue, she glanced over, unafraid to address him. "Okay," she said, "I'm giving you a job now."

Sean looked her way, slightly confused.

"You need to help me navigate out of the downtown core to the freeway. Then, and only then, will we talk freely? Deal?"

Shocked by her bossy demeanor, he nervously agreed. "Umm, sure. No problem."

Pulling away from the hotel, instructed to make a U-turn, she said, "Since you already know my name, I'll introduce you to my children." She glanced in the rearview mirror and added, "Sean Bradley, meet Evan and Ella Anderson."

Evan was the only one to respond, casting a cold wave to acknowledge him. Ella remained immersed in her device and was not paying attention.

"Wait? Anderson?" Sean questioned, believing he had the wrong person.

"You know me as Evily Landy, correct?"

"Ahh, yeah."

"Well, that's my pseudonym. My married name is Anderson." Listening to the GPS instructions, she needed confirmation. "Which way?"

"What?" the actor replied in a fog.

"Which way do I go now? You're navigating, remember?" Evily reminded, frantically scanning the intersection for street signs.

Sean read the screen and said, "Umm, yeah. Go left, then keep going straight. We are looking for a sign that reads I-93 South. You'll then make a right."

"Thank you," Evily said in an uplifting tone while taking the advanced green.

With his heart racing and palms sweating - warning shots fired through his mind rapidly.

What am I doing? Man, you just got into a strange woman's car because she told you to. Are you crazy? And what's with these kids? They don't seem fazed by this at all. What the hell is going on? What did you get yourself into here?

The author glanced his way briefly and cast a crafty smirk before focusing straight ahead.

Moving along, they noticed a large green sign coming into view.

"There," he pointed out. "That's I-93 South."

"Oh, yes. I remember this now. It's a tunnel, I think."

"Seems so," he confirmed.

Stopping the vehicle and waiting for the light to change green, Evily did not make a sound. The action star kept silent, too, and watched the pedestrians walk by.

In minutes, the green arrow illuminated. Evily stepped on the gas, jerking Sean's head backward. Hanging on for dear life, clinging to the upper grab handle while she managed the sharp corner, Sean remained alert on the way down the ramp, strongly questioning her driving skills.

"Stay to the left. That lane hooks up to I-93," he explained, quickly referring to the map.

"Okay. Will do. Thank you." Happy to be going against early morning traffic, she merged carefully into the steady flow heading South before swaying her attention back to him. "Guess you have a lot of questions for me?"

Continuing to stare straight ahead, he answered, "Yes."

"I expected as much. Don't worry. I'll tell you whatever you want to know. But please, do not talk about this in front of the children. I ask that you respect that. Once we get to our destination, I'll give you the okay."

Agreeing with a nod, he added, "Sure. Understood. No problem." With a million thoughts going through his head, knowing this meeting took a different path than he anticipated, Sean noticed her left hand. She wore a wedding band and a large engagement ring, signifying that she was married.

In need of conversation, he casually checked on the kids in the back. Both were listening to something on their phones. That is when he decided to state the obvious.

"So, you're married name is Anderson. Is your husband in Boston with all of you?"

Evily snickered. "No. He had other plans for his life that didn't include us anymore."

Confused by her statement, Sean's mind drifted instantly to his father doing the same thing many years ago.

"I'm sorry. I didn't mean to, umm."

"It's all right. I'm fine with it," she openly divulged while switching lanes. "It was the best thing for all of us."

"Why do you still wear your rings then?"

Laughing, she said, "Wow. You're sharp." Pausing a minute, she willingly revealed, "These aren't my wedding rings. My ex-husband wanted those back. He probably sold them to pay for the divorce lawyer." Peering down at her hand, she clarified, "I bought this set a while ago. If you should know, I wear them to keep the men away. They are a great deterrent. I need to focus on work and my children. These rings make my life less complicated."

"Makes sense," he replied, overly baffled by what she'd said.

Uneasy, he focused on the country setting flowing past his window. Sean's Mother came to mind. She was married many times - not exactly the most stable environment for the children immersed in it all. His childhood was always challenging. Between moving and having count-less nannies and babysitters, he wished one day that he'd have a wife and family that lived an everyday life - one not so dysfunctional.

With their exit fast approaching, Sean alerted Evily that she needed to merge from the freeway into a small borough called Canton. Doing just that, they continued down a country road. Driving through the hamlet, with manor-style homes bordered by white picket fences and patriotic flags hanging proudly, it was strange to be in a rural area for a tournament. The GPS led them past a beautiful lake that sparkled in the sun and over a few small rivers before arriving at the white building called The Ice House. Accented by modern royal blue and black accent stripes, the facility was a recent development based on the newly planted trees bordering the parking lot.

Evan stretched and prepared to depart before his Mother stopped the vehicle close to the main entrance. Evily and her son opened their doors in sync and met at the back. Grabbing his equipment bag while his Mom held the hockey sticks, Sean heard the two talking and curi-ously lent a listening ear.

"Good luck. Play your best and believe in yourself. You earned your spot here, so showcase your skills. Blow them away."

"Thanks, Mom," the young man said, offering a fist punch before heading inside.

"Love you," she whispered so nobody else would hear.

"Love you too."

Pressing the hatch button to lower the tailgate, she waved to her son, who gave a thumbs up. Once seated behind the wheel again, Evily waited until he entered the building before shifting gears and finding a place to park.

Nobody said a word.

Evily headed to the far side of the lot and located a vacant spot in a shady area along the tree line. Pulling into the space, she shut off the vehicle.

"Okay," she said, swiveling around to her daughter. "Ella? Ready to go?"

Not receiving a response, she moved her hand in front of the girl's field of vision. Without skipping a beat, Ella finally looked up. Opening and closing her door, she walked away in a zombie-like state towards the front entrance right on cue.

Unsure what was happening, Sean asked, "So, I go with you?"

"Yes, of course. You do like hockey, correct?"

"I do," he said, closing the passenger side door.

Meeting up with Evily, she remotely locked the vehicle.

"I used to play junior when I was about your son's age. Once, I had to choose between – playing hockey or becoming an actor. Guess I decided to take the road less traveled."

"To me, both choices seem to fall under that category. At least it paid off for you."

"Yes, I suppose so. A lot of sacrifices, though," he clarified.

"I bet there were."

Close to the main doors of the arena, Sean got nervous. There were so many people there. Surrounded by parents, grandparents, siblings, players, coaches, and scouts, they maneuvered through the crowd before walking inside to stand in line and pay the entrance fee.

Sean kept his head down. He didn't want to get recognized and cause a scene without the help of security at his disposal. It got him thinking that maybe this was not a good idea after all. Glancing upward, he happened to catch Evily focusing on him again. Funny enough, it was as though she was reading him like a book in that split second.

Strange, he thought, catching her smirking a second time, looking a little more sinister.

She stepped forward to pay the minimal admittance fee when it was their turn.

Seeing this, Sean reached for his wallet.

Noticing what he was doing, Evily said, "Don't worry. I got it. You're our guest today."

"No, you shouldn't have to pay for me." Handing her a twenty-dollar bill, he added, "Please take it. I insist."

"No, don't be silly. We are dragging you here. It's fine."

Not comfortable with the arrangement, he had no choice now but to go along with it. The ticket was the least of his worries based on the crowd gathered that day.

Advancing past the desk, Evily checked the screens to see where Evan was playing. She quickly discovered the team was assigned rink two. Knowing where to go, the three of them continued up the stairs to their right.

The noise level increased when Ella swung the heavy door open at the top of the stairs. People were everywhere.

Sean tried to keep it together. He knew what would happen if he was spotted. The situation could very well escalate if they weren't careful. Immediately, escape plans started to formulate in his head while scanning the room, looking for emergency exits.

Evily confidently led the way through the crowd while her daughter followed. Sean walked behind them and tried to blend in and not look suspicious. Being six-foot-one and still wearing his ball cap and sunglasses indoors did not help matters.

Locating a few vacant chairs adjacent to the glass windows overlooking rink two, Evily grabbed one for each of them. Not interested in watching the game, Ella dragged hers over to a large round table a few feet away. She opened her backpack, pulled out her laptop, and continued to close off from the world. Seeing this, Sean wondered why she was so antisocial, given that her Mother seemed far from it.

When the buzzer sounded, the crowds in front of them dispersed from the viewing area and snack bar. A space opened up along the glass, so they inched their chairs forward to get a better view of the ice.

Not looking his way once, Evily suddenly stated, "Guess you are wondering how some personal details from your life ended up in the pages of my book."

Aware that he needed to keep his anger in check, Sean sternly replied, "Wow, straight to the point. You know, you had no right to do that."

Facing him, she was prepared for the challenge, already knowing the outcome.

Sean removed his sunglasses. Getting down to business, he asked, "How did you get that information? Who was your source?"

"You'd never believe me if I told you."

Evily watched the Zamboni move from left to right, clearing the ice for the next game. She, too, wanted answers and boldly asked without hesitation, "What made you buy my book, Mr. Bradley?"

Her question hit a nerve. Sean felt like only one person would be controlling this conversation, and that would be him.

"I'm going to ask you again. Who was your source?"

"You will find that out in time." Evily stuck to her guns and did not give him an inch.

"Do you have any idea..." Sean stopped mid-sentence, catching himself raising his voice so much that people looked their way. Adjusting his tone, he started over, almost whispering. "Do you have any idea what you've done? How would you like your entire life splashed across the pages of something you never authorized? Where thousands of people have now read it and know the intimate details of your past."

Pausing, the clever woman appreciated what he'd said but decided to push her luck. "So? Why did you buy it?"

With eyes affixed to the floor, Sean knew he'd probably have to play her game to get answers. Exhaling out of total frustration, hating that he had no choice but to respond, he conceded.

"Fine. You win. Why did I buy your book? One day, I spotted your promo poster in the window at Barnes & Noble."

"And?" she immediately prompted, not giving him a second to think.

"And I went into the store and bought it," he snapped.

"No, you don't understand. A particular feeling drew you to the poster and made you walk into the bookstore, right?"

"I don't know what you're talking about," Sean said, quite irritated, while leaning back in his chair.

Evily shook her head. "Men are the worst at paying attention to details." Her eyes drifted to the ceiling as if speaking directly to it. "This is not going to be easy."

Sean also looked up, then back at her, completely confused. "What are you talking about?"

"You got a weird feeling when you saw the poster. Then you walked away, stopped, and went back to the store to buy it."

Dumbfounded, knowing she was right, Sean tried not to raise his voice. "What? You had someone follow me?"

The author calmly answered, "No, I have more important things to do with my time, actually."

"Then, how?"

"How what? How did I know that happened? How did I know the little details of that particular day?" She started to get snippy. "Do you not think it's odd that you picked my book out of all the new releases available?"

"Look, you owe me an explanation since you're now profiting from my life story." Restraining his anger, he clutched his hands together, gripping them tightly in front of him. *Why is she acting like this?* He thought to himself.

Evily pushed her luck and speedily repeated. "One last time. Why did you feel compelled to buy it?"

Annoyed, he knew he'd have to give her an answer to get anywhere. "The cover? I don't know?"

"Not visual. The *feeling* it gave you," the woman gently clarified, placing her hand over her heart, trying to dig deeper.

He quickly pointed out, "Guys are not good at feelings. Nor do we care about that stuff."

Fixated on him, Evily reached into his soul. "Look, if this is going to work, you must cooperate."

Their eyes met in the most frigid stare.

"If what is going to work? What do you mean? I'm beginning to think you're crazy."

Ella flashed a glaring look of concern, having heard the comment.

Not missing a beat, Evily held her hand up to her daughter to signal that she was fine before addressing him further.

"This situation is far greater than just the words on a page. That story was a means to get you here to this point - to this chair, right here. A gut feeling brought you to the other side of the country to confront a person you've never met. Now, answer my question."

Stunned by what she said, he surrendered and revealed something about himself that many people would not know.

"The title. That's what caught my attention - *Beyond the Grave*. Lately, I've been questioning my mortality. It has sparked a fascination with the paranormal and the afterlife. Is that what you wanted?"

"Good. Now we are getting somewhere."

"I haven't been lucky in love, so I enjoy reading a good story once and a while to fill the void." Focused forward, he wondered how she'd respond.

Evily pounced on his statement. "That's not true."

"What do you mean?" he replied, with barely enough strength left.

"You were very lucky in love - once. You've experienced a love like no other, truth be told. Sadly, it was just for a season. But that love does extend beyond the grave."

"Wait? What did you just say?" Sean picked up on the comment linked to the title of the author's book.

"Again, you'll never believe me if I told you."

"Try me."

"Mr. Bradley, the details hidden in those pages were meant for only you. Nobody else reading it would know who it was referring to."

"How did you know all of this information? Who was your source?" the Hollywood star questioned again.

"I have a special ability. In some religions, it's a charismata gift. In other circles, people describe it as extra-sensory perception. Like a sixth sense."

The actor squinted his eyes in disbelief. "What? You're joking?"

Her hands clasped together in front of her. "I don't know why I know certain things. Events before they happen, thoughts and feelings of people around me. I can hear the voices of those no longer with us."

Outright skeptical, he shook his head, not believing a word. Staring at the floor, he thought to himself. *You traveled all this way just to find out she's nuts.*

Able to read his mind, smirking at the rude comment, she scoffed, "Now, you believe I'm crazy. How do you think I was able to acquire all the information about your life without ever stepping foot in California or speaking to anyone on earth who knows you?"

Analyzing things, he compiled a list of possible sources. "The mainstream media, YouTube, the tabloids, for crying out loud. Who knows."

"They would not have this information. Deep down, you know that."

"Well, thanks to you, the entire planet now knows every ounce of my private life." Sean seemed saddened by his statement.

"Look, as I said before, what I wrote was only meant for you to decipher. Anyone else reading it would never put two and two together. I promise you that." Evily pulled out her phone from her bag. Scrolling through the pictures and videos, she suddenly stopped. "Here, this is my source."

He took hold of her phone and watched the security camera footage she'd pulled up. It showed the outside of a home with sizeable festive stone planters on either side of the snow-covered walkway.

Not seeing anything happening, he asked, "What is this?"

"Watch," she insisted, pointing to the screen.

Suddenly, Sean noticed movement. A faint misty blob slowly appeared from the top of the screen and floated about the space. A second one, smaller in size, joined it as it hovered.

Evily focused on Sean's reaction. His eyes were locked on the shapes moving about.

When the video ended, she reached for the phone and said, "Wait. There's more."

Showing him another recording where the mysterious orbs hovered about Evily's front porch and foyer, Sean suddenly said, "What are you showing me?"

"Not what? Who," she clarified.

"I don't understand."

"Mr. Bradley, where do you think our souls go after we die?"

Uncomfortable with the question, angered at the thought of having to answer her, he blatantly replied, shaking his head, "I'm not religious."

"This has nothing to do with religion. Religion is a product of man. This is about faith in God and belief in the afterlife. Do you believe in a place many describe as heaven?"

He was not sure how to answer that. "I hope there's a heaven."

"You hope, or you know?" the author prompted.

"Hope."

Evily flashed a sad expression his way with a sympathetic tilt of her head. "You only hope there is a heaven? Why?"

"I once lost two very special people, and I *hope* they are together and at peace."

"Your wife and daughter?"

His eyes locked to hers yet again.

"You are here because I have a message from them."

Hitting a nerve a second time, Sean flashed a shot of anger. He returned her phone, put on his sunglasses, got up from the chair, and left.

Evily raised her sights to the ceiling and whispered, "He's not ready."

5

Thursday, July 25th
Canton, Massachusetts

Life is about choices. Some we regret, some we are proud of. Some will haunt us forever. ~ Graham Brown

Enraged, the Hollywood star stormed down the stairs. Dodging people on the way out, he forcefully hit the crash bar on the main doors with both palms, causing a stir amongst those standing outside the arena. Embarrassed, with all eyes on him, he quickly veered to the right and went around the corner of the building.

Behind the Ice House was a small park. Following a path into a wooded area, Sean arrived at a bench under a tall, shady tree while his thoughts drifted to his wife, Janie, and their baby girl. Taking a seat, missing them terribly, it seemed Evily had reopened the wounds he thought had healed many years before.

Grief never ends when you lose someone close to you, he thought. *It just changes shape as the years pass by.*

Reminded that the two most important people in his life were gone, he felt alone. After their passing, he worked a lot, which seemed to help his mind avoid feeling sad most of the time. It distracted him from expelling any emotion. Given Evily's claims, he did not know what to do. Finding himself in a weird predicament, Sean remembered how long it took him to accept the devastating loss. A feat that was once an impossible task long ago. Those years were his darkest—something he wouldn't wish on his worst enemy. Despite how Evily discovered what she did, he was curious about these orbs. He'd never heard of such a thing. With an abundance of questions, he found himself needing to know more about this apparent connection to Janie and his daughter.

Deep in thought, Sean caught a bit of movement from the corner of his eye. Something white in color. Turning his head to the left, a couple of butterflies floated by freely. He marveled at the tiny creatures frolicking in the breeze, watching them linger. A feeling of peace washed over him as they fluttered. Slowly ascending into the leaves above his head, the contents of Evily's book flooded back. In the end chapters, he recalled the two spirits attached to white butterflies that appeared when the main character experienced bouts of grief and mourning. It was their means of communication in the story. They would always arrive when least expected, but timely nonetheless. The skeptical Sean suddenly looked away and figured it was all just a coincidence.

Sitting in silence, he didn't know what to decide. "Stay or go?" he said to himself.

He didn't believe in a God, prayer, or heaven. All of it seemed foreign and far-fetched.

But what if it's not? He wondered if there was more to this gift of hers. *Is that the only way she truly knew of these things? What if there is life after death?*

Needing to test whether Evily Landy was for real, he opted to go back inside. Upon returning to his seat, he planned to pose a question to the author. If she answered incorrectly, he would hire a taxi to take him back to Boston and catch the first flight out to LA. If she happened to be correct, he made a deal with himself.

"Listen to what she has to say with an open mind. The woman has gone to great lengths for a reason. Logically, you need to know why."

After calming himself down, Sean walked into the building and climbed the stairs to the viewing area. There, he found Evily's attention fixated on Evan's game that had already started. With her head on a swivel, following the plays, she did not acknowledge his presence.

Sitting beside the author, he watched Ella glance over at him. She was not happy with how he had treated her Mother.

Evily briefly caught Sean's reflection on the glass. Not saying a word, she refocused on what was happening on the ice below.

To break through the silence, he asked, "What's his jersey number?"

Hesitating, she pointed at Evan when he made his way to center ice. "Seven."

Winning the face-off, they watched the players from both teams move back and forth, from one side of the arena to the other at high speed. Not saying a word, inching to the edge of her seat, Evily saw Evan score. With hands raised to her chin, quietly cheering, her son looked and pointed in her direction, adding a fist pump.

"Okay, that's one," she whispered.

"Great goal. Top shelf. Nice," Sean stated, still feeling awkward.

Needing to make amends, she divulged, "He's been playing since he was four. Like many kids his age, it's been his dream to play in the NHL. God willing, he will."

"Ms. Landy?" Sean said, ready to pose the test question.

Evily picked up on the lack of interest in what she'd just said. It angered her. "What?" She abruptly replied before her eyes brightened unexpectedly. "Wait... Two butterflies. They visited you in the park. Both white, correct?"

Utterly lost for words, Sean said, "How? How did you...."

"Know?" The author finished his sentence. "You have a test question for me too. Do you want that answered now?"

"Sure." He was in awe of her confidence.

"Ella. Her name was Ella."

Sean tried to take a breath, but the air in his lungs seemingly escaped him. A sinking feeling took over, and disbelief spread through his body. While sitting in silence, his eyes welled. Not acknowledging her answer, he gathered his thoughts. "Umm, nobody... Nobody would know that." He cleared his throat and tried to wipe a tear away without her noticing. "We didn't divulge the name we chose for her. It was only known to Janie and me. All we told our family was that it was a baby girl. Nothing else."

"So, did I pass your test?"

"How? How did you do that?" he asked, totally fascinated. His words softened, along with his facial expression.

"Pictures flash through my mind. Other times, I hear the odd word, sometimes a sentence. Through the years, whatever I either visually, audibly, or symbolically picked up on started to line up with moments in my life—thoughts presented by friends, kids at school, and even strangers on the street. I didn't know what to do with it for the longest time. Then, I felt compelled to research it more. One day, I spoke to a pastor at a random church I passed by. Drawn inside, I walked into his place of worship. It seemed like it was for a reason. He answered my questions and taught me about these divinely conferred gifts given to certain people - gifts granted for a purpose. A mode to help convey and restore faith in others."

"So, if you supposedly know things in advance, did you know Evan would score?"

"Yes," Evily boldly revealed with a half-smile. "He's not done yet, either. Two more to go."

"A hat trick?"

So sure of herself, she turned to him and said, "Yes, one hundred percent."

"Does he know this in advance? Do you tell him?" Sean fired back questions.

Evily sat up straight in her chair. "No, never. He needs to experience life without interference."

"Guess this will be another test?" Sean said challengingly.

"You have very little faith. Very skeptical. Eventually, you'll see. Faith will soon return to you. Only then will your life change."

Sean stared at her. She was oddly wise beyond her years. While returning her attention to the game, Evan scored again. Celebrating before pointing to his Mother, she silently applauded, sending positive vibes his way. It was amazing how she encouraged him without saying a word. The two had a powerful mother/son bond. Her body language said it all. It was something he wished he'd had with his Mom. Sadly, she never attended any of his games, let alone offered that type of support. She was always too busy working.

Making it through a very stressful second period, barely saying a word to each other, Evily knew Sean was thinking a lot about what was said between them thus far. Before going into the third, the Zamboni flooded the ice. While the rink returned to a glass-like state, Evily focused on Ella and found her drawing on her tablet. Getting up, she walked over.

"So, what do we have here?"

Ella slid her headphone off one ear.

"It's beautiful." The woman smiled, hovering over her daughter.

The young girl showed the different views of the lake house she'd designed, all nestled in a rocky crest. Her eyes were bright and showed a glimmer of excitement. Able to see what was on the tablet, Sean was surprised by the girl's architectural talents.

"Well, done. This may be the best one yet," her Mom complimented.

Ella's face lit up as she giggled. "That's what you always say."

"I know. Each design keeps getting better and better. It is so exciting for me to see what you create. Every house is so unique." Evily patted her shoulder lovingly.

"Thanks, Mom."

Covering her ears with her headphones again, Ella continued her project. Her Mother went back to her chair.

"She has a knack for that," Sean said kindly.

"Yes, I think so too. Ella is very talented. One day, she'll become an architect. These designs will eventually be part of her portfolio."

An uneasiness blanketed them both. Sean didn't know what else to say. His mind went blank. Evily quickly picked up on it.

"So, you haven't been on vacation for a long time. Does this trip to Boston count as one?" she asked, already knowing the answer.

"Ahh, I suppose. In a way," he said, wondering if she was reading his thoughts. It was true. He hadn't taken a vacation in years. Sadly, he'd made thirty-seven movies instead.

"You have a lot of work ahead of you still?"

"What do you mean? Like acting, work?"

"Yes. That is your job, isn't it?"

Not liking the sarcasm, he replied, "Ah, yeah. I just finished up the promo for a new movie. The premiere is next week. I hope to take some time off after that. There are a lot of opportunities available to me if I choose to sign on, but right now, I feel like I need a break."

Evily nodded strangely.

"What is that?" Sean gestured, pointing to her, getting a weird vibe. "What does that mean?"

"I see I'm not the only one with a sixth sense."

"No, really... What is it?" he asked again.

"Nothing." Evily looked down at the ice, happy to see the Zamboni had done its job.

Both teams skated to their designated benches to prepare for the third period. Evily sat up straight in her chair, ready to watch.

Sean knew there was something she wasn't telling him, but what?

When Evan looked her way, it prompted her to whisper, "Okay, boys. Let's go." As he skated for the face-off at center ice, she held her hand over her heart and then pointed at him. Her son did the same.

"Do you know if they will pull this out?"

"Yes, I feel it will end in a 3-1 win." Evily was certain.

Looking at the scoreboard, seeing that it was 2-0 with 20 minutes left, he figured the outcome was possible.

Just as the puck dropped, the author felt she should explain something. "You know, sometimes what I do feels like a curse. Because of this constant need to help others, my life is not my own."

"I'm sure it's tough," Sean replied, not understanding the gravity of her gift.

The play ended off-side, making Evan's line head to the bench for a shift change.

"You know, sometimes I don't have a choice in the matter." There was a level of sadness in her voice.

"You always have a choice," he naively replied.

Shaking her head, she needed to make him understand. "I spent the past seven months writing, editing, and publishing a book that would bring you to this seat beside me. I took this on willingly, mostly because your girls were so sweet. I couldn't say no." She paused. "Look, this is your chance to experience something completely life-changing with your wife and daughter. All in all, I felt compelled to help them and you."

With a bit of attitude, Sean smirked. "I can't thank you yet."

Flashing an unhappy look, the author said, "Oh, don't worry, Mr. Bradley. You will."

6 |

Thursday, July 25th
Boston, Massachusetts

Good or bad, it's the little surprises that keep life interesting. ~ Tadahiko Nagao

The spectators got rowdy in the final minutes of the third period. It was coming down to the wire as the opposing team was trailing 2-1 at the blow of the whistle. Some disgruntled parents shouted at the referees for handing out penalties that allowed Evan's team to go on a power play. Feeling stressed, Evily and Sean focused their attention on what was transpiring.

Fuming after his team got scored on during the last shift, Evan looked up at his Mom, showing frustration. She held three fingers up while he skated to the face-off to start the play.

Nodding his head, he knew what to do.

"Here it comes," she mumbled when her son easily won possession of the puck. Passing it to his winger, bolting towards the opponent's net, Evily said, "Come on, boys. You got this."

The players all converged into the far corner. Evan curled around the back of the net, knowing the puck was about to break free. Strategically moving into position on the opposite side of the goalie, covered relentlessly by an opposing player, the talented athlete kept jostling for position, ready for the pass. Suddenly, his winger broke from the pack and diverted the puck in Evan's direction. Snagging it on his stick, he fired the shot and watched it fly over the goalie's blocker to score.

With arms raised, the teammates skated past the bench for celebratory high-fives.

"3-1." Evily clapped, pointing to Evan, as he sat down for the shift change.

"There are still four minutes left in the period. A lot can happen."

Evily turned to Sean and tilted her head. "Says ye of little faith."

"We will see," he replied, moving his weight forward, resting his elbows on his knees - chin upon his clenched hands.

"Yes, we will, Mr. Bradley. Care to wager?"

Sean's eyebrows went up. Glancing over at Evily, he asked, "You want me to bet against your kid?"

"You, Sir, are already betting against him. Not me. I just thought I'd make it interesting."

"Yeah, I think I'll pass on that. You seem to have a few aces in the hole," Sean chuckled, sitting on the edge of his chair. Tilting it forward, balancing on two legs, he focused on the plays, knowing the two of them had somehow managed a truce. That got him thinking. "You know, all the Mr. Bradley, Ms. Landy stuff is quite annoying." Hesitating, he suggested, "Look, can we drop the formalities?" His hand reached out between them. "Hi. I'm Sean. Nice to meet you. And you are?"

"Evily. Nice to meet you, Sean." She obliged, understanding his intentions.

Greeting each other civilly, the actor felt a weight lift off him. "Pleasure," he said, happy to see her finally offer a friendly smile.

The last few minutes of the game took an eternity. So many turnovers. Multiple shots on goal. The players worked to their max while the clock dwindled to zero.

"Fourteen seconds left," she confirmed.

Sean knew that the score would be what the author had predicted.

When the buzzer echoed through the arena, Evily stood up when Evan and his team cleared their bench to celebrate their win.

"That's game," Evily confirmed. "Like I said. 3-1."

Knowing she was right, Sean happened to catch Evan pointing to his Mom in the gallery above. Smiling, he placed his hand over his heart. She did the same.

"It's like the two of you have your own language," he observed.

"I can hear what he's thinking, but he can't hear me, so I try and communicate what I can. He and I have been through a lot to get to this point. It's been a long road."

Not sure what she meant by that, Sean stood idly.

Walking over to her daughter, Evily tapped her shoulder. "It's over, Sweetie. Ready to go?"

The young girl again slid one headphone off her ear. "Yeah, sure."

Uninterested in her brother's team's victory, she packed her things neatly in the bag and pushed the chair in before joining her Mother.

Sean stayed quiet and walked alongside the ladies down the staircase. In the process, a few people looked his way strangely.

Leaning over to Evily, he whispered, "Think I'm going to start attracting unwanted attention. We should probably leave the building."

Evily took note of Sean's observations and agreed. "Yes. I think that would be best. I'll text Evan and tell him we will be waiting in the parking lot for him."

People continued to stare and whisper on their way to the lobby. Making it through the main doors, they broke away from the crowds gathered outside. Ella walked slightly ahead of the famous actor and her Mother.

"So, I guess I was right about the score, huh?" she pointed out, a little proud of herself.

"Beginner's luck," he joked.

"Oh, Mr. Bradley, I haven't been considered a beginner since I was five years old."

Offering a content chuckle, Sean knew now what he was up against but still didn't know if she was for real.

Feeling that the actor continued to be somewhat skeptical despite her proven talents, a bit angry at him, everything considered, she stopped in the middle of the parking lot.

"Your flight left yesterday at 8:15 am. While waiting at the assigned gate, you highlighted parts of my book with a bright yellow highlighter. Scenes you later wanted to question me on. People took pictures of you with the book in hand. My sales just went up forty-six percent in the past twenty-four hours. Thank you for that, by the way. Your flight number was 1433. You are staying at the Godfrey Hotel down the street. Suite #4002. You booked the room until Sunday since you snooped on my social media pages and found out the tournament lasts until then. This morning, you grabbed a black coffee at Café Nero with a double shot of espresso. Waiting in the lounge inside my hotel, you got impatient. About to leave, you heard us talking after exiting the elevator. Initially, you came here to confront me. Now, hmm, I believe that anger has diminished. Am I right?"

Halted dead in his tracks, amazed by what she spilled, he knew she was entirely correct on every detail.

"Well?" she demanded, recalling one more thing. "Oh, and before I forget. You found two coins in your room. One is a dime, the other a quarter. I strongly suggest you check the date on those." Speedily passing by him, she left the famous actor in the dust.

Dumbfounded, he ran up behind her. "Wait? How did you know about that?"

With hands on her hips, she stood by the truck. Her facial expression said it all. "So, am I right?"

Sean paused before confirming, "Yes, you are correct on all accounts."

"Look, Mr. Bradley.' She immediately corrected herself. "Sean. You are here because they wanted you to come. Your wife and daughter have a message to give."

"So, you truly believe Janie and Ella orchestrated this whole thing?" he sincerely asked. "You and I meeting like this?"

"They did. This situation has been months in the making. Why would you be here otherwise?"

"I wanted to know where you got your information. That's why I came."

"Look. The bottom line is they gave me every quote, every memory, and every facet. The entire plot was their idea. I just embellished the fictional story around it. Sean, they want to settle your soul."

"What does that even mean?" He looked at her, confused by the context. "Are you asking if I've grieved? If so, I can truthfully say I'm fine. It's taken a lot of time to get to a where I've accepted their death and moved forward."

"Have you?" She awaited his response.

The Hollywood actor said nothing. He was lost for words, knowing she was right.

"Part of this process is you being honest with yourself. I promise to help you and your wife and daughter, but you have to trust me, period. I'm giving of myself – selflessly, I might add. Above all that, you are invading our family vacation, by the way."

"I never asked you to do that," he snapped back.

Disappointed in him, she shook her head. "No, you didn't. I'm doing this out of the goodness of my heart because I promised your girls I would. And I keep my promises. Now, you need to stop this doubting Thomas routine and listen."

The author's words settled in deeply.

He wanted to know what Janie needed to tell him. *Was there something wrong?* He thought. *Are they trying to warn me? Or are there words left unsaid?* Pondering everything, he said, "Alright."

"I want to relay what messages they have. After that, what you choose to believe is all up to you."

Sean went silent.

Evily pressed the remote to open the truck for Ella to get in. Slipping behind the steering wheel herself, she started the engine. Cooling down the interior, now suffocatingly hot, Evily saw Evan exiting the arena's front doors. Leaving for a second, she went to help her son, who was lugging his hockey bag and sticks.

Standing beside the open passenger door, the actor turned to Ella, sitting in the back, and asked, "So, is your Mom always like this?"

The girl sincerely replied, "No. This is the first time she's ever felt a need to help them."

"Them?" Sean questioned.

"You know. The orbs." Ella created a circle with her fingers to help clarify things for him.

"Do you see them too?"

"Yes, but I don't hear them as she does." Ella put on her headphones.

Leaving the young girl to get comfortable in her seat, Sean waited for Evily and Evan to return. His gentlemanly nature surfaced. Walking to the back of the vehicle, he opened the hatch for the athlete to throw his bag inside.

When they approached, Evan said, "Thanks, Mr. Bradley. "Lifting the heavy bag into the cargo area, he carefully placed his hockey sticks at an angle to avoid scratching the interior.

One by one, they piled in.

Evily glanced behind her in the rearview mirror. "Amelia's, Evan?"

"Absolutely," her son replied. "I'm so hungry."

His Mother entered the restaurant into the GPS app. Soon, their SUV pulled away from the arena with the other parents. Each family was happy to celebrate this win and looked forward to the games scheduled the following day.

Realizing the Andersons were now going out to dinner, Sean said, "Look, I don't want to interrupt your family time."

"You'd better get used to it," she pointed out sternly.

"Why?" He wasn't sure what she meant.

"Because it seems you will be around us for a few days."

"What do you mean?"

Laughing, she added, "You'll see. Buckle up and enjoy the ride."

7

Thursday, July 25th
Stoughton, Massachusetts

You learn a lot about someone when you share a meal together. ~ Anthony Bourdain

The sun-cloud mix gave the New England area a break from the intense summer heat. Arriving in the suburb of Stoughton, Evily pulled into Amelia's - their favorite upmarket Italian restaurant. Since it was so early in the day, the place was quiet. Knowing a crowd would develop within the hour, Evily thought their timing was perfect. She was thankful they beat the afternoon rush. Finding a spot to park in the shade along the tree line, she cracked open the windows and popped the sunroof for ventilation.

"Evan?" she said, grabbing his attention. Maybe open your bag and spread your equipment out to dry."

"Yeah, alright," he replied, doing what she suggested.

They waited for him in front of the vehicle, barely saying a word.

Sean felt awkward about going inside to eat with the family. *What do I say to them? How will they react to a stranger sitting at the table?* He was sure it would be weird and worried about how he would be perceived.

It didn't take long for Ella to get impatient with her brother.

"Hurry up, Evan!" his sister shouted. "I'm hungry!"

"Yeah, yeah. I'm coming," he said, not overly concerned about her level of urgency.

As they approached the entrance lined with sculpted shrubbery and seasonal flowers that added a pop of color to the various shades of green, the Anderson family led the way. Sean Bradley followed, still feeling like he was about to infringe on their family dinner.

Not sure how to approach the situation, he said, "Hey, umm, if you guys want to eat alone, please, by all means…"

Evily shook her head. "Sorry. We don't do things that way. You will eat with us." Easing off on her bossy demeanor, she clarified, "I mean, if that's okay with you?"

"Yeah. I'm fine with it if you are."

For a brief second, he didn't feel the usual loneliness. Recalling how often he'd eaten by himself in restaurants, Sean felt like it never got easier or less uncomfortable as the years went by.

Following Evily and the teens, they ascended the stairs and reached the stylish hostess desk beside an impressive glass-enclosed wine cellar.

"Table for four, please," Evily requested, realizing it had been a while since she'd said those words.

The hostess acknowledged her while giving Sean the eye.

He instinctively caught on. People always gave off the same vibe every time he stepped out in public, but now, after years of practice, he could see it coming a mile away. Nervous, hoping the girl wouldn't cause a scene, the actor decided to strike up a conversation with Evily's son.

"So, Evan. Congrats on the hat-trick, man."

The athlete smiled. "Yeah. Thanks. It was a good game."

The girl check-marked their table on the seating chart with menus in hand and said, "Right this way."

Leading the group through the restaurant, she presented the family with a crescent-shaped booth tucked in the corner of a room with a large stone fireplace. Happy with the table, the Andersons gravitated to one side while Sean stayed a comfortable distance away and sat opposite them.

The young woman distributed the menus and explained, "Your waitress will be with you shortly to take your orders."

"Thank you," Evily replied, watching the girl walk away and briefly glance back at them for a split second. She had read her thoughts and felt Sean's uneasiness while he began to peruse the daily specials. Thankfully, the place was relatively quiet since they'd just opened for lunch. She knew the actor simply wanted to eat his meal peacefully and hoped his presence wouldn't ruin their dining experience.

Wanting to spark some normal conversation, he said, "So, Evan? What's a good post-game meal for you? I'd always gravitate towards high amounts of protein."

Evan replied without having to think about it, "I'm going heavy on the salad."

"If Evan had his way, he'd be a vegetarian," his mother confirmed.

"Yeah. Mom has to bribe him sometimes to eat chicken or steak." Glancing over at her brother, the young girl giggled.

Evan shot his sister a look from across the table. He was not happy.

Approached by their waitress, everyone knew what they wanted. Efficiently recording their selections on her notepad, the girl left to submit their orders and tend to a few other tables. Almost in sync, the teens simultaneously picked up their phones to immerse themselves in their online worlds. Creating an empty silence between them, Sean and Evily sat there, lost for words.

In need of interaction, the actor asked, "I assume you've eaten here before."

"Yes. I believe this might be our third, no, maybe the fourth visit. After playing, Evan is super hungry. Since we found this place, it has become a post-game tradition."

Not wasting any time, their waitress returned to deliver their heaping house salads. Sean was surprised that Evan had ordered two portions for himself.

Catching the actor's reaction, Ella humorously stated the obvious. "See! Vegetarian. Case closed."

"So what? Eat clean and green. That is my motto," Evan replied, ready to dive into the plates of lettuce and veggies.

The table erupted with light-hearted laughter.

Picking up his fork, Sean noticed the family stop and bow their heads.

Quietly praying with the teenagers, each concluding with an "Amen," Evily unrolled her napkin to locate the cutlery.

The whole praying thing felt foreign to Sean Bradley. A little panicked, he didn't know how to interact with them. It was intimidating.

Realizing their guest was uncomfortable, Evan decided to help him out. "So, your last movie was pretty badass."

"Oh, yeah?" Sean looked over at the hockey player with a smile. His eyes brightened.

"For sure. It was cool. My friends and I all saw it. The action scenes were wild."

Now halfway through his Caprese salad, Sean appreciated the compliment. "It's always nice to hear when someone loves your work. When your audience says they were entertained."

"Mr. Bradley used to play hockey too, Evan." Focusing on the actor for a split second, Evily added with a squint of one eye, "Umm, goalie? Is that correct?"

Still amazed by her strange ability, reminded he had not mentioned what position he played when they spoke of it, Sean replied, "Yeah. I did."

The athlete had just finished devouring his first plate of salad. "Wow, Goalie, huh? That's a tough gig. I think you have to have nerves of steel to play that position. Our goalies always seem a little nuts."

"You got that right. You gotta be nuts to have guys firing frozen pucks at you like that." Laughing, he said, "I always hated getting scored on. Felt like I let the team down when that happened. I made sure it wasn't often, mind you."

Evan could relate. "I hate when that happens on my shifts. If I'm on the ice, I think about whether I could have done something differently to have prevented it. You know, the goals against don't only reflect on the goalie's skills?"

"Suppose that is also true, but I felt the responsibility fell on my shoulders."

During the lunch hour, more patrons converged on the restaurant, and soon, a noticeable hum filled the air. For Sean, this sparked concern. He stayed alert and positioned his right hand to shield his face from the crowd while eating. Evily noted his apprehension when their pasta orders arrived.

It didn't take long for Evan to dig in. Even after having a double appetizer, he was still famished.

Ready to taste the first bit of her seafood spaghetti with scallops, mussels, and shrimp, Ella took her fork and neatly swirled some pasta with the spoon. Closing her eyes, she savored it. "Oh, this is so good. Yummy."

Sean looked about the table, hoping to know more about the family. The strange situation he was in wasn't far from his mind, either. "It seems you know so much about my life; I'm wondering about yours."

Evily continued eating. After politely swallowing her last bite, she asked, "What would you like to know?"

Sean thought for a second. "Well. Where are you from?"

Ella giggled. "That's easy. Chicago."

"Downtown or burbs?" he questioned.

"Suburbs." Evily felt like this would become a game of twenty questions. Fully aware that Sean had been stocking her social media over the past week, she had a feeling about what he would say next.

"Really? You live in Chicago and have a pool?"

Evily stopped and pretended to flash a look of shock. "Wait. How did you know that Mr. Bradley?" she asked suspiciously, fully aware of what he had done.

Sean froze the second every set of eyes around the table glanced over at him. "The truth is, I kind of scouted you out before coming here," he confessed. "For a few days, actually."

Rolling her eyes and another fork of pasta, Ella sarcastically responded, "Yeah, no, that's not creepy at all."

Her mother turned to her. "No, it's only fair. Everyone does it to him."

"Yeah, umm, that's not entirely accurate. They can't check my social media because I don't use any platforms," Sean divulged while sipping his sparkling water.

"Wait? Nothing?" Ella was in disbelief. "Like no accounts for anything?"

He shook his head and proudly replied, "Nope. Nothing. I feel like - for one - they'd be a waste of time. A distraction, and - two - people would harass me too much. There are a lot of haters out there - people intent on making your life miserable. I don't think I could handle reading all the negative."

Evily could feel his sadness and insecurity, something that surprised her. "I can see that," she sympathized.

"Wait. I'm sure it wouldn't be all bad," Ella debated. "There would probably be a lot of fans leaving positive comments too."

"Like how much they want to marry me?" Sean chuckled. "No thanks."

In complete agreement, the young girl repeatedly nodded, "Oh, yeah. No, no, no. Fair enough. I hear you."

"What else?" Sean pondered some more questions for the family. "Obviously, Evily, you write full-time, correct?"

"Yes, I write independently. Now and again, I do some freelance work for magazines. It's perfect because that way, I'm flexible enough to be there for these two whenever they need me."

"Yeah, if it weren't for Mom, I wouldn't be able to play hockey," Evan added quite bluntly.

"Oh? Why?" Sean thought that was a strong statement.

Evan wasn't afraid to tell the truth. Both he and his sister were well accustomed to their situation.

"Yeah, my dad's not too interested in my hockey, or my life for that matter. Being a lawyer, he's usually too busy and is never around. We don't talk much anyway."

"We aren't exactly a priority to him." Ella agreed with Evan.

Their mother's facial expression said it all as her head tilted slightly with a sorrowful look.

Sean didn't know how to respond. It was information he didn't expect. "Sorry to hear that, you guys."

"It's fine," Evan replied. "We don't need him anyway. Mom's got our back, right, Sis?"

"Right," Ella said firmly without hesitation.

Turning to Evily, he saw her face reflect a mixture of emotions.

"Thank you, you two," she said with tearful eyes. "I know it has been hard."

"Yeah, Mom's encouraged me to pursue architecture, something I truly love. Dad keeps telling me I'm going to law school so I can work at his firm one day. Take over the family business." Ella seemed so frustrated while shaking her head.

"Ella, we talked about this. You can do whatever you want in the future. This is your life, your decisions, and yours alone."

"I know. But, a part of me doesn't want to disappoint him at the same time." Looking down at her partially eaten plate, Ella exhaled.

"You could never disappoint anyone." Her mother reached over and squeezed her hand, getting her daughter to crack a smile.

Amid the deeply rooted conversation, Sean discovered that there was more to this family than he realized. The kids had been affected by the parent's divorce, and Evily had a lot to do with their upbringing. She was their cheerleader - always encouraging them from what he could gather thus far.

Surrounded by silence, out of the blue, Sean divulged, "You know, I never knew my dad. He left when I was five. It was tough growing up without a male figure in my life. My stepdads never paid much attention to me."

"Stepdads, like plural?" Ella posed, wanting to confirm what he said.

"Yes. There were three of them."

She was shocked. "Wow..."

"It's alright. I got through it. If anything, it made me stronger. It showed me how not to be in the future. How not to act towards my children."

"You have kids?" the young girl questioned sincerely.

Caught off guard, he replied with a hint of sadness, "Umm, no."

With impeccable timing, their waitress stopped by the table to take away their plates.

Knowing they had stumbled upon a topic of conversation Sean wanted to avoid, Evily asked, "Would anyone like dessert?"

Both teenagers declined, as did Sean, knowing he needed to watch the splurging between now and the upcoming movie premiere.

"Just the bill would be great, thank you," Evily requested with a smile before the girl departed.

"What is my schedule like tomorrow, Mom?" Evan wasn't sure.

"If I recall, there are two games: one early morning and one late afternoon. You have a tour of the University of Massachusetts arena and the campus. It'll be a long day, so you'll have to get some rest tonight."

Their waitress returned with the billfold in hand. The moment the girl placed it between Sean and Evily, the actor quickly slid it his way.

"Wait? What are you doing?"

Sean casually replied, "Taking care of the bill," not making a big deal of it.

Evan and Ella looked over at their Mom, intrigued by how she would react.

"You can't do that," she stated.

"Just did," Sean said, quickly handing the woman the billfold with the cash payment nestled inside while she strolled by to assist another table.

"Thank you so much. Guys, say thank you to Mr. Bradley for dinner."

They did what their mother asked of them.

"Okay, so where are we off to now?" Sean said with enthusiasm.

Evan stood up from the table and pushed in his chair. "Well, I guess we should get back to the hotel so I can prep for tomorrow."

The Hollywood star was excited for the determined athlete. "Good idea," he said. "It sounds like it will be a busy day."

Leaving the dining room, the teens moved down the hallway to the main entrance while the adults followed behind. At a distance, they heard a woman trying to get someone's attention.

"Excuse me, Sir!" their waitress called out while chasing them down. "Wait! I have your change!"

Sean immediately turned around. Finding the girl stopped a few feet away, she reached out with a few bills for him.

Putting up his hand, he quickly replied, "That's quite alright. Please keep it."

"Wow, thanks," the girl said with a smile. "Please dine with us again soon." Hesitating, she nervously blurted out, "I'm sorry, but are you Sean Bradley?" The young fan locked eyes with his.

He kindly answered, "Yes, I am."

"I knew it!" Taking out her phone from her apron pocket, she took a chance. "Do you mind if I grab a picture?"

"No, not at all. Happy to."

Evily took the phone from the girl standing anxiously beside her favorite action star. "Ready? Big smiles." Snapping a few photos, she handed back the device, wondering if the hostess would show up with the same request.

The girl gushed at the pictures Evily took. "Oh, that's awesome! Thanks again. Appreciate it." She was turning bright red.

"It was nice to meet you," Sean concluded before walking out the door, holding it open for Evily to pass through.

When they exited the building, the two walked a few feet apart.

Trying to catch up to the children, the author said, "Thank you for dinner. You didn't have to...."

"Yes, I did," he interrupted. "From what I've gathered, you've worked seven months to selflessly do something for me, although I don't fully know what that entails yet. Regardless, I would do anything for my girls." Pausing, he added, "It feels so strange to say that."

While walking alongside Sean, a series of bright flashes blinded Evily without warning. Losing sight, she abruptly stopped and tried to keep her balance in the middle of the parking lot. Hands out to the side, wavering, she slowly knelt on the ground.

Sean noticed something was very wrong. "Evily? Evily, what is it?"

Unable to answer, she watched a sequence of images flicker. There were no voices this time. In seconds, her sight returned.

"You okay?" he questioned, seeing her eyes drift upward to meet his.

"When we get back to the hotel, we should go somewhere and talk."

Concerned by her tone, he asked, "Is everything alright?"

"Yes. I just need you to understand a few conditions they've put on us."

"They?" he repeated.

"Janie and Ella."

"There are conditions now?" Sean chuckled, knowing his wife all too well. "That sounds like something she'd say."

"Look, I feel like they're running the ship, and I need to help them steer. That's all."

"Okay, I get it. Don't worry. If they want me to do something, I'll do it."

Arriving back at the truck, Ella opened her door when her mother unlocked it remotely. The teens were too immersed in their devices to notice what had happened to her.

"Oh, no! Mom!" Ella shouted.

"What is it?" Her mother's guard went up.

"That's so gross!" Ella stated, covering her nose.

Evan opened his side door. "What?" he said, somewhat nose blind, fluffing off her reaction to the ripe smell of his equipment wafting from the vehicle.

Relieved it was nothing serious, Evily and Sean sat in the front seats and closed their doors. Immediately, Evily turned on the blowers and opened the windows. All Sean could do was chuckle to himself.

"Don't know why you guys are complaining. It's not that bad." Evan seemed embarrassed.

Being the supportive Mom that she was, Evily said, "Don't worry. We'll give it a couple of minutes. It'll be okay."

Glimpsing over at Sean, she flashed a subtle grossed-out expression.

Evan caught his mother. "Hey! I saw that!"

Chuckling, she apologized, "Sorry, Evan. It is pretty bad. But I'm sure every parent from the tournament is dealing with the same thing."

8

Thursday, July 25th
Boston, Massachusetts

Learning to trust is one of life's most difficult tasks. ~ Issac Watts

Evily kept a close eye on the road while their vehicle inched along at a snail's pace. The freeway traffic was heavy and barely moving on the way back into Boston. An hour into the trip, having hit a lull in the conversation, the writer stayed quiet while her two teens slept in the seats behind them.

As they approached the downtown core, she asked, "Sean, could you watch the Navigation system for me again and let me know where to turn?"

"For sure. No problem," he replied, ready and willing to help.

They could see the city skyline in the distance. Directing her towards their hotels, Sean pondered the day's events so far from morning to present. Humorously recalling his planned altercation with the author, he looked over at Evily in the driver's seat, knowing he had greatly misjudged the woman. Deep down, Sean started to trust her somehow. Shifting his sights out the window on the right-hand side, he rested his elbow on the ledge and used his thumb to support his chin.

What do Janie and Ella need to tell me after all this time? He thought.

Evily happened to look his way, having heard those very words.

Catching her, he asked, "I assume you probably got all that?"

Focused forward, knowing he was concerned about the impending experience, she hesitated before nodding, "Yes. I'm sorry. Can't help it."

"It's fine. Strangely, it kind of makes it easier, you know. I don't have to explain myself. Embarrassingly, I might add. Sharing is usually tough for me. It's good that you understand where I'm coming from without needing clarification." With a few seconds of silence between them, he said, "Don't get me wrong; it's still kinda weird," Sean chuckled, causing Evily to smile. She knew he was right.

While maneuvering through the city center, the truck finally stopped on Avery Street outside the Ritz Carlton Hotel. The kids woke up when the valet attendant opened the back door to greet them. Evan got out and stretched before repacking his hockey bag. Ready for a well-earned break, in desperate need of a shower, with his prized hockey sticks in tow, the athlete started walking into the lobby like a zombie, leaving everyone else behind. Ella lingered and waited for her mother's instructions.

Passing the young girl her access card for the room, Evily explained, "Mr. Bradley and I are going to talk a minute. Go with Evan. I'll be there shortly."

Watching her daughter disappear inside, the valet took the key to the truck and moved it to the garage below. Evily didn't know how to explain what she needed to divulge. This caused them to stand on the sidewalk in silence awkwardly.

"So, I'm just going to rest for an hour. Maybe freshen up a little. I was thinking of taking a walk by the harbor later. Want to join me? We should talk through a few things."

A ray of sunshine reflected off the building across the street, cloaking Evily with bright light. Sean found it hard not to stare. Her eyes had suddenly become so blue.

"Sure. I can do that," he replied, quickly looking away, realizing the author must have picked up on his thoughts since she lowered her head bashfully. It was nerve-wracking knowing she could hear every sentence in his head. "So, ahh, I'll meet you back here in an hour?" he asked, wanting to confirm their plans.

"How does 4:30 sound?" Pausing a second, Evily had something else come to mind. "Oh, you brought running shoes, correct?"

"Matter of fact, I did." He had not pegged her for a fitness nut.

"Good. I usually take a three-mile walk. Are you okay with that?" she challenged.

Up for it, Sean knew it wouldn't be any different than working out with his trainer. "Yeah, I could go for some serious cardio. Maybe we can grab a coffee along the way?"

"Sure, why not? Afterward, I'll check to see if the kids want a light dinner. You can join us if you like."

"That sounds nice. Thank you." Sean slid his hands into his pockets. He didn't know why she made him so nervous.

"Perfect," she answered, not sure what more to say.

"Okay, then, I should get going. I'll see you back here at 4:30."

As he walked away, Evily stood in front of the Ritz Hotel's main doors. Looking back a couple of times, he raised a steady hand to bid her goodbye before rounding the corner.

Unaware of the crowds along Washington Street, the Hollywood star felt a bounce in his step. His feet seemed to float above the pavement. At the same time, his mind analyzed how the day turned out so differently. It was hard to even think of getting angry at the author now. She was a caring person and a wonderful mother, willing to share her mysterious gift with a total stranger.

Very intrigued, wanting to know more about Evily Anderson, the real person behind the pseudonym, he thought, *What is her story?*

Walking through his hotel lobby, Sean stepped into an empty elevator that eventually opened on the fourth floor. Approaching his room, he tapped the card against the lock. With a click, it allowed him access to the suite. Recalling what Evily said about the coins, he went directly to the window and found each in the same place. Staring at them, he picked up the dime between his fingers and checked the date.

"2006," he muttered, taking hold of the quarter and flipping it over. "2006? They are both the same year. What are the odds?" Sean thought a moment. In disbelief, he said, "No, it can't be. 2006?" Having repeated the date a third time, he whispered, "How is that possible?"

He held the coins in the palm of his hand, recalling the year Ella and Janie passed, not fully realizing the significance of his discovery. As most people would, he chalked it up to coincidence and set them on the left side of the desk before having a seat on the end of the bed. That is when he felt it. The heaviness he'd felt all these years seemed a little lighter. His heart didn't feel as weighed down, and it was easier to breathe.

So strange. He thought, running his hand across his chest. *I wanted to destroy her life. I hated her for what she did. And now.* He shook his head. *All of this is just crazy.*

Janie and baby Ella quickly came to mind. It was hard to believe that they'd somehow orchestrated this meeting. All of it still seemed quite surreal. Unable to pinpoint what message they needed to pass along, he hoped that in the next hour, Evily would explain more about what was to come - how this gift of hers worked and what to expect.

Moving into the bathroom, he washed his hands and splashed some water on his face. Deep in thought, he compiled a list of questions that would open topics of conversation during their walk. All of it made him feel anxious.

"Okay, my man, promise you'll keep an open mind with all this," he said, staring at himself in the mirror.

Willing to do just that, he remained slightly skeptical regardless of the signs beginning to appear all around him. In need of rest, trying to ignore the jet lag plaguing him, Sean set his alarm so he wouldn't be late to meet up with Evily. Resting his head on the pillow, he fell asleep quickly without giving it a second thought.

9

Thursday, July 25th
Boston, Massachusetts

Strangers are just friends waiting to happen. ~ Rod McKuen

Believing he had closed his eyes for a brief nap, Sean's phone alarm suddenly went off and filled the room with an intrusive sound that startled him from a dead sleep. Slowly getting his bearings, he rolled out of bed with one eye open. Dazed, the middle-aged actor sat on the edge of the mattress and recalled everything that had happened thus far. All of it was not a dream. This crazy day was for real.

Knowing he had to meet up with Evily, it didn't take much to motivate him. Interested to see Boston harbor, he changed into his workout clothes and tied his running shoes before passing his hand through his hair, concerned about the grey creeping in lately. Slipping on a hat and sunglasses, ready to leave, he took a deep breath, trying to remember the last time he went for a walk like this. Sadly, he knew it had been years.

The hallway was quiet on the way to the elevators. Not a soul was around. Stepping inside the lift when the doors parted, thankful to have it to himself, Sean gathered his thoughts while descending to the main floor. Prepared to move swiftly through the lobby, he checked the time, relieved that he was not running late. Able to anonymously mingle amongst the patrons, he felt a rare sense of freedom. Luckily for him, most people were immersed in their own agendas. Nobody was paying attention. It was a nice change. To them, he was just another tourist.

"I could get used to this," he said, feeling almost human.

Leaving the Godfrey, Sean stayed alert. The last thing he needed was to let his guard down. Amidst the theatre district crowds, dodging pedestrians, not wanting to be recognized, he inserted his earbuds and walked with his head down the entire way. Almost there, about to cross the road, he spotted the author standing outside the front doors of her hotel. Evily was giving her legs a quick stretch. She was dressed impeccably from head to toe, wearing black cropped tights and a royal blue tank, with a light grey jacket knotted around her waist. Not noticing him, he watched her reposition her small crossover bag with one strap slung from shoulder to waist. It held a single water bottle nestled inside. Sean felt overly bland in all black, except for a hint of burnt red trimming the bottom of his Firestarters. Free to dress the way he wanted, he did not miss his assistant's fashion advice.

Scanning the busy intersection, Evily spotted the Hollywood star. She waved with one hand and held an extra water bottle in the other. Sean had no choice but to greet her with a smile.

"Hello, again," she said while he dodged a vehicle passing by slowly. "This is for you."

After stashing his earbuds in their case, he took the bottle from her.

"Thank you. Appreciate that. I'm a bit early. Hope you don't mind."

"No. Not at all."

"Did you have a nice break?" he asked.

"Yes, Evan had a shower and is relaxing. Ella was drawing and talking with friends online when I left, and I got to close my eyes for about forty minutes. Something very much welcomed. I find these trips mentally exhausting at times. Because I am the mom, and no one else is helping me, I always worry about being one step ahead. It takes a toll after a while." Believing she had just revealed a list of useless information, the writer added, "Long story short. I am well-rested and good to go. How about you?"

"If it makes you feel any better, I did the same. My internal clock is off, for sure."

"I guess so. Forgot about that. You are what? A three-hour time difference?"

"Yes, that's right."

"We are only a difference of an hour. It's manageable," she stated, concerned whether he had enough energy for the trek. "Still up to it? I mean, if you are hitting a wall, it's okay. I know how that is."

"No, no. I'm good. I've got to try and get on East Coast time." Stretching his legs, he asked, "So, where to first?"

"Well, usually, I head towards the port and link up with the Greenway." Evily changed her hand's direction as she explained the route. "It will safely connect us to the harbor front. You'll get to see the boats and the view. It's beautiful, by the way. After that, I wrap around and head toward Boston Common. It's a nice loop."

"Great. Lead the way," Sean said, extending his arm outward for her to go first.

"Alright, follow me. We'll take the same street we drove down this morning. It's just up here," she said, moving south on Washington.

Sean didn't know what to talk about with her. So many subjects came to mind, leaving it in a muddle.

Should I ask questions about the girls, her work, or this so-called gift of hers? Maybe I should ask about her life in Chicago, perhaps her ex-husband, or how she intends to receive these messages from Janie. His mind reeled in a million directions.

Once again, Evily turned to him, squinted her eyes, and concentrated.

"What?" he questioned with a snicker.

"Hmm," she replied with a mischievous look.

"What did I do?"

"Nothing," Evily said, having heard him think through a list of topics. "So, what do you want to know first? Shoot."

"Have to say, this whole mind-reading thing is kinda freakish. No offense," Sean accused while fidgeting with the water bottle in hand, cracking it open to take a sip.

"I know. I know. I'm sorry. I can't help it. Your inner voice is so loud. It's hard to ignore." Evily thought a minute. She knew she had to stop doing that or at least make it not seem too obvious. It had to be done subtly in a way that wasn't bothersome.

Another awkward silence followed Evily's heavy train of thought. The only thing she could do was pick up the pace. He had many questions but didn't know where to start.

"First, I am trying to figure out why Janie and Ella visited your front door?" Sean posed, really wanting to know the answer. "Out of all the people in the world, why you?"

"Yes, that's a tough one. I can't fully answer that. Maybe in time, they'll reveal the reason to us. At this point, I assume it is because of my abilities. Maybe the writing part was a bonus. I don't know. Next question?"

"How can you be sure it was them?" He was doubtful.

"Because they told me. Janie and Ella Bradley."

"Did you know it was me who would show up?"

"You specifically? No."

"Why?"

"Do you know how many Jane Bradley's there are out there? I did an internet search once but found over a hundred obituaries spanning a few years. It could have been anyone, and there was no record of your daughter."

Knowing she was right, he said, "That's true."

Evily continued to walk at a fast clip and got into a grove while Sean struggled to keep up. It took only minutes to reach the Greenway. Crossing the street at Leather District Park, located within the gap between the two highways, they followed the path leading to a building with a mural painted on one side.

"This mural is different every time we come here. Once, it was a hobbit-looking person, and then there was a sci-fi theme. Sometimes, they create something thought-provoking. This time, it's two giant swallows." She found the birds interesting like they were a sign.

"Wait? Sci-fi? I haven't heard that reference for eons," Sean humorously pointed out. "Isn't that considered an '80s term now?"

Evily smiled while using the crosswalk to move south on Congress Street. "Maybe so. Hey, you're older than me by exactly sixteen months if you are insinuating that I am the fossil here."

He quickly raised his hands between them, hoping he hadn't offended her. "No, no. That's not what I meant," he said in his defense, reminding himself - *never question a woman's age.*

"You got that, right," she responded with a smirk.

Evily caught herself doing it again, making his eyebrows raise, somewhat annoyed. It was amusing how she kept him on his toes, but the author knew it would drive a wedge that could ruin everything if she continued. That was not an option, given the circumstances. She had a job to do and had every intention of following through on her promise to Janie and Ella. It meant a lot to them.

Close to the seaport, Evily turned to her left. "This path will bring us to the harbor," she explained, hoping to settle things down.

While veering towards the water and distancing themselves from the busy road, Sean was happy to see the crowds of people disperse, making him feel more comfortable. Finding the tall ships from yesterday, he stopped and rested his hands along the back of a bench to take in the sights and catch his breath.

"I passed this place on the way to the hotel."

"It's The Boston Tea Party Museum," Evily revealed while standing beside him. "Want to take a look?"

Sean surveyed the number of people surrounding the attraction. "Umm, no. I think I should pass. I'd probably get bombarded."

Evily could feel his hesitation and disappointment. "Is it always like that?"

"Like what?"

"Do you always get mobbed by fans? Make decisions based on the risk?"

"That depends. Some days are worse than others. So far, we're doing okay. One fan photo is manageable."

"What would happen if a group of people recognized you here?"

"Well, truthfully, it's kind of like a tsunami. One person leads to two, then twenty, then a hundred. You get the idea. The moment a picture gets posted of me on social media, the tabloids get word. They send their people, and I become a moving target. Every paparazzi could take upwards of five hundred pictures in a short time. They then sell them to magazines that will misconstrue the story to suit their narrative. Don't get me wrong; I love my fans. But things do get out of hand. The situation can also get ugly, turn on a dime, and intensify. It escalates quickly."

Optimistic, Evily replied, "Well, hopefully, our walk will be uneventful."

"You know, because I am walking with you, maybe people wouldn't give it a second thought," he said.

"Why? What's wrong with walking alongside me?" she quizzed, putting him on the spot, wanting him to clarify.

"What I mean is, there's no security flanking both sides of me, and not one black SUV is tracking my whereabouts. I don't even have an entourage around." He thought a minute. *People will just see us as a couple out for a walk.*

After giving off that vibe, Sean got nervous. Had she heard him?

Evily played along, pretending she missed it. "So, then you're safe?"

"Suppose so. Still have to be careful. Look, I have a lot of experience with crowds going crazy. If that happens, please distance yourself. That way, you won't get hurt," he warned, concerned for her safety.

"I think I'm the kind of person who would not abandon a friend who needs my help. Just saying. We could outrun them, you know."

Sean laughed. "Yeah? Maybe."

Leading the way down an alley beside the InterContinental Hotel, Evily's shortcut took them back to the main street jammed with tourists. Connecting with the more sparsely populated boardwalk on the opposite side of the bridge, she watched the harbor view captivate him.

Step by step, they only strolled a short distance before having to turn a corner. Filled with excitement, Evily knew the Boston Harbor Hotel arch would be the next attraction on the agenda. The author prepared to take note, waiting to see his face, when he spotted the gigantic American flag hanging proudly in the domed hall. She loved mentally documenting people's reactions. It gave her a real-life reference that made describing specific experiences in her fictional stories easier.

Almost there, Sean's eyes soon fell upon the massive flag. The closer they got, his gaze drew upward. He was amazed at the height of the ceiling and the intricate architectural elements.

Nearing the entrance, he stood under the arch.

"This is incredible," he said, admiring the details.

"I know. Isn't it beautiful? It's even better when lit up at night. Every time I see it, I still have the same reaction."

The handsome actor exhibited a boyish grin while moving about in a circle. Happy to see him this way, she backed off and watched from a distance while he soaked it all in.

When the astonishment wore off, Sean scanned the space, losing track of Evily. Amidst the crowd, it wasn't hard to spot the pretty woman with light-brown hair leaning against the stone retaining wall about thirty feet away. He noticed she was staring at someone intently. Following her field of vision, he found a man dressed in a dark suit carrying a briefcase. Meeting with colleagues, shaking their hands with a forced smile, he stood outside the main doors of the building, having a conversation.

Sean joined Evily. "Do you know him?"

"No," she muttered. Focused on a translucent orb hovering over the man, she said, "His son passed away suddenly. It has only been a few months."

Her eyes fell shut while her heart started to beat erratically. Clutching her chest, feeling dizzy, she found it hard to breathe.

"Damon was young. Athletic. A blood clot stopped his heart from beating." Stressed, she could feel the depth of the father's grief. "There is a void in that man's soul—a missing piece," she said. "The boy is showing me an image of his dad sitting vigil at his bedside in the ICU. Alone, late at night, holding his son's one hand in both of his, he rested his forehead upon their tightly bound cluster and begged and pleaded for a miracle, asking God to spare his only son. The young man with such a bright future was popular and loved by many." Evily paused. "Little did he know, sixteen-year-old Damon was making the journey into the afterlife at that very moment. Not looking back, greeted by an older white-haired relative with a short, white beard, he passed through the light willingly with a look of amazement, knowing they needed him on the other side."

Stunned to hear what she was revealing, Sean just listened.

Tilting her head, Evily was confused. "The mother is filled with guilt and pain. This has put stress on both parents. Her heart aches for her boy. But she harbors a secret she will never share. Struggling, she wakes up often at night to grieve in silence. His death was preventable but nonetheless meant to be. Being perfected in a short time, he fulfilled his long years, for his soul was pleasing to the Lord; therefore, he took him from the midst of wickedness. Yet the people saw and did not understand, nor take such a thing to heart, that God's grace and mercy are with his elect, and he watches over his holy ones." Quoting the bible verse, Evily added, "The mother feels she gave her son the wrong advice."

Unsure of the cryptic message, the author's eyes drifted open as the man walked into the hotel lobby, and the orb disappeared. Whispering a prayer for him to settle his soul and that of the grieving mother, a tear drifted down her face. The boy was a year younger than Evan. She could never fathom him suffering a fate such as this.

Breaking away, she turned her attention back to Sean. Their mood turned solemn. He was fascinated by what had happened.

"Shall we go?" Evily asked rather casually, not about to explain herself any further.

"Wait. Can I ask you something?"

Aware of what he was about to say, she replied, "The answer to your question is no. As a rule, I never interfere in people's lives. That man struggled to get up this morning and travel to this meeting. The last thing I want to do is disturb his progress. For him, the wound is still very fresh."

Agreeing, he nodded, recalling the days, weeks, and months after Janie and Ella had died. He hated anyone bringing up their passing and thrusting him back into the memory of their departure.

Leaving it at that, he questioned, "So, what's next?"

Evily changed gears and said, "The harbor walk continues that way all along the water."

Realizing she wanted to move on, he said, "Lead the way."

10

Thursday, July 25th
Boston, Massachusetts

There's something more to life than what we see on the surface. ~ Adyashanti

Zigzagging, following the pathways, Sean's mind flooded with more questions. Enjoying the beautiful view, he hoped Evily would just pick up on his thoughts so he didn't have to ask. He was still in disbelief and found it hard to fathom the most bizarre situation he had ever encountered. The circumstances were well beyond comprehension.

"So, what did you need to talk to me about?"

Evily glanced over, then looked straight ahead. "Yes, umm... So, remember today, in the middle of the restaurant parking lot, when I happened to pause a second before we left?"

"Yeah, that was more than just a pause," he replied, not fully understanding what had transpired.

Knowing he was right, she explained, "Well, I got a brief message from your girls. That rarely happens, by the way. It was quite out of the ordinary."

Not sure where their conversation was heading, he nodded and said curiously, "Really? What did they say?"

"So, remember the orb videos I showed you?"

"Yes."

"Well, this Monday, Janie and Ella want to visit you at 2:44 am."

In shock, he asked, "What do you mean, visit?"

Explaining things further, Evily said, "They will appear in orb form…"

"At 2:44 in the morning?" Sean interrupted before Evily had a chance to elaborate.

"Yes. Why? Does that have significance to you?" She looked for clarification, feeling confusion radiating off him.

"Ahh, yeah," he said, clearing his throat and lowering his head. "That's Ella's time of death. Janie passed hours later, about 6:20 am."

"I'm so sorry… I know this is hard. They probably used the time to validate that what I am saying is true."

"I understand."

"So, technically speaking, the orbs are Janie and Ella's souls or spirits. They usually prefer to appear in peaceful locations. The closest place I have to that is my beach house."

"Okay…"

"Thing is…" Evily paused, hoping she wouldn't keep stumbling on her words. With anxiety running high, she now needed to drop yet another bomb on him. "The thing is, my house is in Cape Cod. That was their message today. Go to the Cape. 2:44."

"Where's that? Is it close?" he questioned, not knowing the geographical area.

"It's about an hour and fifteen-minute drive, give or take."

"So, how will that work then?"

"First off, I can't leave for the Cape until Evan's tournament ends. I'm afraid you are stuck with us until then. That's if you choose to stay, of course."

Sean did not respond.

"Between now and Sunday, you will need to find a vacation rental in the town of Dennis. Maybe a hotel or a house nearby. I would ask you to stay with us, but I don't feel comfortable with that. No offense."

Sean stayed quiet for a brief second. "Umm, none taken," he whispered, feeling overwhelmed, almost unable to string a sentence together.

"While there, we will wait for them to appear at that time. When they do, Janie and Ella will speak through me, and I will relay their message."

Evily could feel a battle going on inside him. This trip was more than he bargained for. He also struggled to believe everything she said, understandably so. He hadn't grown up in a faith-filled home. For a non-believer, it is challenging to process things you cannot see, hear, or touch. It is hard enough for a faithful follower to grasp it all.

"They could appear to you once or three or four times. I don't know. Part of it is up to you, too. You mustn't be skeptical. If you are, they won't visit. The connection between their world and ours won't open."

Pausing again, Sean looked out over the water.

"This is a once-in-a-lifetime opportunity. A chance to get the closure you need." She hoped he would agree.

Thinking it through, knowing he had to be back in LA for the premiere, he said, "Can't you just give me the message without going there?"

"No. Janie and Ella haven't revealed that yet. I know they want to share something with you, but for that to happen, you need to be present for it to materialize."

Not quite at the harbor walk's end, Sean and Evily stopped to take in the unobstructed view of the busy oceanfront. The salty air was welcoming and fresh. A packed whale-watching vessel passed by while Sean started processing what she had just proposed. Undecided, he looked at all the ships of many sizes spread out on the water. He was impressed by a few large yachts parked along the berths.

"I think my friend Harry has a yacht here somewhere. I recall him talking about it years back. For the life of me, I can't remember its name." Knowing he was stalling, Sean suddenly turned to her without further delay. "Okay. I'll, ahh - I'll go to the Cape." His heart was drawing him there.

Evily nodded. "That's good. I'm glad," she added with a sympathetic tilt of her head, concerned about how complicated their situation was becoming.

"I will get ahold of my assistant. He'll arrange accommodations for me." Part of him wondered what he had gotten into while the other was contemplating how to break the news to Max.

"Good. I'll send you the address later." Relieved, Evily picked up on his energy.

Scared of the unknown, he still possessed such love for Janie and Ella, even though it had been years since their departure. All in all, she couldn't blame him for going quiet. This request was a tall order.

"You are welcome to hang out with us between now and Sunday. I hope it won't be too boring for you."

"Thank you for that. But I don't want to intrude on your family time. Appreciate the invitation, though. You have enough on your plate without worrying about me, too." Sean felt bad.

"Don't be silly. For me, it was nice having another adult to talk to today. Usually, Ella does her own thing, and I watch the game alone."

He got quiet. His thoughts seemed a million miles away.

"So, will you stick around until we leave for the Cape on Sunday? Evan has five games left. It should be an exciting weekend."

Nodding his head, offering a subdued smile, he said, "Yeah. I'll stay."

Evily left the conversation there. She knew he needed time to think. At that point, he realized he'd be extending his trip by at least five days. It was something he hadn't anticipated.

A little overwhelmed and in need of a distraction, Sean tried to think of the name of Harry's boat. Amid their silence, he heard a phone vibrating and chiming inside Evily's crossover bag. "Everything okay?" he asked.

"Yes, all good." Reading the text from Ella, she looked up and said, "Everybody is fine. Evan is sleeping." Typing a message back, she said, "I told her she'd have to wake him or he won't sleep the rest of the night. We've got a long day tomorrow."

Sean pondered that thought. "So, you really don't mind if I join you guys?"

Surprised, Evily said, "No, not at all. As long as you're okay with sitting in a hockey arena all day?" Putting the phone away, she waited for his answer.

"Yeah, I'm up for that. Enjoyed watching the game today. I mean, despite all the drama, it was some fast-paced hockey - kind of exciting, actually." Sean paused, still unsure if she was genuinely okay with him tagging along.

Evily read his mind. "Don't give it another thought. You are more than welcome." She hoped to put him at ease. "We need to be on the road early, though. Evan's first game is at 9:00 am at the Canton rink. We must leave well before eight in the morning to get there on time. Afterward, we head to the UMASS Lowell campus to visit the Tsongas arena for a tour. Once that is over, we'll have a few hours off before his next game at the New England Sports Village in Attleboro. All of the driving will make for a long day."

The tall actor stood there, not batting an eye at the schedule. "I'm no stranger to a hectic pace. Count me in."

"Alright. Don't say I didn't warn you," she laughed.

The sun's rays filtered between the buildings downtown while the two avoided the crowds mingling outside the New England Aquarium. Crossing Atlantic Avenue, staying within the Green Way, they continued past the North Market carousel. Evily thought it best to veer right and remain on the parking garage side of Clinton Street rather than venture through the shopping district. Wanting to stay out of the public eye, Sean wholeheartedly supported her suggestion.

About to run out of steam while making their way between the Great Hall and Sephoria, they took in the sights around the Samuel Adams statue, keeping a safe distance from everyone.

Crossing Congress Street, standing at the bottom of the towering steps outside City Hall, Evily playfully shouted, "Race you!"

Caught off guard, Sean saw the author ascend the staircase at lightning speed. Up to the challenge, he, too, exploded into a sprint, skipping every second step. Struggling near the end, Evily turned to see him close behind. Out of breath, they both stood at the top. Sean felt pain in his knees. Rubbing them seemed to help.

"Too much wear and tear on the joints over the years?" She could feel the aches and pains he was experiencing.

"Think I've taken on too many movie stunts. Possibly made some dumb decisions that had long-term consequences, also," he laughed, knowing it was all a sign of getting old.

Moving slower, Evily pointed out a golden teapot around the next corner. It was a Starbucks.

"Interested in an iced coffee?" Having finished their waters a while ago, she knew they'd need something to keep them going for the second half of the walk. "After that sprint, I think it's a break well-earned, don't you?"

With a nod of his head, he replied, "Sure. I could go for that."

Approaching the shop, Sean casually opened the door for Evily to go first. Once inside, they stood in a line-up of about ten people. It didn't take long for the whispers to start. Evily had heard their thoughts only seconds beforehand. When she glanced over at him, her worried expression confirmed it all.

Out of the blue, a teenage girl asked, "Excuse me. Are you Sean Bradley?"

Caught off guard, not sure how to answer, Sean's heart sank. Needing to respond, he hesitantly replied, "Yes."

The teen immediately started to shake uncontrollably, almost breaking into hysterics. In a high-pitched voice, she said, "OMG! I'm a huge fan! Can I take a selfie?"

"Umm, sure. No problem," Sean calmly replied. His heart began to race, knowing what was about to happen.

Overhearing them, everyone turned and pointed their phones toward the famous actor. People gathered around when he smiled for the girl's photo. In seconds, the once orderly line for coffee disintegrated. The volume inside the shop became deafening.

Trying to remain calm, he briefly looked at Evily and said, "Remember what I told you. Safe distance."

She nodded her head.

The patrons were mobbing him a few feet from where she stood. Watching fans go out the door, proud of their celebrity pic, Evily noticed some of them showing their selfies to those passing by, inevitably pointing inside, revealing the star's location. Word was spreading fast.

"I've got to get us a cab," she mumbled amid the chaos. Catching Sean's attention, she said, "Get ready to move. Keep watch outside."

"I'll try," he said while Evily walked onto the street, leaving him to contend with the craziness.

Every person was jostling for a perfect picture, leaning against him, wrapping their arms around his waist, or resting a hand on his shoulder. One girl even kissed him on the cheek - an action he neither welcomed nor condoned. The fans even got angry and started pushing and shoving. A frenzy that quickly escalated. Needing to get out of there, inching his way towards the exit, taking photo after photo as more and more people entered the cafe, he started to get overtaken. No longer able to control the situation, he glanced outside repeatedly. Spotting Evily waiting across the street after hailing a white car with lime green and brown markings, she held the back door open, waving for him to hurry.

"Thank you, everyone. Sorry, I need to be on my way. Thank you," he said, weaving swiftly through the crowd. Bolting out the door, dodging traffic, he darted toward the cab stopped along the curb.

Evily jumped in the back seat and slid over, allowing Sean to slip in beside her and close the door.

"Go! Go! Go!" she instructed the driver.

"Where too?" the man asked while accelerating, seeing the mob Sean had just escaped.

Needing to get them to safety, Evily told him, "The Godfrey Hotel, please." Traveling down Tremont Street, she turned to Sean. "Are you alright? You're not hurt, are you?"

"No, I'm good." The actor took a deep breath.

The taxi driver kept nosily peeking in the rearview mirror.

"When you said tsunami, you weren't kidding," she confirmed, having now seen it firsthand.

"This is going to be bad." Sean leaned back in the seat and rested his head, totally frustrated.

"What do you mean?"

Whispering, he explained, "Remember what I said about the tabloids? If only one of those people posts a photo of me on social media and tags it in Boston, there will be a paparazzi frenzy. I won't be safe anywhere."

Turning onto Avery Street to backtrack to the Godfrey on Washington, Sean said to the driver, "Can you stop at the Ritz first?"

Evily turned to Sean.

"Look, I'll call you later. For now, I need to arrange a few things. What is your cell number?" Pulling his phone from his pocket, she did the same. Upon exchanging numbers, the actor's mind raced a mile a minute.

She felt so bad for putting him in this position. "I'm sorry…" she said moments before the cab driver stopped outside her hotel.

"For what? That wasn't your fault. It's my problem."

Evily reached for the door handle. "If we hadn't gone on the walk, this wouldn't have happened."

He seemed pretty calm. "Don't worry. It'll be alright. I promise."

Stepping out of the cab, she reminded him, "Make sure to call or text me later."

"I will. Give me about an hour. If you need to, go ahead to dinner with the kids. I'm not sure if I will be able to join you." That saddened him.

"Okay. I'll let you know when we go downstairs. We will be eating at the...." The author stopped herself, knowing the taxi driver was listening.

Motioning with her eyes to the guy in the front seat, Sean acknowledged, "Got ya. I'll keep you updated."

Evily closed the door before the cab pulled away. She waited until it turned left at the corner before walking inside the lobby to head upstairs.

Sean didn't say a word on the way over to the Godfrey. He was too busy compiling a list of calls he'd need to make once he returned to his room.

When the taxi arrived at the hotel, the man glanced in the rearview mirror and asked with a Boston accent, "You're Sean Bradley, right?"

"Umm, yeah," Sean replied, passing him money for the fare.

Taking out his phone, he asked, "Do you mind? My boys are huge fans."

"No. Not at all."

The driver held up his camera as Sean posed for the photo, leaning forward from his back seat.

Having gotten a few pictures, he said, "Pleasure meeting you, Mr. Bradley." Offering a gentleman's handshake to Sean, the driver looked at him directly and said, "God Bless. Have a good evening."

Taken off guard, breaking ties with the driver, not sure how to respond, Sean found it hard to leave his sights. For whatever reason, he felt a sense of peace at that moment. What was it about the Godfrey Hotel that attracted faithful people?

"Thank you," he muttered appreciatively before getting out and closing the door behind him. Their meeting seemed a bit surreal. But he didn't fully know why.

Once inside the hotel, he refocused and immediately sent a text asking Max to call him.

Within seconds, his assistant's face showed up on his phone.

Answering, Sean said, "Hey, Max. Hate to bother you, but we got big problems here."

11

Thursday, July 25th
Boston, Massachusetts

Fame and fortune, how empty they can be. ~ Elvis Presley

Reaching the fourth floor, Sean opened the door to his suite and heard it fall closed behind him, giving a sense of relief. He'd spoken to his assistant on the way up and knew the wheels were in motion to get some help brought in. Prepared for this, Max had made a call while Sean was on the other line with him. Within minutes, security personnel were dispatched to the Godfrey and would most likely arrive within the hour.

Hating that his freedom was short-lived, he sat on the bed and flopped backward. Lying there, staring at the ceiling, he was thankful for the time he did have. It had been a while since he could move about freely in public. Part of him was angry, believing he should have been more careful. Enjoying the walk with Evily, he'd gotten caught up in the moment. Sadly, the consequences of his actions ruined the day. Unable to change things now, he figured he'd text her an update.

Grabbing hold of his phone, he typed.

SO, I'VE HAD TO ARRANGE FOR SECURITY TO BE BROUGHT IN. IT'S JUST A PRECAUTION. DID YOU GO AHEAD TO DINNER?

Evily immediately responded.

NO, WE HAVEN'T GOTTEN THAT FAR YET. SECURITY? WHAT DOES THIS MEAN, THEN?

Sean let out a frustrated sigh.

UNFORTUNATELY, THERE WILL BE GUYS WITH ME TWENTY-FOUR-SEVEN NOW.

Her response bubbles completed their repetitive cycle, over and over. Wondering what she would say next, the whole Cape Cod situation floated around in his mind. That was one bomb he had yet to drop on Max. The extended trip seemed appealing since going there would mean a change of scenery that would hopefully offer some renewed anonymity.

Given what had happened, maybe this is good, all things considered, he thought.

Evily's reply popped up on the screen.

SO, WHAT DO WE DO? WILL YOU BE ABLE TO JOIN US FOR DINNER?

Sean thought for a minute, trying to figure things out. He knew he couldn't leave the hotel at this point.

APOLOGIZE, BUT I HAVE TO STAY HERE AND ORDER ROOM SERVICE.

Every bit of emotion flowed through his words. Evily could feel it. Not seeing her thinking bubbles rambling, he texted,

I'LL KEEP YOU POSTED - YOU GO AHEAD TO THE RESTAURANT. I WILL CHECK IN LATER. BTW, WHAT IS THE ADDRESS OF THE COTTAGE IN CAPE COD?

12

Thursday, July 25th
Boston, Massachusetts

Fame is not your friend. ~ Aaron McGruder

Evily typed the cottage address and added some additional information on the town of Dennis and the Corporation Beach area. Pressing send, she felt to blame for the day's events.

"Why didn't I see this coming?" she quietly asked. Troubled by what happened, she sat down on the edge of the bed.

"What's wrong, Mom?" Ella was puzzled by her mood.

"Well, my walk with Sean kind of got out of hand."

"Oh? How's that? What do you mean?" the girl questioned intriguingly.

"A couple of people inside Starbucks recognized him. We should have never gone in there," Evily recounted, shaking and lowering her head. "A crowd of people gathered wanting pictures. Really, it was more like a mob. Now, he is waiting for security to arrive. From now on, they will escort him wherever he goes."

"That sucks. I would never want to be famous. Freedom is underrated. Couldn't imagine not being able to go wherever I want, when I want."

Evily listened to her daughter, who was quite wise for her young age. "Yes, you are so right, Ella." Resting her phone on the side table, she asked, "Are you both hungry? Want to grab a bite before bed?"

The hockey player never turned down food. "Yeah, sure. I could eat." Getting up, he grabbed some clothes from the open suitcase on the dresser and started watching YouTube while heading to the bathroom to change.

"Ella? How about you?" her mother prompted for an answer.

"Yeah, I could go for something small. I'm still full from lunch." Her daughter started packing up her computer and tidying up the desk area.

"Okay, then. We will head downstairs in about ten minutes."

The Anderson family got ready and made their way to the Artisan Bistro. While waiting for the hostess to greet them, Evily felt something was missing.

"Good evening," the young woman said.

Breaking away from her thoughts, Evily replied, "Good evening. Table for three, please."

13

Thursday, July 25th
Boston, Massachusetts

The secret to happiness is freedom. The secret to freedom is courage. ~ Thucydides

Almost at the end of a very long day, Sean was exhausted. Waiting for security to show up, he had no choice but to order room service. About to pick up the phone to call the concierge, he thought of Evily and the teens going to dinner without him. It had been nice to be a part of a family, even though they were technically strangers he'd only met that morning. For some reason, he felt an inexplicable warmth from the Andersons. They had this uncanny ability to make a person feel welcome.

Sitting at the desk, leaning back in the chair, he ran his palm over the flat surface. Immediately, he noticed something was missing. The two coins that he'd placed there were gone.

"I am sure the maid service wouldn't have taken them." Sean looked on the floor around the desk. He felt guilty like he'd lost a piece of Janie and Ella. "I should have paid more attention and taken better care of them," he said.

In the midst of it all, he heard a knock at the door. Walking past the windows, he stopped dead in his tracks and took two steps back. With his sights affixed to the window ledge, the air left his lungs, leaving him almost unable to breathe. Moving closer, he confirmed his suspicions. The coins were back in the same place he'd initially found them yesterday.

"Is this some kind of joke?" he whispered to himself. Picking one up, he checked the date.

"2006," he said quietly before doing the same with the other. "2006. These are my coins." He smiled.

The person knocked a second time. But this time, the rapping was louder. Tearing away from the peculiar finding, slipping the coins into his pocket for safekeeping, Sean continued around the corner and cautiously answered the door. A man dressed in a three-piece suit with a visible name badge stood in the hallway waiting for him.

"Good evening, Mr. Bradley. My name is Lawrence Costello. I am the hotel manager. About fifteen minutes ago, I received a call from...." Pausing, he read the name off a piece of paper. "...a Maximillian Tanner. He asked that I assist you."

Not surprised to hear that, Sean invited the man in, but Mr. Costello outwardly declined, opting to stay in the hall.

"From what I understand, security will be arriving shortly," he updated, keeping his distance. "If there is anything we can do to make your stay more comfortable, here is my contact information. I have written my cell number on the back. You can contact me directly." The man stayed calm and professional throughout the entire speech.

"Thank you, Sir. I appreciate that," the actor said, taking the card from him.

"Upon arrival, I will escort your staff here to meet you. Arrangements have been made for the guards to be located just across and down the hall." The man pointed to the assigned rooms, each located to the left of his suite.

"That's great."

"Will there be anything else?" The older gentleman was unfazed by the celebrity.

"No, I think I am okay for now."

Nodding, Mr. Costello said, "Very well then. I will be on my way."

When he left, Sean allowed the door to close behind him automatically. Rounding the corner, he stopped and pulled the coins from his pocket before placing each on the desk. Staring at them, perplexed by their presence, he had a seat in the office chair, knowing he now needed to call Max to discuss the subject of Cape Cod. It was a conversation he was dreading. Dialing the number, fidgeting with the coins, sliding their positions from left to right, he heard Max answer after the first ring.

"Hey, Sean. What's happening now?" Max sounded hyper. "Everything okay?"

He could feel his high-strung friend was about to go from zero to sixty. "I'm fine, Max. Calm down. It's all good. I'm in my room and just got a visit from the hotel manager. Hopefully, security will arrive shortly."

"So, you are coming home. Do you need me to book a flight?" Max assumed presumptuously.

"Umm, about that...." Sean hesitated, wondering how to phrase his next sentence. "I need you to do something else. But you'll have to keep this under your hat. Do you hear me?"

Max's heart sank, knowing the actor only made that comment when he was up to no good.

"I will be in Cape Cod from this Sunday to Wednesday." The actor scrunched up his face and fidgeted with the coins. Not hearing a word on the other end, he figured his assistant was not in favor of his request. Resting his elbow on the desk to prop up his head with his hand, he was not in the mood to explain things further. "Please don't argue with me on this one, and don't ask questions either."

Able to recognize his friend's sincerity and fatigue in his tone, Max could tell there was definitely something going on beyond just a simple confrontation with the author. But what?

"Cutting it kind of close, aren't you? I mean, the premiere is Thursday night."

"I realize that. Look, I'll tell you everything when I get back. But for now, I really need you to do this, okay?"

Remembering his promise to always be there for his friend when he needed him the most, Max agreed to help. "Yes, understood. What do you need?"

Sean sent him the address of Evily's beach house. "Any chance you can find me a place to stay close to the town of Dennis? Somewhere in the vicinity of Corporation Beach, preferably."

"Well, I'll see what I can do. I can't promise anything, though. It's high season. Vacation rentals there are usually booked months in advance. Inventory will be scarce."

"Please, just do what you can."

Max got worried. "I'll start working on that right away. Maybe I can call in some favors? See if anyone from here has a place there or knows someone who does."

"Thanks. I'll make sure I'm back in plenty of time." The Hollywood star exhaled. "Maybe send the jet to an airport in Cape Cod."

The phone went silent.

"Are you sure you're alright?" his assistant asked, the sharp edge of concern cutting through the silence. "You sound... off. Did something happen?"

"Dude..." Sean sighed, not knowing where to start. "You'd never believe me if I told you."

14

Thursday, July 25th
Boston, Massachusetts

The greatest glory in living is not in falling but in rising every time we fall. ~ Nelson Mandela

Noticing that dusk was fast approaching, Sean hung up the phone with Max. The light posts along the streets below illuminated, bringing the city back to life while the day slowly ended. Confident he would secure accommodations at the Cape within hours, he took a deep breath. Max always made things happen. At times, it seemed he used some sort of magic to honor his requests.

"If I can depend on anyone, it would be him," Sean said while looking out over the city. He hoped this trip would be well worth all the effort he'd gone through thus far. Thinking of his girls, Janie and Ella, he knew it was. "After all this time, what message do you have for me?"

Beginning to get impatient, Sean felt caged. At that point, he would give anything to leave the hotel. Thankfully, room service arrived to offer a short-lived distraction.

About to sit down and eat his food, another knock came on the door. Rounding the corner, Sean figured it was Mr. Costello and the guards. Opening it, he found the older gentleman standing in the hall alongside two muscular guys dressed in black. Both looked intimidating and lethal.

"Hello again, Mr. Bradley," the manager said.

"Hi, gentlemen. Please come in."

Entering the room, one security guard seemed overly forward with the introductions.

"Mr. Bradley, my name is Ben, and this is my associate, Tim. We are with Executive Protection Services."

Immediately, Sean detected Ben's Aussie accent and shook each man's hand. "Nice to meet you both. Thank you for coming."

"It's no problem, Sir. They had us on stand-by yesterday," Tim revealed.

Sean's eyebrows raised, knowing he'd have to have a little chat with Max later on. That said, he understood his friend was only doing his job.

"Just want to reassure you that everything will be fine from here on in. Should things get heavy, we have another two guys waiting in the wings."

Not liking the idea of being surrounded by so many, Sean hoped it wouldn't come to that. "Sounds good. Let's take one day at a time."

Mr. Costello passed along another business card. "Here are the men's room numbers," he said. Picking up on Sean's fatigue, he assumed their client wanted his privacy. "Alright, gentlemen. Let's get you settled. We will leave Mr. Bradley in peace."

On their way out the door, Ben confirmed, "Let us know if you need anything. One of us will start the night shift shortly."

"Perfect. Thanks." Sean forced a smile and watched them, hating the thought of relying on security again.

Walking back into the room, passing the bank of windows, he sat down feeling antsy. Out of the corner of his eye, he noticed a visitor's package resting on the right-hand side of the desk. Upon flipping the folder open, the pictures of Boston Common caught his attention - it was the park he was supposed to visit with Evily today. Knowing there was so much more he wanted to discuss, out of the blue, Sean decided to text her and ask if she wanted to meet up. It was now dark, so it would probably be safer, all things considered. Quickly rummaging through his suitcase, he recalled packing a dark-colored hoodie. With his phone in hand, he typed.

Hi, Evily. How are things going?

Within seconds, her reply bubbles appeared on the screen below his message. He waited patiently, wondering what the author would think of his idea. Hopefully, she wouldn't mind the guards accompanying them.

Evily's text showed up.

Hi, Sean. We are doing okay. The kids and I went to dinner downstairs for a small bite to eat. We just got back to the room. So, you want to go for a walk in the park?

Sean laughed. She already knew what he was going to ask. In response, he texted a ghostly emoji face, followed by one rolling its eyes to remind her of the creepiness of her text. After making his point, he typed his reply.

What time?

Fidgeting, he waited for the author to confirm their plans.

How about fifteen minutes? Does that work for you? We can't be out too late, though. It will be an early morning tomorrow. Are you still able to join us?

Contemplating her question, he knew the last thing he wanted was to be cooped up in the hotel room for the next three days, afraid to venture out anywhere. Peering through the window, seeing all the people on the streets below, Sean had looked forward to seeing Evan play but didn't know if that was a wise idea.

Sure, I can meet you in front of your hotel in fifteen minutes. I'll have two guys following me, so don't freak out. They'll stay a safe distance away. As for tomorrow, I can't see why I can't go. Nobody would expect me to be outside the city. So, yeah, I'll join you. The Henchmen will be with us, though.

Within seconds, Evily sent a response.

Is that what you call them?

Chuckling to himself, he figured nobody in their right mind would mess with these guys. They were huge, ex-military, and looked pretty mean even though they were well-spoken.

Well, that and Bruisers or Goons. I like Henchmen, even though they would never harm anybody -Well, unless necessary, I suppose. While on the job, their main objective is to get the principal client out of danger. Not confront it. Sean paused and added, I will see you shortly then.

Her thought bubbles rambled on.

Alright. See you soon. It will just be us. The kids are tired. Evan needs to reserve his energy for tomorrow, and Ella already has plans with friends from back home.

Putting his phone down on the desk, nervous about being alone with her, he quickly stood up and slipped on his hoodie before texting back a simple thumbs-up sign. Dressed and ready to leave, he looked at the card from Mr. Costello with the room numbers of the guards written on the back. Exiting his suite, he knocked on the door closest to his. In a timely fashion, both men appeared simultaneously. That is when he discovered these guys were very much in sync.

"What can we do for you, Mr. Bradley?" Ben asked, standing militarily with his hands positioned behind him while the other guard listened in.

"I'm meeting a friend outside the Ritz Hotel down the street. We are taking a walk through Boston Common." Sean wondered what the two men would say. In his experience, executive protection always complied with the client's requests, but he wasn't sure what their mandate would be here on the East Coast.

"Right away, Sir. One minute," Ben replied.

The two disappeared into their rooms. Within seconds, both emerged with access cards in hand and earpieces affixed, efficiently checking comms on their way down the hall. Each was still dressed casually, in all black, to blend with the night as much as possible.

"This way, Sir," Ben said, leading the way. "When we reach the street, we will give you some space, but I suppose you know the drill."

"Yes, unfortunately. I don't anticipate a problem, but you never know."

Back in familiar territory, the Henchmen on either side steered him away from the guest elevators. Sean got the feeling they were well-versed.

Apparently, Mr. Costello gave the two guards authority to use the maintenance lifts to avoid the crowds.

Reaching the ground level, Ben and Tim led Sean to the side door of the building. Before stepping out onto the street, he pulled his hood over his ball cap and kept his head down. The brim angled over his face more than usual. Walking along Temple Street, they took the long way to bypass the hustle and bustle of the theatre district.

After veering left, moving across Tremont, they hit the aroma of freshly brewed coffee lingering in the air. That was hard for Sean to ignore. Passing a place called the Thinking Cup, the actor stopped and instantly noticed the number of people inside.

Ben stepped forward. "Would you like coffee, Mr. Bradley? We can get it for you."

Sean felt helpless, as he was at the mercy of his surroundings, and these two guys were the only people who could bridge the gap.

"Umm, sure. Can you make it two? Both small." Sean dug into his pocket for some money. "Grab for yourselves, too, if you'd like."

"Thank you. We are good," the Aussie said. "How do you take it, Sir?"

"To make it easy, order two regular decafs," their famous client replied, giving him a few bills.

The big man walked inside and stood in line to wait his turn. Tim moved about ten feet away and kept a sharp eye on his client and the activity around them. Within minutes, Ben returned with the drinks in hand. Handing the celebrity his coffee and the change, Sean took hold of the tray and pocketed the coins.

"Thanks, man." Sean hated the idea of not managing the simple task himself, but given the situation, he did not have a choice.

Continuing along their way, the three soon reached Avery Street, just south of the Ritz. Sean stopped on the corner and called Evily on the phone. Peering towards the hotel, he could see that she was already standing outside the lobby, facing Washington Street. He assumed that she was watching for him to appear from that direction.

"Hello?" she said, answering on the third ring.

"Hey. Look to your left."

Sean raised his phone above his head when Evily swung around.

She quickly spotted him, and the light from his phone screen stood out in the dimness of night and waved while ending their call. Within minutes, the author was a mere twenty feet away, greeting him with a happy smile. "Hello. I see you made it unscathed."

"Guess so," Sean replied, keeping his head down, unable to hide behind a pair of sunglasses. "Umm, Evily, that's Ben and Tim." He pointed in their direction. Each man offered a subtle nod. Nothing more.

Acknowledging with a slight wave, she brought her attention back to Sean.

"Here. I got you a coffee. I didn't know how you take it, so I guessed and chose regular. Is that okay?"

He passed her the small white cup with a black logoed sleeve.

"Thank you. Appreciate that."

"Both are decaf. Thought I'd have trouble sleeping otherwise."

Her face brightened. "No, that works for me too. I'm the same with caffeine after hours."

Experiencing a lull in their conversation, seemingly emerging whenever they first see each other, Sean and Evily inched to the corner of Avery and Tremont.

"So? Ready for our walk through Boston Common?" she asked, slightly apprehensive given the creatures she usually encounters prowling at night.

"Yeah. I'm looking forward to it."

"Great," she chuckled, knowing he wouldn't be saying that if he saw the things she did. "Shall we, then?"

"Sure." Sean seemed lost for some reason. Not himself.

Sensing he was tired from the day's events, Evily knew something else was amiss.

Once the walk sign illuminated, they crossed the street. The security guards hung back a few feet, giving their client space. Moving along the paved path, the two soon faded into the shadows.

It only took seconds for Evily to pick up on Sean's thoughts.

Addressing it, she whispered, "You've been thinking a lot about Janie and Ella."

Surprised she clued into that, he said, "Yes, more so than usual." Pausing a second, wondering if he should tell her about the coins in his room, she turned to him.

"The coins? You found a connection, correct?" Evily waited for him to confirm her suspicions. She knew her abilities still surprised him.

"Yes, the date on both was 2006," he answered in awe.

"Did you notice their sizes?" Evily wrapped both hands around the small coffee cup, loving its warmth.

"Well, one was a dime; the other a quarter." He didn't know what else she was referring to.

Reading him, she clarified, "Firstly, they are in the shape of the orbs. Ella's, you will soon see, is small, and Janie's is larger. To me, what you have experienced is a sign. A means of communication."

In disbelief, he silently doubted what she said, even though his gut feeling somehow knew she was right.

"No skepticism, remember? You need to work on that."

Her straightforwardness caught him off guard. It was like she had some sort of superpower - a power he had yet to understand.

To lighten the air, Evily asked, "So, have you ever been to Boston before?"

"No, never. First time," he revealed, taking careful sips of the hot coffee.

"Every year, I walk through this park with the kids. Sometimes by myself. It is in the heart of the city but seems peaceful. Evan has been participating in this tournament since he was thirteen. We always look forward to it."

"You are so proud of him," Sean pointed out.

Evily smiled from ear to ear. "Yes, of course. I am proud of them both. They have unique personalities, with different likes and dislikes. Evan is outgoing. Ella is more reserved. Both talented in their own way."

"It must be hard being a single mom."

"You know, when the kids were younger, I won't lie. It was challenging. Now that they are older, it has gotten a little easier, but still busy nonetheless," she divulged. "I think things would have been far worse if I hadn't gotten divorced." Knowing she said too much, Evily changed the subject. "So, on a happier note, we just love this area of town. What do you think so far?"

Sean paused a second. "I haven't seen much of it, but I loved the harbor today. The city is not what I expected. I thought it would have a New York City vibe, but it doesn't."

"No, it is not at all like New York. Maybe it's the proximity to the ocean or the historical landmarks. For sure, the people here are welcoming. Most are super friendly." Evily couldn't pinpoint what he was thinking but could not ignore the weird feeling she got from him. "Are you alright after that commotion earlier today?"

"I suppose so. It's not like that hasn't happened often before. Enjoyed having a little freedom, though. Unfortunately, reality hit." Exhaling, he added, "You'd think I'd be used to the attention after all these years."

Pondering a moment, she wanted to say her piece without further delay. "Look, I've been thinking a lot about this entire situation, and I want to apologize."

"For what?" he asked curiously.

"For bringing you all this way."

"What do you mean? I came on my own accord." Sean was confused.

"Technically, yes, but I was the reason behind it. This morning, when we met, you had such anger. I'm sure your life is stressful enough without adding this to the mix." Taking a sip of her coffee, she added, "Sometimes the messages I get are hard to read and understand. Other times, they are as clear as day. In this case, with Janie and Ella, I hope I am interpreting it right. Honestly, they are acting a bit secretive."

"Secretive?"

"Well, it's mostly the short messages that seem to be flashing past from time to time."

"You know that every chapter of your book was spot-on - every detail. I'm pretty sure whatever vibes you're getting from them are probably valid, too," he revealed, staring straight ahead.

"They haven't told me about their plans for you. I'm also limited by what they are willing to share."

Sean and Evily stopped briefly to watch a doubles game on the tennis courts brightly lit in the middle of the park. Walking along in silence, they eventually hit Charles Street and cautiously mingled with a few pedestrians before crossing the road.

Moving to the other side, breaking away from the crowd, he said, "Like I've said before, if Janie and Ella want me here for any reason, then I'll do whatever they ask."

"I'm happy to hear that. You have to be patient, though."

With a nod, he replied, "No problem. You just guide me as to what I need to do."

"I'll try my best," she said with a smile.

15

Thursday, July 25th
Boston, Massachusetts

It is during our darkest moment that we must focus to see the light. ~ Aristotle

The beautiful gardens flanking the path seemed ominous now in the shadows. Certain areas housed multiple sets of red and yellow eyes, causing Evily's guard to go up. She quickly clenched her fist on one side and clutched the coffee cup tightly on the other while her heart hammered in her chest. The darkness always brought about unease and a sense of fear. To this day, that never changed.

Noticing her look about, almost peering over her shoulder like someone was following her, Sean asked, "What is it? Is there something wrong?"

Nervous, her sights moved to the walkway below their feet.

Sean gave her his undivided attention. "Are you okay?" he prompted again.

Not sure if she should divulge that at least ten entities were lingering nearby, Evily decided to keep that to herself, knowing he was not yet ready to learn about the fine line between the spiritual realm and their own.

"Yeah. I'm okay," she said bravely with a slight waver in her voice.

The creatures never hurt Evily, but if given a chance, they easily could. Each just hovered, feeding off of her fear and apprehension. It caused this indescribable, sick feeling to fill her stomach. Like their presence was a poison seeping under her skin and into her veins, causing her blood to curdle. She could hear faint growling and gnashing of teeth - a familiar sound she knew all too well. Not saying much, she focused on her thoughts and flushed out all the negative, replacing them with feelings of love for her children and the connection developing between her, Sean, Janie, and baby Ella. Aware of the future and what was to come, she could see it as plain as day. Concentrating on ridding herself of any dread-laced emotion, she took another deep breath. Within minutes, they disappeared.

With not a word said between them, she was happy to move along to the well-lit suspension bridge just ahead. Emerging from the darkness, the author gradually relaxed when they stepped into the light. The lagoon looked so magical. Inching their way across, the two could see ducks floating with their bills nestled under their wings for the night. The weeping willows bordering the shoreline swayed gently in the breeze. Their rustling leaves emitted calming sounds, creating a form of welcomed white noise.

Stopping in the middle of the bridge to marvel at the city lights reflecting off the water, Ben passed by casually to take up his position on the opposite side while Tim stayed put.

Concerned about what she needed to convey, Evily figured it was best to just come out with it.

"Do you want me to share more about how I met your girls?"

Leaning against the pillar, Sean turned to her and said, "I'd like that."

Evily started at the beginning. "It was the second week of December. We were preparing for the holidays. I'd been in my office jotting down some new story ideas. While sitting there, a cool breeze wafted through the room. A shiver rolled down my spine. For whatever reason, I needed to get some fresh air and decided to look at the Christmas lights on the house. Outside, walking around the yard, I heard a child's voice. It belonged to a little girl. That is when I saw the orb. She told me about her mother and revealed small details about her Dad. How he missed them so."

Paying close attention, Sean looked away upon hearing that. Evily knew those words were painful for him.

"In the days that followed, a woman's spirit was adamant about making contact with me. Spilling her story, I recorded every word she shared on paper. The same night, the little orb brought along a guest. It was her mother. That is when I made the connection between the two souls. Both the mom and daughter would appear at my door after dark in the weeks that followed. They would reveal certain things, which I continued to record. Sometimes, they would show me images. While writing in my study, they often imposed certain thoughts in my mind. From those details, I created this fictional story with similar elements. Dan, the main character, met Laney at a promo party for her friend's rock band. That was similar to how you and Janie met, correct?"

"Yeah, Janie came to hang out at the bar with a girlfriend that night. As she walked through the front doors, I knew I had to meet her," Sean clarified. "There was a mysteriousness about her: dark brown hair, dark eyes, and a bright smile. I loved the fact that she thought I was just some guy. She hadn't recognized me at all. Guess that added to the overall attraction."

"She said your first date led to a second, then a third. You frequented a hotel restaurant close to where you happened to be living. On another date, you drove up the coast on a motorcycle? Is that right?" Pausing, not knowing if the statement was valid or not, feeling like she was guessing at times, Evily turned to Sean and waited for an answer.

"Amazing," he quietly confirmed, nodding his head. "When she agreed to get on the back of my bike and trusted me, that's when I knew it was serious." Sean got off the book's topic and wanted to know more about Evily's gift. "When did you realize you had this ability?"

"As I mentioned, I've seen orbs since I was five or six. That's my earliest recollection. Over time, I could feel emotions off them and associate thoughts that were popping into my head while around them. I could even pinpoint their purpose based on their color. That spread to hearing what people were thinking, even knowing what was coming next in the future. Sometimes that is vague since every decision and choice in life brings about a different outcome or branch."

"What colors are Janie and Ella's orbs?"

"Theirs are a white translucent mist. It means they have a heightened connection. A peaceful, healing blue appears at times."

Missing them beyond words, Sean longed to hear more.

"Shall we keep walking?" Evily was getting tired and wanted to head back.

"Sure."

They descended the stairs on the other side of the bridge and followed the waterside path under the trees. The Henchmen kept a close eye in the darkness.

"Can I ask you a personal question?"

"Oh, boy," she replied, already knowing what he was about to say.

"What happened between you and your husband?" Thinking he may be prying, Sean backtracked a bit. "But, it's okay if you don't want to share that. I'm just curious. I noticed today that the kids didn't hold him in very high regard."

Evily snickered. "Yes, isn't that the truth." Waiting a moment, wondering how to phrase her answer, she stopped. "Long story short, he cheated on me with his secretary. I know that is an old cliché, but it's true. Her name is Jennifer. She is perky and young and beautiful. Now, he is her problem. Not mine."

Stunned by her bluntness, Sean said, "So sorry to hear that," as they continued down the path.

"Oh, don't be sorry. I feel like we are better off without him. When he and I first met, he was the nicest guy. He'd do anything for me. In the courtroom, though, he was ruthless. I feel that the lines blurred between work and family somewhere along the way. Day after day, the cut-throat world he is privy to inevitably changed him. You become a product of your environment over time."

"I can relate to that. I think that's my life in a nutshell."

"But, deep down, it didn't change you."

"This is true." He knew she was right.

"You are a compassionate person. Not selfish or self-centered."

"I hope I'm not. Now and again, I try and reevaluate things to stay on track. My assistant, Max, usually tells me if I become too *Hollywood*. He keeps me grounded."

"Well, then, Max is a great friend to have," Evily confirmed genuinely.

"Yes, I think so too. He's been there since the beginning."

The darkness of the night sky paled in comparison to the city lights when approaching Arlington and Boylston. About to pass a historical monument, Sean stopped and read the plaque.

"It's William Ellery Channing. He was a Unitarian minister, if I recall. Please do not make me connect with him or explain his life's story because I am drawing a blank."

"Alright then," Sean laughed at her exaggerated exhaustion.

"I know, I know. I'm sorry. I get grumpy when I'm tired." She needed to be truthful. Usually, she found it hard to function by the end of the day since her brain felt fried.

Surprised by her humor, he laughed again. "I think everyone gets grumpy when they are at the end of their rope."

Heading towards Tremont Street, Evily mentioned, "So, are you sure you're okay with the whole Cape thing?"

"Yes. Why wouldn't I be?" In seconds, Sean realized the gravity of what would take place. Having the chance to speak to his wife after all this time made him feel emotional.

Evily zeroed in on that. "They wish to give you closure. It's something you've wanted all this time."

"You're right. Everything happened so fast that day, you know. I didn't even get time to say goodbye. In a blink, both were just gone."

"I can only imagine," she said sympathetically, adding, "They also want to strengthen your faith too. It's important to both of them.

Janie knows that this is going to be easier said than done. You are very skeptical - always needing proof and validation."

"So you've said," Sean confirmed. "She's right, though. Nobody knows me as she does." Thinking about meeting Evily earlier that day, he asked, "Truthfully, did you know I was coming to Boston? Is that why you weren't surprised to see me this morning?"

"Oh, believe me, I was surprised. As I mentioned, I knew a person connected to them was coming. I had no idea it was going to be you. I won't lie. I was a little star-struck initially."

"Really? You played it pretty cool." With a tilt of his head, he flashed a smile. "To be honest, you caught me off guard. I was intimidated."

"How on earth can you be intimidated by me? Seriously. That's ridiculous." Evily Landy blushed.

"A strong woman has that effect on people. You straight out told me to get into your car and immediately took control of our conversation from the second I said your name in the lobby."

Recalling the strength and confidence that Janie also had, a sad look came across Sean's face. It plunged him deep in thought. Evily could hear a few things surface about the book and how this day developed.

"Please don't be angry about the story. Nobody but you will know the details. That's what they told me. The story will make sense to only one man. Guess that is you. It was a means to get you here. Now, we need to find out why."

"Yes, we do," Sean agreed.

Evily and Sean crossed the road at Avery Street with the Henchmen close behind. Arriving at the Ritz hotel entrance, Sean tossed away his empty coffee cup into the recycle bin. Evily did the same. The valet greeted them with a nod while passing by the front doors.

"What time did you say Evan's first game is tomorrow?"

She thought about their schedule. "It starts at 9:00 AM. We need to be there forty-five minutes to an hour before. It means we have to leave here by 7:30 at the latest."

"You're sure it's okay that I tag along and watch?"

"Of course."

Sean had an idea. "How about I swing by and pick you guys up?"

Always on her own, never relying on anyone, she did not know how to respond. In the grand scheme of things, he was still a stranger to them.

"What about Tim and Ben?" she questioned, buying time.

"Oh, don't worry, the guys will be hovering. They have a vehicle and will follow us."

A look of uncertainty flooded her face.

Needing clarification, Sean said, "Tell me the truth. Does this whole thing bother you? I mean, me invading your time here, not to mention having security now hovering around? I don't want you to feel uncomfortable or anything."

"This situation is quite out of the norm for me, but surprisingly doesn't feel weird." Contemplating his question, going against her cautious nature, she answered, "You can pick us up if you'd like."

"Thought me driving would take the stress off you. Give you a bit of a break."

Evily looked his way and felt a sense of sincerity and chivalry. "Thank you for that."

Sean nodded, not knowing what more to say.

"So, the kids and I will meet you here then. I'm warning you. It'll be a full day with two games and a university tour. Sure, you are up to spending that much time with us?"

"Yeah. I think it will be an exciting experience." He added, needing to bring about some humor, "You know, I'm also interested in your predictions for the scores. It'll help me believe in this crazy gift of yours."

"After everything that's happened today, you still need proof?"

"Once a skeptic, always a skeptic."

"Well, we will see about that. Prepare to be amazed," Evily said, pointing her finger at him.

Standing a few feet apart, with arms crossed in front of his body, he said, "You know, today wasn't so bad. Meeting you has been an eye-opening experience, to say the least."

"Well, I'm happy to hear that. I'm not the horrible villain you painted me out to be now, am I?"

"How did you...."

The author flashed a confident expression while tilting her head.

Grinning from ear to ear, lowering their sights to the street below, Sean repeated, "Villain? Right." Instantly, he felt his heart beating out of his chest, and his palms got sweaty, making him rub them together.

"Well, on that note, I will bid you good night. We will see you bright and early," Evily confirmed with a chuckle. "Remember 7:30. Don't be late."

"Don't worry. I won't be. Trust me."

Bashfully, she replied, "I'm going to try."

Sean started walking across the street. Turning, he said, "Night, Ms. Landy."

Evily smiled. "Night, Mr. Bradley."

Waving to him while he walked up the street with his two Henchmen a few feet behind, Evily waited until they rounded the corner before going into the hotel. Privy to more than just general conversation, Evily innocently honed in on his thoughts and could feel a strong connection developing. Torn, she didn't know what to think. Was he getting too close?

On the elevator ride to their room on the tenth floor, she hoped to quiet her mind enough to get some much-needed rest but feared it would be a long night.

16

Thursday, July 25th
Boston, Massachusetts

Someday, everything will make perfect sense. So, for now, laugh through the confusion and smile through the tears, be strong, and keep reminding yourself everything happens for a reason. ~ John Mayer

Not wanting to take the long way around, almost too tired to go any further, Sean walked along Washington Street, past the outdoor cafes filled with people. Surrounded by the hum of conversations everywhere, he kept his head down, hoping nobody would recognize him amidst the crowds. Luckily, his hotel wasn't far, and the theatre district was quiet since the patrons were nestled in their seats, taking in the shows.

Thinking back to how angry he was at the author, those feelings seemed to have miraculously changed. In his mind, that horrid woman and Evily were now two totally different people. She wasn't at all what he painted her out to be.

Funny how things work out, he thought.

Learning that Janie and Ella had arranged all this seemed spooky at first. Now, he was anxious and excited at the same time. There was this anticipation to hear from them, but a sense of sadness loomed, knowing he might just find out why God took both of them that day. Sean often thought it was a form of punishment for his choices in life. Being so busy, he also knew he took Janie for granted. It was something he wished he could have taken back. Thinking of a silver lining, he figured, just maybe, after this experience is over, the guilt and grief he's been carrying all this time might lighten. But that wouldn't change the fact he still missed them every day. Even all these years later, the pain was still very much there.

About to walk through the doors of his hotel, Sean raised his sights to the sky above and said, "Love you both." He then passed through the lobby to turn in for the night, curious to see what the next few days would bring.

Meeting up with Ben and Tim inside, they headed to the fourth floor using the maintenance elevators. Along the way, he wondered why his heart raced, and his palms sweated while he said good night to Evily. A part of him could not deny that he was beginning to care for the family after only one day.

How is that even possible? I hardly know them, he thought to himself.

When the doors slid open, Sean stepped out into the hall and informed the guys of their morning schedule. The two men immediately provided their famous client with a plan of action before bidding him good night.

Alone in his room, moments later, staring at four walls, Sean checked on his coins. Once again, they'd moved from the desk to the window sill. Recalling what Evily said about the sizes of the orbs and it being a sign, he suddenly felt a closeness to Janie and baby Ella. The thought of his girls made him smile. Leaving the coins where they were, he got ready for bed. It had been a crazy day. So much had happened.

Exhausted beyond words and having difficulty focusing, his head hit the pillow. Hoping to get a good night's sleep, he rolled over and felt a cool breeze brush past his face. He assumed the air conditioner vents were angled downward, but he was too tired to get up and see if he could adjust them. Pulling the covers to his chin, he braved the chill and fell asleep. Little did he know, he had company.

17

Friday, July 26th
Boston, Massachusetts

It's not about what happens to you but how you react to it that matters. ~ Epictetus

Hardly sleeping a wink past three o'clock, Sean got up with his alarm that morning. Turning off the annoying sound, he slowly sat up, feeling his age. Tired, with aching joints, especially his knees, he fell back into the pillows, wishing he could sleep in a little longer. Staring at the ceiling, thinking more about the day ahead, the idea of spending time with the Andersons gave him a boost.

With a shower out of the way, his senses awakened more and more. Looking forward to the hockey games that would allow him to relive his youth through Evan, his thoughts drifted to Ella, not wanting her to feel left out. At some point, he hoped to spark a conversation that would prompt the young girl to share more about her love of architectural design. Not sure how to do that exactly, he figured a door might open, making it easier to pose the right questions. It was hard to think that his Ella and Ella Anderson would roughly be the same age. He wondered what a conversation with his daughter would've been like - whether or not they would have been close or even gotten along. This he would never know.

"It was nice to see Ella finally break out of her shell at lunch yesterday. Guess she is not as quiet as I initially thought."

Her quick-wittedness resembled that of Janie's. Very sharp. Full of energy. Pausing, Sean could hear his wife's joyful laugh. It was a memory that would emerge while recalling all the happy times they shared. His Janie, with a smile that would light up a room. Not a moment would go by when he didn't miss her beyond words. Sometimes, the pain was hard to bear.

Breaking away from memory lane, he looked in the mirror and returned to reality. "I guess we will meet again soon," the actor said quietly, unsure what that would entail.

Dressed casually in jeans and a dark t-shirt, he topped it off with a black ball cap. Trying to think of something nice to do for the family of three to say thank you, he wondered if he should grab breakfast To-Go for everyone. While setting his grey hoodie on the end of the bed, he located the hotel menu and called down to the concierge to place an order.

Hanging up the phone not long after, Sean second-guessed himself. "Hope everything I selected will suffice. But really, who wouldn't like breakfast sandwiches with bacon?"

Ready to get moving, glancing at the time, he called the valet to bring his truck from the garage.

Texting Ben and Tim, Sean reminded the guys to meet him out front by 7:15. Not surprised to hear that one was waiting downstairs for the trucks and the other was outside his door, ready to depart, Sean finished up a few last-minute things before heading out. Sending a quick text to Max, he requested an update on whether he had yet secured a vacation rental in the town of Dennis. After pressing send, forgetting it was four in the morning in LA, Sean felt terrible for a split second, then went about his business believing it was one of the hazards of the assistant's job.

Nervous about picking up the family, he contemplated what information Evily could divulge today. Still somewhat skeptical, he wished her gift could explain why he lost his wife and daughter so tragically - a thought that had weighed on him for years.

Venturing out the door, Sean found Tim waiting for him.

"Good Morning, Sir," the Henchman greeted.

"Morning, man. Sleep well?"

Tim didn't know how to answer that. Clients never asked him how he was - ever.

"I, umm, slept good, Sir. How about you?"

"Barely got four hours," Sean said while they walked down the hall. He always told the truth straight up and never sugar-coated it. "That's what happens when you get old."

Unaccustomed to casual conversation, Tim wasn't sure what to say in response. He was used to being seen and not heard.

Deciding to discuss the impending weather forecast, the two men soon arrived in the lobby. The first order of business was to pick up breakfast. Next on the list was to locate Ben. Finding him already out front, standing beside the Escalade, waiting for them, Sean watched his Land Rover pull up seconds later.

With his hat shielding his face, hiding behind a pair of sunglasses, Sean greeted the woman standing at the concierge desk. On the counter behind her, he noticed a couple of sturdy paper bags with corded handles sitting to one side with four hot drinks on one tray and two cold smoothies secured in another.

Reminding himself of his alias for this trip, he stepped toward the desk and said, "Good morning. I'm Mike Waters. I called down earlier about the breakfast order."

With a bright smile, the woman with light brown hair replied, "Yes, Mr. Waters. We have it right here. It arrived moments ago. The valet also has your vehicle outside."

Happy with everything neatly packaged, he touched the coffees to be sure they were still hot. The smoothies for Evan and Ella were strawberry-banana flavor. One was marked with the word *whey* to signify Evan's protein shake. Something the athlete would appreciate, he was sure.

"The vehicles are ready," Tim communicated, hearing Ben relay the information through his earpiece. "I'll help you bring everything out."

While exiting the hotel, Sean bolted for the Land Rover out of habit. Ben had already opened the driver's side door for him while scanning the street for anything usual. Swiftly ducking inside, Sean got comfortable and placed the bags in the passenger seat while Tim handed him the drink trays.

"Hey, I got you guys some breakfast sandwiches, and these coffees are yours," he said, passing it all to Tim. "On duty or not. You need breakfast."

"Thank you, Sir. Much appreciated," Ben said from a distance.

"Yes, thank you, Sir." Tim concurred, realizing their client was very different than most.

Before leaving, the actor needed to clarify something – a minor pet peeve of his.

"Can you guys do me a favor and not call me Sir? It's too formal."

Ben interjected. "How would you like to be addressed? Umm, Sir..." Scrunching up his face, he added, "Sorry. Force of habit."

"It's fine. You know my alias for the trip. Use that if you need to be formal in public. Otherwise, Sean is fine. Unfortunately, you will be stuck with me for a while."

Each nodded their head.

"You got it," Ben said, keeping it light.

"Okay, let's get going. We can't be late," the action star clarified, starting the engine.

Carefully taking the drinks from the tray and placing one into each center console cup holder between the front and rear seats, Sean was anxious about what the day would hold. Noticing the guys glancing back in their side mirrors, giving the signal to proceed, Sean pulled out behind the Henchmen.

With one last look at the time, he said to himself, "Perfect. 7:25. We will be there right on schedule."

The trucks turned left on the first street as Ben drove towards Boston Common Park. Wrapping around to the Ritz hotel, about to call Evily and tell her he was almost there, Sean saw them standing outside the main glass doors while the caravan drove towards them.

Evily waved as he stopped along the curb in front of the Andersons. The teens looked confused.

Swiftly getting out to help the family with their baggage, Tim was intent on keeping his client from showing his face.

With a press of the button, the Land Rover tailgate opened. Sean listened to their Mom explain what was happening. Okay with it, Evan swung his equipment bag into the cargo bay along with his carefully placed sticks. The young Henchman opened Evily's door and the back passenger side for everyone to slip in so they could be on their way in a timely fashion.

"Good morning, everyone. How did you sleep?" Sean said, peering out from the driver's seat.

"Morning. We had a good night," Evily answered while standing beside the posh SUV, about to get in beside him. "You sound chipper."

"Wow! This is a nice truck," Evan said, surprised by the luxury brand, jumping in behind Sean.

"Thanks. It's a rental," the actor laughed while closing the tailgate remotely again. "Morning, Ella." He greeted the young girl standing on the sidewalk with a look of uncertainty.

Tim continued holding the door open, waiting for her to make a move.

"It's okay. Jump in. I hope you don't mind me driving today. Thought I'd give your Mom a break." Not receiving a positive reaction, he added, "Hey, I got you a strawberry smoothie and some breakfast. Interested?" he said, hoping she would accept it.

Ella silently nodded with a hesitant smile. He could tell that her guard had gone up right away. Contemplating what he did wrong, he wondered if their change of plans set her off. Or was it his second intrusion on the family's vacation that she didn't like?

Taking a seat, Evily turned around to check on her daughter and was happy to see her slowly give a thumbs-up sign.

Figuring how strange this whole scenario must be, Sean tread carefully, not wanting to make her feel uncomfortable. He could feel that she was being overly cautious when it came to him. Almost leery. Maybe a bit fearful. *Guess I have a lot to prove to her,* he thought, wanting to be patient and kind to the girl.

When everyone had buckled up, he watched the teens look around before explaining what he had in the bags resting on the center console. They'd already taken a sip of their smoothies.

Evily was thankful to see two coffees sitting in the holders between them.

"Have you eaten breakfast yet?" he asked, hoping his hunch was correct.

"No, we haven't. Sadly, we got up a little later than expected and ran out of time. Funny. I was going to ask if we could stop somewhere before the game," the author said.

"Well, now we are ready to head out. No need for that." Sean handed the one bag to Evan and Ella. He gave Evily the other one and said, "I got one for each of us, too."

"Oh, perfect. Thank you so much."

Evan looked at the word written on the side of his cup. "Hey, you got me a protein shake. Thanks, man."

"You're welcome." Sean smiled, knowing that what he did helped them out this morning. "So, where are we headed? Same place? Do you have the address of the arena?"

"Sure do. Let me find it." Evily took out her phone and found the information she had used yesterday. Looking at the screen, he punched it into the built-in navigation system. While it calculated the route, Sean texted the Henchmen the details.

After flipping open his coffee tab, he took a sip before checking his mirrors and pulling away from the hotel. Carefully making the U-turn, he drove toward Tremont Street and turned left into the morning traffic flow. The Henchmen followed while the Land Rover maneuvered through the many streets to link up with I-93 south. It wasn't long before the trucks disappeared into the tunnel beneath the city.

Seeing the light of day in the distance, moving along slowly as they merged into bumper-to-bumper traffic, Sean broke the silence surrounding them and said, "If you think this traffic is bad, you should see it in LA. This is nothing. Sometimes I'm stuck, not moving for thirty minutes at a time, maybe more."

"That would be horrible," Evily replied while they finished their sandwiches. "Chicago is bad too. But not like that."

In the rearview mirror, Sean saw the teens enjoying their food and smoothies. Afraid to communicate with them, he said, "So, Evan. Big day today."

"Yep. I'm ready. Feel rested. Not tired. Once I get there, the adrenaline will kick in."

"Good luck. Looking forward to watching the games."

"Yeah, thanks. Appreciate that." Evan leaned back, closed his eyes, and inserted his earbuds. Still sipping his smoothie, he started listening to a motivational podcast to help him focus on the upcoming game.

Noticing Ella was dozing off, Sean moved his attention to Evily. "So, did you guys go to bed late last night?"

"No, not really. Those two were asleep by 10:30. I was shortly after. You?"

Eyes affixed to the road, taking a sip of coffee, he revealed, "Well, I slept for about four hours. After 3:00, I tossed and turned—too many thoughts rolling through my mind. I also kept feeling this cold draft in the room. It was strange."

Evily knew precisely where that draft was coming from. Not wanting to scare him, she thought she'd leave that for a time when he was more confident in the whole topic of the supernatural.

Keeping the conversation simple, she said, "Guess that's my fault. I gave you too much to think about."

"No, that's a good thing. It helped me recall the happy times spent with Janie. Things I'd almost forgotten about."

"I'm pleased to hear that. Part of this experience is about rekindling your connection with them beforehand. By doing this, it fuels their ability to appear. Sometimes, if someone has not emotionally connected to the souls that have passed, it doesn't work. This walk-through memory lane is good. It's a step in the right direction."

The chiming of Sean's phone interrupted their conversation. Safely glancing at it, secured in a hands-free holder, he read the message from Max.

"Looks like my assistant got me a place in Dennis. It was one of the only rentals available close to you."

"Well, that's great news. One week is all you need. Janie and Ella will have said what they needed to by then. At least you were able to get something. Being so late in the season, I wasn't sure if you would."

"Umm, Evily, I thought you should know that I must head back to LA on Wednesday night. I can't stay a week - only a few days. The premiere is on Thursday, and I have a full schedule. Does this change things?"

"I'm sure they are aware of it. I wouldn't worry." Evily thought for a minute. "Just to give you a little more validation. Correct me if I'm wrong, alright?"

"Okay." He was intrigued.

"Hmm. Let me see." Concentrating, she looked straight ahead and said, "You already had a few rather successful movies under your belt, with a certain level of fame to go along with it, when you met Janie. Once you were together a little over six months, you bought her an Asscher cut diamond with a simple platinum band and proposed on the beach off the PCH at sunset. It wasn't long after that you found out you were expecting Ella. The two of you opted for a small ceremony out of the public eye. Weeks later, you started filming a big movie. Long days. It was hard on Janie. She didn't see you much."

Lost for words, Sean paused to process everything she'd said. "Yes, that description does differ from how you described my character in the book."

"Well, that information wasn't meant to grab your attention. Only the intricate details were. For some reason, while recording what Janie was passing along to me, I could see the ocean and sunset in my mind. The Hollywood sign, palm trees, things like that. Most of the book is a work of fiction, but I intertwined many of Janie's details into the plot. I figured I'd write it as a tragic love story."

"I guess that's one way to describe it."

Evily felt bad. She wished she could take back the comment.

Immediately, what she said rekindled a series of memories. Sean's tone changed. "I remember every second when I asked her to marry me. The feelings I had. Even the expression on her face when I proposed. I'll never forget it. We were so happy to be expecting Ella. It brought us closer together."

"I'm so sorry, Sean. I didn't mean to describe it in that way."

"It's fine. That's what it was - a tragic Hollywood love story. I'm sure I am not the only guy in the world who has suffered through something like that. Certainly won't be the last."

"I apologize."

"Look, if I haven't told you already, everything you've said is unreal. Even though I am still somewhat skeptical, I'm beginning to believe more and more in your gift."

"Still not fully convinced, huh?" Evily perked up.

Laughing, Sean said, "Baby steps, Evily. Baby steps."

"I'll take that. Whatever we need to do to get you where you need to be."

Hearing the navigation system tell them to merge off the highway, Sean followed the directions and headed south on 138 into a more rural landscape. He recognized the road from the day before and knew which way they were going.

Evily took a chance and asked point-blank, "Are you angry with God for taking them from you?"

Almost choking on his coffee after taking a sip, he realized that was a fully loaded question. Sean exhaled. Not knowing how to answer her, he looked out the side window and forward again. Checking on the Henchmen, happy they were keeping up, he replied, "Yeah. Maybe at the time." He stumbled on his words and cleared his throat. "It seemed the universe took away the love of my life and the chance to be a dad to a beautiful little girl. I felt I was being punished or something. That I wasn't worthy of that level of happiness."

"That's a natural human reaction."

"I mean, people say everything happens for a reason, but what possible reason could there have been to take away my family?"

"You must let go of any resentment. I know this is easier said than done. They are both in a good place."

"Up until now, I was doing okay. It's been tough to see families walking together. Like a mom, dad, and a little girl. I often wonder what could have been, you know?"

Seeing the arena coming into view, Evily said, "Let's continue this conversation inside. You need to vent. It will help heal your soul. I promise."

She seemed so convinced of that. It made Sean believe she could be right.

Arriving at the Canton arena, he pulled into the parking lot. The black Escalade was close behind them. Based on the number of cars everywhere, they knew the building would be full of people. Not as worried as he was the previous day, happy to have now security waiting in the wings, Sean took a deep breath before stopping outside the front doors and shifting the vehicle in park. Evan had already opened his eyes and looked pumped and ready to play. As the mother of two got out with her son for their usual ritual, they met at the back as the tailgate raised for Evan to grab his equipment. Listening intently to another one of Evily's motivational speeches, Sean turned the air conditioning down so he could hear her better.

"Have confidence in your abilities, and be tough enough to follow through until you reach your goals. That is a quote from Felicity Luckey. She is an author, too. Today, her quotes are a great source of inspiration to athletes of every sport. Evan, lead your team by example. Show them courage, strength, and determination. Inspire them to do the same. Support them, and they will support you." She smiled. "Most of all, don't forget to have a little fun along the way."

"Thanks, Mom." Evan nodded in agreement. With a fist bump, they ended their conversation before he disappeared through the doors into the arena. Evily returned to her seat in the truck, prompting Sean to move along and find a parking spot. He was simply amazed by her parenting skills.

Reversing into a shaded area, the actor popped the sunroof and surveyed the premises. Ben pulled up and backed in beside them.

"What time does the game start again?" he asked, seeing crowds of people gathering outside. "One must have just finished."

"He plays in less than an hour." She looked at the time and confirmed, "Forty-five minutes, to be exact."

Ella leaned in between the two seats. "Are we going in or what?"

"Maybe we should let the crowds die down," her mother replied.

Ben and Tim got out of their vehicle and walked over.

"Stay here with Tim," Ben instructed. "I'm going inside to scout things out."

Agreeing, Sean, Evily, and Ella stayed in their seats and waited for him to return. It was probably best since there was too much time between now and the start of Evan's game. In that span, something could go very wrong.

"Do you think you'll get recognized here?" Ella asked.

Turning to the young girl, utterly unfazed by his fame, he replied, "It's always a possibility."

18

Friday, July 26th
Canton, Massachusetts

What you get by achieving your goals is not as important as what you become by achieving them.

~ Henry David Thoreau

With the sun beating down on the parking lot and the heat rising with every passing minute, Sean, Evily, and Ella watched for Ben to make his way back. The actor felt guilty for dragging the Andersons into his life. It wasn't fair that they, too, had to suffer the consequences of fame.

"I'm so sorry. If you want to go ahead inside, please do. It's taking this guy forever. I know you want a good seat when the previous game finishes."

"Don't be silly. We can't leave you behind," Evily affirmed, spotting the burly protection agent exiting the front doors. "See! There he is."

The three of them got out and stood with Tim between the SUVs.

Upon his return, the lead Henchman, explained the planned strategies for this arena location. "Tim, on the far left-hand side, is an emergency exit. Park there and wait for further instructions."

"Roger that," Tim said confidently, finding a seat in the Escalade.

"Sean, you can move ahead inside when you're ready. I have scanned the viewing area upstairs. Given the number of people there, I won't be far," Ben confirmed.

The actor turned to Evily. "Is that okay with you?"

"Yes, of course. Whatever you need," she replied, knowing he had no choice.

Deciding to leave her bulky tote behind, Evily only took a sweater and her cross-over bag, intent on traveling light. Locking his truck, Sean walked alongside Evily and suddenly reached out his hand to her.

Confused and unsure of what was happening, her guard went up.

"Please take the key just in case I need to leave early with these guys. That way, you can drive out of here, and we can arrange to meet somewhere safe. Think of it as our Plan B."

Somewhat relieved, she said, "Alright." Taking hold of the SmartKey fob, she slipped it into a small zippered pocket in her bag.

Just outside the entrance, Sean pulled the brim of his hat down to hide his face, hoping not to get noticed, while Ben followed at a distance. Able to weave through without incident, the famous actor grabbed the door handle and swung it open to allow Evily and Ella to enter first.

Amidst the crowd, he thought, *So far, so good.*

While standing in line at the ticket table, the actor caught Evily before paying their fees. Prepared, he quickly slipped the lady behind the desk a fifty-dollar bill, taking the author by surprise. Shooting him a look, he raised his hand to stop her from saying anything.

"No, I've got this one," Sean stated before confirming with the woman behind the desk, "Admission for four, please."

"But, you are our guest, remember?" Evily tried to debate the issue while the ticket lady listened to their conversation.

"It just feels weird - you buying my ticket. On top of that," he said under his breath, "I have the Henchman with me too. Really, it should be the other way around anyway."

"Why? Were you born in 1955?" she giggled.

"Close. '64. You're nine years off."

Ella walked beside her Mother and pulled on her sweater, interrupting their banter. "You guys are making a scene. Can we go now?"

People were casting a few looks their way, and whispers were floating in the air.

"Remember, we need to blend, Mother," Ella taunted, rolling her eyes and shoving her Mom along.

Sean trailed behind them with his head down. Climbing the stairs, they arrived at the top to find large groups of people. Immediately going into defensive mode, he kept his hat and sunglasses on, which seemed to bring more attention to himself, but that said, no matter what he did, it would be no different. Maybe it was his confidence. Maybe his good looks. But Sean Bradley stood out no matter how he tried to mingle anonymously.

Evily caught on right away. "You need to relax. You're sending out a vibe."

Not knowing what she meant, he thought, *What vibe?*

Quickly spotting three empty chairs close to the glass, they took a seat with their backs to the room full of people. Sean could see the reflection of everyone behind them without making eye contact. A few feet away, Ben found a seat against the wall near his client, optimizing his one-hundred-and-eighty-degree view.

Reading the room, the author leaned over to Sean. "Don't worry. You're good. The rumor mill has subsided for now." Right then, she picked up on his thoughts. "Sure, if you want to, we can talk further about our conversation from last night. You know, continue where we left off."

Freaked out by her statement, Evily realized she had heard his inner voice, but he hadn't said anything.

"You are doing it again."

"So sorry," she said, shaking her head. "Sometimes your thoughts are so strong; I think you verbally spoke."

It was true. Sean did have a few things to ask. Glimpsing her way, he knew she was about to say something but was trying her best to refrain.

Raising his index finger, he said, "No, I ask the questions."

Nodding, she agreed with a smirk, giving him the floor.

"So, can I ask about you? Your life to date? It seems you know everything about mine." he whispered to her.

Given the circumstances, that was only fair. "What do you want to know?" she asked.

"Based on what was said yesterday, the kids made it clear that they don't speak to their father. But do they have any relationship with him at all?"

Expecting that topic of discussion to surface, Evily glanced at her daughter and saw her watching a movie with headphones over her ears. Given their previous conversation, Evily felt a need to share the ugly truth.

She took a deep breath and said, "So, his name is Peter. Everyone around us thought we were the perfect family. Lawyer, writer, and fortunate enough to have a boy and a girl. Little did they know, the nightmare I was living in behind closed doors."

Sean flashed an overly concerned expression and gave her his full attention.

"Evan and Ella were younger at the time. We walked on eggshells a lot. Long story short, I didn't want them growing up in a split home, but things were pretty bad. I stuck it out for as long as I could. Thankfully, his affair started with his secretary. I say it that way because he was preoccupied and not around much. That was a good thing. When we separated, he moved out. We hardly saw him during that time. His mistress didn't like kids but certainly loved the lifestyle my husband provided. You know what I mean? Invitations to the most elaborate parties, luxury vacations, a fancy car, a penthouse apartment, things of that nature. After finalizing the divorce, Evan was probably the most affected. He was so angry. Ella just felt abandoned and thought her father didn't love her. I tried my best to be there for the two of them. In the end, their Dad showed his true colors. It was something Peter could never take back. To this day, the kids do not trust him."

Evily fidgeted with her jacket zipper, deciding what more to say. It had been so long since she'd shared this with anyone.

"According to the courts, he had the right to see them every second weekend. They never wanted to go. I struggled with that since I could feel everything they felt inside. The fear, the anger, the uncertainty. All of it. After a while, he started canceling, using work as an excuse. The truth is, he couldn't be bothered with the drama. Eventually, he did not show up when he was supposed to on his scheduled Friday nights. The kids and I were always relieved about that. These days, he doesn't see them at all. They are no longer part of his life. I can't remember the last time we had to deal with him. He has never been to one of Evan's games to this day. You happen to be the first spectator who is not his Mom or sister."

Sean leaned forward and rested his elbows on his knees. With his sights on the rink, he followed the Zamboni while it cleaned the ice, not knowing what to say in response.

Evily felt it - the pain rckindled from hearing a similar story to his own.

Reminded of his Father abandoning him and never having a relationship with the man, the hurt he suffered resurfaced. By the age of eighteen, Sean remembered he'd only seen his father once in thirteen years. It was hard knowing Evan and Ella had suffered through that as well.

Not letting on that she'd heard his thoughts, Evily waited for him to say something.

"I came from a home with similar circumstances. I totally get it. Sorry, all of you had to experience that."

"In the end, we've made it through and are now stronger than ever. My children are so close to me - it's all a mother could wish for. They have my back, and I have theirs. Through thick and thin."

The seriousness of that conversation got sidetracked when Evan's team skated out on the ice for the warmup. The players circled on their end, taking shots on goal amid a series of drills. The action helped change the course of their solemn mood. Both were ready to witness some great hockey.

"So, any predictions on the score for this game?" he questioned.

"Well, let me see," Evily said light-heartedly. "I believe it will be a three and O victory."

"Wow. Impressive. Clean sweep, huh? How many goals for Evan?"

"Sadly, just one, I think. That's okay, though. As long as he gets on the score sheet."

The coaches gathered the players alongside the bench for their pep talk. Ready to do battle, the Raider's name echoed once through the arena before the lines took their places. Some families in the crowd called out words of encouragement while Evan and his teammates skated to center ice for the face-off.

With the puck drop, their team won possession. Over the next ten minutes, the players went back and forth, struggling for offensive control. The referees blew the whistle many times in the first period and handed out penalties, given the rough body checks and dirty play erupting because of the rivalry.

By the start of the second, it was still a no-goal game. The boys looked tired on both sides. A minute-thirty into the period, Evan broke out on a rush when their defense set up left-winger Luca for a breakaway. His parents cheered when the forward sniped the puck top left!

"Yes," Sean said aloud with a single clap of his hands. Turning to Evily, he found her quietly clenching hers together with excitement, watching for Evan to look their way. He wondered what gesture she would offer her son.

After they ran through their traditional bench fly-by, Evan's eyes found his Mom in the viewing lounge. She placed her hand over her heart and pointed at him. He gave her an empowered fist pump with a smile to light the building, then covered his heart and pointed at her.

Grateful to witness such an amazing bond between them, he knew these two kids were probably the luckiest in the world.

"You can do this, boys. Come on." Whispering to herself, silently cheering during the changeover, she did not notice Sean staring at her.

Today, he saw Evily Landy-Anderson in a new light. She seemed more like a friend now versus the vicious woman he had come to confront. Hearing what she shared about her ex-husband and how the divorce affected the kids, his protective instincts stirred inside him.

It strengthened their connection and made him more mindful of the family's situation.

When the team skated off the ice at the end of the second for a much-needed break, the Zamboni emerged to flood the rink.

Evily could feel that Sean was doubtful the Raider's team would win with a 3-0 victory. Reading his thoughts, she said, "So, you don't think they will pull out two more goals for the win?"

Sean was still astounded by her sharpness. Suddenly, out of the blue, the actor froze when he faintly heard his name mentioned nearby. When he saw a reflection of someone stepping forward, his heart sank as they got closer and hovered directly behind them. Lowering his head, he exhaled. All he wanted was to watch the game in peace.

"Excuse me," the female voice uttered nervously. "Are you Sean Bradley?"

Afraid to turn around, he slowly swiveled to lock eyes with Ben before greeting the teen with a forced smile.

"Yes," he said aloud, knowing the room would soon erupt into a frenzy.

"Oh my god! I knew it was you. I can't believe it!" The teenager repeatedly bounced up and down in the highest-pitched voice known to man. "Can I get your autograph? Take a selfie? Oh my gosh! This is so exciting." The shrillness of the girl's excitement made him squint his eyes and want to cover his ears.

In seconds, her reaction set everyone else off. Immediately, Ben stood up to control the crowd. They started pointing at Sean and taking pictures from a distance.

Standing tall, seeing several eyes on him, he took the girl's pen and signed the hockey program she'd shoved in his face. While autographing it for her, she pulled a phone from her pocket and skillfully took several pictures. Within minutes, a few other people gathered around to do the same. Evily felt his frustration. He figured his freedom had now come to an end for sure. From here on in, he'd be looking over his shoulder. Everywhere they go, he'd be waiting for the ball to drop.

Ella turned to see the commotion unfolding, surprised by the swarm of people encircling Sean. Ben had his arms widely outstretched, creating a barrier between the people, Sean and the Andersons.

"Mom? What's he going to do? At this rate, I'm pretty sure he won't be able to watch the third period."

"Ben will control things," she said, "Then, I will step in and ask for privacy when the game starts."

Seemingly putting on a happy face for his fans, secretly, the veteran actor was tired of all the attention. After years of this, he'd hoped people would forget about him, especially now that he was over fifty. Sadly, with the premiere coming up next week, he knew that would not be the case for a while.

Ella noticed the teams returning to the ice. She bumped her Mother's arm to let her know.

The author looked back to find Sean talking to a group of star-struck people who were still lingering around, asking him countless questions. Being charismatic, he answered everything cordially while Ben stood by his side to keep the peace. She sensed that the famous Hollywood star was overwhelmed and seemed almost angry.

Standing up, she politely asked, "Thank you, everyone. I'm sorry. Can we steal him back? The game is resuming."

Met with a few leud comments from the peanut gallery, Ben made the fans back away. Sean thanked everyone and took a seat.

"You okay? Thought I'd save you."

"Appreciate that. I never want to be rude, but people don't know when to stop," he whispered under his breath, with Ben standing stoically behind them.

"Don't worry. I don't mind being the bad guy if Ben doesn't want to be," Evily chuckled, seeing the Henchman glance down at her. Giving him a playful nudge and a wink, she got him to crack a partial smile just as the referee blew the whistle for the teams to return to battle.

19

Friday, July 26th
Canton, Massachusetts

Settled in for the third period, Sean and Evily watched Evan skate out for the face-off. When he looked at both of them, his Mom held up two fingers. Nodding, he understood what that meant.

Sean turned to her. "Wait? Did you just tell him how many goals to score?"

"No. I simply said the team needs to score two goals," she chuckled, knowing what she did was neither here nor there.

Glued to the team's every move, the spectators watched the clock dwindle minute by minute. After spending so much time on their end, the puck finally broke out, allowing Evan and his teammates the opportunity to move up the ice in formation. The athletes could smell blood. Sent a precise pass from his winger, snagging it on his stick, Evan instinctively aimed at the five-hole while his eyes distractingly spied the top left corner to psych out the goalie.

"Goal!" Sean shouted. "Nice."

Silently celebrating, Evily grasped her hands together with a white-knuckle grip and hoped the group of boys would have enough in them to finish out the game. Sean could see she was nervous, sitting on the edge of her seat.

"Don't worry. They've got this," he said.

The author turned and flashed an uncertain smile.

"Now, who has little faith?" he laughed.

"Even though I know what the score might be, I still have this element of doubt. What if I'm wrong? What if the circumstances change?"

"Well, let me see. So far, you hit the mark on every detail of my life and the game yesterday, so I think you're good."

The puck dropped again with ten minutes left. The players scattered and passed up and down the ice at lightning speed. Evan's team was working hard to ward off their competition - a known top-three team from last year's tournament. The air got thick as the game escalated. Multiple penalties stacked players into the box. Exhaustion plagued both sides.

Evan took a seat on the bench to recover from the last shift. Encouraging his teammates, he saw them gain possession. The second line stormed past center and skated alongside the boards to charge the net between the overwhelmed defensemen. Confidently firing off the shot, the goalie stretched out to snag it, but the puck trickled over the tip of his glove. The spectators held their breath as it seemingly fell in slow motion past the line behind the goalie. Aware he didn't have it, he dropped to his knees, turned around, and lowered his head. There it was, sitting in the back of the net.

"Goal!" Sean said, clapping his hands.

Evily calmly exhaled and said quickly, "Yes. Perfect. Okay."

"Are you always this calm?" Sean thought she'd be bouncing off her seat.

Laughing, she said, "Believe me. I am bursting inside. I can't let my nerves get the better of me. It's so hard."

"I bet." Knowing he hadn't had this much fun in a long time, Sean felt the need to say something. "You know, umm, I want to thank you for allowing me to join you. It's nice to think of something other than work for a change."

"Oh, you're welcome. At least it is helping you pass the time."

Little did she know, it meant more to him.

Evily watched the players whiz by the bench, grabbing high fives on the way past. Things got tense. After checking the clock and the number of penalty minutes for both sides, she realized the Raider's team would be on a power play for forty more seconds.

In the final minutes of the period, the boys held their lead. After managing multiple turnovers, sustaining penalties, and fighting through a few fights, the clock counted down, and the buzzer sounded.

"That's game," Sean said, overly excited about the win.

The entire team left the bench shouting. Each skated to the goalie and piled on top of him to celebrate. As the Zamboni prepared to clean the ice, many spectators stood to applaud the team's efforts. They assembled in a line for the handshake before parting ways. Evily could hear the thoughts of so many people. It was like a million radios playing a different station all at once. Overwhelmed, she knew Sean Bradley was the common thread.

"I think we should head out to the truck now. You're about to be surrounded," she warned.

Ben's guard went up. Returning to reality, Sean asked him to move in and control the crowd.

"Ella, get ready to go," her Mother said.

On the ball, the girl quickly got up from her chair and packed her phone away. Sticking close to her Mom, she was not sure what to expect.

All Sean could see were countless bodies moving towards him and cameras flashing from every angle. Trying to be polite, he smiled at everyone and waved, taking the odd photo. Amidst the mayhem, Ben quickly carved a path through the crowd and alerted Tim they were on their way.

"Follow me," Ben instructed calmly.

Leading them through the private Scouting Lounge, Evily, and Ella followed the Henchman. Sean kept the two of them in his sights, more concerned about their safety than his own. Descending the stairs toward the rear exit, Ben's hands hit the crash bar to open the door. The sound loudly echoed through the deserted space. The three escaped and found Tim waiting outside with the Escalade parked a few feet away.

Allowing the girls to get in first, Sean found a seat before Ben shut the door behind him. Thankfully, nobody followed.

Sitting there, Evily texted Evan.

Great game! So proud of you! FYI - Sean had a few fan interruptions between periods. We've gone ahead to the truck to wait for you.

Evan replied minutes later.

Okay. Hey, Good News. My coach asked me to speak to Four different university coaches. From what he says, they sound interested.

Sean saw the mother of two raise a hand to her face. Her eyes quickly welled.

"You okay?" he asked, concerned something was wrong.

Emotional, she couldn't look at him. "Umm, yes. Everything is fine. I'm just happy. Some coaches want to talk to Evan."

"Well, that's awesome." He felt honored to witness the touching moment.

"I only want the best for him." Evily caught Ella looking her way. "I want the best for both of you. My only wish is that you are happy in life, especially in your chosen career paths."

"That's what you always say," Ella pointed out, having heard this speech many times before.

"You'll see one day when you have a family. That is the job of a mom, Ella."

"Oh, I almost forgot." Evily took the Land Rover key from her bag and reached out to Sean. "This is yours."

Unexpectedly grazing his hand underneath hers, he watched her drop the fob in his palm. Time stood still at that moment. Nervous,

Sean hoped she hadn't heard his runaway thoughts because if she did, she'd know that there was just something about her that he liked.

Very aware of that, Evily's heart skipped a beat. *How could that be?* she thought. *He is a famous actor, and I am just an author who prefers writing in the shadows.* Opting to stay quiet and not bring attention to the incident, she focused on the view of the park. Questioning if the actor was getting too close, she wondered if allowing him to spend time with them could be detrimental in the long run. Curious to peer into the future, her visions blurred. That was a sign that it was unstable and not yet concretely written. There were too many undecided variables left to chance.

Uncomfortable, the two stayed quiet while Tim parked beside the Rover. Sean passed the key to Ben so he could start the engine and cool down the cabin before they got in. It was best to stay hidden in the Escalade until Evan returned to join them.

Watching intently, Ella noticed her brother walking out the front doors. She alerted her Mom.

They saw the team gathered around the coaches. One of them handed out envelopes to each team member while they received further instructions. When the meeting broke, Evily went to help her son with his sticks. He looked exhausted.

"Okay, Ella. Guess we should change vehicles," Sean instructed after Ben gave the word.

Both got out and found a seat in the Rover. Popping the tailgate for Evan to store his bag quickly, Sean watched the mother and son make their way across the parking lot.

The tall hockey player strode confidently toward her, his broad smile impossible to miss. After a brief exchange, he handed over his sticks, then unexpectedly pulled her into a warm, one-armed hug.

Sean watched in amazement as Evily, momentarily speechless, gently patted her son's back in silent pride. A tear slipped down her cheek as she wiped it away, and the two walked off together, chatting and laughing with an ease that filled the air with warmth.

When they reached the truck, Evan shoved his stuff in the back. Opening the zipper, he took out his equipment to dry before getting in and collapsing in the rear passenger seat. They saw most of the team looking on with eyes glued to the famous actor chauffeuring the family today.

While Evan settled in, Sean glanced in the rearview mirror and said, "Great game, man."

"Thanks. It was a tough one. Can't believe we bounced a top team. After the game, a few coaches wanted to speak to me, Luca, Matteo, Makaio, and Cole. They will be sending information on their schools and the athletic scholarships available. I gave them my contact information."

"Congrats," Sean replied, noticing more people staring.

Taking a breath, the teenager then dropped a bomb. "And, oh, by the way, everyone on the team knows you're Sean Bradley, and most are wondering what you are doing watching the games with my Mom. Thoughts?" Evan chuckled, humorously catching the actor off guard.

The two adults did not know how to respond to that. Both were now concerned about what would await them at the Tsongas Center.

Turning to his mother, he said, "The team is going straight to the university. Guess we'll have to get something to eat later." Scrolling through his social media, slouching in his seat, he was unfazed by the family's odd situation.

Needing to change the flow of things, Sean asked Evily, "So, where are we off to now?"

"Umm, let me check the email."

"Oh, Mom. Here is the information on the UMASS visit." Evan passed her the envelope he'd received from the coaches.

"This is the school's address," she said, pointing to it on the bottom half of the page.

Keying it into the Nav system, Sean passed the info along to Tim, who was standing outside his door. Excited to take part in the school tour, never having done this himself, the former junior player felt he could live vicariously through the talented young man, if only for a moment. It made him wonder what his life would have been like if he hadn't pursued a career in acting.

Evily heard certain things ramble through his mind. Picking up on his silent thoughts, she caught wind of some resentment and regret. "Why on earth would you ever regret becoming a successful actor? Look at the opportunities it has awarded you."

Stunned by her outburst, Sean and the children were surprised by her statement.

"Where did that come from?" Ella asked, thinking her Mom was off her rocker.

"How about we stay out of my head for a while, okay," Sean chuckled, making light of the statement.

With a smirk, his gaze focused straight ahead. Receiving a text from Tim permitting him to leave, he shifted the truck into gear and slowly drove out of the parking lot.

Realizing what she had done, Evily, once again, had invaded his private thoughts and announced them for all to hear.

Driving along, Sean tried desperately not to think of anything. But Evan's words sunk in. How would he explain spending time with a mother of two teenage children? If the press got a hold of this, it would spread like wildfire in a matter of days.

At the same time, Evily watched the scenery go by, finding it hard to refrain from commenting. Not looking his way, a part of her felt like maybe they weren't worthy of being around the famous actor. She feared this could end badly for her and the children, too. Panic set in. How she wished her job here was already over. Looking up to the clouds, she hoped Janie and Ella knew what they were doing. Waiting for a sign from them, Evily sadly received nothing in response.

20

Friday, July 26th
Lowell, Massachusetts

By loving them for more than their abilities, we show our children that they are much more than the sum of their accomplishments. ~ Eileen Kennedy - Moore

Navigating the side roads, Sean merged onto I-95 North with the Henchmen following close behind. Ella was acutely aware of how quiet the ride was so far. She couldn't bring herself to close off from the world by slipping on her headphones. Intuitively feeling the stress between her mother and the actor, the young girl figured she should step in and help them out.

"So, Mr. Bradley?" Ella stated, startling him a bit.

Sean peered at her in the rear-view mirror. "Before we go any further, can I say something?"

Not sure what he was going to ask, the teen with long brown hair like her Mother's nodded, "Sure."

"Can you please call me Sean? The Mr. Bradley thing is too formal."

Ella leaned forward to see her Mom's expression, wondering whether she would approve.

"Don't look at me," she said. "If that is something he prefers, then who am I to argue."

"Okay, Sean," Ella emphasized his name. "What's it like being famous? It seemed you weren't comfortable surrounded by all those fans today."

"Wait…" Evan perked up, wanting to know what he missed. "What happened?"

His Mom explained. "Well, during the flood before the third, one person recognized him and started a small frenzy of people asking for selfies and autographs."

"Really?" Evan looked over at Ella.

She quickly confirmed what their Mom said.

Sean glanced back. "Yes. Sadly, my anonymity at the next game may not exist any longer."

"So, what does that mean?" Evan was worried about what he would say.

"Well, as I explained to your Mom, it happens in waves. It starts with selfies. That spreads to the general population. Then the paparazzi get wind of it." Exhaling, sounding quite frustrated, he added, "Within a few days, we will see photographers lurking around. Hopefully, it won't affect you guys too much. If it does, well, I apologize in advance." Sean knew it would probably be better not to attend any games over the weekend, given what was happening. "I may have to hire extra security to control it all."

"You're joking," Ella said in disbelief. "More Henchmen?"

"Yes," he confirmed. "More Henchmen."

Although the two teens thought it was all pretty cool, they could also sense that it somehow haunted Sean in a way.

"So, as a famous actor, I guess your life is never your own?" Ella sounded so sincere.

"No, it's not. My life is an open book - no pun intended." Sean offered Evily a smile.

The comment made her chuckle.

Interrupted by the GPS voice command, it instructed them to merge off the highway onto Thorndike Street. Ben and Tim were right behind when they crossed a bridge over a scenic river. Making their way through town, Ella marveled at the traditional architecture of some of the municipal buildings along the main street.

Approaching the upcoming intersection, Evan leaned forward and pointed. "Is that it?"

Double-checking the map, Sean said, "Yes, I believe it is." Slowly proceeding through the green light, they entered the grounds of the Tsongas Center. Exiting the first right off the traffic circle, Sean drove toward the entrance to the arena and said, "Here we are."

Finding a shady spot to park, they all got out to stretch after the long drive. In the heat of the afternoon, the humidity was on the rise.

The Henchmen took their positions and scanned their surroundings.

Evan stood there, admiring the size of the facility, realizing his dream of becoming an NCAA athlete was within his grasp. His Mom caught the priceless look on her son's face and walked over to put her arm around him.

"Excited?" she questioned.

"Hell, yeah," he said before walking towards the front doors.

Hearing Ella's giggly laugh made Sean smile.

She immediately wanted to confirm her brother's comment. "Did he just say hell?"

The actor snickered. "I think so."

Running ahead to join her brother, Ella was so proud of him.

Their mother hung back and watched the two playfully push and shove each other off balance. At the same time, she listened while Ben and Tim devised a plan of action, given the venue's size and the crowd gathered around.

Sean approached the author, seeing her sights affixed upon the teenagers.

Analyzing the scene unfolding before her, she thought it was symbolic. Maybe a foreshadowing of what was on the horizon in the coming years. A fact of life that was inevitable. In a daze-like state, Evily whispered, "I don't think I'm ready to let him go."

"I know. I can't imagine," Sean said from a couple of feet away. Trying to think of something supportive, he added, "But Evan seems ready. He's a good kid. You've raised him right."

"Why do they have to grow up so quickly? It just feels like yesterday that I brought him home from the hospital. A lot of water has flowed under the bridge since then." Coming to her senses, realizing what she said, knowing Sean didn't get that opportunity in life, she immediately backtracked. "Oh, I'm so sorry. That was insensitive. Please forgive me. I didn't mean to...."

"Don't give it another thought. It's fine. Really. It's okay." With silence lingering between them, he said, "Hope you don't mind me intruding on this experience with all of you."

Evily could feel genuine happiness off him. "I'm glad you are here. To be honest, it's kind of nice not going through the day alone for once." Seeing Sean's face light up made her shyly look away.

"Well, shall we?" he said, moving his hand forward and allowing her to lead. He noticed more cars arriving and assumed they were Evan's teammates.

Joining her children inside the arena, Evily found her son in awe. It just warmed her heart. He was excited about the opportunity to see the school. Their family waited off to the side while everyone walked in. Evan's Coach, Jason Pinzino, greeted a man descending the stairs. Exchanging a friendly handshake, the former NHLers officially welcomed the families.

Addressing the team and all the parents, the man said, "Welcome to the Tsongas Center, everyone. I'm Nate Bazin. I'm the coach here at UMASS Lowell. I'll be showing you around this afternoon. Believe the tour will take about forty-five minutes to an hour, depending. If you have any questions, please feel free to ask. Let's get started!"

The group climbed the stairs into the stands and walked along the perimeter of the arena's upper bowl. Evan stood along the railing, looking down at the ice surface, amazed by the number of royal blue seats.

"Can you see yourself playing here?" Evily asked while standing to one side of him. His sister was on the other.

Sean stayed back and looked at the family of three from a distance.

Nodding, her son replied, "Yeah, for sure. This feels real now. Like a dream about to come true." Evan soaked it all in as his Mom stayed close. "All my life, I've worked so hard for this moment. This one year will either make or break me. At this point, I hope I'm good enough. I pray for that every day."

His Mother placed her hand on top of his, resting on the railing. "You are. Don't let anyone tell you otherwise."

"I love this game. Seeing the ice down there makes me want to suit up right now," he said confidently.

Intently watching the mother and son move along to keep up with the group, eavesdropping on them from time to time, Sean turned to find Ella lagging a few steps behind. Slowing down his pace, he decided to keep her company.

"So, Miss Ella. What do you think about all this? You know, with your brother eventually going away to school."

Ella crossed her arms in front of her. Deep in thought, she looked forward and then turned to the actor, seeming more like a friend than a stranger.

"Umm, well, I think he needs to do what is best for his future. Mom and I will be fine. He will visit us, I'm sure, and we can visit him on weekends, too."

"Yes, I think all of you will adjust. It will take a little time." Wondering about her future plans, he added, "Where do you see yourself going after attending high school? Your Mom said you want to be an architect."

"University of Chicago, of course. I can live at home with Mom and attend classes during the day. A perfect scenario for her and me."

He could hear the excitement in Ella's voice. She seemed to have given this a lot of thought already. "It's good that you have such a solid plan."

"I figure Evan will be playing in the NHL or Europe by then. Mom will need me," she added. "It will just be her and I. We will probably watch Evan on TV."

Sean's future flashed before him. He knew nobody would be there waiting in the wings when he got old.

I guess I'll have to pay someone to do that, too, he thought.

Ella looked his way and offered a strange expression.

A bit paranoid, he wondered if the girl had the same gift. Had she heard him, too?

21

Friday, July 26th
Lowell, Massachusetts

You don't build a bond without being present. ~ James Earl Jones

That afternoon, Sean walked with the Anderson family through the arena, athlete's academic center, gym, and residence. Ben and Tim followed, never allowing their client to leave their sights. The actor could hear his name whispered throughout the tour, making his guard go up. That and the constant staring was something he'd gotten used to over the years.

Evily took notice of his uneasiness. "Everything okay?" she asked.

"For now, I suppose," Sean quietly pointed out, "It's fine."

"Yes. I don't need to hear their thoughts, either. They aren't shy about it." The author paused. "Do you want to go back to the truck?"

"No, I'm okay." Sean chuckled unnervingly. "It's like I'm in high school again, and a rumor about me is spreading through the halls."

"Hang in there a few more minutes. It shouldn't be much longer." Evily saw another player's Mom wave her over. "Sorry, Sean. Excuse me. I'll be right back."

"Sure. No problem."

Instantly, Evily could sense Kristen's nosey nature erupting.

"Evily! How are you? Long time no chat." Fictitiously pointing out a few things on the bulletin board to their right, Kristen leaned over and whispered, "Okay, tell me the truth. What's up with Mr. Hollywood? Everyone has been watching you two. Are you dating Sean Bradley?"

"No, of course not. He's just a friend." Evily was unwilling to share anything more with the overly rumorous woman, always looking for a scoop.

"Huh," she huffed. "I thought we were friends."

"We are. But it's the truth. There is nothing to tell. He's just a friend of the family." The woman still didn't believe her. "Listen, umm, I've gotta get back, okay."

As Evily walked away, the hockey mom outwardly replied, "Yeah, sure. You do that. Don't want to leave that handsome man by himself for too long. Someone may snatch him up."

Standing beside the celebrity again, having stayed away from the crowd, he was happy to see her return.

With a somewhat sexy smirk, he caught Evily off guard when he said, "What was that all about?"

She mumbled, "Oh, enquiring minds want to know."

"Really? What did she say about me?"

"You know, she had the audacity to ask if we were dating. I mean, how ridiculous?" Fluffing it off, the author felt strange. It was such an uncomfortable topic of conversation.

Laughing, he said, "That's not so ridiculous."

Evily blushed with embarrassment after shooting him a surprised look.

"What?" Sean grinned. "I'm just saying."

"Yeah, okay, Romeo. Let's go," she replied bluntly, making light of his comment.

Moving ahead of him, Sean chuckled when she looked back a few times, clearly bothered by his observation. The thing was, she'd tuned into his thoughts. Strangely, she was able to confirm he wasn't lying just then.

During the tour, dark clouds crept into the area south of the university. They assumed the rest of the day would be wet and stormy. Before leaving the Tsongas Center, Coach Bazin asked to speak with Evan and his Mother. His coach also joined the conversation.

Not wanting to stay there, suffering from sore feet and tired legs, Ella decided to go ahead to the truck with Sean. Ben and Tim followed them out the front doors while the team and their parents looked on. Thankfully, nobody stepped forward to bombard the actor, which made the whole experience more tolerable.

Halfway to the Land Rover, the two strolled about five feet apart. Sean attempted to strike up a conversation.

"So, Ms. Ella, how do you love architecture so much at such a young age?"

"Not sure. I love designing homes from the ground up, incorporating various design elements. I started creating about two years ago but have learned a lot in that short time."

"Who's your favorite architect?" he asked, clicking the remote to unlock the truck.

"Well, let me see. There are so many. My Mom got me a subscription to Architectural Digest last year for Christmas. I prefer clean lines, uncluttered rooms - you know, the modern white boxes with unexpected twists. The houses in California seem to embody many of the design elements I love. Inside one issue was an article featuring Paul McClair. He had put out a book called *The Contemporary House*. I fell in love with his balance of glass, earthy tones, and water features."

Sean's eyebrows raised. Once seated behind the wheel, he replied, "Oh, really?"

"Yes. So, to answer your question, I would say Mr. McClair is my favorite architect. Of course, I love Frank Lloyd Wright's Fallingwater House and the Guggenheim. Who wouldn't? But McClair's designs harmonize humanity with its environment. Waterfalls, living green walls, and natural woods blended with sheets of glass that bring the outside in - that's his signature style."

"Impressive," Sean replied, taken by the young teen's expert analysis. Smiling, he said, "I am so surprised you know of him. I, too, am a fan of his work."

About to elaborate, Ella spotted her Mom and Evan exiting the arena, talking with the coaches. "Hey, there they are," she said before returning to their conversation. "So, why do you like McClair's designs?"

Sean took out his phone from his pocket. Scrolling through his photos, he stopped at one and handed it to her. "What do you think of this place?"

Grabbing hold, she looked at the picture. "Wait? Where did you take this? I think it's the house featured in A.D. One of my favorites. That said, I have many favorites."

"Well," he replied, ready to let her in on a little secret. "That is actually – my house."

"Shut up!!" the young girl shouted, giving him a hard shot to the shoulder, making him wince. "You're joking! Tell me you're joking."

"No. Not joking. It's my house." Rubbing his shoulder, he said, "Maybe instead of design, you should take up boxing."

Ignoring his suggestion, she shouted, "No way! Hold on." Ella took out her phone and searched up Sean Bradley's house in L.A. Finding what she was looking for precisely, the teen scrolled through the images, confirming everything he had just said. "Oh, my goodness. Oh, my goodness!"

"Wasn't my picture enough proof for you?" he laughed.

"I can't believe this." Ella was astonished. "It's the most beautiful thing I've ever seen."

"So, maybe if you, Evan, and your Mom visit L.A. sometime, I can introduce you to Paul. He's a good friend of mind – for obvious reasons."

"This is amazing. Of course, I'd love to meet him. Wow, this is crazy! Wait until I tell my Mom. She will be so surprised. Oh, my goodness. I can't believe this." Ella was practically jumping out of her seat. "Do you have any other pictures?"

The girl got out of the back and jumped in the front beside him. Returning his phone, Sean pulled up a few more photos.

"Here is my living room. There's the view from the terrace, by the pool. This is the waterfall and the living wall you seem to love."

She was speechless. With tears developing, clutching her heart, she said sincerely, "I just love it."

Noticing that she got emotional, Sean said humorously, "Hey. Don't cry. Don't.... Your Mom will think I said something rude or mean to you."

"No, she won't. You know this is like a dream to me. I would love to see your house if she ever wants to take me."

"Well, we will just have to convince her. That's all there is to it."

When Evan and his Mother were almost back at the truck, Ella got out of the front and returned to her seat. Eventually, everyone settled in for the next leg of the journey that day.

Exhaling, Evan slid his hand through his hair. "Wow, this day can't get any more amazing."

"Good news?" Sean asked.

"Yes, excellent news," Evily admitted.

"He wants me to play for him after I graduate. I could see myself playing for this school, Mom."

Choking up, quickly composing herself, Evily said, "At this point, Evan, keep your options open. We will apply and move forward with it, but let's not put all your eggs in one basket." Her voice vibrated. She stared forward, biting her lip slightly.

Sean glanced her way, knowing this whole experience was stressful for her. Hearing his thoughts, she raised her index finger, silently requesting that he give her a moment.

"You all right there, Mom?" Evan taunted, knowing she was probably crying again.

Tears flowed silently.

Noticing this, the athlete reached out to hug her from the back seat. "It's okay. You'll still have Ella at home."

That pulled on her heartstrings even more since Ella would then be next.

"I know a day will come when you both have to leave me to follow your dreams. It's just happening so fast. Some days, I want it to slow down," she said, sniffling while pulling a tissue from her bag.

"Think how nice it will be when sis and I visit."

"Evan, we need to change the subject," Ella interrupted, feeling the pain in her Mother's heart. She also was exploding inside after the conversation she'd had with Sean. "Mom! Hey! Guess what?"

"What?" her Mom said while fixing her face in the vanity mirror.

"You know that McClair house I love in L.A.? The one in Architectural Digest I showed you maybe a year ago?"

Showing her Mother the picture she'd pulled up on her phone, Evily replied, "Oh, yes. I remember that one."

With an abundance of excitement, she shouted, "Guess who owns it?"

Evily turned to her and said, "I don't know. Who?"

Ella pointed to Sean.

"You're kidding?" The author went straight-faced. "No way..."

Sean nodded his head. "Tell me that isn't a coincidence."

"It's such a beautiful home." Evily turned around to Ella. "It's the one with the living wall and waterfall, right?"

"Yes, that's the one. Sean said we could visit L.A. and see it. Can we go, Mom? Can we? Please, please, please?" she pleaded with praying hands.

"Well, if it is okay with him, maybe we can arrange a short vacation when he's free."

"Yes!" her daughter shouted, falling back into her seat. "I can't believe it! This is so awesome."

Noticing that Evan felt left out, Sean suggested, "Maybe we can go to an L.A. Kings' game, too."

Evan's ears perked up. "Really? Are you serious?"

"Sure. Why not? I have many connections. Maybe you could get some autographs. What do you say?"

Evan's mouth dropped. He couldn't speak. "I would love that. Thank you."

"Hey, you two, let's just get this trip over with first. Then, if his schedule permits, we will arrange something. Just a weekend. Nothing more. We don't want to impose." Evily turned to Sean and smiled. She silently mouthed the words, *Thank you* and hoped her kids wouldn't be disappointed if the plans didn't materialize. She knew things between them would fall by the wayside, just not exactly how or when that might happen.

The actor nodded with a smile. "So, Ms. Landy, what is our next destination?"

"Game two is in a different arena. Umm, it's called the New England Sports Village. Here is the address."

Entering it in the Nav, the kids put on their seat belts, ready to go. Sean confirmed the route with Tim, while Ben gave them the thumbs up to proceed. Tiny raindrops hit the windshield while they pulled out of the parking lot. On their way to Attleboro, the clouds got darker the further south they drove.

22

Friday, July 26th
Outskirts of Boston, Massachusetts

Driving south on the Lowell Connector, linking up with the #3 Expressway, the storm clouds looked much darker than before they left the university. The rain, now heavier at times, made everything look so green on either side of them. So many shades. Most much deeper and more defined when soaking wet.

While looking through his social media for updates from friends and the content creators he follows, Evan posted photos from his experience at the Tsongas Center and quickly noticed something pop up.

"By the way, I got bombarded by questions about you during the tour," Evan said to Sean while continuing to scroll.

As visibility worsened, Sean glanced in the rearview mirror once and kept his focus on the road. "Oh, is that right?"

"Yeah. Umm, this may have something to do with it. A fan posted this picture a couple of hours ago. I think it is from the Canton rink," the athlete said, passing his phone to his mom.

"What is it, Evan?" she asked. That is when she saw the picture with the caption – *Met my favorite actor at my brother's hockey game today! #SeanBradley*

Captivated, Ella leaned forward to get a better look. She immediately recognized her. "That's the girl who made all the fuss."

Sadly, Sean knew where one photo was; many more would follow.

In searching up *#SeanBradley*, Ella found a ton.

"Yeah, word seems to be getting around. I've counted, umm, well over, umm, eighty," the young girl said, continuing to scroll.

"Eighty?" Evily questioned in disbelief.

"Yeah, I've lost track now."

With a sigh, Sean said, "That's about right. At least we will be at a different arena for the second game."

Curious, the author started a hashtag search. Hearing the rain pelting the windshield, she was concerned about what this would all mean. Quickly finding a few photos that featured snaps of Sean and her escaping in the taxi cab while on their walk yesterday, she also noticed a few posted of the children. She didn't like their family being in the public eye. Over the years, she always protected them from the spotlight. That was why she used a pseudonym when publishing her books. Her career and family were always kept separate for a reason.

Outwardly continuing the hashtag search, Ella scoured the internet for more information.

Peering back in the rearview mirror at Evan, Sean said, "Sorry, bud. I don't want this to ruin your tournament weekend."

"Are you kidding? All of my teammates are asking when they can meet you. It's awesome!" The hockey player was frantically texting.

Happy to hear it didn't come across negatively, he turned to Evily and found her in a panicked state. "Are you okay?"

"I'm not sure yet," she said, knowing there is a consequence for every action. "I'll explain later."

Now, twenty minutes into their trip, the Hollywood star wondered if they should stop for food. "So, is anyone hungry?"

"Yeah, I can always eat. But just pasta, chicken, and sauce. Maybe broccoli. Need energy for tonight."

Hoping to find a restaurant along their route, Evily changed her search subject.

"Tavolino, at Foxboro Stadium, has pasta and pizza. It's on our way to Attleboro. Are you interested in that? We have four hours before the game still. Lots of time."

"Sure." Inserting his earbuds and reclining the seat, Evan closed his eyes. "I'm going to sleep. Let me know when we get there. It's a long drive, right?"

"Little less than an hour," his mom replied before her son closed his eyes to take a nap.

It didn't take long for Ella to do the same. Reclining her seat, the girl put on her noise-canceling headphones and scrunched a hoodie into a pillow to rest her head.

"Guess our conversation reduced to a party of two, just like that."

Sean laughed. "Yes, it's unreal how they just instantaneously shut down. Don't know how they can fall asleep so fast. I wish I could do that."

"I know, right? It takes me forever to fall asleep these past few years."

Hitting a lull, Sean broke their silence after a couple of minutes and asked, "So, want to talk about the pictures online?"

Evily lowered her head and stared at the black screen on her phone.

"I'm just worried my ex-husband will see them."

Focused on the road, he asked, "Why? What will he say?"

"Let's hope and pray he doesn't say anything. I don't want to deal with that." She exhaled and moved her sights to the scenery rolling by. "Can we just change the subject?"

"Absolutely. What should we talk about then?" He hoped to pose a few questions.

"Pose away. What would you like to ask?" she interjected, having read his thoughts while the rains fell, creating a constant swooshing sound as they drove through the countryside.

"When you do that, I feel like I'm an open book," pausing, he added, "No...."

"Pun intended." Evily finished his sentence.

"Yeah, that."

"Guess it's why my husband left me. He hated it, too. There were no secrets between us. But it wasn't because we each wanted it that way, unfortunately. I know it's bothersome. I apologize."

"No, I didn't mean it in a bad way."

"Sometimes, I wish I didn't have this ability - that I couldn't hear people or pick up on their feelings. It's intrusive."

"To tell you the truth, I think it has its perks. Somehow, it makes communicating easier. I forever keep my cards tight to my chest, if you know what I mean. Oddly enough, I've shared more with you in forty-eight hours than anyone in the past fourteen years. It's been so long since I've talked about Ella and Janie. I mean, they never come up in conversation anymore. I've enjoyed discussing and remembering them freely."

"Well, they have a lot to say to you." Evily paused. Biting her lip, a set of images flashed through her mind. "The day you bought my book, something made you feel heavy-hearted. You were still searching for a gift, knowing that whatever you bought this person, they wouldn't like it because they were expecting something in particular. One gift above all others."

"How do you do that?" He shook his head in amazement.

"It's just a series of feelings mixed with images flashing in my mind. Never know if I'm right unless I blurt it out, and someone confirms it." Looking at Sean, she asked, "So?"

"You're right. When I saw your poster in the bookstore window, I was stressed. I'd contemplated buying a gift for a woman I'd been seeing. Her name is Andrea Branti."

Evily's eyes widened. "The actress?"

"Yeah... Our relationship had been anything but smooth sailing. Full disclosure: we'd only been together on and off for under three months. I was shooting a movie on location for half of it. The truth is, I cared about Andrea, but what we had, I felt, didn't warrant that level of commitment. Long story short, she wanted to get married, thinking it was a good business decision. She believed we could get a quickie divorce if it didn't work out. That, to me, was a warning sign. I did toy with the idea for weeks, especially when I picked up a few things I needed on Rodeo. Passing by the jewelry store where I bought Janie's ring, I couldn't bring myself to go in. I didn't feel the same about this girl as I did about my wife. That settled it. When I left there and dropped into The Grove, that's when I saw your poster in the window."

"Please know Janie veered you off that path and sent you in another direction."

"Funny you say that. Within hours of returning home, I broke up with her. That night, I started to read your book." Sean was stunned. "This is unbelievable. It's almost addictive."

Closing her eyes and squinting, Sean kept glancing over at her.

"Guess you really need to focus?"

"No," she giggled. "I'm just messing with you." Met by disappointment, Evily knew he wanted to hear more.

Shimmying around in her seat, she said, "Okay, okay, wait. Let me think a moment."

Sean turned off the I-95 to Highway 1, anticipating what she might divulge.

"Why do you leave your lights on at night? Strange. Don't you like sleeping in the dark? You never turn them off."

"Yeah, I forget to sometimes."

"Well, that's not what I see," the author prompted, empathically picking up on his feelings while images flickered in front of her.

He got nervous. "Okay, you know, that whole thing is hard to explain."

Believing he wouldn't share his thoughts on the subject, Evily checked on their location. "Well, let's see, you've got eleven minutes to spill everything."

Inhaling, holding it in, he revealed a secret he's never told anyone. "To this day, nobody knows this. I mean, not even my best friends. You probably can already guess what I am about to say."

"Kind of, but continue."

"What is this? Gang up on Sean Day? Holy smokes..."

"No, this is Janie being worried about you and wanting you to feel happy and, most of all, safe. It is a fear that spans back before her death."

"You're no stranger to this, so I suppose I can tell you straight up."

"You see ghosts. Just say it. I see ghosts."

"Yeah, so...." Sean muttered. "What does that mean?"

Shifting her body to face him, she asked excitedly, "White or misty black ones?"

"Ahh, both sometimes, I think."

"Oh, really? Interesting. And that has caused you to be...." The author prompted him again, but this time with hand gestures intermixed.

"It has prompted me to be..." Sean's tone changed as he whispered, "Somewhat afraid of the dark."

"Hallelujah."

"Hey, it's not something I'm proud of. I play a badass on-screen but hate sleeping without a light on at night. How embarrassing."

"Janie visited your house a few months after she passed. You saw a white shadow near the entrance to your bedroom. Correct?"

He thought a moment. "That happened so long ago. Truthfully, I didn't know if I was hallucinating or not."

"You weren't. Did you feel a chill in the air?"

He thought for a minute. "Not sure. Maybe. I'd have to think more about that." Pausing, Sean tied in a conversation they had earlier. "Is that why I felt the cold draft in my hotel room? Was Janie there?"

"Yes, they both were."

His hair stood up on the back of his neck at that thought.

Hesitating, Evily had to ask while getting mixed signals. "The night you saw Janie's ghost outside your bedroom door, you were overly distraught and in pain. Something bad happened earlier that week."

Sean nodded. "Despite being a memory forever ingrained in my mind, if it's okay, I'd rather not elaborate on the details just yet." To keep her from invading his privacy, he intentionally repeated lines from his latest movie to throw her off. He didn't want her to know what had happened - especially the evil thoughts that had taken over and almost won.

With images flashing through her mind, Evily could get the gist of what had transpired. The makings of that fateful day were better left unsaid. It was a dark secret he'd kept to himself all these years, and he wanted it to stay that way.

Veering into the turn lane with Foxboro Stadium on their left, he said, "Time's up."

23

Friday, July 26th
Foxborough, Massachusetts

When there's an elephant in the room, you can't pretend it isn't there and just discuss the ants.

~ Ellen Wittlinger

Sean turned onto Patriot Place and followed the signs, with Tim and Ben following close behind. Directed into the parking lot by attendants controlling traffic, he was surprised by the size of the venue and how impeccably maintained the grounds were.

Immediately spotting the restaurant he thought Evily had suggested, he asked, "Is that it?" while pointing to the building with orange awnings.

"Yes," she answered before swiveling around to tap Evan and Ella's knees to wake them gently.

The teens opened their eyes and stretched. Never having visited this area before, they scanned their surroundings. With fields and forests to one side, hotels, shops, and a massive stadium on the other, they saw so many cars and loads of people around the state-of-the-art village celebrating the sport of football.

"Time to grab some food, guys," their Mother said.

Moving along slowly, the SUVs adhered to another attendant pointing to a few spaces at the back of the lot. Evily noticed the sky was beginning to clear. Unfortunately, the break in the weather would be short-lived, as another storm in the distance promised a second wave of rain and severe thunderstorms.

The football stadium looked like it had its own zip code. The signage revealed that an International soccer tournament was taking place nearby—seemingly a match between AC Milan and SL Benfica. Many fans wore jerseys for one team or the other as they walked past, heading toward the event. Sean was concerned about the crowds.

"Look, we will just keep to ourselves. Maybe nobody will recognize you if you wear a hat and sunglasses," Evily said.

"Maybe," the actor replied, not convinced.

Getting out of the vehicle, the group joined the Henchmen. Ben even looked apprehensive.

"We are heading toward the orange awnings marked Tavolino," Sean told them while locking the truck.

"Alright," Ben replied. "We will have eyes on you the whole time. But if I call it, we are gone."

Sean nodded, knowing a frenzy could be inevitable in this setting. But he didn't want to impose restrictions on the Anderson family. It wasn't fair to them. Since it was earlier in the day, he thought just maybe there wouldn't be as many people waiting for a table.

Making their way over to the Italian eatery, they looked like a very unconventional family. The Henchmen were overly muscular, dressed all in black, and seemed out of place. It caused a few people in the crowd to look at them curiously.

When they approached the front doors, Sean could see that the restaurant was still buzzing, but thankfully, there wasn't a line to get inside.

Greeted by a lovely hostess at the front, Evily stepped forward when the girl said, "Welcome to Tavolino. Table for six?"

"Yes, Thank you," she said, with slight hesitation, realizing the girl had added in the security guys. "Is it possible to find a table tucked away somewhere in the back?" Evily turned to Sean while the girl checked the seating chart. She whispered to him, "Is it okay if the guys join us? I didn't want to correct her."

Sean nodded that it was fine.

Dressed in a form-fitting black dress with a colorful scarf around her neck, the woman turned and grabbed their menus. The bistro was about half full. Flashing an intrigued facial expression, she strangely scanned the six of them. Suddenly, her eyes fell upon Sean. "Please follow me," she said in a monotone voice.

Passing an impressive circular wine cellar while walking toward their assigned table, peoples' eyes gravitated in their direction before the hostess turned and presented them with a crescent-shaped booth in the far corner.

"Is this okay?" the hostess asked.

Evily graciously replied, "Perfect. Thank you so much."

"No problem. Your waiter will be by shortly."

The author focused on her while she walked to the front. It didn't take long for the girl to take out her phone and look at the screen. She wanted to confirm Sean's identity, believing he resembled the guy she saw on a movie poster last weekend.

"Great," Evily said under her breath.

"What?" Sean questioned, deciding where everybody should sit based on Ben and Tim's security requirements.

"Nothing. It's okay," Evily said, sitting down beside her children, not wanting to add to his stress.

Sliding into the booth beside Evan, Ben joined the family to watch the restaurant from that vantage point while Tim and Sean sat in the chairs facing them.

Happy to put his back to the crowd, the Hollywood star removed his sunglasses and set them in front of him.

"Think we will have to make this a quick dinner," Evily warned, acutely aware of the hum beginning to erupt.

"You alright eating here, Sean?" Evan was concerned, adding, "We can take our orders to go if we need to."

"No, it's fine. Don't worry. The guys will handle things."

Scanning their menus, a young man arrived, seeming quite overwhelmed. Being new to the job, he was stressed, even though this was nothing compared to the evening rush.

"Hello, everyone. My name is Marco, and I will be serving you today. I'm sorry to keep you waiting." He opened his notepad and asked, "So, what can I get everyone to drink?"

As he went around the table, the young waiter took everyone's orders. Soon, he got to Sean. Immediately recognizing the actor, his eyebrows raised. "Holy shit," he said under his breath. Quickly backtracking his statement, the waiter tried to smooth things over, mortified by his reaction. "I apologize. Please forgive me." Embarrassed, he added, "Mr. Bradley. I'm just such a huge fan. I wasn't expecting, umm...."

The table erupted in laughter at the young man's reaction and quick recovery.

"It's quite alright. No worries," the famous star responded, trying to stabilize the situation. Staying calm, seeing patrons in his peripherals taking pictures, he said, "Marco, we need your help. Can you get us out of here as efficiently as possible? Maybe within an hour, preferably?"

"Yes, Sir. I certainly can. You can count on me, Mr. Bradley. Absolutely," he confirmed with an abundance of energy. "Let's finish your drink orders, and we will move on to entrees. I'll make sure your food is delivered pronto. I got you covered."

When Marco left them, he seemed to drift into overdrive. Their beverages were delivered in minutes, followed by their entrees not long after.

Once everyone had their pasta dishes set in front of them, their waiter offered freshly grated parmesan and milled pepper before issuing a request.

Getting Sean's attention, he asked, "Would it be totally out of line to take a picture with you, Sir?"

Happy to oblige, Sean responded, "No, not at all. We will do that before we leave."

"Of course, yes. Thank you. Appreciate that."

Before he departed again, Sean added, "And Marco, please keep our agreement between us, if you know what I mean."

"For sure. No problem."

Seeing the guy pull his phone from his pocket, Sean glimpsed over at Evily. "He's going to text his friends, isn't he?" Sean knew he would.

Evily squinted her eyes. "No. He is just checking the time. He's ensuring we get out of here at the top of the hour."

Having prayed over their meals silently, the kids focused on their devices while eating. Sean decided to strike up some conversation, knowing the patrons wouldn't interrupt if they were talking amongst themselves.

"So, Evan and Ella?" He said to get their attention. Each teen looked his way. "What's life like for you back in Chicago?"

Setting the devices down with one hand, forks in the other, the teens prompted each other to go first.

Ella smiled, a little flustered at being put on the spot. "Well, I'm going into grade eight this September. My best friends are Maya and Daisy. I'm not sporty like Evan. Umm, so, the yearbook and the school newspaper are kind of my thing. Next year, I'm looking forward to art and drafting classes when I hit high school."

"What do you do for fun?" the actor queried, taking a bite of his salmon with asparagus and risotto.

"My friends and I go to the movies. Sometimes, we hang out at the mall. They all come to my house during the summer because of the pool. None of them have one, so yeah. That's it."

"How about you, Evan," Sean said, moving on to the hockey player.

"I usually hang out with friends."

"And his girlfriend," Ella taunted her brother. "Her name is Alana. She's a soccer player."

"Knock it off, Ella." Refocused on Sean's question, he explained, "My friends and I usually play a lot of sports together. Mom put a concrete hockey rink in the backyard for me a few years ago."

Sean lifted his napkin to wipe his mouth politely. "You're pretty fortunate to have someone do that for you."

Evily blushed, proud to take the credit.

"Yeah, I know. Anyway, we flood it in the winter, and my friends come over to play hockey. In the summer it's a ball hockey and basketball court. Pretty cool. We're the only ones with anything like that."

"Yeah. You're a lucky guy."

"I think so. Mom's done many things like that for us over the years."

Interjecting, Ella turned the tables on Sean. "So, how about you? What do you do for fun? I bet you have big parties at your house."

He shook his head from side to side. "Unbeknownst to the general population, I lead a very quiet life. I've never thrown a big party. Only have the odd dinner, but that's all. My home is my haven. A place where I can escape the Hollywood bit. I've gone bowling. That's always fun. Sometimes I go to the movies."

"Bowling and movies?" Ella scrunched up her face, expecting more. "Really? Nothing cool like skydiving or surfing?"

"Well, sadly, the business part of my job means the production company owns you until the movie wraps. So, when you're under contract, there are no risky activities. No extreme sports. Always having work means I don't get to have that type of fun."

Evan nodded his head. "Makes sense. Hockey players have the same clause in their contracts."

"Precisely. There are times I ignore the stipulations and drive up the coast on my motorcycle. It helps me to think or rehearse my lines. There's nothing but me and the open road."

"That's so awesome," Evan said partway through his pasta dish.

"You didn't mention any friends." A little concerned, Ella noticed he spoke a lot about being alone.

"I have friends. A handful of them. You keep four, maybe five, close to you when you get older. Everyone else becomes an acquaintance. When I see my close friends depends on whether I'm on location or not. If I'm at home, we do things together. While away shooting a movie,

I create friendships with the crew working on the set. Other actors, assistants, stuntmen. I get along with everybody." Stopping a moment, he asked, "So, what about you, Evily Landy slash Anderson? What do you do for fun?"

Her daughter swiftly answered, "Nothing."

"Ella..." Evily was surprised. With a slight pause, she said, "It's not like I don't have fun."

"Mom, all you do day in and day out is take care of us and write," the teenager firmly stated.

"That's my job. I wouldn't have it any other way."

"I know, but we feel bad sometimes when we go out with our friends and leave you alone at home," Evan commented thoughtfully.

"Don't be silly. I retreat into my books - the world of writing. The characters are my friends, and they help me escape my life for a little while. That, to me, is fun."

Sean flashed a look of shock. "You don't have any friends?"

"No, she doesn't," Ella verified.

Defensive and feeling ganged up on, the woman tried to save face. "That's not true. I have Soph and Lily, umm, Julia, and Anna."

"Oh, yeah. When did you last speak to them?" Ella could see her Mother felt defeated.

"Okay. Truth be told, I withdrew into a quieter life when the divorce was final. Our friend circle mostly consisted of my husband's friends and wives. Everyone felt awkward after the split. That's when you truly know who your friends are. Where a person's loyalty lies."

The table went quiet as Evily bowed her head and fidgeted with her napkin.

"Mom, I had no idea. I'm sorry." Ella felt horrible. "I didn't know."

On a positive note, Sean said, "Well, if it's any consolation, I hope you'll consider me a friend now?"

"Thank you." Humbly locking eyes with him, Evily was happy to hear that.

In need of a conversation shift, Ella posed a few questions to the Henchmen, both of whom decided not to answer, let alone participate. She even tried to pull out of them if they were married or dating. Sitting, eating their food, with eyes peeled, they both shook their heads and stayed silent.

Nearing the top of the hour, Evan immersed himself in his phone after finishing dinner. While they waited for the bill, he scrolled through his texts. He found countless requests from his teammates, asking that he introduce them to Sean. Some made jabs about his mom that were borderline offensive. Ignoring it, he knew he would have to shut down the drama at the next game.

When Marco returned with the billfold, he placed it on the table and took out his phone.

"Do you mind? Is it okay now?" their waiter asked.

Sean stood up. "Sure."

The Henchman shielded them from the patrons looking over, curious about what was happening. Handing Ella his phone when she offered to take the photo, the guy nervously leaned next to the Hollywood action star. Upon snapping a few pics, she passed it back to him.

"Thank you so much. Appreciate it. I'm so excited about the sequel getting released next week."

"Happy to hear." Sean always liked it when fans were excited about his movies.

Evily handed Marco her credit card, prompting the young man to pull the POS machine from his apron.

"What are you doing?" Sean said.

"Paying for dinner," she laughed. "You snooze, you lose."

There was nothing he could do. Marco had already slid the card through the machine and hesitantly passed it to the author.

"Thank you. But you know what that means?" the actor stated. "I get the next one."

"We'll see," she said, punching in her tip and pin before handing it back to him.

"Thank you so much, Ma'am," Ben said to Evily.

"Yes. Appreciate it, Ma'am," Tim added.

The group got up from the table, about to leave. In an instant, the restaurant erupted. People converged from all angles, phones in hand. Before they knew it, a line was developing in front of the actor. The Anderson family stepped back in case things got out of hand.

Transforming into Hollywood star Sean Bradley, he graciously greeted his fans while the Henchmen managed the crowd. While taking a few fan photos, their group noticed the whole restaurant was slowly filing toward them. It was crazy. Amidst it all, Sean could feel his phone buzzing in his pocket. The ringing was constant. He knew someone was desperate to get a hold of him.

Marco returned to clear their table.

Surrounded by fans, Sean glanced over at Evan and noticed him checking the time on his phone several times. The teen was getting impatient. He knew they had to get going. Turning to Ben, he gave the Henchmen the signal to step in.

"Thank you, everyone. That's it for today," Ben said, holding everyone back.

Tim started to move the Andersons toward the front doors but noticed a mob of people out front, some with telephoto lens cameras. He knew the photographers got tipped off by the patrons' posts over the past hour. They weren't all fans and certainly weren't there for the food.

Corralling the family back toward the rear of the restaurant, Tim informed Ben, "The crowd out front won't be easy to get through. Word must have circulated quickly."

Scouring the restaurant, Ben found an EXIT sign inside the glass-enclosed private dining room.

Quickly spying it, too, Sean waved Marco over.

Willing to do anything for the actor, he said, "Yes, Mr. Bradley?"

"Hey Marco, can we speak to you privately for a moment?"

"Sure. Of course." Marco brought everyone into the divided space.

Ben shut the glass door behind him while Tim pulled the drapes. Pointing to the exit sign, the lead Henchman asked Marco, "Can we use this door?"

"I can't see why not. It isn't an emergency exit. That's the designated entrance to this party room."

The head security guard sprung into action. "Great. Let's get a move on."

Slipping his head out to see if the coast was clear, Ben waved the group onward. He propped the door open, accounting for everyone on the way out. Crossing the laneway, dodging the puddles here and there, Ben proceeded toward the trucks, hoping nobody would see them leaving.

Dark clouds once again were moving in from the south.

"The calm before the storm," Evily whispered.

"Go, go, go!" Ben advised the group to shuffle along. Motoring, with head down, hat, and sunglasses on again, Sean did not look back.

"Is this really necessary?" Ella whined.

Sean was quick to explain. "Believe me. Evan would've missed his game if we had exited through the front into that mob."

24

Friday, July 26th
Foxborough, Massachusetts

From a tiny spark may burst a mighty flame. ~ Dante Alighieri

The wind swirled around them, and the trees swayed from side to side. Thankful to make it back to the trucks without incident, the sound of car doors closing caused a sigh of relief.

Sean leaned his head back against the headrest and took a deep breath. Quickly starting the engine, he remembered someone had called his phone. The Hollywood star removed it from his pocket and found a string of texts and missed calls from Max and his agent, Sheri. Connecting to the hands-free system onboard, he waited for Sheri to answer.

"Sean! My God. What's happening? The tabloids are reporting that you are in Boston. Why didn't you inform me of this trip? Now I have a shit-load coming through requesting comment."

"Sheri, calm down."

"No, don't tell me to calm down. This is not how we do things at my agency – especially with the upcoming premiere next week. I told you, no negative press. The tabloids are going to have a field day with this one. Why the hell are you on the East Coast?"

"It's a long story. Personal business." Sean rolled his eyes and looked out his side window.

She jumped all over that statement. "You don't have personal business! Your business – is my business!"

"I realize that." Sean glanced over at Evily and raised his eyebrows, knowing Sheri was furious.

"You need to fly back to LA now."

"No. I have to be here a few more days." Sean knew how she'd respond to that.

"Absolutely out of the question! I want you back here by tomorrow morning."

Sean shook his head. "Sorry, Sheri. I have to do this. Make it happen."

There was dead air between them.

For him to respond that way, she realized there was something wrong. Breaking their silence, she questioned, "Max says you're at The Godfrey. Correct?"

"Yeah. Why?" Sean put the truck in reverse and drove out of the parking lot, causing the Nav system to recalculate and continue where they left off. Hearing a ping, he saw the picture Sheri sent. Clicking on it, he found a group of photographers camped out across the street from his hotel. While turning onto the highway, heading toward Attleboro, the storm converged, unleashing heavy rains, thunder, and lightning. At the same time, he counted at least thirty people waiting for him outside the Godfrey.

"Honestly, Sean, I've had to go into damage control mode here." Her voice sounded beyond frustrated and stressed.

"I haven't done anything wrong, Sheri. Just needed a little getaway. That's it."

"You've given me no choice then," his agent firmly stated. "Additional security is being dispatched to the hotel. Max came clean. He said you've already got two guys with you. This will now require more eyes. Who are the other people in the photos? How are they involved in this?"

Sean glanced over at Evily and the teens sitting in the back. All of them were listening in on his conversation. "They're friends."

"Well, I hope your *friends* know their faces are about to be splashed across the tabloids. Be prepared that this may land on entertainment news within hours."

"What?" Evily said out loud, grabbing her phone.

"Wait? Are you on speakerphone?" the agent queried.

"Maybe?" Sean said.

"You let me go on talking like that with kids in the car?" Sheri went into overdrive, knowing two teenagers were involved.

Evan laughed while leaning forward. "Hey, we aren't kids!"

Sean illegally took his phone in hand and continued driving with it, melded to his ear. If she was freaking out this badly, things must be pretty bad.

"Just tell me your plan."

Everyone in the car could hear the woman's voice but couldn't decipher her words. There seemed to be a lot more to this than meets the eye.

Evily worried about what people back home would think, especially what would happen if her ex-husband got wind of it.

"You've booked me in at the Ritz? Really?" Sean repeated, knowing Sheri had no idea that Evily was staying there.

Hearing their banter, the author was confused.

"Alright. I'll do that. Send me the guys' contact info. I'll text them when we're heading back to the city." Nodding his head, he offered a few one-word answers. "Yes. Yeah, sure. Okay. Alright. Bye." Sean hung up the phone and merged onto I-95 South towards Attleboro.

Evan laughed. "Wow. It sounds like you're in trouble."

"Guess I should have given her a heads up. Thought I'd be okay for a few days on my own. I never get to escape anymore." With one hand on the wheel, resting his opposite elbow on the window ledge, Sean held up his head while his mind reeled.

"I think you may have miscalculated this situation," Ella cleverly stated.

Evily could feel the depth of Sean's stress. He was thinking of so many things all at once. It was beginning to give her a headache. Sadly, she couldn't tune it out.

The GPS directed them off the highway into South Attleboro within ten minutes. When they arrived at their destination, they noticed that this facility also looked brand new. The parking lot had not even faded yet. The asphalt was still entirely black, and the lines appeared freshly painted.

Sean found a spot to park just as the rains subsided and a hint of sunlight broke through the clouds.

"I guess you can't go in and watch this game then?" Evily figured he'd want to avoid the crowds for a while.

"Oh, no. I'm coming in. It'll be okay. Sometimes, if I don't acknowledge people, they get the drift. If I act rude towards them, don't take offense," he warned.

The Henchmen met with their client the moment he exited the truck. He let them in on his conversation with Sheri and the plan for their return to Boston's downtown core.

Evan quietly got out and walked to the back of the vehicle while this was going on. Lifting the tailgate, he packed up the equipment scattered across the cargo space. Piece by piece, making sure everything was accounted for, he was tired but knew he'd get a second wind when he entered the change room. That's when it dawned on him. He would now have to shut down the rumors about his Mom and Sean. A distraction he certainly didn't need right now.

Almost halfway across the parking lot, Evan heard his Mother call out to him. Stopping, he turned to find her running toward him.

Seeing the two together, Sean assumed she was offering some inspiring words to the young hockey player. Glancing their way periodically during his conversation with the Henchmen, unable to hear the wisdom Evily was conveying, he watched Evan acknowledge her. When their conversation ended, she concluded the ritual with a hug. She hung onto him tightly this time, but in seconds, he pulled away, seemingly anxious to get going.

Sean jogged over. "Evan, wait!" he said, making the hockey player stop again. "Good luck, my man." He put out his hand to offer a handshake.

"Thanks," Evan replied, knowing he was trying his best to be supportive. Before going on his way, he turned and said, "Hey. It's been nice having you in the stands."

Happy to hear that, Sean gave him a nod. "Sure thing."

The second her son entered the building, Evily prayed a silent prayer. With eyes drawn upward, she immediately noticed something in the sky.

Not sure what she'd spotted, Sean and Ella looked in the same direction. So did the Henchmen. There, high above them, was a rainbow. But not just any rainbow. This one was strangely different. Inverted, it looked as though heaven was smiling down upon them.

"Wow, look at that," Sean said, pointing to the unusual sight. He immediately took a few pictures.

Producing an enlightened expression, she turned to the Hollywood star and asked, "Remember the butterflies you saw the other day in the park under the tree?"

He replied, "Yes."

"Well, that was a sign that the girls were watching over you."

In awe, he stared at the rainbow smile with bewilderment.

"This is yet another message." Evily let her words sink in while the rainbow got brighter and brighter against the darkened sky.

"I have never seen anything like this before." He felt a warmth enter his heart. His body went from being stressed to a state of weightlessness. It was something he could not explain.

The sun's rays broke through the clouds to shine down on them. With eyes closed, she looked up and allowed the light to invigorate her spirit.

All of it seemed surreal to Sean - almost magical.

When the phenomena began fading, Evily could hear what the Henchmen were thinking. Initially, they thought she was just an ordinary mother of two. Now, they knew something was special about her. She had this mysterious gift. It scared them in a way. Intimidated, she seemed almost supernatural to them - like she was an alien or a witch.

"Don't worry, Ben," the pretty woman said on the way past the security detail. "I won't cast a spell on you."

Ben's eyes widened in fear, unsure if he should believe her or not. He turned to Tim in disbelief, a might concerned for his well-being.

Chuckling, the ladies walked by the muscular men with eyes still glued to the rainbow in the sky. Joining them, Sean locked the truck with a click. He realized Evily was playing a joke on his two security guards to keep them on their toes. Not only did they have a famous actor to contend with, but some kind of witch or wizard about to hex them both.

Distracted by their thoughts, the gifted woman quickly discovered she hadn't heard one unspoken word from Sean since seeing the rainbow moments before. Her mind quieted the further they moved from the Henchmen.

At the entrance to the arena, the sun peeked out from behind the clouds again. Now, descending toward the horizon, it showcased brilliant colors of oranges and reds before they went inside. Stepping through the main doors, they noticed it was pretty quiet. There weren't any crowds. It helped Sean relax and allowed him to let down his guard.

Since it was a late game, Evily figured it might be the last one of the day for this location. That would explain the absence of people.

Keeping his sunglasses on, they walked through the vestibule. Sean pulled his hat down to cover his face while passing by a small group gathered on one side of the lobby. Standing in line at the ticket table, dodging a few spectators and players, Sean paid their admittance fees while Evily checked the screen to find out where Evan was playing.

Seeing they scheduled the game on the Premiere Rink, she walked down the hall to the right, hoping to find a table close to the glass.

The Henchmen took their positions on either end of the long and narrow viewing area. The arena's scouting box was just a portioned-off bit of real estate in the hallway bordering both rinks. Pretty close quarters if they needed space.

Peering out the windows at the ice surface, Evily and Sean stood around the bar-height table, waiting for the game to start.

Ella found an empty spot near the coffee shop, not far from them. Sitting at the table, she set up her tablet to work on her latest house design. Before fully settling in, she decided to grab a bottled sweet tea. Counting out the exact change for the cashier, Ella knew not everyone appreciated her precision.

The Henchmen kept a close eye on their group and tried not to bring too much attention to themselves.

While people were leaving, Evily searched for unclaimed chairs. About to pick one up and bring it over, Sean stopped her.

"Here, let me get that for you," he said.

Without question, she stepped back and allowed him to help. He lifted the chair and brought it to their table, allowing her to have a seat while he got one for himself. This gentlemanliness did not go unnoticed. She was used to doing things alone all these years, most times having no choice. In her lifetime, never had anyone done something so nice for her.

The ice below them was dormant. Across the hall, on the opposite side, a warm-up had started. Evily could tell based on the echoing booms of the pucks hitting the boards in succession.

There were so many questions floating through Sean's mind at that moment. Sitting in the chair, he focused his sights on the surface of the table and asked, "So, if you don't mind, can we discuss the orb visit some more?" With a short pause, Sean thought about what he wanted to say.

Evily assumed the rainbow had sparked more questions and had a hunch it ignited his faith. Strangely, though, she didn't know for sure. His thoughts were still silent.

"I'm curious about the experience and how it works," the handsome actor posed. In a matter of days, he would have an opportunity to talk to his wife and daughter. Part of him was scared, while the other half didn't want to screw it up.

"Where do I start?" Evily said, wondering how to explain things. "As I said before, you need to create a connection for them to appear, blending your life today with the thoughts and emotions associated with memories from your past. This connection needs to grow from now until we reach the Cape."

"Okay, I can do that. Then what?" Sean listened intently.

"Don't be worried about communicating with the girls. I will translate their words and dictate them to you. You, in turn, can speak directly to them."

"Got it." He rubbed his palms together, noticeably anxious about the upcoming event.

"One last thing – absolutely no skepticism of any kind. Like none. They will not show up if you don't believe in this or have doubts. The negative energy will prevent their visit. The door won't open."

Feeling enormous pressure, he nodded at every detail she outlined before Evily shared the best part.

"After this experience is over, when you see Janie and Ella, hear their words, speak to them, you will forever have a connection if you foster it. They will always be near you. You just have to ask them for a sign. Pose a question and make it as detailed as possible. Then watch and see what happens. Your response may come in the form of synchronized numbers on a clock, perhaps butterflies flying by. Ladybugs. Rainbows. Birds. Things from nature create the answers you seek. Depending on the bond you've established, they will sometimes interact with electricity or music. It is the most amazing thing. Once you experience it for yourself, you'll understand."

"Strangely, I think I already have. Somehow, I knew it was them when those butterflies showed up." He smiled and lowered his head.

"You miss them to this day. Sadly, I don't think you'll fully heal from this level of loss."

"No, I don't think so either. It haunts you. Often, grief creeps in when I least expect it. It's kind of like a life sentence."

Evily could feel his pain, and the void left behind was evident. "This is why you need to have faith. Without it, life is pretty meaningless. Don't you think? Going about your days believing all of it will just end and nobody will think of you ever again, like there is nothing to move on to afterward. It's a depressing thought."

"I suppose that's where I'm at."

"I can tell you from experience that I have seen the makings of the afterlife. I don't share this often with people. But years ago, I had a strange thing happen. Around that time, I was frustrated and doubting my abilities – almost rejecting them. I blacked out after suffering the onset of severe chest pain late one night. I thought it was a heart attack. With limbs going weak and my focus fading, I lay on the floor as a beam of light hovered above me. It was so bright, but it didn't make me squint. The feeling of peace it exuded was indescribable. I felt nothing - the pain disappeared instantly, and so did the suffering, the uncertainty - just hope and love remained. I never passed beyond the light as some people have." Thinking, she added, "Regarding Janie, I'm sure you are curious about how they crossed over. She will probably share this experience with you. It will put your mind at ease. All we wish for those who have passed is that they are safe and happy. That alone provides closure to the soul."

Sean stayed silent. She could sense that what she shared was enlightening.

Evan's team began to trickle out onto the ice for the warm-up. Checking on Ella, she found her laughing and talking with friends online.

Because Sean hadn't said anything more, Evily said, "Hey? Are you doing okay?"

Sitting back in the chair, a little hunched over, Sean seemed miles away. "Yeah," he responded somberly. "Yeah, I'm okay."

Still unable to hear his thoughts, she could only empathically read emotion off him. It seemed his mind had turned to radio silence.

"Can I ask you something?" she questioned.

"Sure," he replied, slowly raising his sights to meet hers.

"Are you afraid to die? The fear of this inside you is very intense."

He tilted his head down and looked away. "See, for me, this is the thing... I feel like I'm leaving nothing behind. Nobody to carry on my family name and memory. Haven't even done anything meaningful to be considered worthy of entrance to the afterlife." Stopping, he added, "Years ago, when starting my acting career...well, let's just say, you do things you are not proud of. Things that you wish you could change or wouldn't have done. Things that a higher power would shun."

"The higher power you're referring to is God," Evily freely witnessed while the ice was a buzz with players.

"This is easy for you. It's like second nature. My mother never discussed faith in our home. I wasn't in a family who'd go to church every Sunday. I'm assuming that's the kind of upbringing you had since you are well-versed. I don't have any religious education. Never in all my years have I opened a Bible. Do you know how many hotel rooms I've stayed in? Each had a Bible in the drawer, and never, not once, did I open one. There's been so much time wasted. Maybe I'm questioning my mortality now because I'm older. It's making me reevaluate my entire life." He leaned his body forward and rested his forearms on the table.

Evily reached over and rested her hand on his right arm. "It's good to have those thoughts, but you can not change the past. It's what you do from here on in that counts. Are you with me? I can help."

"Okay," he said, ready and willing to adhere to her advice.

A few people stared at them while the teams skated around in circles. Both quickly pulled their chairs closer to the glass and kept their sights forward, using the reflection on the window to watch for anyone passing by.

When the game was about to start, Evily saw that Evan wasn't in the starting line-up as the players prepared for battle.

Is something wrong? She thought. He always played in the first line.

A nameless centerman took the face-off to win possession of the puck. Their right-winger snagged it on the fly and skated down the boards, searching for a teammate to pass to. Bombarded by the defense, he found the centerman approaching the goalie at high speed. The puck got loose after both teams broke from a scuffle mid-ice. Bravely battling to control the play, the winger shot the puck like a bullet and found the mystery player's stick. In an instant, he sniped it top shelf for the team's first goal.

"Holy cow," Sean said. "Who is that guy?"

"I have no idea." Evily wasn't sure if the boy had played on their team the day before or this morning. His skating style did not look familiar.

"Any idea of the final score yet?" he asked, intrigued by what she might say.

She thought for a minute. "Think it will be a 5-0 win."

With a look of surprise, Sean turned to her and said, "Really? That's awesome."

"Yes, this new player will score three. Evan, two."

He watched the team switch lines. "At least he will be on the score sheet, correct?"

"Yes."

Evan skated out to center ice for the face-off. Glancing up at his Mom, he had a look of defeat. She placed her hand over her heart. He, in turn, reluctantly did the same.

"You'll be okay," she whispered, moving her hands into a praying position. She hated when her children were troubled but knew her son would rise above in the end.

Mindful of how she handled herself, Sean knew most mothers would get defensive and talk negatively about the other player. Not Evily Landy. She stayed calm and collected. Not one mean comment escaped her mouth.

The first two periods ultimately showcased the unknown centerman's talents. He had brought the game to a score of 3-0, all on his own. The rink-side scouts were impressed. Evily could feel her son's disappointment. Luckily, the two boys were never on the same line.

Skating off for the break before the third period, the Zamboni made its appearance. Suddenly, there was a shift in the air. On the rink to their left, the game was finishing. Evily's head was on a swivel. A soul was reaching out. Spotting a woman walking past their table, the author sensed she had been outside on the phone, crying. Her eyes were red and swollen, and she clutched a tissue in her left hand. Returning to her chair by the glass, she showed very little interest in what was happening on the ice. It was like her mind was elsewhere. From time to time, she glanced up at the ceiling to stop the tears from rolling down her cheeks.

Sean recognized the expression on Evily's face. "What is it?" he asked, knowing something was wrong.

"Her sister is having a bad day." With her sights glued to the woman, the feeling she was picking up on got stronger. A tingling spread into her hands and feet. Soon, she noticed a faint translucent orb hovering over the woman. "Her nephew passed away in a car crash about five months ago. Her sister is having great difficulty coming to terms with the devastating loss of her son."

Images appeared and blacked out Evily's field of vision. Startled, she rested her palms flat on the table to stabilize herself. Flashing one at a time, a series of memories scrolled through her mind.

"His name is Oren. He was eighteen and came from a loving family. To everyone, his future was so bright and promising. They thought of him as the man of the house." Reading the clock that appeared, she whispered, "12:41 am was his time of death. He died instantly and did not suffer from his injuries."

The young man stepped forward with a bright smile. He was so handsome.

Evily's eyes filled with tears. "He is sorry that his departure caused so much pain."

Oren's spirit turned toward his Aunt sitting along the viewing windows. In an instant, Evily knew what he wanted her to do. Unfortunately, that was not how it worked for her. She never intended to be a medium who spoke for the dead. That is why she wrote the spiritual messages in her books. If fate allowed the right person to read the story, then they would receive the information sent from the afterlife. Evily was very strict on this rule. She never directly interfered in a person's life.

A calendar appeared. Year after year, the wind blew each month away until it reached February.

"He lived 6788 days," she revealed concretely.

Fascinated by it all, Sean listened.

"Strange," she said, pausing a moment. "Remember the father we saw the other day? The man at the arch? The one who lost his son?"

The actor nodded.

"He passed away sixteen days after Oren. That boy - I think his name was Damon - lived 5688 days. They were a little over three years apart. Most people forget that we all have an expiry date - a limited number of years, months, weeks, minutes, and seconds. From the time we take our first breath, the clock begins."

What she said was profound. Tormented by his mortality, thoughts of death and what comes next always crossed Sean's mind.

"Do you know how long Janie lived?" he asked.

Evily concentrated. "10,343 days."

Stunned, he said, "Wow. I never thought about it that way. Makes me wonder how long I'll live?"

Her eyes drifted open, and she stared at him from across the table.

"Please don't tell me you know my end date..."

"I don't know when you will die. We don't know the day or the hour. But you have lived 21,192 days as of today. An amazing, adventure-filled journey thus far."

Sean agreed.

"Don't worry. You have a ways to go yet. That is, as long as you don't do anything crazy." Winking at him humorously, Sean figured she knew what he did many years ago. Something stupid that could have cost him his life.

Her attention gravitated toward the tearful woman again. "You know, the forces of evil were well aware of who these two young men would become in the future. How strong they would be. At an early age, both were a force to be reckoned with. Everyone was grateful to have known them. These spirit-filled teens would have grown to be strong-minded advocates of faith. Evil benefitted from their departures. Those left behind to mourn are bitter and blame God for taking away their children."

When she realized what she'd said applied to Sean, Evily backtracked. "I'm sorry..."

"I can certainly relate to what you just said. That, too, was me."

"Soon, you will discover that Janie and Ella, like these two boys, are safe in a beautiful place filled with love. A place most could neither fathom nor describe."

Oren presented another memory to her. Closing her eyes, Evily broke into a smile.

"He was met by a heavenly angel and welcomed into the Kingdom with open arms. Applauded by those awaiting him, he immediately felt at home."

Blinking repeatedly to stop the tears from flowing, she said prayers for the Aunt and Oren's Mother.

"He is determined for me to pass along his messages..."

"Are you going to do it?" he asked, glimpsing at the frail woman.

"I don't interfere in other people's lives."

"But, you are bending that rule for me. Why is my situation any different?" Sean asked blatantly.

There was silence between them. Evily focused on the Aunt again. She was being pulled in her direction and felt compelled to speak to her even though she knew she shouldn't.

"I mean, you agreed to mediate a visitation between Janie and Ella. Why? Why help me and not that woman?"

Caught off guard, not a hundred percent sure how to answer that, Evily hesitated. "That is a good question... With Janie and Ella, it is different. When they shared their story, they also held some details back. I suppose I'm a bit curious about all the secrecy. They also made me feel like you were in danger and I needed to help. Believe me. I do not normally extend myself the way I have in your case. It is rather unusual for me."

"Well, thank you for that. I appreciate everything that you're doing." Evily smiled.

"But why can't you grant Oren's Aunt the same experience?"

Sensing the woman's pain and desperation, knowing that speaking to her could very well help the family, she knew it went against her better judgment.

"He touched the lives of everyone who met him - outgoing, confident, and kind. A shining light is how he was described by many. Oren welcomed Damon at the gates the day he crossed over. He helped him transition. The two instantly hit it off. They have been given heavenly tasks and have willingly embraced their new jobs." Squinting, she revealed, "Oren says he is there to welcome a multitude of children who will soon flood the gates. Damon is to do the same." She was not sure what that meant.

Trying to wrap his head around their conversation, Sean didn't have much to add. Like a fish out of water, he felt like he was in over his head and had a lot to learn.

Evily broke away from the soul's connection, determined to stay true to her convictions.

The two watched the Zamboni leave the ice after the flood. Ready to drift into the third, the nameless centerman skated out again to have the first crack at the puck. Evily noticed Evan look over from the bench. She slowly raised two fingers in the air without thinking anything of it.

"Hey, are you giving him a heads-up again?" the actor questioned.

Evily felt for her son. "All I'm doing is encouraging him. It will give him the confidence to run the play and score. Watch."

Sean analyzed Evan's movements after the shift change and immediately noticed a difference. Exhibiting a more confident façade, he battled more in the corners and looked for opportunities to rush the net. He encouraged his teammates before the plays. They kept the pressure on their opponents, and then unexpectedly, the puck landed on Evan's stick, and he fired off the shot!

Evily stood up and shouted, "Goal!" Embarrassed by her reaction and her loudness, she quickly covered her mouth and cowered into her chair.

Sean offered her a high five, which she happily accepted. The joy on her face was priceless. Most would say it was just a goal in a hockey game, but to him, it showcased a Mother's love and hope for her child. Evan skated by the bench to celebrate with his team. Switching lines, his Mom could see the centerman, and Evan was now talking and laughing. They even tapped gloves.

Her face brightened. "Maybe they'll become friends instead of rivals," she said sincerely.

Sean saw Evily smile from ear to ear. His heart skipped a beat in the process. For the first time in years, a spark inside him ignited. Something he never thought possible.

25

Friday, July 26th
Attleboro, Massachusetts

I don't think I realized that the cost of fame is that it's open season on every moment of your life.

~ Julia Roberts

With two minutes remaining, now down to the wire, Evan's team was up 4-0. Slowly, their opponents were running out of gas. They could see fatigue settling in. The turnovers were not lightning-fast, and their players had no breakaways.

As the clock dwindled, it seemed Evily's prediction was incorrect.

"Guess it's going to end in a 4-0 win. Not five," Sean questioned.

Evily did not bat an eye. "Just wait. You'll see."

With exactly forty seconds remaining, Evan skated for the face-off in the opponent's end. Sean watched Evily's hands clench together so tightly her fingers turned white. Constantly biting her lip, she watched the referee drop the puck with an intense look on her face. Evan passed to his winger. Setting himself up, skating behind the net, he battled with the defense to get in the clear. That's when his teammate took a shot. It rebounded right in front of Evan with thirteen seconds left. Amidst a mass of bodies, Evan seized control and fired to the left of the goalie's skate.

"Score!" Evily and Sean shouted simultaneously.

The author's fists were flying high in the air. Looking at Sean, she said, "You were saying, Mr. Bradley?"

"I hate to admit, you were right," Sean conceded.

Locking eyes with her son, Evan and his teammates piled on top of their goalie. He had done a great job the past couple of days. It was amazing to see.

Ella began clearing her things from the table and packing them into the backpack. "So, I guess that's game, Mom?"

Spotting Oren's Aunt walking by them, Evily hugged her daughter. She said, "Yes. We should probably get Sean out of here, just in case. Come on, let's go." She still felt Oren's presence.

The Hollywood star heard her suggestion and signaled to Tim and Ben that they were now on the move. He kept his head down and did not make eye contact with anyone. Having witnessed Evily's focus on the woman, he leaned over and asked, "So, are you going to say something to her?"

Worked up, she nodded.

Sean raised his eyebrows, wondering how her conversation would go. Would the woman be angry at her for interfering, or would she embrace the news with open arms? He did not know.

When they reached the main doors, Tim took the lead and guided them to the parking lot. Upon seeing the blue sky, Sean immediately looked up. The clouds had dispersed, and the late-day sun was shining brightly.

While walking along behind the woman, the translucent orb was still hovering above her. Evily kept her distance. Before she got into her car, the author knew it was now or never. Approaching, she said, "Excuse me. Are you Stefania? Oren's Aunt?"

"What?" she said, overly confused. "How do you know him?"

"My name is Evily. I have an unusual gift. Your nephew wanted me to give you a message." The author chose her words carefully.

Stefania quickly covered her mouth with her hand. Giving Evily a nod, she was speechless.

Ella, Sean, and the Henchmen looked on, unable to hear what they were saying.

Somewhat skeptical and a bit scared, Stefania stood silent, ready to hang on to the stranger's every word. With watery eyes, she listened.

Hearing Oren's voice, Evily repeated, "He says his departure caused everyone enormous pain. It was preventable, and he takes full responsibility for his passing. A lapse in judgment cost him his life and could have caused his friends to suffer the same fate. For that, he is truly sorry."

Focusing, unable to look at Stefania, she added, "He says, please tell Mom I am not alone, and she doesn't need to worry. Thank her for always being there for me without fail. I will forever love her. We have an unbreakable bond. She feels that."

Stefania cried and tried to restrain her emotions.

"He says, I'm sorry I disappointed her."

His Aunt quickly shook her head. "No, he could never disappoint anyone."

"He says, I did. She had such hopes and dreams for me. Now, none of those things will come to pass."

The woman was heartbroken.

"He says, tell her - thank you for being there for my mom all these months. She could not have survived without you."

Emotional, trembling uncontrollably, she nodded and said, "Yes."

While seeing the scene unfolding before them, Sean got a lump in his throat. Uncomfortable, he crossed his arms in front of his chest and clenched his hands into fists.

"Oren says, I know how much you've sacrificed to help her and the burden you carry."

"It is not a burden. Please tell him not to think that."

"He is listening." Pausing, Evily confirmed, "Tell Mom, for my soul to rest, she needs to let me go as hard as that will be. I am safe. I am happy, and most of all, I am at peace. She needs to focus on Little Bro. Tell him he is doing a great job, by the way. Very proud of him."

Stefania smiled. "He started a charity in his brother's name that benefits children in the community. So far, he's raised over ten thousand dollars."

"He says, make sure you tell him I know what he is doing. I will forever watch over him and Mom. I am not gone. I am always in your heart. He says he loves you all."

Hearing that, Stefania broke down. Evily inched forward with open arms and allowed the woman to fall into them. Holding onto her, the Aunt whispered, "Thank you. An angel must have sent you to me today."

"Yes," she said, seeing the translucent orb hovering above them slowly fade. "That angel's name is Oren."

Fingers trembling, the woman wiped the tears from her face, unable to speak.

"I won't keep you. I'm sure you have somewhere to be." Evily didn't know what more to say.

Shaken, the woman said, "Thank you. Thank you so much. Bless you."

"You're very welcome. Enjoy the rest of your day. God bless you and your family as well."

Evily waved to Stefania, who had already pulled out her phone. As she walked toward the truck, she could hear the emotional woman speaking to Oren's Mother. She hoped the family would heal from their loss in time, and she believed the message she conveyed today would be a good starting point for them.

A few feet from the trucks, Evily stopped.

"So?" Sean asked. "Looks like that was successful."

"Yes, it was, but I can not make a habit of it."

Unlocking the truck, the three jumped in, happy to be safe and sound. Evily texted Evan and told him they'd be waiting outside. All he sent in return minutes later was a thumbs-up emoji.

While waiting, Sean and Evily did not say a word. Nor did Ella. Fatigue was slowly setting in.

Looking at the author, Sean could sense she was troubled by what had happened. "Penny, for your thoughts?" he said.

Ella immediately chimed in. "Mom, what you did was amazing. I mean, helping that family like that..."

Her Mother interjected. "God-willing, they will be okay. It will take some time."

Leaving it there, not elaborating further, Sean and Ella did not push or ask further questions.

Overall, it had been a very long day, and everyone was exhausted. But now, upon his return to the hotel, poor Sean had to deal with additional security.

"So, how will this work when you return to the Godfrey? Can they move you to the Ritz without being seen?" Evily wondered.

He thought for a second. Then, checking his phone, he found a series of texts from Sheri. After reading them, he knew the plan.

"Well, it seems I'm supposed to arrive in front of my hotel. The paparazzi will get pictures. I will head inside, and my decoy, another security guard dressed to look like me, will exit a while later to throw off the photographers. They'll think I'm leaving for the airport with a suitcase in hand." He added, "Apparently, I'll leave from a designated service exit, head over to the Ritz, and immediately go underground. We will jump on an elevator and go straight to the Presidential Suite."

"Oh, fancy," Evily smiled.

Before forwarding Sheri's text with the phone number of one of the new security guards, Sean raised a hand to get the Henchmen's attention. Ben checked his phone, immediately called the guy, and gave his client a thumbs-up. His name was Ivan, and the other guy was David.

Sean's phone soon chimed with an update. Needing confirmation, he asked, "We are heading back to Boston when Evan comes out, correct?"

Nodding, Evily said, "Yes. Thankfully, we have finished for the day." She could hardly wait to get back to their hotel.

Conferenced in on a call between Tim, Ben, and Ivan seconds later, Sean confirmed, "Yeah, it looks like we are about an hour outside Boston."

Hearing the plan devised by the security staff, the actor listened intently.

"I'll be dropping the family at the hotel first, right? We'll meet you there. Yes, we'll head to the underground parking and find you. Perfect. Yes. Okay. Bye." Sean ended the call.

"There's Evan," Ella said, seeing her brother exit the building.

The tailgate lifted at the touch of a button, allowing the athlete to fling his equipment bag inside the vehicle. Evily easily read her son's mood.

"Ready to go?" Sean questioned, closing the hatch for him.

"Yes, ready," Evan replied, jumping into his seat and buckling up.

"Everything okay? It was a great game," his Mother said.

"Yeah, it didn't start that way, but it worked out in the end. I am exhausted, though. Like, mentally and physically spent..." He reclined his seat and tried to get comfortable.

Pulling out of the parking lot with the Henchmen close behind, they soon connected with the highway, leading them back to the city's center. It was a quiet ride home. The athlete fell asleep quickly, as did Ella, leaving Sean and Evily to talk some more. She felt uneasy about what he needed to do tonight but knew everything would be fine.

"Are you going to be okay? This switcheroo thing isn't going to be a problem, is it?"

"No. It happens all the time. Sometimes, when things get too heated, we switch bases. Just have to make sure nobody sees me do it. It's gotta be fast."

Sean could feel that the author was worried. He could hear it in the tone of her voice. "What is it? Do you know something I don't?"

"Umm, no. I think it will go off without a hitch. That's my gut feeling." She seemed certain.

"Perfect. Happy to hear that."

The two went silent again. Evily stared straight ahead.

Glancing over a few times, Sean asked, "How about you? Are you doing okay? Did I do something?"

"No, not at all. I'm just tired. It's been a stressful day, and the games usually take a lot out of me. My brain feels a bit fried. Honestly, I was thinking about Evan going off to college next year. There will be a lot of changes. Ella will be going into high school when he moves out. I'll have two graduates in June. I feel like I'm not prepared for them to grow up. I know that's silly, but it seems almost seventeen years have passed in a blink."

"I can't imagine how difficult that'll be." Sean lent a sympathetic ear.

"The kids are right, you know. I don't take time to have fun. Any free time I have, I take advantage of it. That way, I get some writing done without any interruptions. The way I write requires concentration and quiet. I'm quite productive when the kids are out of the house. But for the first ten minutes, it is deathly quiet. It bothers me sometimes."

"Maybe you should get a few outside activities of your own? Or re-connect with those friends you mentioned. Perhaps they'd like to catch up? If not, do something to meet people and make new friends. Hell, call me up, and we can hang out."

"Well, thank you for the offer. I think you will be far too busy for that. The rest is easier said than done. That part of my life is over. I feel like I don't need that close friend relationship anymore. It seems like a waste of time and energy. Perhaps I've been away from the social scene for too long. I don't know what I'm missing."

"Maybe so, but I'm sure you'd like to vent to someone once and a while or talk out your feelings?"

"No." Evily chuckled. "No, not really."

"I get it," Sean laughed. "I love the time I have to myself. I read. Watch TV. Order-in dinner. Sleep."

His passenger giggled.

"Don't laugh. I often don't get to do those things because I work so much."

"Oh, when you put it that way, I guess so. Can't imagine what your life is like back in LA. People constantly surround you. We've had a small dose of it so far. Don't you get tired of it?"

"The crowds and being harassed all the time for pictures, yes. The acting part, definitely not."

On the outskirts of Boston, the city lights came into view. Descending the ramp into the thick of the downtown core, Evily pulled out her phone and secretly did a hashtag search of Sean's name. She was shocked to find hundreds of posts featuring her, Sean, and the kids on countless social media and tabloid sites. Reality struck. Worried beyond belief, unsure how this would play out, it scared her to the core. What had she done? What would this do to her children? Her career?

At the same time, ready for the next order of business, Sean focused on driving. He recalled how often he'd done a switch before and hoped it would run smoothly, as Evily predicted. Maneuvering the one-way streets, they soon approached the hotel's underground parking and slowly veered right to drive down the ramp. They located the valet office on the first level and saw another SUV with two men waiting, both dressed in black.

"That must be them," Sean stated.

Shifting the truck into park, Evily woke up the kids and got them to remove their things from the Land Rover, making sure nothing was left behind. Sleepy, Evan slung his equipment on his shoulder. His Mother took hold of his sticks while Ella placed her backpack on one shoulder. Double-checking everything, Evily saw Sean walk over to greet the big security guard named Ivan. There was a younger-looking guy, but she could not fully see his face in the dim light. Shaking hands, the famous actor listened to his instructions while Ben and Tim scanned the perimeter, understanding their role.

Before the family disappeared inside, Sean turned and said, "I will be back soon. I'll text you when I get settled in my room."

From ten feet away, Evily nodded and said, "Alright." Lingering a moment, focusing on the outcome of what was about to happen, her face brightened. "Good luck. Everything will be fine."

26

Friday, July 26th
Downtown Boston, Massachusetts

It's all done by smoke and mirrors. ~ Anne Brooke

In the seclusion of the parking garage, the Henchmen split up, each knowing their job. Ben disappeared from view, tasked with meeting the hotel manager, securing the Presidential Suite, and arranging additional rooms for his security personnel. Ivan and Tim were in the second Escalade, ready to move into position outside the Godfrey. Eager to get this over with, Sean found a seat in the back of the Land Rover. The security agent named David got in behind the wheel. Receiving the signal from Tim, both vehicles quickly moved out.

Appearing above ground, turning right, and heading toward Washington Street, Sean leaned forward and said, "So, David. Are you ready?"

"Yes, Sir. Do you have any questions?" the man replied.

Sean detected a familiar accent but couldn't put his finger on it.

"No. Sadly, this is pretty much standard issue, I think," the actor revealed, unfazed by it all. "Hey, I hope you don't mind me asking, but are you German?"

"Yes, Sir." Focused on the task at hand, David did not offer further details. Turning left on Washington Street, he continuously scanned the space around them with his eyes peeled.

The guy was not one for conversation, so Sean decided to stay quiet. Surrounded by families, couples, and retirees flooding the sidewalks— all happily moving about and having somewhere to be—he figured most were on summer vacation. Concerned about the number of paparazzi waiting for him, he assumed that number might have doubled since earlier this afternoon.

Hating the silence inside the truck, needing to say something, Sean asked David a general question. "So, have you been working security detail a while?"

"Yes, nine years, Sir."

"Very good. Appreciate your help. Things got a bit crazy here. Hopefully, we can slip out Sunday morning and gain a little freedom for a few days."

"Yes, I'm sure some normalcy is always a luxury for people in your business," David acknowledged.

"This is very true."

Inching through the entertainment district, very lively for a Friday night, Café Nero was bustling with people enjoying the warm evening air. Many crowds gathered about the theatres, with tickets and playbills in hand, anticipating the doors opening.

As he approached the Godfrey Hotel, David quickly reviewed the procedure. He could see the ominous mob camped out on the street ahead, which caused the traffic to move slowly.

"Just to recap, Sir." The new Henchman reminded militarily, "Go straight inside to meet the hotel security. They are awaiting your arrival. Head to your room and gather your things. Tim will already be there packing up. Ivan will wait in another SUV on the opposite side of the hotel. Follow them and proceed to Site B. Clear?"

"Clear," Sean said, taking a deep breath. He watched the photographers jostling for better viewpoints and spotted a few paparazzi wolves at the building's left-hand corner, less than fifteen feet from the main doors.

"You see that?" Sean pointed to the three men, who were preparing to rush in forcefully for a photo.

"Yes, copy that, Sir. Don't worry. I'll alert their security. You make a straight shot inside."

"Will do," Sean confirmed.

David alerted the team via comms of the group assembled to the left of the building. Security outside the Godfrey was immediately on it.

Slowly rolling closer and closer to their drop-off point, David turned on their emergency flashers. This signaled the police and the hotel security staff that their VIP had arrived. The photographers erupted. Everyone began shouting the actor's name, asking him to look their way, even before showing his face. The sound was deafening.

Always around so many people, he often wondered if a crazy fan was lurking in the shadows - someone intent on harming him or, worse, ending his life. With camera lenses pointed at their target, Sean slipped on his sunglasses. Surrounded by lights flashing, that horrible thought crossed his mind for the millionth time.

A few uniformed men went into action, each highly trained to handle the circus unfolding on the street. It was madness. They strategically protected the vehicle, with eyes peeled, ready for the actor to make his appearance.

Inches away from parking outside the main doors, David said at the last second, "Remember, fast and efficient."

"Got it," Sean confirmed.

David came to a stop.

With security on either side of the entrance and police holding back pedestrians, Sean took a deep breath. Peering inside, he noticed the staff gathered around to greet him. Awakening his celebrity persona, he knew what he needed to do. It was show time.

"Ready?" David said before getting out to help him.

"Ready," Sean confidently responded.

"Here we go."

David left the driver's seat and quickly opened Sean's door. Bombarded by countless bursts of light bouncing off the buildings and adjacent windows, the celebrity found it hard to focus. The strobe effect infringed on every angle.

"Go! Go!" David shouted above the volume of the crowd. Time seemed to move in slow motion. Flanking the movie star, he quickly got him through the main doors.

Not given time to think, the Hollywood star rushed into the lobby to join Lawrence Costello, the hotel manager. Security politely asked guests to step aside and make way for the VIP. Walking along to the elevators made Sean feel very uncomfortable. He hated to inconvenience anyone.

"Good evening, Mr. Bradley. So we meet again," the smartly dressed older gentleman with thinning white hair and tiny glasses said while swiftly moving his famous client along with guards on all sides.

"Nice to see you, Mr. Costello."

On schedule, the group piled into the elevator and shielded the Hollywood star, who moved to the far back corner.

"Upon arrival at your suite, we will wait in the hall for you to gather your things, Mr. Bradley," the manager instructed before throwing in a positive comment. "I trust your stay has been pleasant until this point?"

"Yes, it has. Perfect. Thank you."

"Good to hear, Sir."

Sean compiled a list of things he needed to do, knowing he was running on a tight timeline.

When the elevator opened on the fourth floor, the two security guards and Mr. Costello stepped off and continued with their guest to his room. Accessing his suite, Sean went inside while the gentlemen waited for him. Thankful for a minute to himself, he walked into the bathroom and splashed some water on his face. Drying it with a towel, he tried to stay focused. Reminding himself that this trip and everything it entailed was well worth the trouble, he suddenly felt pulled in two directions. Drawn to his beloved wife Janie and their baby girl Ella, he also gravitated towards the Anderson family.

On task, he gathered his things. Stuffing his clothes into the carry-on, he double-checked the bathroom and left his hat and sunglasses out to give to Tim. Sure he had everything, he unplugged his laptop off the desk and slid it inside his brown leather satchel.

About to leave, reminded of the coins, Sean walked over and took them off the window ledge. Stuffing them in his pocket for safekeeping, he changed into a hoodie and pulled the hood over his head. With the satchel strap positioned across his chest and suitcase in tow, he scanned the room one last time before opening the door to find the group still waiting. Tim was ready for action. It was his turn now.

Mr. Costello went into business mode, standing straight and tall to make a good impression. "We will take the service elevator to the street-level service doors. Ivan is waiting for you there, Sir."

"Yes, Thank you."

Handing Tim his hat, sunglasses, and the jacket he'd been photographed in many times before, Tim donned it all and said, "See you shortly, Mr. Bradley. I'll return these things to you afterward."

Nodding his head and passing over his suitcase, Sean replied, "Sure thing."

The team was ready to move. Tim went downstairs to the lobby to meet David, who was waiting outside in the Rover. At the same time, the hotel team was leading the actor down the hallway toward the service elevators. They didn't have to wait since an empty one had been stationed and locked in place for his departure. Upon approach, the group stepped inside, along with Mr. Costello, who turned the exclusive access key, allowing it to descend.

It was a quiet ride. Nobody said a word. All that Sean heard was the beeping of the elevator passing each floor. One security guard held their group steady when the doors opened on the lower floor until the other checked to see that their route was clear. They only saw a house-keeping maid walking by with her trolley cart loaded with fresh towels and toiletries. Staring at the actor while she walked past, the men held Sean back until she was at a distance. Finally signaling them to move forward, the group approached the service exit. Prepared for anything, they found Ivan standing alongside a black SUV. Ready to transfer his client, the man swung open the back door the second the actor bolted onto the street. Ducking his head, Sean slid into the vehicle, thankful for the dimness of the night since the shadows helped shield him. Successfully securing his client, the newest Henchman quickly got behind the wheel.

Radioing David, Ivan confirmed, "Package is loaded. Heading out."

"Roger that," David said with eyes on Tim, fast approaching from inside the lobby.

In an instant, the photographers went crazy, believing it was Sean Bradley. David waited patiently before opening the rear door on cue for Tim to swiftly walk out with his head down, hiding under the jacket. Stashing the baggage in the cargo bay, David calmly got into the driver's seat and quickly pulled away. The cameras continued to flash, making it hard to see. Headed to the airport for the next phase of the plan, David and Tim kept an eye out for anyone following them.

On their way, David radioed Ivan. "Rover is taking flight."

With the decoy now en route, causing a distraction, Ivan moved along Temple Place to turn left on Tremont. That is when he noticed headlights behind them. Concerned, he thought it could be photographers tailing.

"We are taking a detour before returning to the Ritz," Ivan suggested. "I know it's an inconvenience, but I believe if you want to stay at that hotel, we can't take any chances. We don't want you compromised. I was supposed to pick up David and Tim at the airport after first dropping you off at the Ritz. We are changing the plan."

In agreement, the Hollywood star made the best of it. "Well, this way, I get to see more of Boston. Haven't done too much of that yet." He thought about his walks with Evily and the memories he'd take with him after leaving the city. "No more sightseeing, I suppose..."

"I would advise against that, Sir."

Once again, Sean felt like he was limited and caged. Captive to what fame had created.

Ivan explained to the team via comms, "Change of plans, gents. We might have a tail. Prepare to rendezvous in thirty minutes."

The team answered, confirming Ivan's instructions.

"Again, sorry, Mr. Bradley. Please sit back and enjoy the ride. We will get you to your destination as soon as we can."

Ivan kept a close eye on the vehicle in the rearview mirror. Turn after turn, it was still following them. Heading for the airport, hoping to blend in with other SUVs, Ivan moved into the airline limo lane and waited. For the first time, there was no sign of the car.

Simultaneously pulling away with three other Cadillacs, he kept up with them and intentionally changed lanes often to confuse anyone who may have been following. Stopping in front of the car rental terminal, picking up David and Tim outside the main doors, and transferring the baggage, they headed back into the downtown core, thankfully without anyone following this time.

Able to rest easy, Sean slumped in the seat and let the city pass by in a blur. His thoughts turned to Janie and Ella. Now, one day closer to being granted the opportunity to speak to them, he felt enormous pressure. He hoped their connection was strong enough for them to appear. Those thoughts prompted a review of his trip so far.

How crazy this experience had been - very unexpected in so many ways. Being around the Anderson family felt normal. There was just this ease to it all. It was like they had been part of his life for years. He could never be angry at them for anything, especially after they embraced him the way they did.

Faintly hearing music playing on the radio, Sean recognized a familiar tune. It caught his attention immediately, making him close his eyes. The 80's song by John Waite reminded him of the first fight he and Janie ever had. Recalling that night, tired and jet-lagged, having just returned home after shooting on location for three weeks, he found her sitting in the dark crying. She was pregnant with Ella and felt alone in their marriage. In hindsight, he believed she chalked it up to hormones in the end, but the two had words, causing both to retreat to different corners of the house. Frustrated beyond, not wanting tension between them, Sean heard this song cut through the silence. It was her way of expressing that she did not miss him while he was away. That, in his world, she did not feel important or loved right now. Hearing the song's lyrics made him want to find her. She was hurting, and he needed to make things right. Upon reaching the living room and seeing her sitting on the sofa, emotionally distraught, with tears streaming down her cheeks, he cautiously approached as the chorus filled the room. Offering her his hand, she took hold. Pulling Janie in close, they danced, immersed in the peaceful moment. Kissing her forehead, he dried her tears.

"I missed you so much," she whispered.

"I know," he said, hugging her tightly. "I missed you more."

Able to recall the expression on her face and every emotion he felt that night, his heart ached. When the song ended, his eyes drifted open. Abruptly pulled back to the present, the SUV emerged into the downtown core.

Strange how these memories flooded back after all these years just because of a song.

Torn between two worlds, he remembered his therapist's words, encouraging him to focus his energy on the present. Years from now, he would have the opportunity to reunite with the past.

27

Friday, July 26th
Boston, Massachusetts

Life is about change. Sometimes, you have to roll with the punches. ~ Caroline Manzo

After driving around for almost an hour, Ivan finally signaled to pull into the garage leading to the Ritz Hotel's underground parking. At the bottom of the ramp, the valet had reserved them a spot close to the security office under Ben's watchful eye. He awaited their return, wanting to end the day with his client safe and sound in the penthouse. Greeting the crew, the men didn't waste time on pleasantries. Whisking their client over to the elevators, the Henchmen surrounded Sean. Not long after, the actor found himself outside his suite high above the city of Boston.

Opening the door with the card key, Ben handed it to Sean. "Here, Mr. Bradley. This is yours."

The actor counted three and realized that Ben and Ivan had the other two. Once again, his life wasn't his own; someone else had control.

"We all have rooms across the hall from you. Should you need assistance, I've marked the doors with a red dot." Ben wheeled in his client's suitcase. "I've checked everything over. It's secure."

Only acknowledging with a nod, the actor was exhausted and quite hungry. The group left the room, closing the door behind them. Venturing into the sizeable space, far too big for one person, he found the bedroom and fell backward onto the fluffy duvet comforter, sinking a few inches. Able to take a breather, resting before starting the shower, he felt compelled to text Evily and tell her he'd made it back. It was something he promised he'd do when he left. Certain she'd be worried, he pulled out his phone and wondered what he should say. It was now evening and probably too late for them to meet. All that said, he decided to keep it simple.

Hi Evily. I made it to my room. They put me on the twelfth floor. What floor are you on?

Sean waited for her to respond. Two seconds later, she texted back. He assumed she was patiently waiting by the phone.

Glad you've returned safely. We are on the 10th floor. 1006. The kids are sleeping, and I have been writing. Is there a plan for tomorrow?

Despite spending the day together, Sean was strangely disappointed that he wouldn't get to see her tonight. That feeling reinforced the strong connection that was developing.

Interested in talking for a little while? I'm ordering some food. Can we discuss tomorrow's schedule over a late-night bite?

His fingers hovered over the keys before pressing send. When reading back the words, his heart raced. In a way, it was like he was asking her out on a date. Not allowing himself to back out, he bravely sent the message and waited as Evily's thinking bubbles kept him in suspense.

When her reply popped up, Sean exhaled and could breathe again. It read,

Sure. I'll drop by.

He responded nervously.

I'm just going to have a quick shower. Give me fifteen minutes.

Without hesitation, she sent her reply.

Sounds good. See you then.

He set his phone down on the bed and paused for a second. It wasn't hard to see how complicated his life had suddenly become. He found himself liking the author. But that said, it seemed she wasn't interested in him that way. Evily remained entirely focused on the task at hand. It made him think he should do the same. After all, they'd gone through so much to get him to this point.

Jumping into the shower to rid himself of the remnants of their hectic day, Sean wrapped himself in a towel and opened his atrociously packed suitcase, knowing Max would have a bird at the sight of it. Not wasting time, he changed into a clean pair of athletic shorts and a T-shirt and headed out to the foyer.

Upon rounding the corner, the first thing he was on the hunt for was the room service menu. Finding it on the dining table, he wasn't sure what to order. While perusing their options, he had difficulty deciding what his guest might like. Anxious about seeing Evily outside the whole Evan and Ella family unit again, it felt weird since she was the one intent on connecting him with his wife and daughter. Mulling over their situation, he analyzed every angle. His heart went out to Evily and the kids. The fact that he grew up with similar family circumstances, being a product of divorce, helped him sympathize with their situation on another level.

Selecting a few appetizers and wine options, Sean called in their order. Seconds later, a gentle knock came on the door. Opening it, he found Evily standing in the hallway with arms crossed. Her hair was pulled back in a ponytail, spiraling over her left shoulder. With her makeup freshened, more natural than made-up, she casually wore black tights, a tank, and a thin, fuchsia yoga jacket that seemed to help give her cheeks a rosy tone.

"Hey," Sean said, standing off to the side, clearing a path. Noticing what was on her feet, he teased, "Nice slippers."

Evily smiled and peered down at her furry black Fluffita slides - a staple for any girl's wardrobe. "Don't mock my footwear. Comfort is always key for me," she chuckled. "No judging."

Sean put both hands up in front of him. "No judgment here," he confirmed, secretly agreeing with her statement.

Scanning the space, she timidly inched inside, surprised by the grand entryway. The two stood awkwardly as the door closed behind them.

"Wow, this is amazing. Guess being a movie star has its perks."

"So that you know, I didn't book this suite. My staff did. I usually go for something comfortable and less flashy. The room I had at the Godfrey was pretty simple. Bathroom, bed, desk, and a chair."

Moving across the black and white checkered marble floor, Evily noticed a powder room to the left. Looking around, she said, "You even have an office?"

"Guess I do. I haven't looked in there yet."

When they moved into the main dining area, Evily's mouth dropped. "Oh my! Is this all for you? It's beautiful."

Anxiously taking in every nook and cranny, they passed the oblong dining table with a shimmering circular chandelier above it. Peeking around the petition in the middle of the room, Evily entered the well-appointed living area with leather chairs, a crescent sectional, a linear fireplace, and views overlooking Boston Common from every vantage point. Stopping to admire the decor, she wasn't sure if she should sit or stand.

"Please. Have a seat anywhere you like." Waiting for her to choose a spot, he said, "The drinks and appetizers I ordered should arrive shortly. With everything going on tonight, I haven't had anything to eat yet."

"That's fine." Evily sat down in the middle of the curved sofa. "The kids and I ordered room service a while ago. Evan was too tired to go out anywhere."

"I bet. He's had a busy day."

Still unable to hear his thoughts, she was concerned about how Sean was doing. It was strange how everything had happened so quickly after seeing the rainbow. It was like a higher power had changed her rules of engagement. "So, how did the transfer go?" she asked. Clutching a throw pillow, trying to get comfortable, she sat cross-legged on the sofa.

"It was good, but took a little longer than expected." Recalling the song on the radio, he said, "Before I forget, something odd happened too."

About to share the makings of his experience, unsure if it meant anything, they heard the sound of a door chime.

Evily looked his way, believing he had company.

"That's just the butler service announcing their arrival in the pantry," he revealed. It was entirely normal to him.

Surprised, she nodded, realizing their worlds were very different.

Sitting a few feet from her, Sean said, "Guess he'll be in shortly."

As predicted, an entirely proper and immaculately dressed older gentleman rounded the corner.

"Good evening, Sir. Ma'am. My name is Leonard. I will be your butler this evening."

"Nice to meet you, Leonard," Sean said, getting up from the sofa to shake the man's hand. "What do you think, Evily? Do you want to stay here, or would you prefer we sit in the dining room?"

She thought for a second. "No, here is good. We can keep it casual. Less fuss."

A shiver rolled down Evily's spine. Without warning, a translucent orb appeared and hovered in the corner of the room behind the man. A sweet-looking older woman with wavy white hair and stylish glasses was attached to it. Fairly short, barely five feet tall, she looked on with a smile and said her name was Eleanor and revealed she was Leonard's wife. Not wanting to do this again, Evily turned away from the soul about to request her help. Shimmying on the sofa, she tried her best to face the opposite direction, but she could still see the orb in her peripheral vision.

Sean advised, "Leonard, if you have everything on a wheeled cart, you can just bring it in, and we can serve ourselves."

With a nod of his head, he replied, "As you wish, Sir."

Thankfully, when the butler left the room, so did the woman's soul.

Returning to his spot on the sofa, Sean said, "Right, what were we talking about?"

Before she could say anything, Leonard returned, pushing a fancy trolley with a selection of appetizers and three bottles of wine. Two were chilling in an ice bucket, and the red was at room temperature. He removed the fresh floral arrangement from the middle of the coffee table and set it down nearby. The ice bucket took its place along with glassware, two plates, and rolled cutlery - all presented beautifully to perfection.

The two waited for him to finish before they continued their conversation. The orb reappeared, causing a chill to blanket Evily. Fidgeting, she zipped up her jacket and held the collar around her neck.

Standing back from them, the butler said, "Will that be all, Sir?"

"Yes, thank you. Appreciate it," Sean said before the gentleman disappeared from the room.

The actor turned his attention back to Evily. "So, where were we?"

In a daze, she did not hear a word. Fixated on Eleanor's desperation, Evily felt their eternal love that had transcended beyond the grave. It made her blurt loudly, "Excuse me, Leonard?"

The gentleman returned to the room. "Yes, Ma'am."

Not knowing what was happening, the actor recognized Evily's expression and the tone of her voice.

"Forgive me, but is your wife's name, Eleanor?'

The man's face said it all.

"The reason I ask is that..."

"She is here, isn't she?" he asked. "I can feel her."

When he said that, the hair on the back of Sean's neck stood on end. He searched the room from left to right.

Evily said, "Yes. She is."

Tears developing, the man pulled a handkerchief from his jacket pocket.

"I have a message from her. Would you like to hear it?"

Unable to speak, he agreed. His legs weakened, making him sit down in the closest chair.

Closing her eyes, Evily concentrated on the images Eleanor sent her. The woman's voice was so calming and soft-spoken. "You miss the sound of her voice. The sweetness it encompassed."

Leonard lowered his head. "Every day," he muttered.

"She is so happy you didn't sell the house. She says thank you."

"The lawyer said it would be better if I did. But I couldn't bring myself to do it. That is why I have this job. She is in every corner of that house, and I intend to keep working for as long as possible so I can live there with her. We have so many memories..."

"I often walk with you in the garden, she says. When you read by the window, I sit and rock in my chair alongside you."

Leonard confirmed, "Yes. Yes. That does happen."

"When you fall asleep, I am there."

"This is true. The scent of baby powder fills the room every night." Leonard shook his head in disbelief at what he was hearing. "This is absolutely amazing, my dear."

"She says she misses you, but she is never far away. No matter how many years pass, her love for you has never faded. It remains just as strong as the day you first met."

Shifting his weight forward and listening to what the author was saying to the butler, Sean rested his elbows on his knees and clasped his hands in front of him.

"She's showing me a cute little dog with floppy ears. Grey and white in color. Small enough to pick up with one hand. She's holding her tightly. Cuddling her close."

"Yes. That is Stella. She died not long after Eleanor. I often wondered if she had passed away because she missed my wife. Those two were always two peas in a pod. At times, I felt like a third wheel," he chuckled before the sorrow returned. "What I would give to see my Eleanor again..."

Evily thought a moment. Approaching the man, she said, "Do you trust me?"

Looking up at the woman, she seemed almost angelic. Captivated but fearful, Leonard nodded, not saying a word.

"Close your eyes," she instructed, lifting her hand to the man's face. Letting it hover, she, too, closed her eyes.

The man's expression immediately brightened, and a smile emerged. He instinctively raised his hand in front of him as if reaching out to cling to something.

"Oh, Eleanor. How I've missed you, Sweetheart." Tears streamed down Leonard's face. "She's so beautiful."

It was such a powerful moment. Sean was in disbelief.

Watching the butler wave to Eleanor, Evily said, "She is always there for you. When you need her, close your eyes, and she will appear."

He nodded.

Evily lowered her hand, prompting him to open his eyes.

In awe, Leonard stared at the woman who had given him the greatest gift he could have ever received.

Happy to have helped him, she grabbed hold of Leonard's hand when he reached out to her.

"Thank you," he mumbled, wiping his face with his handkerchief. "God bless you," he said.

With arms outstretched, she gave him a kind-hearted hug.

"Please excuse me." He left the room silently.

Honing in on his thoughts and emotions, Evily could sense his happiness, but after receiving the messages, a sadness loomed when he realized he was still alone on earth without his Eleanor. In an instant, a wave of exhaustion hit Evily like a brick. Moving to her spot on the sofa, feeling a bit dizzy, all Sean could do was stare.

"That was incredible," he said as she recovered.

"Yes, but I fear he misses his wife now more than ever. This is why I avoid meddling in people's lives—it only sets them back."

As the moment settled, she shifted her attention to the array of plates before them: stone-fired Margherita pizza topped with fresh tomatoes, ricotta, and basil; lobster tacos; and a charcuterie platter brimming with deli meats, cheeses, spicy nuts, chutney, and slices of freshly cut French loaf. Everything looked delicious. Turning to him again, she found the actor still sitting in amazement.

"What?" she said.

"You're kidding, right?" He turned and glanced across the room before swiveling around to lock eyes with her again. "That was unreal."

"Okay, enough. You're creeping me out," she stated. "Can we not talk about it?"

He nodded while switching gears from what he'd just witnessed.

Hoping to change the subject, she said, "This could feed an army?"

Sean came to his senses. "As I said earlier, I haven't eaten since our afternoon lunch. That's a long time for me to go without food." He stayed quiet a moment longer as the experience resonated, then said, "Umm, please, help yourself. So, red, white, or, umm, what do we have here?" Checking out the other bottle, he added, "Or Rosé?"

"Think I'm in for the red."

"Absolutely. Red it is." Sean grabbed the bottle opener and skillfully poured two glasses.

Handing one to her, he said, "For you."

"Thank you."

A nervous expression came across his face when he sat down and pulled the coffee table closer to access the nibbles he'd placed in front of them.

"So, what happened earlier?" she asked, taking a sip from her glass.

"Oh," he recalled. "Like I said, weirdest thing. I think it may have been another sign?"

"Really? That's great." She was intrigued.

"It had to be. Can't explain it otherwise, although it could have just been a coincidence. But somehow, I don't think so. Janie popped into my mind when I heard a song on the radio, and it brought me back to one specific memory." He sounded excited and very upbeat.

"So tell me the details." Evily set her wine down on the table and grabbed the throw pillow, clutching it tightly.

"While I was driving with the Henchmen, long story short, we had to pick up Tim and David at the airport and then drive back here. On the way, the song, Missing You by John Waite - do you know it?"

Evily thought a second.

With his unrelenting talent, Sean started to sing the lyrics.

The sound of his voice took her aback. "Oh, yes. I know that one," the author confessed.

"Well, it came on the radio and immediately brought me back to a time with Janie years ago. She was pregnant with Ella, and I was on location, shooting a movie for almost a month. I hadn't seen her at all. We'd just spoken on the phone. Back then, there was no Facetime or anything like that." Leaning back against the sofa, Sean looked to the ceiling to remember all the details. "So, as the song played, I saw the two of us having our first argument. Janie was frustrated that she'd been alone for weeks, and I was exhausted from working. I don't know how the fight started - what even sparked it? Regardless, we ended up retreating to different ends of the house after having words. It was so quiet. Then suddenly, that same song began playing from the stereo in the living room. Hearing it - needing to make amends, I got up and followed the music. There, I found Janie sitting on the sofa, crying. As I walked over, all I did was offer her my hand. In the process, I did not say a word. She stood up and danced with me. When I kissed her forehead, she said, *I missed you so much.* Remembering that moment gave me the same feeling in my heart. Like I relived it for a reason. Was this a message from her?"

"It is quite possible. I would say yes. Especially because the feeling you got was so strong. Did you feel like you were there?"

"Definitely. It was as though I had left the world for a minute. When the song ended, it seemed like I fell back into reality and found myself in the SUV."

"There are times they communicate through music. You might even find that the lights may flicker on and off, a faucet may turn on, and of course, don't forget there's the appearance of nature too."

"Never would I have thought this was something that would ever happen to me? For years, I felt like she and Ella were just gone, you know. It felt like they had disappeared off the face of the earth. A double funeral was not exactly what I hoped my future would include."

His last comment engrained itself in Evily's mind. This man had buried his daughter and his wife at the same time. He'd lost everything in one day.

"I don't know how to respond to what you just said. Even to say things happen for a reason doesn't make sense in your situation. Why do some people pass away and others stay here? We are not to question it despite being human to do so. One day, you will know why. You'll just have to wait until then."

Sean smiled at her, lost for words. "Any chance I can see the videos of the orbs again? You know, the ones you showed me?"

"Yes, of course." Taking her phone from her pocket, she scrolled through her videos.

Sliding closer to her, Sean took Evily's phone when she handed it to him. She purposefully used an accent pillow as a buffer to keep him at arm's length. One by one, Sean watched the videos she'd pulled up. It was fascinating to him.

"That's truly them?"

Evily nodded.

He still found it difficult to wrap his head around that concept.

It was then she saw Sean Bradley in a different light. He spoke softly of Janie and Ella.

Sean handed her the phone. "Are there more?"

"Yes. Let me see." Scrolling to the next one, she again handed it back.

Amazed, he watched the little orb that was more active than the larger one. "This is incredible." Sean glanced over at Evily. His eyes locked with hers, causing a profoundly intense stare. "How can I ever repay you for all the trouble you've gone through this past year? I mean..."

She quickly broke away. Her heart beat rapidly. *What is happening?* she thought. "Umm, you don't need to repay me. I'm happy to do it. I promised them I would help, and I keep my word." Uncomfortable, Evily knew what she had to do. While checking the time on her phone, she said, "It's late. Think I should get going."

"Yeah, umm...alright."

Placing both feet on the floor and slipping her fuzzy slippers back on, she could see he was disappointed to hear her say that. She knew if she stayed, it could ruin his chances of connecting with Janie and Ella. That was something she couldn't leave to chance.

"I guess tomorrow will be a busy one?" he confirmed.

"Yes, it is usually an intense day—there is much riding on that game. Will you be able to join us?"

"What arena is it at?" he asked, slightly concerned.

"Canton. The first arena we went to."

"Is that the one with a ton of people?"

"Yes, unfortunately."

He knew he'd be setting himself up for trouble by going there. The last thing he wanted was to bring negative attention to the Anderson family.

"Would you be okay if I stayed here?"

"Of course. Based on what's happening, that might be best."

"That location was pretty active. I also feel like my presence could disrupt Evan's focus. This is a big opportunity for him."

Impressed that he considered how this would affect her son first and foremost, she nodded. "Yes, it is."

"Would he be disappointed if I don't go?"

"Possibly, but he would understand why," Evily said. The fact he continued to think of Evan and not himself did not go unnoticed.

Sean followed her into the foyer.

Always paying her way, she asked, "Can I contribute to your buffet bill?"

Shaking his head, he said, "Are you kidding? No, out of the question. Besides, the Henchmen will probably help me devour it all."

Arriving at the front door, she decided to peek in on Leonard standing in the pantry. "I just wanted to bid you goodnight."

His face brightened. "Good night to you as well, my dear." Still emotional, he added, "Thank you so much. I will forever remember this night. I will carry it with me always."

"Remember what I said. She is always with you. Take care."

Sean stood back, listening in.

When Evily turned her attention back to him, he was unsure what to say.

"So, we will see you tomorrow at some point?" Fiddling with her phone in hand, she watched him open the door for her.

"Yes, for sure," Sean replied before asking, "Do you want me to walk you to your room? That way, you'll get back safely."

"No, no. It's alright. I'll be okay. I'm used to being alone, remember?" Evily offered a half-smile.

The actor acknowledged her while leaning against the edge of the door. "I'll text you in the morning."

"Okay." Evily walked out into the hallway. Ben was there standing guard. "Night, Ben," she said.

"Night, Ma'am."

"Make sure you text me the updates on the scores. I want to hear your prediction, too," Sean whispered as she walked away.

Turning around, squinting her eyes a second, she opened them widely and said, "Sadly, I think it will be their first loss."

"No. Really?"

"Yes, that's what I'm feeling. The game will be tight, though. Possibly a score of 2-1."

"Well, a one-goal deficit isn't so bad. Tell me the team at least loses it in overtime."

Shrugging her shoulders, she said, "We will have to see."

Watching her step into the elevator and disappear, Sean asked Ben to invite the guys over to help eat the food he ordered. Closing the door behind him, hit by the silence, he could faintly hear his phone ringing in the bedroom. Following the ringtone and locating it, he noticed he'd missed several calls from Max and Sheri, along with countless texts in the past hour and a half. Their messages dropped yet another bomb. Something he expected but was still unprepared for. Pressing play on the entertainment news video sent to him, he was afraid to hear what the tabloid outlet would divulge, given the thumbnail displayed.

To this breaking news just in! We have a Sean Bradley sighting in the city of Boston. Not a place he is known to frequent. It seems the action star is visiting a woman there. Sources have confirmed that her identity is that of best-selling author Evily Landy. Many photos are surfacing of the couple and their movements around the New England coast. In true Sean Bradley fashion, he has taken the time to stop for fans. The couple's recent visit to a coffee shop resulted in a flurry of activity, causing the two to leave in a hurry. A fan took this picture as they escaped in a cab. We have crews on the East Coast ready to find out more. With the upcoming movie premiere in under a week, you'd think he'd be in Los Angeles prepping for that. Love is in the air, people! Mainly in the city of Boston!

Sean sat down on the end of the bed. "Oh my, god," he said aloud, wondering what she would say.

Until then, the photos and videos on social media were only fan-driven. The mainstream hadn't picked up the story yet. But this? This was different. Aware of how they operate, Sean knew the family's connection to him could destroy their life.

Hoping Evily wasn't asleep, Sean texted her.

Sorry to bother you, but we really need to talk about something.

Her thinking bubbles erupted a few seconds later.

Sorry. I just got into bed. Can this wait until morning?

Deciding to hold off, he figured he'd call Sheri and Max first to ask for advice. Evily's identity was about to be blown up in the media, and there was nothing he or anyone else could do about it. Typing a response, he said,

Yes. But we need to meet first thing. Text me when you get up.

All he received in response was a sleeping emoji face.

Sean fell back onto the bed. Frustrated beyond, he was scared about what this could mean for the Andersons. Knowing he couldn't sit back and just let this happen without a fight, he thought of a plan to counteract what would occur. He needed to prepare for anything and felt an obligation to protect this family at all costs.

Sheri called with absolutely perfect timing. Seeing her picture on the screen, he rolled his eyes, not wanting to answer. Slowly picking up the call, he listened and then replied, "Yes, I know. I'm aware."

28

Saturday, July 27th
Boston, Massachusetts

Integrity means that if our private life were suddenly exposed, we'd have no reason to be ashamed or embarrassed. Integrity means our outward life is consistent with our inner convictions.

~ Billy Graham

Before eight o'clock in the morning, Evily's phone began ringing and chiming steady. She'd received countless messages and tags on social media from readers wondering what was happening. Barely coherent, she viewed the popular entertainment news feed sent to her by her publicist, Angela. Speechless, she didn't know what to do as her body went numb, knowing this would produce a damaging blow to her family and her career. Seemingly falling through the mattress, simultaneously spiraling out of control, Evily angrily got dressed and tied her hair back before heading up to Sean's suite.

While stomping in her UGG slippers down the hall to the elevators, she texted Sean.

Get up!!! I am coming to your room!!!!

The actor barely slept five hours but woke immediately upon hearing the notification and reading the message. He figured Evily had seen the news. In hindsight, he should have insisted they meet last night to discuss things. Now, the author was on her way up. Given the number of exclamation marks in her text, he knew she wasn't happy.

Frantically getting dressed, not having time to brush his teeth thoroughly, he heard someone pounding on the door. Rushing over, he flung it open to find Evily having a heated discussion with Ivan.

"I need to speak to him now!" she declared, shaking her finger at the protection agent.

Sean looked on humorously as the petite woman paled in comparison to the Henchman's overpowering stature. Giving Ivan a nod, the guard put up his hands, losing the battle between them.

"Thank you, Ivan. Finally," the author said in a huff.

Swiveling around to pound on Sean's door again, she was surprised to see him already standing there.

"Oh, you're here."

Sean stood silent.

All business, she stated, "We need to talk."

The actor stepped aside with an outstretched arm to invite her in. Ivan looked on, happy he didn't have to deal with the frazzled woman anymore.

"Good luck, Sir," the Henchman chuckled. "She's a lively one."

Sean smirked. "Yeah, thanks."

The door swung shut. Sean walked in to find Evily hysterically pacing the floor in the dining room. With one hand on her hip, the other melded to her forehead, about to have a heart attack, Evily couldn't even speak as a million scenarios flooded her mind.

"What do we do about this? Seriously? What they posted is a lie. We are not together. We are certainly not dating." Stopping, she pointed her finger at him. "See! This is the thanks I get for doing something good for someone. What is this going to do to my kids? What is everyone back home going to say? My ex is going to have a hay day." Almost carving a path into the floor, she continued walking with her hands fluttering at high speed around waist level.

Sean crossed his arms in front of him and waited for her to finish venting.

Once the panic attack subsided, she pulled out a dining chair and collapsed.

The Hollywood star tried to infuse some humor into an otherwise bad situation. "You know, that outburst right there was worthy of an Oscar nod."

"This is not funny!" she voiced angrily.

Ivan's eyebrows raised, having heard her shouting from the hallway.

"Come on, Evily. It's a tabloid news feed. Nobody pays attention to those." Unfortunately, Sean knew otherwise but wanted to bring her down a notch.

"What do you mean?" She tried to catch her breath. Elements of calm were flashing across her face intermittently.

"How many people would believe we," Sean paused, moving his finger back and forth between them, "You and I would be a thing?"

The petite woman slumped in her chair. "Wow... Thanks, Sean..."

Immediately taking a knee in front of her, he backtracked his words. "I didn't mean it like that."

"Sure feels like you did." Evily realized what he was saying. Raising her sights to the ceiling, she asked, "Why? Why did you do this to me?"

"Hey, are you blaming Janie and Ella?"

Evily stood up as Sean stayed a safe distance from her.

"No..." The author's chin dropped to her chest in defeat. "No, I know it's not them." She walked over to the window. "When did my life get so damn complicated?"

"Let me guess. It's when you met me?" Joining her, standing almost shoulder to shoulder, he knew what had happened wasn't exactly ideal. "Can I tell you something?"

"Sure," she said calmly with arms crossed.

"From my experience, these things blow over when something new comes up. By tomorrow, we will be old news."

"Are you sure?" Knowing there was nothing they could do, she asked solemnly, "You're just not saying that to calm me down, are you?"

"Perhaps, but I'm sure everything will be fine, though." His voice was steady, but his gaze softened as he stepped closer. Slowly, he opened his arms, the movement almost instinctive, and to his surprise, she allowed it. Sean wrapped her in a gentle embrace, the warmth of her body fitting against his in a way that felt so perfect it defied words.

Evily's arms slid tentatively around his waist, pulling him a little closer. He responded by holding her tighter, resting his chin lightly atop her head. Her hair tickled his skin, and as she nestled her head against his chest, he knew she could hear the steady rhythm of his heartbeat. The moment felt like it stretched beyond time, as an unspoken connection formed between them.

Caught off guard, Sean instantly felt very protective of Evily Landy—something beyond unexpected. For the first time in what felt like forever, he wanted to shield someone, to be their strength.

But as the silence wrapped around them, Evily's thoughts began to swirl. The solace she found was undeniable, yet a stark reality tugged at her heart. She realized what this moment might mean—for her, for Sean, and for the delicate, precious bond he still needed to foster with his late wife and daughter.

Her breath hitched softly, the weight of it all settling in her chest. This was more than just an embrace—it was a step toward something that could change everything. Understanding the gravity of it, the author abruptly stepped back. With a shocked expression, she looked into his eyes and pressed one hand against his chest. Standing at arm's length, she didn't know what to say.

"Sorry, I, umm...." Sean knew she was uncomfortable. "I didn't mean to...."

"It's fine. We are both mature adults...." She didn't know where to look.

Drawn in, Sean couldn't help but stare into her eyes.

"I think a little distance today might be good," Evily whispered.

Clearing his throat, regrettably conceding, he said, "Yeah, sure. I need to deal with some backlash anyway."

Evily nodded. Then, as if a veil lifted, she noticed how handsome he was while he stood in front of her. With hair styled perfectly and a mature grey speckle along the sides, his face expressed sympathy and concern. She felt a sudden shift. A battle of feelings erupted - something she hadn't experienced in years. Walking to the door, shell-shocked, she felt like she had betrayed Janie and Ella. Forced to regroup, she knew her loyalty was to them, especially when it came to Sean Bradley. They were her priority.

Standing in the foyer, he broke the silence between them and asked, "Can you still text me the score of the game as it unfolds?"

"Sure," she said in a shallow tone. "It starts at 1:00. We should be back by 3:30 or so. I'll let you know when we return."

"Do you want one of the Henchmen with you today? You know, just in case?"

"I think we'll be fine. Nobody would know me otherwise. You know, without you around stealing the attention." Those words slid off her tongue too easily. "I'm sorry." She shook her head. "That's not what I meant. What I mean is - I am a nobody. The world doesn't care about author Evily Landy. I don't exist, and I liked it that way."

He witnessed a few tears running down her cheeks. Sean's heart sank. She was succumbing to all the stress. Jostling with this overwhelming need to comfort her, he knew he couldn't.

"Well, if it's any consolation, I am very thankful to have met you, Evily Landy slash Anderson."

Offering a smile, drying her face with her sleeve, she whispered, "Thank you," before glancing at the time on her phone. "Look, I need to get going."

"Don't worry about the tabloid stuff. My people are dealing with it."

Evily nodded solemnly, knowing the damage was already done. All she could do was move forward. Approaching the door, Sean reached out to open it for her.

Seeing Ivan standing outside, she felt so bad.

"Sorry for attacking you, Ivan. I apologize. Please forgive me."

"No problem, Ma'am. It's all good."

Thankful to hear that, she shuffled, almost mournfully, down the hall in her slippers. The two men watched her leave. Sean waved while she waited for an elevator. Before long, the author disappeared.

Addressing Ivan, Sean instructed, "I'm going to need one of you following the Anderson family to the Canton rink in case things go south."

"For sure, Boss. No problem."

Leaning on the edge of the door, he added, "Make sure you don't miss them leaving. Things could get ugly today."

"Roger that."

Sean let the door fall shut. Standing in the foyer, running both hands through his hair, he took a deep breath, processing everything that just happened. Passing the accent table at the entrance to the bedroom, he stopped and looked at his reflection in the mirror. His face said it all. Resting both hands on the edge of the marble table, he leaned forward and knew right away.

"You're falling for her, man. How did this happen?"

29

Saturday, July 27th
Boston, Massachusetts

Within the hour, Sean met with David to coordinate surveillance on the Andersons. Standing inside the foyer of his suite, he had specific instructions for the newest Henchman.

"I want you to follow the family today to the town of Canton. We need to keep an eye on them. I believe they are heading to the Ice House for Evan's hockey game around eleven."

David noticed Sean was worried. Standing militarily with his hands behind his back, he replied, "No problem, Sir. I will watch over them and make sure they are okay."

Not having met David yet, Evily and the teens wouldn't know who he was, so that worked out well.

"Hover around the arena and only intercept if necessary. Send me updates along the way via text."

"Yes. Will do."

The younger Henchman was up to the challenge. Exchanging cell numbers, David headed out to prepare for the day.

Sean felt confident about his decision while walking into the office on the far side of his suite. It gave him peace of mind and allowed him to focus on what he needed to handle. The main objective now was to calm the rumor mill. Still unsure how to do that, he strategized with Max and quickly developed a plan to distract the press from focusing on the family.

30

Saturday, July 27th
Boston, Massachusetts

Life is a series of mistakes, followed by long periods of damage control. ~ Linda Poindexter

At eleven-thirty, Evily and the teens left the hotel. David confirmed their departure time with Sean. Wishing he had joined them and not stayed behind, the actor hoped Evan would understand why he was absent today. That's when the thought crossed his mind.

Did I just let Evan down like his Dad, Peter, has so many times before?

Analyzing it from that perspective made him feel sick. He never intended for all of this to happen. Had he hurt this family in more ways than one?

Torn between feelings for Janie and baby Ella and what was developing with Evily and the teens, Sean tried to strike a balance. He focused on the past to help fuel his connection with the orbs and stayed mindful of the Anderson family's involvement in the present. There were times he was overwhelmed by it all.

Sheri and Max started contacting him frequently. Simultaneously watching the television mounted to the wall, disappointment washed over him when the entertainment news featured photos and commentary involving the Andersons, the Henchmen, and him. Relaying that updated information to Sheri, she, in turn, dealt with it on her end. Scanning the myriad of emails forwarded from her, each looking for a comment on *#SeanBradley,* he took a break from damage control and immersed himself in the secret project he was working on with Max. Paragraph after paragraph, he believed it would help resolve life's problems.

Drawn to the sports segment of the news hour, a welcomed distraction from all the drama, he saw that the New York Yankees were in town to play the Red Socks tonight at Fenway. A dream ever since he was a boy, he immediately made a few calls. Tonight was one ball game he didn't want to miss. Excited to surprise the teens with a fun-filled night out, he wondered how Evily would react. In the end, would it help him make amends with her? Or was it too late?

31

Saturday, July 27th
Canton, Massachusetts

Life is always full of surprises. You never know who you are going to meet that will change your life forever.

~ LiveLifeHappy.com

The Andersons arrived at the Ice House in Canton just after the top of the hour. As they circled the parking lot, the Mother of two could feel her kids seemed off. Their energy had changed, and sadly, she knew this could be the reason for Evan's upcoming loss.

Finding a spot under a small tree at the far end, she shifted in park and watched Evan get out, stretch, and open the back hatch. Slugging his equipment bag onto one shoulder, the athlete grabbed his sticks. About to get out and offer her usual words of encouragement, he stopped her.

"Mom, can we not do this right now? I just need to go."

What he said hit her hard. Shocked, she replied, "Yeah, sure, honey." Pausing a moment, she added, "Good Luck."

"Thanks. I'll see you after the game."

"Alright. I love you."

Evily felt she was to blame. Because of what had happened the past few days, she expected an element of spiritual warfare to creep in and reveal itself. And it did. There are repercussions for going above and beyond to witness to someone and to save their soul. They had become a target, and she knew that opposing forces would unrelentingly bombard them from that moment onward. For them, this battle would continue until Evily fulfilled her promise to Janie and Ella. But there were no guarantees their life would return to normal even then. Doing this was a life sentence.

Praying for her son while he walked away, she let him go, having faith that he would be protected. Meeting up with a few teammates just outside the arena entrance, she watched a smile emerge upon his face while mingling with the guys and could hear their upbeat hockey-related banter. This gave a sense of relief. Once he walked through the main doors into the building, she figured he'd be okay. Standing alone in the parking lot, Evily soon returned to the driver's seat.

"So, Ella, do you want to go inside or wait a bit?"

"Wait," she said, with hopes of enjoying the quiet time before having no choice but to go inside.

That left Evily with time to think. Since Thursday, dealing with Sean was an eye-opening experience. Not only had his thoughts been mysteriously blocked from her watchful mind, but now future events attached to him reflected a void or black hole. A nothingness. Something very unfamiliar to her. She then thought about the souls she helped. Going against her convictions, she assumed she'd probably worsened their situation. Why hadn't she seen any of this coming? There was not one warning sent to her from above.

Typing in #SeanBradley on her phone, she found even more photos of her and the kids. A tension erupted inside her chest. She didn't know how to stop it. The whole world knew about them, and there was absolutely nothing she could do about it.

Desperate, she raised her sights to the sky in a moment of faith and whispered, "Please help me. Tell me all of this is going to turn out okay?"

With impeccable timing, a customized platinum Land Rover drove past with a vanity license plate. It displayed the letters BRADLY. Another vehicle parked across from them had a bumper sticker with the number nineteen on a pair of red socks inside a white circle. Not yet fully understanding the significance of the signs, she smiled. It surprised her every time little miracles happened, especially after receiving a small acknowledgment when she needed it most.

32

Saturday, July 27th
Boston, Massachusetts

Happiness doesn't result from what we get but from what we give. ~ Ben Carson

Going mental while staring at four walls, Sean communicated with Max and Sheri for hours. Despite dealing with all the social media requests for comment, the rumor mill was far from contained. On top of that, he had not told either of them about tonight's plans. It made him wonder if he should give them a heads-up. Believing nobody would know they were even there if he played his cards right, Sean opted to keep it to himself and ask for forgiveness later.

Still working with Max on their special project, Sean emailed him what he'd written and closed his laptop. Happy to receive a text from Evily shortly after, updating him on Evan's game, Sean noticed the final score, knowing Evily was right. The team had lost 2-1 in overtime. In the grand scheme of things, he hoped the young athlete would not take it to heart. One loss out of six games was something to be incredibly proud of.

Seeing that Evily was sending another message, he waited.

Evan's team is in the semi-finals tomorrow at 10:30 am in Marlborough at the New England Sports Center.

Right then and there, Sean decided that he would attend that game regardless of what complications could arise. He forwarded Ben their

Sunday schedule and noted that it was pending confirmation from Evily in the coming hours.

Given a moment of clarity, he knew he had made a mistake in light of how the day went. While trying to protect the family, he inadvertently abandoned them instead. A feeling he could not shake since he vowed years ago never to be the man his father was.

Amidst the heavy self-reflection, the phone rang, startling him. It was Sheri.

"Hey. What's up?" Sean asked when answering the call.

Sheri paused a minute, then huffed.

"Spit it out. What is it?" He was almost afraid to ask.

"I got a call from the producer. They are concerned about the recent headlines. You and Andrea were supposed to be the glam couple at the premiere. Now, it seems she's gotten wind of this fling you're having out East and is breathing down their neck and mine."

"She doesn't own me. My relationship with Andrea all this time has been a sham, and you know it." He was beyond frustrated. "My judgment was clouded for a while, but no more."

"Look, I realize that is the case. I have been hearing it from you for a while. You should have taken my advice and ended it sooner," she paused. "Listen, you're a good guy. I get it. But now, this barracuda is looking for blood."

"What could she possibly do? Never mind, it's not even an issue. If they don't want me to walk the red carpet, I won't do it."

"Well, it's exactly the opposite. They are demanding you continue your relationship publically until two weeks after the box office opening." Sheri was serious.

"Not a chance. You and I know nothing in my contract states I am obligated to do that. You will call them back and say Sean Bradley will complete his contractual obligations by attending the premiere, walking the carpet, and giving any necessary interviews. He will not continue a fictitious relationship with Andrea Branti. End of story."

Frazzled, she knew he was right.

"I've been in this business a long time and built a reputation for being an upstanding man with integrity. Always professional. I'll be damned if I am going to compromise that."

Sean hated anyone controlling his private life. It wasn't anyone's business.

"Look, I need to go," the action star said bluntly.

"Sean? When are you returning to LA?"

The actor exhaled. "Not yet. I still need to deal with a few things here. When I return, I'll fill you in. Until then, you need to trust me."

There was silence on the other end.

"Fine. I can't stop you. Just think before you leap, please."

Sean snickered. "Sure will."

After hanging up, he opened his laptop and Googled Evily Landy. A striking photo of her appeared. Taken at a book launch in Chicago, she looked so happy. Leaning back in his desk chair, he spun around in a circle. Spying her photo with every rotational pass, dressed in a black-short-sleeved knit top, with her hair cascading over both shoulders, he knew her smile must have brightened the hockey arena today.

Slamming the laptop closed again and checking the time, Sean opted to bribe Max into organizing a dinner in his suite for everyone before going to Fenway. Calling Ben right afterward, the Hollywood star informed him of the arrangements he'd made for the night and asked him to create a plan of action to keep everyone safe and sound.

33

Saturday, July 27th
Boston, Massachusetts

Variety is the spice of life. We all want surprises. ~ Tony Robbins

Time dragged on while waiting for the family to return to the hotel. Pumped about attending the ball game, the Henchmen seemed upbeat, given the amount of activity within the suite. Sean felt anxious about the plans he'd made. He hoped the Andersons would be just as excited as he was.

Determined to keep a balance, reminded of what Evily said about connecting with Janie and Ella, he reached into his pocket to pull out their coins. Looking down at the dime and quarter, he knew the countdown was on. Tomorrow, they'd be traveling to Cape Cod for the much-anticipated meeting with his wife and daughter. Thinking about their schedule for Sunday, he received a call from David.

"Hey, man," Sean said, anxious to hear his report.

"Hello, Sir. The family is just pulling out of the arena. I am right behind them. Depending on traffic, we should be back in about forty minutes to an hour."

Concerned if anything transpired, the actor asked, "So, how did it go?"

"I went inside and sat at a distance. People were whispering. Probably not something she wanted to hear. I believe that's why she and her daughter were wearing headphones. Maybe they were trying to drown it out."

"Hmm..." Sean said, wishing he had been there. "Thanks, David. See you shortly, man."

"You got it, Sir."

Calling Evily, he hoped she would agree to join him tonight. Nervous, he dialed the number and waited for her to pick up. She answered on the fourth ring.

"Hello?"

"Hey, umm... Just checking in to see how the afternoon is going?"

"We are fine. How about you? Did you have a good afternoon?" Evily replied.

The actor chuckled to himself. "It was uneventful. That word describes my last four hours. It certainly wasn't a fast-paced hockey game. That said, things needed to get done." Pausing a second, he asked, "So, I've ordered dinner. It should be here within ninety minutes, I believe. Can you guys join us? I've invited the Henchmen too. We can celebrate our last night in Boston. What do you think?"

There was silence on the line.

"Hello, Evily?" He wondered if their call had dropped.

"Yeah, I'm here."

"Oh, thought I lost you." Sean quickly realized the meaning of what he had just said. To cover it up, he asked, "What do you think? Dinner? Please don't say no."

"Mom!" Ella shouted from the back seat. Her voice seemed far away. "Sean! We will be there!"

Initially disappointed about his loss, Evan was happy to hear from the Hollywood star. "Sounds great, man," the athlete said.

"Perfect, so I'll see all of you in a little while?"

"Guess so. I'll text when we are on our way up," the author confirmed.

"Okay. I'm looking forward to it. Bye."

"Bye."

So thankful Ella and Evan weren't mad at him for not tagging along today, Sean felt like he could breathe freely for the first time in over six hours. Executing stage two of his plan, he texted Ben, Ivan, and Tim to drop by for a meeting. He wanted to be briefed on the agenda for the evening before the family returned.

Within seconds, there was a knock at the door. Ben unlocked it with his key card, and all three men converged in the office, ready to discuss things.

"So, gentlemen," Sean said. "I want to be invisible tonight at Fenway. Tell me how we are going to do that?"

34

Saturday, July 27th
Boston, Massachusetts

The adventure of life is to learn. The purpose of life is to grow. The nature of life is to change.
~ William Arthur Ward

While panning the suite from left to right, Sean was elated with how everything looked. The staff had draped the dining table with crisp, white linen and set it for eight before beautifying the room from top to bottom with colorful fresh flowers. Now, all they were waiting for was the food to arrive.

Pacing about his bedroom moments after, trying to be patient, peering out the window at the view, he watched the sun begin its descent ever so slowly toward the horizon. Sporting designer jeans and a white collared shirt, Sean hoped he wasn't over-dressed.

His phone vibrated on the nearby side table. Anxious energy filled the air while he walked over to read the message.

Hi. We are on our way.

Excited that the family would be there shortly, Sean smiled and sent her a thumbs-up emoji before heading to the foyer. Upon turning the corner outside the bedroom, the sound of the butler chime filled the room. Going to check on who was assigned to them this evening, he happily found Leonard in the pantry.

"Leonard, my man. Good to see you." Sean greeted the elderly gentleman with a handshake.

In return, he happily said, "Good evening, Sir. Your food order has arrived, and everything is ready."

"Thank you. I appreciate that. My guests are on their way." Sean could tell the man had a bounce in his step. He was more bubbly, and his face was bright. Privy to his incredible experience last night, he knew the reason why, too.

Right then, the security team walked through the door. David included.

"Guys, the Andersons will be here shortly. Ben, have you briefed David on tonight's little surprise?" Sean asked, rubbing his palms together.

"Yes, all good."

Faintly hearing banter outside in the hallway, he recognized Evan and Ella's voices. Opening the door, he found them chatting amongst themselves.

Evily stood back and let her kids greet Sean first. They were pretty excited to see him. In between the pleasantries, Sean's eyes soon found hers. She tried not to smile.

"Hi," she said. "Thank you for having us. This was a nice surprise."

"Thanks for joining me." Moving aside, he said, "Please, come on in."

Suspiciously looking at David, she noted, "I think that guy was at the arena today. Happen to know anything about that?"

"Not a thing." The movie star moved toward the dining room, fluffing off the comment.

Evily rounded the corner. Immediately, her sights fell upon the table, beautifully set with candles down the center, intermixed with fresh flower arrangements. Clutching her heart, she was speechless. Sean walked up and stood beside her.

"Is it too much? I mean, I just let them do their thing."

"It's lovely."

The sincerity in her voice made the afternoon of prepping all worthwhile.

Not wasting any time, nervous about letting the family in on his surprise, the actor gathered everyone around the table.

"Now that we are all here, flowers and dinner aside, I have another surprise for you all."

He immediately noticed the expression on Ella's face.

"A surprise? Really? Truly?" With her hands clenched in front of her, she eagerly waited to hear what he was about to say.

"Yes, Ella. Really, truly." The actor's heart melted at her reaction.

Evan stepped forward and stated what everyone else was thinking. "Well, don't keep us in suspense. What is it?"

"Do you like baseball?"

"Yeah..." Evan immediately replied, lingering on the word, not skipping a beat. "Why?" Evan was about to explode.

"Well, I've arranged for a box at Fenway to see the Yankees play the Red Sox tonight. I want all of you to join me."

Ella's face lit up as she tugged on her Mother's arm.

The Henchmen offered subdued smiles that paled in comparison to Evan raising his hands in victory.

"Yes! That's awesome!" the teen voiced with an abundance of enthusiasm.

Sean turned to Evily and noticed she didn't seem as happy about it. He quietly took her aside while the teens mingled with the security guys.

"Is everything okay?"

"I am not sure." There was a fair bit of uncertainty in her voice.

"You don't want to go to the game?" he asked, concerned.

She hesitated.

"Did I do something wrong?"

Evily moved into the office. Sean followed.

With a worried look, she inquired, "Won't people see us in the stands? What if more pictures circulate?"

"I've made special arrangements for us to arrive after the game starts. By doing that, it should make us invisible. We will be escorted to the box using the private entrance and elevator. The space is all ours."

"So we don't have to sit in the crowd?"

"Well, not if you don't want to."

A little excited, she confessed, "Truth be told, I've always wanted to see a game at Fenway."

"Oh, yeah?" He was relieved to hear that. "This is a dream I've had since I was a kid. I couldn't pass it up."

Seeing Evily, Leonard walked over to greet her. "Good evening, Ma'am. So happy to see you."

She took hold of his hand in hers and clung tightly. "How are you doing?" She asked.

"Very well, thank you. I still feel what happened yesterday was a dream. I am so thankful. You have an amazing gift." Elated, Leonard explained, "I did what you said. I asked Eleanor to visit me in my dreams, and she did." Tears developed in his eyes.

"I'm so glad." Reaching out to him, she gave him a warm-hearted hug. "Keep your faith strong, Leonard."

"Yes, I will, Ma'am." After he pulled himself together, he announced, "Everyone, please take your seats. Dinner is served."

Hearing him, Sean turned back to Evily. "So, we're good?"

Nodding, she answered. "I suppose so."

The group gathered around the dining table. Sean pulled out Ella and Evily's chairs for them to have a seat before finding his place at the end. Raising his glass, his guests followed in unison.

"Thank you, everyone, for joining me tonight. First off, congratulations to Evan on making the semis tomorrow. Well done, Sir."

Forgetting about the loss, Evan took a bow. "Appreciate that."

"Here's to our last night in Boston and our adventures at the Cape. I have no idea what awaits us there, but I'm excited to visit. Cheers."

"Cheers!" the group said in unison.

That was Leonard's cue.

Each guest removed the domes from their plates, revealing a bright red steamed New England lobster with chips, garlic butter for dipping, and flakey biscuits.

Casually giving out tacky lobster bibs, Sean said, "What? Did you think this dinner was going to be formal? That's not my style, folks."

35

Saturday, July 27th
Boston, Massachusetts

Baseball is a good thing. Always was, always will be. ~ Stephen King

After the East Coast-themed meal, the group parted ways to prepare for the ballgame. Within half an hour, they all met outside Sean's suite before piling in the elevator to descend to the parking garage with Ben leading the way. Tim was waiting in the Escalade XL when they arrived, ready to escort their client and the Anderson family to Fenway. Ivan and David had parked behind him.

When approaching the trucks, the teens jumped in the very back while Sean and their Mom occupied the space in the middle. Once everyone settled in, the caravan left the garage.

Amidst an abundance of conversation from all angles, they made their way to the legendary baseball field. Yielding to fans crossing the road dressed in team colors, Sean leaned forward and explained to Tim that they needed to find Gate E on Lansdowne Street. Ben pointed out the orange cones that came into view when they rounded the next corner. Turning on their emergency flashers, Tim slowed the vehicle to a stop. Rolling down the window, a few security guards spoke to Ben before moving the cones aside for the group. In front of a set of guarded wooden doors, the guys parked the SUVs. Each secured the premises while the Fenway team gathered around to support the Henchmen. Familiar with the routine, Sean watched for the signal. Unsure what to do, the family waited for further instructions.

From the front seat, Ben turned around. "Walk straight inside the building. Stay together. No straying," the security guard advised. Nodding to Sean, he exited the vehicle and opened the door for the actor and Evily to step out, allowing Ella and Evan to escape the back row.

Leaving David with the SUVs, Ben and Ivan took the lead with Fenway security. The teenagers, along with Sean and Evily, closely followed. Tim brought up the rear. Swiftly moving through the entrance and over to the elevators, they soon arrived at the premium suite marked L-24, situated along the third baseline.

The family entered first. Immediately captivated by the sounds coming from the open glass panels, they heard the crack of the bat echoing through the stadium as the crowd cheered.

"Looks like it's 1 - 1 at the top of the third," Evan revealed, checking the monitor on the right-hand side of the room.

The Henchmen moved over to the bar stools lining the glass to scope out their location.

Ella timidly inched her way out onto the balcony. Sean went to check on her.

"What do you think, Ella?' he asked.

"This is amazing. I've never been to a baseball game before. Dad would take Evan to see the Cubs but said it was no place for me."

"Well, I think everyone can enjoy watching a baseball game. Don't you?"

Nodding her head in agreement, offering the brightest smile, she said sweetly, "Thank you for inviting me."

"You're very welcome. If you need anything, don't hesitate to ask, alright? Whatever you want. There's a full snack bar over there and a selection of drinks. Help yourself."

"Okay." She took a seat and marveled at the stadium and all the people.

His heart went out to the young girl.

How could a father deprive her of simply seeing a ball game? he thought. Sean found the author looking over. He wondered if she had overheard their conversation. Approaching, he asked, "So, Ms. Landy? Everything good?"

"Thank you for this. She is so excited. Must admit, I'm feeling quite spoiled right now, too."

"Happy to hear that. It's about time you had a little fun."

Bashfully lowering her head, Evily suddenly heard who was up to bat. Catching the announcement on the television screen, she read the player's name. Jackie Bradley Junior. Initially, she thought the connection to the vanity plate at the arena earlier today was Sean.

"Bradley?" she whispered, recalling the nineteen on the bumper sticker.

Seeing the player step up to the plate, swinging the bat, she checked his jersey number. It was #19. That is when she knew. This was where they needed to be.

"What is it, Evily?" Sean asked, seeing her pleasant reaction.

"Nothing. Nothing at all." She watched Bradley Junior hit a home run and knew there were angels in the outfield tonight.

36

Saturday, July 27th
Boston, Massachusetts

Life throws you curveballs, but you either learn to swerve them or hit them like there is no tomorrow.

~ Sadie Christman

Tucked away in the Marvin Suite, staying out of the public eye for most of the game, Evily and Sean watched from a bar-height table close to the glass. They allowed Evan and Ella to venture out to the stadium seats to immerse in the whole Fenway experience. Tim sat with them while Ben guarded his clients. Ivan stayed close to the main door.

Smack dab in the middle of the eighth while rooting for the Sox, the crowd began to cheer as a cheeky tune flowed through the stadium.

"Sweet Caroline!" Sean said. "Evily, you have to see this."

The two joined the Henchmen and the teens on the balcony. They found all the spectators on their feet for a well-deserved stretch break. Everyone began enthusiastically belting out the lyrics to Neil Diamond's song. It was a sight to behold. Evan and Ella watched the jumbotron and everyone waving, shouting, and dancing. The teens were so happy, clapping and singing along with the fans. Evily thought it was an excellent way to end their time in Boston.

That is when Ella pointed and said, "Hey, Mom! Look! That's us!"

Shocked to see their faces flash across the enormous screen, Evily fearfully retreated inside, horrified by the public spectacle. Sean followed behind her, leaving their group to enjoy the intermission.

"You okay?" he asked, already knowing the answer.

"I thought you said anonymity?" She paced the floor, breathing erratically.

"It'll be fine. It was just for a split second," he explained. "That was not something I could control."

In the background, they could hear the crowd shouting the song's chorus.

"You're not worried?" she questioned, wondering if she was over-reacting.

"We leave for the Cape tomorrow and won't be back here after that. It'll be fine. Trust me."

"I am trying to." Not sure how to explain herself, she said, "Honestly, I'm not used to all the attention. I know it is normal for you. But right now, my life is being disrupted in a way that could have drastic consequences. This could destroy everything." Evily was so panicked she could barely breathe.

Sean didn't fully understand what she meant by that but knew he needed to calm her down.

"I think you're getting ahead of yourself. Look, can we just enjoy the rest of the game? We must leave at the beginning of the ninth, or we'll have to wait until the crowds disperse. I know Evan has to get some rest, so technically, we have only twenty minutes left, give or take."

"Can we go? As much as I want to stay, my priority is to keep my kids safe. I don't want things to get out of hand with thousands of fans in one spot." Frightened, Evily shook her head. Her confidence was slowly decreasing, and a level of insecurity was beginning to surface.

Troubled by her reaction, Sean signaled to Ben without giving it a second thought.

She felt so bad. "I'm so sorry," she said. "I've ruined your evening."

"No, you didn't. It's okay. You're right. We can't let your guard down."

Ben came inside to hear Sean request that he round up the troops.

Grabbing two bags stuffed with Red Sox swag, Sean walked over to Evan and Ella. He could see that they were disappointed about leaving. Passing their gifts along, he said, "These are for you guys."

"All of this is for me?" Ella exclaimed, peeking into the bag filled to the brim.

Sean smiled. "Yes. I hope you like it."

Her face brightened from ear to ear. "That's so nice. Thank you so much."

Evan tried to stay composed and not look too excited. "Wow. Thanks, man. That's awesome. Appreciate it."

"You're very welcome. Glad you enjoyed the game."

Ready to depart, Ben and Ivan stuck close to Evily and Sean while Tim was assigned to protect the teens. Descending in the elevator, they made it to street level. Fenway security created a barrier around them while the group inched through the crowd outside the main doors. Surrounded by flashes from phones lighting up the space around them, Evily tried to emulate Sean's stoic reaction to it all, but she couldn't bring herself to move her hand from blocking her face. Not fazed, he looked straight ahead, owning it, and didn't let the situation control him. Approaching the truck, Ella and Evan got settled in the third row when Ben swung open the door. Once they were secure, Evily slid into the middle seat. Sean sat beside her.

Safely in the confines of the vehicle, thankful for tinted windows, David and Ivan simultaneously pulled away from the curb and drove off down the street, yielding to a few pedestrians crossing the roadway. It was a very quiet trip back to the hotel as a battle raged inside Evily. A list of repercussions for her actions began revealing a series of red flags. Her stomach felt sick.

In the stop-and-go traffic, it took almost forty minutes to return to the Ritz. The Henchmen split up and made a short detour to ensure nobody had followed them.

Listening to the radio, finally pulling into the hotel's underground parking, they heard that the final score of the Red Sox's win over the Yankees was nine to five. Their SUV stopped in front of the doors leading to the elevators while Ivan went ahead and parked. One by one, the group got out and gathered around. Instructed to go upstairs, David secured Sean's suite while Ben, Ivan, and Tim escorted their client and the family to their room.

Standing in front of the elevator doors, Evan said, "At least the Sox had a better day than I did. Thank you for taking us, Sean. Haven't been to a ballgame in a long time."

"Glad you had fun, my man." Taking a chance, Sean asked, "Is it okay if I join your Mom and sister tomorrow? Don't want to miss the semis."

"It's okay with me. Thanks."

"Sure thing. Looking forward to it."

The ride to the tenth floor was quiet. Everyone seemed tired, having had a hectic day. Escorting the family down the hallway, they soon arrived at room number 1006.

"This is us," Evily said, waving her card key over the reader to open the door.

Evan presented his hand to give dap to Sean. Understanding the gesture immediately, Sean grabbed the athlete's raised hand and bumped opposite shoulders before parting.

"Thanks for everything. Tonight was fun," the teen said.

"You're welcome. Get some sleep. Big game tomorrow." Sean was flattered by the male bonding moment.

Ella then stepped forward sweetly. "Thank you for taking us to the game and, oh, for the gift bag, too. Tonight was awesome."

"You're very welcome, Ella."

About to walk into the room, the girl hesitated and turned around. With open arms, she innocently embraced Sean and then left. "Goodnight," she said before disappearing inside the room.

"Night, Ella," he replied, surprised by the unexpected hug.

As she disappeared inside, Evily stayed while the door fell closed.

Security took a walk down the hall to give them some privacy. Nervously slipping his hands into his pockets, Sean stood a few feet from Evily. He felt like they were on their first date, and they'd reached an awkward moment before he had to step forward and kiss her goodnight. His stomach looped at the thought while his mouth went bone dry.

"Look, umm, I hope all this didn't cause you too much stress. It wasn't my intention." He was uneasy. "Just wanted all of you to have some fun."

Evily picked up on his intense emotions, hoping he wouldn't act on them. "I know it came from a good place," she said with great sincerity.

"So, what time do we need to be on the road tomorrow?"

Looking at the ceiling, she tried to remember the details of the schedule.

"The game is at 10:30. We have to be there an hour before. That's 9:30. So that said, I'd say we should aim to leave by at least 8:40. It's a forty-five-minute drive."

"Okay. I'll make sure the guys and I are ready." Pausing a moment, he added, "Want me to drive with you and the kids, or would you prefer if I followed along with the Henchmen?"

"Whatever you like. You can ride with us if you want."

Sean felt temporarily sidetracked from their primary purpose for being there. The lines were blurring, it seemed. Needing to clear the air, the actor asked, "Look, are we...are we good? I know sometimes I come across too strong... Some people don't like it," he rambled on, lowering the tone of his voice, knowing he'd divulged too much.

"Don't worry. We are good. Remember, you should focus on Janie and Ella over the next few days. You've come all this way to hear from them. I can do my part, but you must do yours too."

"I understand."

"I am determined to keep my promise to your girls," Evily confirmed. He nodded.

That conversation left them lost for words.

When she opened the door a crack, she heard the teens inside getting ready for bed. "Thank you for a memorable evening."

"You're welcome. Thanks for joining me."

Evily felt like she had ruined his night entirely with her negativity. At the last second, she turned and said, "You were right, you know. It was nice to get out and do something fun, all things considered." Smiling from ear to ear, she whispered, "So, on that note, goodnight. We will see you in the morning."

"Night, Evily." He raised a steady hand. "Yes, bright and early."

A mix of feelings hit Sean when she walked inside and closed the door. There was this hold she seemed to have on him. A grip he could not sway from, nor did he want to. His heart sank while standing there. Raising his hand, he gently pressed it flat against the room door for a second. Feeling defeated, he lowered his chin to his chest before turning and heading back down the hallway to the Henchmen waiting for him a short distance away.

Little did he know, but Evily had seen what he did through the peep-hole on the other side and felt every bit of emotion radiating from him. The intensity of it made her cry.

Meeting up with the three security guards, Sean was embarrassed at how the evening ended. Unfortunately, the men had witnessed the pretty woman reject him.

"Ben? My man. Do you think she had fun?" he asked, looking for a third-party insight.

"For sure, Sean," he concurred with his famous client. "Absolutely."

"Yeah, I think so too. Well, let's get some sleep, gentlemen. Big day tomorrow. Semi-finals and the Cape. Get ready. It is going to be fun."

Shortly after, Sean and the men reached the twelfth floor. Having discussed tomorrow's schedule while walking down the hall, everyone turned in for the night. The actor declined night duty service to ensure they got a good night's sleep.

The room seemed so empty when he locked up. He hated being alone. It was a feeling that haunted him for years. Pouring a glass of red wine, he walked around the living room and dining room area.

Peering out the window to the night sky above, he said, "Guess I will see you soon, Janie." Glancing over the city, leaning his right arm on the glass window, he suddenly felt a draft. Startled, he looked around. It was like someone had whisked by him.

Where did that come from? He thought, scanning the room. Knowing there couldn't be anyone there, he suddenly caught a familiar scent.

"What is that?" he whispered as the smell lingered.

Intent on finding the source, he noticed it was more concentrated in the center of the room. Searching around, he only saw a white down feather on the floor. Bending to pick it up, he briefly caught the strong floral smell again. But this time, he knew what it was exactly.

"Dior, J'Adore, 1999," he whispered, remembering Janie's favorite perfume.

37

Sunday, July 28th
Boston, Massachusetts

Everything you've ever wanted is on the other side of fear. ~ George Addair

With their suitcases packed, Evily scanned the room while the kids gathered the last of their things. Ready to head down to breakfast at the Artisan Bistro, not having told Sean that was their plan, she opened the door and said, "Okay, guys. Let's get going."

Evan hoisted his equipment bag onto his shoulder. Even with his sticks in hand, the young hockey player managed to squeeze out into the hallway.

Ready to leave, slipping on her backpack, Ella maneuvered both her suitcase and her brother's down the corridor toward the elevators.

Taking one last look around, the Mother of two grabbed her cross-over bag. Fixing the strap across her chest, she did the same with her laptop case. Hearing the constant chime of her phone every thirty seconds, she ignored it while pulling her hair out from under the straps resting on her shoulder. The room door closed behind her once she stepped out into the hall. Swiftly moving to join the kids, she was happy to see Evan had held an elevator for them. Each jostled for space. His equipment bag took up at least half. Intent on packing their luggage in the truck before grabbing something to eat, the doors soon opened at P-1.

Stuffy and humid, they found their truck in the dim parking garage. With a click of a button, the back hatch raised. Each gathered around to pack their things, hoping to maximize the space. Amidst the chaos, Evily heard voices close by. Seeing the Henchmen packing their SUVs, laughing and joking amongst themselves, she knew they would have to pass by them.

After locking the vehicle, she said, "Ready for breakfast?" Met by hungry stares, she said, "Okay. Let's go."

On their way back to the elevators, she saw David, Tim, and Ivan.

They noticed the Anderson family right away.

Both Ella and Evan waved to the guys.

"Good morning, everyone," Ivan said respectfully.

"Morning, Ma'am." David and Tim each followed suit.

"Good Morning, gentlemen," Evily greeted formally. "How are all of you this morning?"

"Very well," Tim said. "And you?"

"We are fine. Thank you. Just heading upstairs to grab some break-fast." Evily could hear their thoughts. Before departing, she said, "I guess we will be seeing you shortly."

"Yes, Ma'am. We will be ready to depart on time," Ivan confirmed.

"Wonderful."

On their way to the elevators, Evily tapped into the Henchmen's conversation. They were surprised that the family had not included Sean in their morning plans.

The author exhaled and heard her phone alert go off again for the hundredth time. Frustrated beyond, she was afraid to look at it.

Arriving at the hostess podium inside the Artisan Bistro, Evily could smell the aromatic smell of eggs and bacon filling the air. She did not see hide nor hair of the Henchmen or Sean at the restaurant. Assuming the star had ordered room service, she felt guilty for not asking him to join them, mainly because he had gone through so much trouble to make their last night in Boston special, regardless of how things ended.

Given a booth to the right of the place, Evily and Ella took a seat to one side while Evan slid in opposite them. Greeting their waitress, the teens and their Mother knew what they wanted to order. Not wasting a minute, Evily informed her of their time constraint. The girl assured them they would be out in under forty minutes.

Evily's device continued to chime.

"What is with your phone? Who is texting you?" Ella asked curiously.

"It's nothing," she said, silencing the ringer. "It's just work."

Casually looking at the notifications, she found a slew of texts from her publicist, Angela, intermixed with countless emails and social media requests from strangers. There were even some messages from people she hadn't spoken to in years, each suddenly declaring they were best friends overnight. Frustrated, she had no choice but to ignore each message and follower request, knowing there was a mountain of damage to repair when they returned to Chicago. Texting back Angela, Evily read her replies. She was imploding with everything going on so early in the morning. That's when she saw a message pop up on the screen out of the blue. The name gave her chills that rolled down her spine. It was one person she never wanted to hear from, but she knew it was just a matter of time.

38

Sunday, July 28th
Boston, Massachusetts

Your life doesn't get better by chance; it gets better by change. ~ Jim Rohn

The streets below were quiet for a Sunday morning while Sean finished packing. Anxious about the next stage of his journey, he knew he would be hearing from his wife and daughter in a few short hours. Everything still felt surreal. Trying to stay positive and not dive into an ocean of doubt, he kept thinking of their visit with anticipation, hoping their connection would be strong enough to open the door between worlds.

He arranged for breakfast to be delivered that morning, hoping Leonard would be there as requested. After witnessing his experience firsthand, Sean wanted to see the man one last time. Wheeling his suitcase toward the front door and rounding the corner, Sean noticed the older gentleman working in the pantry.

"Good morning, Leonard," the actor said happily.

He still seemed to have a bounce in his step. "Good morning, Sir. How are you? Sleep well?"

Not wanting to bore him with his insomnia struggles, he replied, "Yes. Not bad. But, a lot on my mind these days."

"Well, breakfast is awaiting you in the dining room. It arrived a few moments ago. Can I offer you freshly brewed coffee?"

"Yes, that would be great. Appreciate it." Moving along to the table, he had a seat. Wanting to discuss a decision he had made in the early morning hours, Sean said, "So, Leonard."

The butler walked over with an insulated coffee pot and poured him a cup.

"Please sit with me for a second."

Leonard did just that, unsure what was happening. He was not used to interacting with his guests in this manner.

Taking a sip, Sean set the mug down. "I was thinking more about your situation - how you work here to afford the cost of staying in your home."

"Yes, Sir. As long as I am able, I will continue to work. I am determined to live out the rest of my days there, so I will do what is necessary to make that happen."

Wrinkled, the man's face looked a little tired. Sean assumed he had a life full of interesting stories to tell. He wished he had the time to talk with him more.

"Well, I want to help you with that."

"I beg your pardon, Sir. I don't understand." Leonard looked at him, confused.

"What I am trying to say is... I want to give you money to get rid of your debts and pay your taxes on the house - have maintenance done whenever you need it. Maybe hire someone to tend to your gardens." Handing him a card with his contact information written on it, he got up from the table and walked into the office. Returning with a piece of paper and a pen, he added, "Can you write down your full name and address here for me? Put your phone number also. My assistant will be in touch with you to arrange things."

"Sir? I, umm..." Leonard began to shake. He was in shock. "No, no, I can not possibly..."

"I insist. You have left a lasting impression on me. I just want you to enjoy your life and not worry about losing your home. Please let me do this for you." Sean slid the piece of blank paper and a pen in front of him.

His eyes filled with tears as he got up from his chair with open arms. Sean did the same. Embracing him, the actor, in turn, offered a manly pat on the back. "Everything is gonna be okay. Don't worry. I will make sure of that."

He nodded in disbelief, unable to respond. Pulling his handkerchief from his inside pocket, he wiped the tears from his face, trying to control his emotions, failing miserably. Leonard took a deep breath and exhaled before sitting down. Reaching into his jacket, he took out his reading glasses.

Watching him write the information with a shaky hand, Sean called Max to arrange a lump sum payment to start. Taking a blank check from his wallet, he filled it out and handed it to Leonard.

His hand dropped to the table when he saw the amount. "This is too generous." Tears streamed over his cheeks.

Sean could see his worry melting away. It seemed a stress-free life was now within the kind man's grasp.

"I am giving you this money, so you don't have to work unless you want to. Wanting to work and having to work are two very different things."

"But..."

"No, buts."

Sliding his contact information over to Sean, he asked, "How can I ever repay you?"

Sean took a photo of the man's information and sent it to Max. "You can send me a letter once and a while and let me know how you are doing. If I'm ever in Boston, I'll be sure to visit."

"I can certainly do that. I look forward to seeing you again also." Leonard heard the Henchmen at the pantry room door. "Excuse me a moment," he said before going to assist them.

"No problem at all." While lifting the stainless steel dome off his plate of food, Sean's heart felt full. Believing everything happens for a reason, he thought about all the things that had to transpire for them to have met. None of this would have materialized if he hadn't had issues with the photographers and needed to change hotels. Sean felt like things worked out the way they were supposed to. Wondering what the rest of the day would bring while pouring a bit more coffee to warm up his cup, he noticed the room seemed so empty. Recalling the laughter and joy surrounding the table last night, he believed the group felt like a family. Shifting his thoughts to the scent of Janie's perfume, he knew it was a sign of things to come. Within hours, he would be conversing with her and Ella.

"They need to be your priority right now," he whispered, reminding himself of the task at hand. "If not, you will miss out. That's not an option."

Eating quietly, hating the silence, he wished he was at work, surrounded by people and the hustle and bustle of the set. That was where he felt the most at home.

About to finish his last bite, a knock came on the door.

Leonard appeared from the pantry to answer it. Glancing around the corner, he said, "Ben is waiting for you, Mr. Bradley."

"Thank you."

"Absolutely, Sir," he said before going to tidy up.

Taking his coffee cup with him, Sean met the lead Henchman in the foyer.

"Morning, Sean. Sleep well?" the retired navy seal asked.

"Nope. It has become a habit, I'm afraid."

Following his client into the dining room, Sean set the cup down on the table.

"Coffee?" the actor asked the Henchman.

"No, thank you. Just had one."

Ben stood tall with his hands positioned behind his back. "The men are ready to move out when you are. Our bags are in the trucks." Pausing, he added, "Thought you should know, the guys saw the Anderson family doing the same this morning."

"Wait, they haven't left, have they?" An anxiousness fell upon him.

"No, Sir. They returned upstairs. I assume they went for breakfast."

Sean didn't know what to think of that. "Thanks for the update. Appreciate it."

"Sure thing. I'll wait for you in the hall."

"Sounds good. I'll be there momentarily."

Hearing the door close, Sean scoured the large room to ensure he had everything. Going to the office, he packed his laptop and cords before checking the bathroom and bedroom one last time. Strolling through the living room, thoughts of Evily and their conversations still gave him a sense of warmth. Moving past the windows, so did their unexpected embrace. It was something he could not ignore. Even though he didn't want to, given the importance of the next few days, he thought it best to back away from Evily for the time being. It seemed the feelings he was having weren't mutual. Or maybe they were, but Janie and Ella were the reason for her hesitation.

"Besides," he said quietly, "You need to focus all your energy on connecting with them. Nobody else."

Soon, he hoped to get the answers that had plagued his life for so long. God willing, this would bring a bit of closure and peace of mind, knowing that his wife and baby were okay.

Bidding farewell to a room full of memories, carrying each with him, Sean walked over to Leonard, standing by the door.

"Thank you for everything, my friend." Sean reached out his hand to the man.

Shaking it, the only thing Leonard could say was, "Thank you so much, Mr. Bradley."

"Please, from now on, call me Sean," he said, offering a side hug and a pat on the shoulder. "You contact me if you need anything. I mean it. Don't hesitate, okay."

Leonard nodded, lost for words. "Yes, I will. Thank you from the bottom of my heart."

Pointing his way, Sean smiled. "Make sure you write me. I hope to see you again soon."

"I look forward to it." He looked as though he'd lost a million pounds of stress. "Safe travels today."

"Yes, thanks. I hope to have an experience tonight similar to yours."

"Best of luck. I will pray for you." Leonard dried his eyes again.

"Bye for now." Sean opened the door and wheeled his luggage into the hall. There, he found all four men waiting in the wings.

"Morning, gentleman," he announced confidently, turning on the Hollywood charm. "Heading to the Cape today. Are you guys excited about that? Little sun and surf?"

Each offered some casual banter as they walked down the hall to the elevators. The men were glad their client sounded upbeat and did not seem scarred from the night before. Thankfully, the air was light on their way downstairs.

Once on the parking garage level, Ben commandeered his client's suitcase and slid it into the back of the SUV. With the men ready to go, Sean wondered if he should text Evily and confirm their plans for the day. Opting to be patient and wait, he opened the Escalade door and had a seat.

Minutes later, he could hear the sound of happy banter. Confirming it was the family exiting the elevator lobby, he spotted the teens happily heading his way. Evan arrived first, with Ella following close behind. Sean noticed their Mother stayed further back.

"Hey, man. Good morning," Evan said, offering the same dap as before.

"Hello, Anderson family. How are we all doing this morning?" Sean asked.

His sights drifted past the kids to Evily, seemingly hiding behind them.

Ella piped up. "We're good. I had waffles and syrup. My favorite breakfast here. How about you? What did you have?"

"Well, let me see. I had some traditional bacon, eggs, and toast. You know, breakfast of champions." Turning to Evan, he said, "Speaking of champions, ready for the game today?"

"Yeah, for sure. I got a goo,d solid sleep and ate a decent breakfast. Now I'm ready to play."

Evily looked at the time on her phone. "Speaking of that, we'd better get going."

Sean clapped his hands enthusiastically. "Alright, your Mom says it's time to leave. Where are we off to?"

"Marlborough arena," Evily replied.

Pulling up the address on her phone, she passed it along to Ben, who already seemed to know where they were heading.

Sean received mixed signals as the teens moved toward their vehicle parked a few rows over. Making eye contact with Evily, he asked, "So, should I drive with you?"

Already a few steps ahead of him, she turned and replied, "Sure, I don't mind. The kids will probably sleep. At least I'll have someone to talk to."

He knew she wasn't in the best of moods based on her tone. It made him wonder if she was still angry with him for the blow-up on social media or if there was something more to it. The last twenty-four hours were a lot to process. He couldn't blame her for being upset but hoped they could move past it.

On her way over to their SUV to join the kids, not saying a word, Sean sneakily increased his pace to try and catch up to the family. Afraid the entire trip would be a silent one, the actor knew he'd have to tread carefully.

Opening the vehicle remotely, Evily slipped behind the wheel while her children settled in the back.

Sean got in on the passenger side just as she was about to punch in the arena's address. At one point, he was going to ask if she wanted him to drive but quickly abandoned that course of action. Both of them buckled up when the Nav system calculated their route.

"Everybody good?" she asked.

Not receiving a response, she found Evan with earbuds in his ears and Ella sitting with her tablet on her lap and headphones in their usual position. It was almost as if the teens wanted the two of them to talk.

"Guess it's just you and me," she said, putting the truck in reverse.

"Guess so."

Slowly passing the black trucks, Evily waved to all four Henchmen. Sean stayed silent while they climbed the exit ramp. The best thing he could do now was to help her navigate toward the highway. Maybe then, things would lighten up.

Turning left onto the street above, zigzagging over to Tremont, they made a series of turns before merging onto I-90 West. Entering the tunnel running under the city, Sean couldn't take the tension between them. Unsure how to phrase his question, he decided to blurt out the first thing that came to mind.

"Hey, can I ask you something?"

Evily immediately picked up on his complete desperation. She knew he was beating himself up for no reason. The blame fell on her shoulders, and she needed to fix it. "Look, I need to apologize," she said. "You've done nothing wrong. I have a lot on my mind this morning. People from back home are coming out of the woodwork. They've seen the pictures online. That's been a whole ordeal. Those who know me as Evily Anderson have now made a connection to my author pseudonym. And, of course, if they knew me as author Evily Landy, they now know I have children - something I've tried to keep private all these years for obvious reasons. The world is not a kind place. On top of that, I'm no longer writing behind a curtain anymore. I guess you could say I find myself in a pickle, and there's nothing I can do about it. That said, I realize I blew the whistle on your life per se, so maybe this is karma, but given the information from Janie and Ella, I'm not fully convinced that's the case."

Sean understood her frustration. "I'm sorry my presence here has caused all this. Suppose I should have been more careful and tried to stay out of the public eye. I've missed having an ordinary life - a life where nobody knows me. I know I signed up for this - that fame goes hand in hand with losing it all. Guess it was a choice I made. I'm sorry. You shouldn't have to suffer because of it."

This conversation left them at a crossroads. To cut through the lingering silence, the famous actor decided to share his experience from the night before.

"So, I may have had another one of those connection situations with Janie last night."

Surprised, Evily turned to him, intrigued to hear more. "Really?"

"I was thinking about everything that has happened since I arrived in Boston. That is when she came to mind. I felt a cool breeze when I looked out the window over the city."

"Yes, there it is. That's great." The author smiled, knowing he'd made progress.

"Wait, there's more."

"There is?"

"So the Christmas before she passed away, I bought her some Dior perfume. It was a scent that always lingered when she was there – even when she wasn't. After they passed, I left the hospital and returned home. The moment I walked in the front door, the first thing that hit me was her smell. I will never forget it. Last night, the cool breeze had the same scent. I'm not even sure if it is available in stores anymore."

"Amazing. I am happy you are receiving all types of signs. That's very promising. It means the connection you share is strong, and there is a pretty high probability that you'll get to communicate with them tonight."

"You think so?"

"Yes, I do."

Thankful to hear her voice returned to a sincere and uplifting tone, Sean tried to relax and hoped their conversation would continue to go as smoothly. Peering down at the GPS, he noticed they still had almost a thirty-five-minute drive ahead of them. Passing Boston University, Sean saw the Henchmen making a move.

"What are they doing?" Evily asked, concerned about the SUVs boxing them in the front and rear.

"They are creating a convoy perimeter. It's a standard thing."

"Oh..." Evily said, her eyebrows raised, learning something new yet again.

About to hit the outskirts of Boston, the sun was shining brightly.

Out of the blue, she faintly heard her phone ring. Peering down at it in the holder, she saw who it was. Frantically pushing the cancel button to ignore the call, she focused on the road ahead. In seconds, it rang again. This time, she turned the phone off completely.

"Who is that?" Sean queried.

"Umm, nobody important."

He realized she did not want to divulge that information, so he left it alone.

The humidity had reduced due to the storm that had rolled through the day before. Surrounded by shades of green, Sean felt like he could breathe again. Instead of being immersed in a concrete jungle, all he could see were wide open spaces—fields and forests.

Looking forward to the trip to Cape Cod, he asked, "So, what is the town of Dennis like?"

The author's face lit up immediately. "Oh, it is so quaint—lots of mom-and-pop shops. The house is on Corporation Beach. It can get busy in the summer months. There's always a bunch of people around. We usually go to Mayflower Beach on Monday. There are crowds, but everyone is overly distracted by the sun, sand, and ocean to care. Do you ever go to the beach in California?"

"Truthfully, no. Not at all. I do drive along PCH from time to time, though."

In the thick of stop-and-go traffic, Evily concentrated, giving Sean time to think of more conversation topics. Wanting to be prepared, he compiled a list of questions he would ask if Janie and Ella showed up that night.

"Can you run me through the orb visitation process again? I mean, what happened when the girls appeared to you?"

"For me, I know when they are near. I get a chill, then a tingling starts in my chest and works its way out to my hands and feet. This feeling would draw me to the front door, almost like it was pulling me there. Now, that's not to say that this will happen to you. You may have a different experience."

"After you get that feeling, then what?"

Slouching in her seat, she relaxed a little more. "I usually concentrate on the things around me. One time, snow fell, and the wind rustled a few dead leaves on the trees. I concentrate on the sounds of nature, and within minutes, the translucent orbs appear. They generate a hint of light and leave a tiny mist trail that dissipates as they move. While each hovers, I can faintly hear words and sentences. Sometimes, I'm given images and feel emotions. It's almost magical." She paused, giving way to a smirk. "That's if I believed in magic. Which I don't, by the way," she laughed.

The atmosphere lightened.

Effortlessly picking up on his feelings, she added, "Don't be worried. I know it's a strange phenomenon, but believe me, it will be something that will change your perception forever. You will never be the same once you get proof there is a heaven. Your appreciation for life and the world created for us will intensify. Over time, you'll see the intricacy of nature and ponder how difficult it must have been for God to create all of it. It simplifies things, I think."

Sean nodded his head, trying very hard not to be skeptical. The topic was pretty deep. Unfortunately, he didn't have enough knowledge to offer anything in return.

The Henchmen's SUV signaled ahead of them. Evily followed the truck as it merged onto I-495 North toward Marlborough. Content with them leading the way, not needing to overthink it, she enjoyed the drive through the countryside.

39

Sunday, July 28th
Marlborough, Massachusetts

Sometimes, two people have to fall apart to realize how much they need to fall back together.

- Colleen Hoover

Aware they were about ten minutes out, Evily woke up Evan. Still sleepy, he sat up in his seat and stretched while getting his bearings. She was thankful Ella was still watching her movie.

Winding through the rural setting, Ben's SUV stopped at an intersection in front of them. Signaling right, Evily did the same. The New England Sports Center was directly across from them. Driving along Donald Lynch Boulevard, they made a left into the facility.

Sean could see Evan was getting pumped. "Good luck, man," he said.

"Yeah, thanks. It's going to be a tough game. Think we're playing the top-seeded team at the tournament."

Evily pulled into the one-way drop-off lane behind Ben. In front of the main doors, Ivan and David got out and took their positions as Mom and Son met at the back to get his equipment.

"Good Luck, Evan. I'll be praying for you. This tournament has been another stepping stone towards achieving your dreams no matter what happens. Enjoy the ride, okay? Be safe."

"I will. Thanks, Mom. I'll see you inside."

Evan spotted a teammate walking by. When he joined him, the guy looked at Sean in the passenger seat and noticed security at both ends.

Before the player could say anything, she heard her son say, "Yeah, yeah. Don't worry. I'll see if he will come to the change room to meet everybody."

Seeing the teammate's excitement, Evily said a prayer of protection for the players and returned to the driver's seat. "Guess you will be making the rounds after the game. His teammates want to meet you if that's okay?"

"For sure. I can do that."

Ben gave the signal for the guys to get back in the trucks. Moving past the entrance, a few more players met up with Evan. Each watched the caravan slip by them. Parking near a crumbled rock retaining wall at the far end of the lot, Evily turned off the vehicle.

"Are we going inside?" Ella asked, packing her electronics in her backpack.

Spying Ben walking over to Sean's window, he opened his door to speak with him.

The burly man explained, "I'll go inside first. The guys will stay with you. Once I secure the premises, you're free to proceed. I need to check on the arrangements I've made."

"Arrangements? What arrangements?" Evily questioned while the Henchman walked toward the facility.

"Wherever we go, they usually call ahead and have the manager meet them in the foyer. That man will probably have a place for us to sit that is a little more private."

"I thought we were going to try and blend." Evily leaned forward and rested her forehead on the steering wheel.

"Yeah, no. I think we are beyond that in this environment. Hopefully, the Cape will be different for a few days before things go crazy." Sean was so calm about it.

"Are you saying this will continue when we get to the beach house?"

"I'm sorry. All it takes is one photo."

Ella was listening to their conversation. She said, showcasing her solid problem-solving nature, "Why don't we create a disguise that nobody would even remotely believe it was you?" Her voice ended on a high note. "Like, flashy Bermuda shorts, a t-shirt, and a floppy-brimmed beach hat? Maybe white sunblock lines on your face? You're an actor. So, become a new character at the Cape."

Sean sat back in his chair, imagining what Ella had just described. Tilting his head to the side, contemplating what she suggested, he believed that might not be a bad idea. He'd worn worse costumes in his career. How bad could it be?

"Ella, you may have a point," he replied.

"If that doesn't work, you may have to be nocturnal next week and only emerge for the orb sessions at night. Nothing else," the author stated quite concretely.

Right then, Ivan knocked on his client's window.

Giving him the signal, Sean said, "Okay. We can go in now. Ready?"

The young girl quickly got out and shut the door with her backpack in tow. Her Mom grabbed their arena tote, packed with blankets, water, and a heavy sweater for Ella and herself, before locking up.

Intent on staying anonymous, the handsome actor put on his hat and sunglasses and added a black hoodie to his disguise. When they were partway across the parking lot, he flipped the hood over his head.

"You're not going to walk in there like that, are you?" the young girl pointed out.

Confused, Sean asked, "Why? What's wrong with it?"

"Because you look like a criminal," Ella exclaimed without missing a beat.

Shocked by her observation, Sean checked his reflection in the arena's mirrored glass window. Seeing what she described precisely, he said, "Yeah, you're right. No hood."

"Can we just go, please?" Evily blurted, nervous to watch her son's semi-final game today. Sadly, she already knew the outcome.

He got the feeling something was up based on her snappiness. "Would you like me to carry that for you?" Sean asked, reaching to grab Evily's tote.

Not sure what to say, caught off guard, she handed it to him while inching closer to the entrance.

The three moved along, their shadows close behind them in strategic formation. David was the odd man out. He had to remain at the truck in case they needed to leave urgently.

Meeting Ben at the front of the building, the lead Henchman confidently escorted the group inside and introduced them to an older gentleman named Wes. Not aware of the visiting VIP's identity, the man approached with a smile.

"Hey, Wes. We are back," Ben announced.

Most politely, the manager replied, "Very good. Follow me. Right this way."

Wes didn't have to ask who the Henchmen were protecting. The Hollywood star seemed to stand out from the crowd, no matter how hard he tried to blend in.

Climbing the stairs, the man asked Evily, "Is your son playing in the semis today?"

Proud to respond, she replied, "Yes. My son Evan."

"Well, best of luck to him. I look forward to seeing the game."

All eyes were on the group until Wes rounded the corner to a viewing area between Rinks 1 and 3. Positioned at the far end of the ice, the arena staff had designed a VIP room with trade show booth curtains hanging from portable metal frames so they could watch the game in peace, away from the patrons gathered around the restaurants.

"Wow, Wes. This is fantastic," Sean said.

The gentleman nervously chuckled, star-struck by the famous actor standing only feet away.

Sean reached out and offered to shake his hand. "Thank you so much, Sir. Appreciate it. You have no idea."

"Oh," he said bashfully. "We aim to please."

Escorting them inside the space, the Henchmen stayed along the perimeter to stand guard. Inside, Ella found refreshments and packaged snacks, a table set up for her to work on her house design, and three chairs lining the upper glass.

"Well, let me know if you need anything. Ben has my cell number. I'll be around all day."

Evily addressed the man before he walked out. "Thank you for everything. This is really nice of you."

"Oh, you're welcome. Happy to have you folks here."

Recalling Evan's teammates and the thought of having to go to the locker room hallway, Sean asked, "Hey, Wes. Can I ask a small favor?"

"Sure. Anything."

"After the game, is it possible for you to bring the Raiders team here for pictures and autographs? That way, I don't get bombarded by the circus downstairs?"

"Absolutely. No problem. I'll go and give the coach a heads up."

"Thanks. Appreciate it."

"No problem. Enjoy," the gentleman said before stepping outside the curtains.

Ella was so impressed. Setting up her laptop on the table, she said to Sean, "I could get used to this movie star treatment."

Her Mother looked over with a tilt of her head.

"Well, it's true. Isn't it better than sitting out there?"

Seeing all the spectators buzzing around today, Evily agreed. "Yes, I suppose, but...."

"But what? At least we can now watch Evan without looking over our shoulder all the time."

Evily knew she was right.

While the Zamboni systematically moved back and forth to bring the ice to a glass-like state, Evily and Sean settled in to watch Evan's team warm up. Strangely, the mystery centerman was not on the roster. They figured he must have just joined in for only one game.

The music was loud, and the spotlights moved around erratically, making it feel like an NHL game. When the semi-final was about to begin, the teams stood on their blue line for the national anthem before heading to their designated benches.

"Here we go." The author sat down, clenching her hands together tightly. Repeating her prayer, she took a deep breath.

"So, what is the call on this semi-final game?"

The woman lowered her head, "One and O loss, unfortunately."

"No way... Really?" He was surprised.

She closed her eyes and concentrated. "It's the top team. They will hold them back and make them work for the win. That's the main thing."

Sean leaned forward and balanced on the two front legs of the chair. "So, Evan isn't going to score?"

"No, not today."

The game began right on time with a blow of the whistle. Both teams relentlessly chirped at each other and went full-out from the opening face-off. Evily knew it would be a rough period, given the penalties accumulating in the first few minutes. Even the spectator chatter was overwhelming. Preparing for the worst, she could hear some parents from the opposing team urging their boys to 'take out' Evan's teammates. Her blood boiled. To counteract the evil energy, she continuously prayed prayers of protection for the boys.

By the start of the second, it was still a no-goal game. Evan skated out to center ice and secretively shared his strategy with his players before the puck dropped.

After a couple of turnovers, the author watched her son catch a pass up the middle. His wingers flanked both sides for a three-on-two while converging on the opposing defensemen at full speed. Excited, assuming they might score, suddenly, out of nowhere, Evily spotted a player leave the bench and steam-roll across center ice towards Evan.

"No!" she shouted, alarming Sean.

Time stood still as the player maliciously cross-checked her son from behind to bring him down. Helpless, she watched his stick leave his hand in slow motion and witnessed his body fly through the air uncontrollably. Her legs weakened when he landed head-first into the far corner, sprawled awkwardly, mere feet from the boards. Unable to breathe, her hands shook, and her body trembled. Evan was lifeless.

They watched in horror as the team doctor and trainer bolted across the ice to tend to him. The guy who'd inflicted the brutal, illegal hit looked to his father in the stands, proud to see him applaud his execution. Seeing that, Evan's teammates tackled the player responsible. Full of anger, with fists flying, their equipment littered the surface while the crowd kept shouting with the odd obscenity rising above the noise. In seconds, both sides had cleared the benches to join the brawl. Referees acted quickly to control the fight that exploded, sending each team into a separate corner.

Thankful to finally see the referee's hand point to the ruthless player ousting him from the game, Sean turned his attention away from the horrific scene unfolding. He found Evily shaken to the core with tears streaming down her face, silently praying. This made him instinctively wrap her in his arms.

Clinging tightly, Evily fell into him. Afraid for her son, the arena soon went eerily silent when the boy hadn't moved.

"Please, God. Come on, Evan," she whispered, her voice trembling, barely audible over the roaring silence of the arena. "Just move for me."

Holding her, unable to let go, Sean felt his chest tighten when she said that. "He'll be okay," he murmured, almost as much to himself as to her.

Time seemed to crawl as the coaching staff, doctor, and trainer hovered around Evan, their movements careful and calculated as they tended to him.

Hands clenched and knuckles white, her eyes remained locked on the still figure of her son. Then, she saw a slight twitch—a movement so small it might have gone unnoticed. Her breath hitched as Evan's leg shifted.

Sean saw it, too.

Slowly, the player sat up, shaky but upright, under his own power.

Her hands flew to her mouth as relief crashed over her. "Oh, thank God," she gasped, the words breaking apart as she began to cry.

Legs buckling, she nearly collapsed, but Sean steadied her with firm hands and helped her take a seat on the chair. Unsure if his presence could offer anything meaningful, the instinct to comfort her won out. Pulling his chair closer, he placed a hand gently on her back. His touch was light, tentative, but steady enough to convey he wasn't going anywhere.

As her sobs poured out, feeling helpless, she suddenly leaned into him.

Sean hugged her again. "Don't worry. He's good," he whispered. "He's okay."

They both looked down at the ice, where Evan, wincing but determined, was being helped to the bench. Relief flooded through her as the echoing sound of sticks on the ice and boards filled the arena in a show of support for her son.

Exhaling as her body heaved, she turned and sat up, glad to see Ella immersed in her work, not having seen what happened. Returning her attention to Sean, she distanced herself slightly and caught something raw and unspoken in his eyes. Even his embrace, though gentle and concerned, carried an undercurrent of something she couldn't name but felt deeply. About to speak, her lips parted, but nothing came out. Feeling his hand still resting on her back, it radiated a warmth that seeped into her, grounding her amidst the chaos.

"I was worried," he finally said, his voice low and steady, breaking the silence.

"Thank you for, umm..." she started, her voice trembling again, but not from fear.

"You don't have to thank me," he said, leaning closer, his voice almost a whisper. "I don't mind." His hand slid just slightly, his fingers brushing her shoulder.

She nodded upon hearing that. "I know he loves playing this game, but I hate times like this."

"Yes, I can see why. That was intense." Sean's hand slipped away, but the imprint of it lingered, just as the moment between them did.

Feeling an undeniable shift, for a fleeting moment, the terror soon got replaced by a sense of safety—a welcomed connection she hadn't allowed herself to feel in so long. And just like that, a spark ignited in the unlikeliest of circumstances.

But reality intruded as the roar of the crowd surged. Her gaze flicked back to the rink, where Evan now sat on the bench, surrounded by his teammates.

Evan stayed off for two shifts while getting checked by the doctor. He courageously took his place in the line-up minutes later, ready to play again.

Given what just happened, Evily was furious about this.

By the start of the third, it was still 0 - 0. The crowd could tell the players on either side were stressed. A lot was riding on who would win and who would lose. With four minutes remaining, countless shots on goal, and so many turnovers, Evily knew they would not go into over-time despite reading the thoughts of those sitting around them.

The Raiders team showed some fatigue, and the author could feel their exhaustion. While watching the next shift, Evan's defencemen suddenly made a crucial error. Unable to knock down a knee-height, air-borne puck with his stick, it passed him by, allowing an opposing player to take possession. This left their goalie wide open for a breakaway shot. It all happened in seconds. Their opponents scored.

Watching the team's excitement, she wished it was them who were celebrating. "There's the goal," Evily said disappointingly.

"Guess you were right, yet again."

She lowered her chin to her chest. "I wish I wasn't."

"Did you know he was going to get hit?" Sean asked, confused by her reaction and quite surprised she didn't see it coming.

"Yes, just not exactly when or how. I knew it would happen in that far corner, too. When Evan went in that direction, my heart dropped." The author shivered. Feeling a familiar tingle, she wondered if the angels were above them since she'd envisioned her son being more injured. She believed her prayers had helped intervene.

With only seconds left, the time dwindled. Hearing the buzzer signal the end of the game, the opponents rushed onto the ice to celebrate their win. Doing the same, Evan led the Raiders to their goalie for the traditional helmet taps. They had done their best. It just wasn't their day.

The teams lined up opposite each other on the blue lines while they announced the stars of the game. Each stepped forward when the convener called out their name. Cole and Evan both received a medal for their efforts before the teams broke and cleared the ice.

"Well, that's it. Evan will be happy to get to the Cape now for a well-earned rest," the Mother of two said, feeling a sense of relief, taking a seat beside Sean.

Ben entered the VIP space and interrupted their conversation. "Wes will be escorting the team upstairs within a few minutes. Hang tight." Not sure how to phrase his next statement, thinking ahead, the Henchman divulged his exit plan given the news coverage that had poured out of the media that morning. "Sean, in light of our current situation, I wonder if it would be best for Evily to drive solo to her house with the kids. We don't want to compromise her location."

Evily overheard them.

Not wanting her to drive the whole way by herself, Sean understood what Ben was saying. She felt it.

"It's okay if you have to drive with them. I'm used to getting there on my own. The kids and I have to stop at the store to pick up a few groceries anyway. Don't worry. We will be fine."

"Are you sure?" Sean was disappointed but knew it was probably for the best.

"Don't give it a second thought," she said.

One by one, the team began to trickle upstairs.

The moment Evily saw Evan, she walked over and hugged her boy. He tried to assure her he was okay while fighting to loosen her tight embrace in front of his friends. Letting him go, she sat to the side and watched at a distance.

When the young men gathered around for pictures and autographs, Sean's demeanor changed to that of a confident movie star. It was a great way to end the tournament weekend.

Taking her phone out of her bag, she stared at it. Turning the power back on, a string of missed calls and texts from her ex-husband robbed her of the celebratory moment. He was noticeably angry - a feeling that made her cringe. Ignoring it, she turned the phone off again and slipped it into her bag.

Sean happened to see her do that. He wondered who she was trying to avoid.

Ending the team's forty-five minutes of fanfare, Ben had everyone move out. Filing through the crowds of spectators, not stopping, and skillfully guarding their client and the Anderson family, the Henchmen got them back to the parking lot to load up.

Ready to depart for the Cape, the teens slipped into the back seat of their vehicle, assuming Sean was driving with them. Knowing that wasn't the case, Evily went to close the back hatch of their SUV. Glancing over at the action star talking to the Henchmen, she could feel the stress of this game had brought Sean undeniably closer.

He wore his heart on his sleeve, yet beneath it lay a quiet conflict. She could feel his curiosity drawing him into the present, even though he remained tethered to his past.

Seeing her look his way, Sean walked over. "Are you sure you're okay driving there on your own?"

Secretly preferring his company on the trip, Evily smiled to put his mind at ease. "Of course. Like I said, I do this every year," she replied, trying to act casual.

It wasn't hard to feel a mix of emotions off him. She knew he didn't want to separate from them. Strangely, there was this sadness in his soul. It seemed he felt rejected – like the odd man out.

"We'll catch up with you and the guys at the Cape. Text me when you settle in at your place." She hoped he wouldn't worry.

"Will do," he said while the Henchmen pulled the trucks from their parking spots.

Wheeling the SUV around, Ben stopped right beside Sean and Evily. The other two Henchmen were a car length behind. With impeccable timing, Tim got out to open the passenger door for their client. Doing this made Sean feel obligated to leave.

"Alright..." he said with a great deal of hesitation. "Guess I will see you there in a while?"

Evily nodded. "Have a safe drive."

"You too," he said, getting in the back of the vehicle.

Evily waved goodbye before walking around to the driver's side.

Slowly departing, the Hollywood star kept his eyes locked on the family. He watched the author get into the truck and close her door. At the last second, Evan slipped into the front. He hoped the athlete would help his Mother navigate in his absence. With his heart noticeably aching, the caravan left the arena and pulled onto the highway. The Andersons waved to him while backing out of their parking space. Hating that he was leaving them behind, Sean's protective instincts surfaced. Again, he felt a sense of abandonment. Even though they wouldn't be far apart on the way there, he saw the Henchmen picking up the pace. Driving a bit faster, they created a gap between them.

Desperate to clear his mind, he remembered he'd be speaking to Janie and baby Ella later that night. Before long, Sean heard Evily's voice telling him to focus on his wife and daughter. Reclining the seat, he recalled a series of beloved memories but soon got sleepy in the process.

Opting to rest, he knew there was still a lot to do once they got to Corporation Beach. Unsure of what awaited him, he was excited about the impending experience but scared to death at the same time.

40

Sunday, July 28th
Corporation Beach, Massachusetts

A change of scenery can help everything. ~ Drew Pomeranz

The late afternoon sun flickered across Sean's face. Only hearing the sound of the tires hitting the seams on the road rhythmically, he woke to find them perched high above a narrow river. The SUVs were making their way across the Sagamore Bridge, about thirty minutes from their destination. The celebrity took in the incredible view when they hit the peak before starting their descent down the other side. Inevitably, the Andersons crossed his mind. He wondered where she and the kids were. It seemed Ben had increasingly created distance between them to give Evily anonymity. Glancing back, she was nowhere in sight.

Handed an iPad from Tim, he said, "She's not far, Sir. It looks like they are just coming up on the bridge."

Sean spotted a blue dot inching its way along the digital map.

"You're tracking her?" he asked.

"Protocol, Sir, just in case she needs our assistance. We have maintained a one-mile buffer."

Immediately questioning whether tracking the family was ethical, Sean passed the tablet back to Tim. Despite everything, he felt better knowing the guys were watching over them.

With forests of trees lining both sides of the highway, the drive got boring after that. Sean pulled his phone from his pocket and checked in with Sheri and Max. They were happy that the media frenzy had died down since the morning. The only thing that had surfaced was a few of the team's photos taken with him that afternoon. Feeling more confident that their time at the Cape would give him a break from the public eye, Sean exhaled while the weight of his public life lifted, allowing him to breathe better.

Receiving an update on the rental, Max informed him that a property manager would be on-site when they arrived. Quickly locating the house on the map, he wanted to see its proximity to Evily's place. Discovering that the houses were less than a half-mile apart, not far from each other, and right on the beach, he smiled. There was nothing like waking up to the sounds of the ocean.

Sean gazed out at the blur of passing scenery, his mind wandering to thoughts of Janie. He couldn't help but wonder what she'd think of his feelings stirring for Evily. For so long, he'd kept his promise never to let anyone take his wife's place, but the loneliness had grown heavier with time. Meeting Evily had cracked something open in him—a longing he hadn't dared acknowledge. Realizing what he was doing, he shook the thought away, knowing he couldn't get distracted now. Today was about Janie. Letting his memories drift back to the joy they'd shared— the milestones, the laughter, the quiet moments—he found himself clinging to the hope that it might be enough to bridge the distance between their worlds.

The caravan of SUVs veered off the main highway onto a regional road toward the ocean. Surrounded by dunes and seagrass, Sean and the Henchmen arrived at their destination and pulled into the driveway. Taking command, Ben instructed everyone to stay in their vehicles while he met the woman making her way down the steps to greet them.

Patiently waiting in the truck with Tim, he kept his focus on the quiet street ahead. After a short while, the signal came—it was time to move. From his vantage point, he watched as the woman handed Ben a folder, likely containing the Non-Disclosure Agreement Sheri had sent over. Ben flipped through the pages, his sharp gaze ensuring everything checked out.

When Ben returned, keys to the house in hand, they waited a few more moments. Only after the woman's car disappeared down the street did he step out, ready to proceed with the next steps of the plan.

Authorized to move about freely, Tim opened Sean's door. The minute he stepped out of the vehicle onto the sandy driveway, he peered up at the house, thinking it was simple but welcoming. Immediately tasting the saltiness in the air, he climbed the stairs and walked through the open door. Looking about the casually decorated space, he found a wall of windows boasting an expansive view of the waves rolling in from right to left. Sean was in awe. From the living room, he moved out onto the rear balcony. Standing there, he closed his eyes to feel the winds hitting his face. Given the short distance between Anderson's place and his, he thought he could see their house based on her description.

"Max, you did a great job finding this place," he said quietly, thankful for his assistant's help.

Hearing the Henchmen bring in the bags, Sean pulled his phone from his pocket and texted Evily.

We just arrived. I am not far from you.

Taking a snap of his current location, he sent it to her.

Within seconds, her thinking bubbles appeared. It gave off a warmth that was hard to ignore. *Why am I really here?* He thought, feeling a shift in his priorities.

Evily's text popped up.

Perfect. You are super close.

With a break, the bubbles went active again.

We just stopped for groceries and are now on our way to the house. We Should be there in ten minutes. Are you hungry? We usually get lobster rolls from DPM's Grill on the beach the first night.

He texted back.

Sure. That sounds good to me.

Having arranged to meet with the family in thirty minutes, Sean moved inside to let the guys know he would be heading to Evily's place to grab dinner. Ben confirmed his request and implemented a plan for the evening to ensure his safety.

Room by room, Sean checked out the house, moving through the main floor. Upstairs, he found the primary bedroom, with his suitcase resting on the end of the bed. Not sure what to wear, he opened it and pulled out a pair of shorts and a T-shirt, thinking he'd need to do some laundry sooner than later. Loving the ocean view and seeing the sun descending toward the horizon in the west, he was nervous about tonight. Finally, after all these years, he hoped to get answers. So many questions had eaten away at him and caused such resentment and anger. Ready to heal the grief and sadness, he knew his life would change from that day forward. Little did he know how much.

41

Sunday, July 28th
Corporation Beach, Massachusetts

Sometimes, what you want is right in front of you. All you have to do is open your eyes and see it.

~ Meg Cabot

Shadows fell along the dunes while the sun descended in the early evening sky. At the bottom of the stairs behind the house, Sean took in the sights before immersing his bare feet in the cool white sand. Holding his shoes in one hand, he checked his text from Evily. From what he could gather, he was going to the *bend in the beach*, as she described it. That is where they planned to meet up with him.

Sunglasses on, hat covering his face, he walked along the shore with the receding tides, allowing the surf to pull at his ankles. By this time, many beachgoers had retreated to their homes to eat dinner after soaking up the sun's rays most of the day.

Inching closer to the bend, controlling his emotions, he spotted Evily and Ella waving in the distance. Despite the feeling he got upon seeing Evily, he knew they needed to stay neutral for the time being.

"Hey, guys!" Ella shouted, waving her hands about in the air, jumping up and down to grab their attention. "Over here!"

The handsome Sean Bradley strolled closer, sporting the brightest smile. His Henchmen were not far behind. Right away, he noticed that Evan was not with them.

"Hello there," Evily said when he stopped a few feet away.

Happy to reunite with them, a little winded from the walk, he said, "Hi."

"How was the trip?" she asked, excited to share their little slice of heaven.

"Trip was good. It went by pretty fast."

Overlooking the ocean, she said, "So? What do you think?"

"This place is beautiful." Sean scanned the shoreline. Captivated by the waves, he needed to point out the obvious. "You're missing someone. Where's Evan? Is he okay?"

Ella chimed in on that, quickly cutting off her mother. "Evan is exhausted, but he still has the energy to talk to his girlfriend."

Her mother added, "His body hurts a bit too. He thought he'd stay home and rest."

Sean figured he'd be sore.

"Come on. The food is this way!" Ella waved them on, leading the adults up the wooden steps built over the dunes to the DPM Grill.

Standing in line with only a handful of people around, Sean was mindful of his surroundings the entire time. The ladies knew it was uncomfortable for him, so they hurried along and picked up the order they'd called in ahead of time. Receiving the food, Sean offered to carry the take-out bags back to the house.

Approaching a gravel driveway about a hundred feet from the parking lot, contently inching along at a snail's pace, the group passed the first house and carried on to the quaint grey-shingled home.

A few yards away, Sean immediately spotted two rocking chairs on the covered porch. *That must be a nice place to sit and relax,* he thought.

Ella and Evily opened the front door. Before going in, Sean requested that the Henchmen keep a quiet perimeter.

Knowing the two men would be on duty outside, Evily handed out the food she'd ordered them. "Here, guys. These are for you. I hope you like lobster."

"Thank you, Ma'am. Appreciate that," Ben said.

"Yes, thank you, Ma'am," Ivan nodded.

"I have two more for Tim and David. When you return, I'll send them with you."

Ben smiled. "Sure thing, Ma'am."

After taking off their sandy shoes, they walked into the spacious foyer. With honey hardwood floors and wispy beach artwork on the walls, they moved through the house and into the kitchen, where Sean placed the bags on the large island overlooking the water.

Hearing them, Evan came bounding down the stairs, ready to eat. "Hey, Sean. Good to see you."

Welcoming him in the same manly fashion they'd become accustomed to, Evan reached out his hand to Sean, bumping opposite shoulders while Evily took four plates from the cabinet.

"Have you recovered from the game today?" Aware the athlete had endured five straight days of intense hockey, he hoped he was feeling okay.

"Yeah, suppose so. I'm tired and a little sore from the knock today. Won't lie. But I'm lookin' forward to opening my window tonight and sleeping in till eleven."

"I bet. Don't blame you. You've earned it."

"What can I get you to drink, Sean?" Evily took two glasses from the cabinet. "I need a glass of wine."

"Yeah, that sounds good. Thank you."

The kids grabbed their food and headed upstairs to their rooms, leaving Evily and Sean alone. The author set placemats along the island, with a glass of red wine, a lobster roll, and chips at each setting.

"Guess they are happy to be here?"

Now much more relaxed, Evily said, "Yes, I think out of all of our vacations, this is their favorite."

She took a seat next to Sean. "I love waking up to this view every morning. Love the water, the waves. The serenity. Things we don't experience back home."

"The air is amazing. It was the first thing I noticed."

"I know. It's so fresh." Evily took hold of her wine. "I guess I should make a toast?"

"Sure," he said, raising his glass to meet hers.

"To a successful visit with Janie and Ella tonight. May you find the answers you are looking for. Cheers."

"Cheers to that." Looking at the lobster roll, he said, "So, this is good?"

"Yes, it's delicious. I promise it will be something you'll crave when you don't have access to it every day. Might have a few while we're here."

Sean took a bite, as did Evily.

"What do you think?" She grabbed her napkin to dab the corner of her mouth.

Chewing, savoring an abundance of flavors, he said, "Yeah, it's excellent. The bread is super fresh. Love it. Good choice."

The quiet between them felt heavy, the weight of Sean's thoughts on the upcoming orb visitation from his wife and daughter making it hard to find the right words. Evily seemed to sense his apprehension. Gently, she steered the conversation to lighter topics—sharing tidbits about the town of Dennis, nearby attractions, and the story behind building the house. Her voice was steady and warm, filling the silence without pressing too hard. He listened, grateful for her effort, chiming in here and there with comments that felt just enough to keep things flowing.

After dinner, the two moved to the chairs facing the ocean to take in the deep shades of red and orange dusting the sky.

"We have a front-row seat to the best sunsets here."

At a loss, he simply nodded, letting the moment speak for itself. The view was incredible.

Unable to veer away from the actor's anxiousness, Evily thought she should try and put his mind at ease. "Do you want to go over what to expect tonight? I know we've talked about it, but now that you're here, I can show you more so."

Fidgeting, he said, "Yeah, sure. That would be good. Don't know why I'm so nervous. I mean, it's Janie."

Evily got up from her chair and set her glass of wine on the island. "Here, let's do a practice run."

Sean followed her to the foyer of the house.

Turning to him, she explained, "When you arrive around 2:30 am, I'll meet you at the door. We have to leave it open a crack in preparation for their arrival. I will turn the outside lights off, and this area will have a few candles," she pointed out. "I need a hint of light to catch sight of the orbs. We will sit on the floor over here by the closet door and wait."

Nervous, he hesitated before taking a deep breath. "Alright."

"When they show up, I'll translate for you. I may talk in first-person - but I will repeat what Ella and Janie are telling me. At no time will I be referring to myself in the conversation, so think of me as invisible - that the voice you hear is Janie's or Ella's, okay?"

"Okay." Sean looked perplexed.

"You alright? Ready for this?"

"Umm, yeah. I think so. It seems it's taken a long time to get here."

"Well, we've had a busy few days."

The actor nodded.

She got the feeling he wanted to address what was transpiring between them. Knowing it wasn't a good idea, Evily opted to cut their evening short. "So, because I need to get some sleep, I think we should call it a night. I want to have enough energy to read for you."

He was disappointed to hear that but knew the importance of what was happening in a few hours. "Absolutely," he replied.

Opening the front door, the two walked out onto the front porch.

While he put on his shoes, Evily said, "Okay, so I'll see you at 2:30, then? Don't be late."

"Don't worry. I'll be here."

As they were about to leave, Evily said, "Oh! Wait! I almost forgot the guy's sandwiches. One second." Evily jogged to the kitchen and returned with the brown paper bag in hand. "Here you go," she said. "I hope they like it."

"I'm sure they will. Thank you." Sean took hold of the bag and stepped onto the gravel walkway. "I'll see you in a little while."

"Yes, I'll be waiting."

Strolling down the lane, the Henchmen followed their client. Before leaving her street, Sean turned to wave and bid Evily goodbye. She, in turn, did the same.

The guys hung back while Sean went on ahead of them. He now felt weighted again in his thoughts. Deep down, he wasn't sure if he was truly ready for this experience.

42

Sunday, July 28th
Corporation Beach, Massachusetts

Only in the darkness can you see the stars. ~ Martin Luther King Jr.

Late that night, the house seemed too quiet. Sean tossed and turned in bed. The silence was almost deafening. Used to the sounds of the city cascading over his California home, lulling him to sleep, he rolled on his back and stared at the ceiling. The relaxed pace in Cape Cod was hard to accept. He felt antsy like he needed to be somewhere, doing something, learning lines, anything to push him to exhaustion. It was the same feeling he got when he'd return home after a movie wrapped. An idle mind was never a positive thing for him.

Over the years, the actor always kept going from job to job and location to location, wherever they required him to be. He barely took time off between projects to recover before moving on to the next. That worked for him. It was a distraction—a means of keeping him from missing or even thinking of Janie and Ella in the early days. After a while, it just became a hard habit to break.

Tired from the emotional day, he knew he needed sleep. The last thing he wanted was not to be fully awake and alert to hear from the love of his life and his baby girl, a meeting that was now four hours away.

"What message do they have? What is so pressing that they needed to go to such lengths?" he questioned. "In the end, will I finally understand why He took my family from me?"

It was hard to fathom everything that had transpired over the past four days. The entire situation was extraordinary, a series of events that would be unbelievable to most.

Taking Evily's advice, he kept venturing down memory lane. It was crucial to establish a solid connection with the girls if this was to work. He focused on a span of two years. Sadly, that was all that he had with his beautiful wife. Their relationship moved fast, something he believed would happen when he knew he was truly in love. He could never think of spending his life with anyone else but her. That was the reason he remained single all these years. Nobody else had come close to the connection the two of them shared. They could talk about anything and everything without judgment. She knew his many moods and had ways to calm him down, especially when he felt stressed. She gave him space when he needed it but knew when he wanted to be close. Janie loved him for the man he was, regardless of his faults. He missed her being a part of his life. Such happiness she found in the simplest of things. Being with her wasn't at all complicated. In his mind, she was perfect. All these things brought a tear to his eye.

Switching to thoughts of Ella, it seemed her short life disappeared in the blink of an eye. He recalled the months when she was still safely in Janie's tummy. Moving from side to side, kicking against his gentle hand placed on his wife's baby bump, Sean could still see the smile on Janie's face with every magical moment they sat together, anticipating being a family of three. Concentrating on the love for his little girl then, and on the day of her birth, he marveled at her pretty features and ten perfect fingers and toes. Her tiny, lifeless body was so very fragile. She had a head of dark hair like her mother's. Knowing they'd created this beautiful soul was hard to comprehend unless experienced firsthand. There was just this outpouring of love and abundance of joy that erupted.

Thinking more about that fateful day, he recalled arriving at the Emergency Department and Janie immediately getting hooked up to monitors. Sean could still hear the beeping coming from the machines. Seeing the worry on the nurse's faces as they tried to find the baby's heartbeat, he remembered his wife fretting.

"No. Please, don't say it...." Janie said to the nurse.

Based on their silence, he knew there was no sign of life.

When the doctor entered the room, she looked down at the data printed on the long piece of paper hanging from the machine.

"I'm so sorry. There is no heartbeat. We need to do an ultrasound to see what happened. Afterward, I am admitting you to the labor and delivery floor."

Unable to breathe, holding Janie tightly while her body heaved in his arms, all he could do was clutch her tighter when she cried out with a loud shrill.

Recalling hours after having gone through a horrid delivery, the nurses wrapped their baby in a hospital blanket. Cautiously walking over amidst their heart-wrenching pain, his wife bravely wiped her tears and put out her arms to welcome their little one without hesitation. Gently cuddling her, she kissed her forehead and ran her finger along her cheek. Lifting her tiny hand and resting it on her index finger, Janie wished for a miracle. She would've given anything to see her daughter's fingers move slightly. But that was not meant to be.

Even though those moments were the worst of his life, the two of them somehow found beauty in it all. That is when Janie suggested the name Ella.

It suited her, he thought. *It really did.*

Desperate to escape his tragic past while struggling to return to the present, Sean checked his phone and noticed the time was inching by ever so slowly.

Lying in bed for almost two hours, he opened the window, believing the sound of the waves crashing along the shoreline may solve the problem. Met by the ominous rumbling creating a form of white noise, he stood there appreciating the peacefulness.

Imagining what it would be like to have the orbs hovering above him, Sean needed some air. Upon opening the door, he moved onto the balcony and sat on a red bench while the ocean roared. The moonlight sparkled like diamonds on the water further out. Immersed in the elements, it wasn't long before an internal debate erupted about whether there indeed was a God who created all things. That made him question the intricate details of flowers, trees, clouds, sky, sun and moon, rain, snow - the list went on. Such care and attention infused into every speck of life on the planet. Floating on this small piece of the universe made one feel insignificant amongst all the stars in the heavens. A train of thought he'd never considered before. What was happening? Not only was his mind opening up to the possibility of his loved ones being near, but now he was seeing a bigger picture, things he'd never believed in before.

Maybe death isn't the end of life? His mind raced. *Why am I here? What is my purpose on Earth? Was I supposed to accomplish something more meaningful than being famous?* He hoped that Janie might have the answer, that just maybe, she stood before God years ago and was awarded the secrets of life here on Earth and in heaven.

Knowing he wouldn't get any sleep between now and two o'clock, Sean took a shower before leaving for Evily's place. Anticipating the experience but still terrified and extremely uncertain, Sean took a deep breath.

"Everything is going to be okay. You'll see," he whispered, hoping that to be true.

43

Early Hours of Monday, July 29th
Corporation Beach, Massachusetts

Dreams feel real when we're in them. It's only when we wake up that we realize something is actually strange. ~ Leonardo DiCaprio

Minute by minute, Sean impatiently checked the time, anxiously awaiting the moment he'd anticipated for days. Every ounce of him wished he could fast forward the clock and be on his way. Trying to stay calm, something easier said than done, he thought of Janie and the words he wanted to express the most. There was so much to say.

Maybe she will answer my questions without asking, he thought.

With that said, Sean took a deep breath and closed his eyes. Concentrating on their life together, continuing to do as Evily instructed, he happened to doze off.

While the setting sun cast its day-ending light, Sean found himself on the beach in Malibu. It was the exact location where Janie shared the news that they were expecting Ella. Knowing the spot very well, he scanned the shoreline and noticed the figure of a woman dressed in white, cloaked by the sun's rays. Not sure who she was, his heart told him it was her. Moving closer, she turned around. The white gown flowed gracefully in the breeze, and her long brown hair wistfully cascaded over her shoulders. Blinded by the brightness of the light, he circled to the woman's left. His feet sank into the sand while the water swirled around his ankles. Able to focus more clearly, Sean tilted his head slightly upon finding Janie's loving eyes twinkling when she looked up at him.

"Hello, Sean," she said, her mouth not moving when she spoke.

The voice in his head belonged to her. There was no mistaking it. Like time had not passed, the love they shared returned without fail.

"Hello," Sean said, studying the flawlessness of her face. "I've missed you so much."

Stepping forward, he reached for her hands - each glowing, feeling warm and peaceful.

"Close your eyes, Sean."

Again, not saying a word, he did what she asked and held onto her, still feeling the ocean at his feet. His heart lightened, and his breathing slowed. In an instant, an enormous tree appeared in his mind. It glistened and swayed in the breeze. The air filled with a tranquil melody emanating from the golden grass. The feeling was indescribable. Nothing seemed to matter. His life on Earth, at that moment, became a distant memory. One that he neither missed nor wanted back. It was like his soul separated from the world and went to this beautiful place where pain, stress, fatigue, and worry did not exist. Feeling her hands leave him, Sean opened his eyes to find Janie hovering above the sea.

"We will see you soon," she said, gracefully floating further and further away. "I love you, always and forever."

Frantic, Sean waded into the water and tried to follow, but Janie moved towards the sun descending along the horizon. Slowly, he watched her disappear into the light as if it were a portal. A feeling of loneliness overwhelmed him. Now submerged to his shoulders, the waves became rough and treacherous. Surrounded by darkness, knocked over, and tossed about in the currents, desperate for air, his arm suddenly thrust upward through the surf, guiding him to the surface.

Gasping for air, he suddenly took a deep breath and opened his eyes.

44

Early Hours of Monday, July 29th
Corporation Beach, Massachusetts

Faith is believing the things you cannot see are more real than the things you can see. ~ Karen Wheaton

Disoriented, tossing, and turning, he woke to find himself in bed. The waves outside the window crashed thunderously as the winds increased. Sean sat up, still unable to catch his breath. The room was so dark. Slowly distinguishing where he was, he looked around at the chaotic state of the covers, sheets, and pillows. Switching on the side table light, he inched to the edge of the mattress, needing to plant his feet on the floor. He held his head in his hands after shifting his weight forward.

This process is supposed to bring me peace, not pain and fear. Is this normal? He silently asked himself, recalling what Evily had said earlier. Remembering dreams like this often happened after Janie and Ella passed, he knew it took years for him to sleep soundly at night.

"Wait... What time is it?" Sean questioned with a sense of urgency, grabbing his phone, believing he might have slept through his alarm. His heart sank when the numbers illuminated. It was already fifteen minutes after two. Only partially awake, he said, "I need to go."

Pulling himself together and getting somewhat dressed, he snuck downstairs to find Ben on shift, having made the perimeter rounds moments earlier. Playing a game of solitaire on the dining room table, he remained alert. Immediately standing up at the sight of his client, Ben was surprised to find him fully dressed.

"Where are you off to?" he said, knowing he had not arranged anything prior.

"There is something I need to do," Sean replied, not giving him any information.

Unwilling to let Sean out of sight, Ben silently grabbed the keys to the truck and waited for further instructions.

His client clarified, "I need to go alone, man."

"Sorry, Sir. I can't let you do that. They've given me strict orders."

Hearing this, he assumed the production company was protecting its best interest. Angered, Sean was too tired to argue, so he walked outside with Ben close behind. The movie star took a seat in the front passenger side.

"So, I guess it's gonna be that kinda night?" Ben whispered before getting in behind the wheel and starting the engine. "So, where to?" he asked, unsure what was happening.

"Just head to the Andersons."

Ben's eyebrows raised. Surprised, he quickly texted Tim, Ivan, and David and shared the actor's plans before pulling out of the driveway. Ivan immediately responded and got up to take over his shift.

Heading towards the highway, turning right at the end of the lane, he accelerated the vehicle amid the darkness of night. The powerful truck groaned, disturbing the peacefulness around them. Within minutes, they were close to Evily's home.

About to turn down the lane, Sean put out his hand to Ben. "Stop here," he said. "Stay in the beach parking lot. I will let you know when I am ready to go back."

The actor could tell Ben was questioning what was going on but knew he would never ask. Security personnel always have their eyes open. That said, they also know when to turn a blind eye.

Getting out of the truck and gently closing the door, Sean walked the rest of the way to the grey-shingled cottage. The Henchman kept watching to make sure his client arrived safely at the house. When the porch light illuminated, he moved along as instructed.

Upon approaching the front door, Sean found the author waiting for him. The deck boards on the porch creaked when he passed over to step inside. Surprised to see Evily in her black-framed glasses, he liked her hair tied up in a messy bun. Sporting pajamas and a robe, she looked relaxed and cozy.

"I know, I know. I look horrible, right?" she quickly pointed out after reading the expression on his face. Sadly, his thoughts were still dormant.

"No, not at all." To him, it was the opposite. He thought she looked pretty. Wanting to put her mind at ease, he said, "You look very comfortable." Nervously shoving his hands deep into his pockets, he felt a strange energy flow over him.

"Well, I rolled out of bed, still pretty tired. I didn't think I could get dressed and do the whole shebang." The author flung her hands about as if magically waving a wand, believing she might change her appearance. "You know what I mean? Do my make-up and hair, only to return to bed again. Hope that's okay."

"Yeah, that's fine," he chuckled at her explanation. "So, what do you want me to do?" His mind had gone blank.

Picking up on his slight fear, still unable to hear his thoughts, somehow clouded or blocked by a wall between them, Evily said, "We need to get ready. I'm going to turn off the lights now."

He nodded unnervingly.

Scratching a match alongside the matchbox, Evily sparked a flame that cast a subtle glow across the foyer. Lighting a few candles in the space provided a dull, inconspicuous light before she walked over and left the door open a crack.

"Have a seat. I placed a couple of cushions over there."

Sean looked at the pillows on the floor. Doing what she asked of him, he sat down and leaned against the closet door. Her foyer looked eerie. Resting his elbows on his bent knees, he started fidgeting. Evily sat down a couple of feet away.

"So what now?" he asked, prompting for more direction.

"Well, now. We wait."

"Alright…" Sean scanned the room, peering up at the ceiling.

"So, when they arrive, you'll see Janie and Ella's orbs floating around the room like the ones I showed you in the videos. The candlelight makes them easier to spot. I'll have to concentrate on the messages they are sending. You focus on them. The moment they say anything, I will relay it to you. Think of my voice as theirs."

The Hollywood star gave a thumbs-up as he moved his sights to the floor. His heart pumped a mile a minute. He could hardly breathe as his hands shook.

Evily kept an eye on the time. The closer it got to 2:44, she watched for any movement at the doorway. Across the lane, multiple sets of red and yellow eyes appeared in the forest opposite the house. The veil between the spirit world and theirs was thinner than a human hair. It was easy for them to pierce. Unnerved, trying to control the fear the entities imposed upon her, Evily knew she needed to be brave for Janie and Ella tonight. Nothing was going to stop her from helping the Bradley family. Rejecting the ominous feeling, fighting against it, soon the evil eyes disappeared. Relieved, she prayed prayers of protection for the house and everyone in it. A peacefulness fell upon the space. The timing was perfect.

Overwhelmed by silence, something Sean had come to hate the past few hours, Evily asked him, "So, were you able to get a little sleep?"

"No, not really. Couldn't turn my brain off."

"I figured as much. Don't worry; after tonight, you will," she reassured.

"That's good to hear. I'm exhausted."

Evily's attention diverted from him. He held his breath the second she closed her eyes. When they drifted open again, she checked the time, unable to feel a presence nearby.

"Did you do what I said? You know, try to reconnect with them?"

"Yes." Sean bluntly stated.

Tilting her head, Evily looked his way, not entirely convinced.

"Look, before becoming here, I had this dream." Sean stopped himself. "Well, I don't know if it was a dream or something else. Regardless, it focused on one memory Janie and I shared years ago, but it was more than that." He decided to spare her the intricate details.

"Well, then, that is a good sign."

"Maybe they aren't coming?" Sean questioned with a hint of doubt.

"No, don't say that. I promise they'll be here." She was so sure.

A cool breeze wafted through the door, swinging it open an extra foot. Tightly closing her robe around her neck, Evily focused as that all-too-familiar tingle ran down her spine and into her hands and feet, making her shiver.

Seeing his breath, it was as if they were standing outside in the dead of winter. The hair stood up on the back of his neck. His arms and legs were prickly.

With attention drawn upward, the author asked out loud, "Janie? Ella?"

His heart skipped a beat upon hearing their names.

A bit of movement caught the light emanating from the candles. Sean sat up and pressed his back tight against the door while looking around, losing sight of whatever it was. His hands melded flat to the floorboards. Instantly, a tiny circular orb swooped down and floated playfully about the room – dipping and diving. His eyes widened when it abruptly halted mere inches from his face. He froze, unable to move a muscle.

Evily whispered, "Sean, meet baby Ella."

Flooded with emotions, the actor marveled at the tiny object calmly moving back a few inches, seemingly giving him space. Thousands of crisp, glistening particles swirled inside the orb, creating a marbled pattern. It was like he was seeing the vibrance of Ella's soul.

"I'm going to talk for her now." Evily's eyes remained closed so she could concentrate.

All he could do was nod at the author sitting cross-legged on the pillow, exuding such peacefulness after glancing his way.

"Hi, Daddy," Evily relayed in a soft voice. "You made it."

Barely breathing, he quickly rubbed away the tears pooling in his eyes before they could fall across his cheeks. All it took was one word he'd longed to hear all these years.

"It's okay. Don't be sad," the actor heard Evily say. "Mommy will be here in a second. She takes longer than me."

He was mesmerized by what was transpiring and reminded himself to be strong for them.

Was it indeed her? Was it Ella? he thought.

Mustering the courage to respond, he could barely squeeze out the words he'd always wanted to say.

"How is my sweet girl?"

The tiny orb moved around fleetingly here and there, overly excited by his statement.

Evily spoke. "I'm good. Mommy and I are good. We miss you."

Tears streamed down his face. His heart ached for the little girl he could only hold for a few hours. Her life was cut short through no fault of her own.

"I miss both of you so much," he said, feeling a strange calm overtake him. Almost every ounce of fear his body encompassed instantly faded away. "Please tell me one thing."

Ella's orb swirled about in front of him. "Anything." Evily relayed the word.

"Are you and your Mommy in heaven?"

"Of course, silly. But we don't call it that. To us, it is home. It's so lovely, Daddy. When you join us one day, I will have many things to show you. The tree. The grass. The light. The golden city. It's all so beautiful."

Before he could respond, another cool breeze blew through the gap in the doorway. They watched a larger orb arrive, identical to Ella's, with a hint of blue shining brightly amidst the glimmering particles swirling inside.

"Look, Mommy! It's Daddy! He made it. He's here." Evily whispered, switching to repeat Janie's words. "She says, Hello, my love."

Unable to produce a sound, Sean's eyes welled, and his heart ached for the love of his life. Needing to hinder his gasps, he found it difficult to take in air. Evily reached over and gently grabbed hold of his forearm. Almost like she'd thrown him a lifeline, the author intermittently clenched it tighter, trying to offset the rush of tremendous euphoria invading his senses. What she did helped him stay grounded.

Feeling the pain in his heart, Evily said on Janie's behalf, "I am so sorry I'm not there. I know you feel that Ella and I abandoned you. Please know we didn't. We didn't, my love. We have always been with you. Every step of the way, we've watched over you."

With a pause, Evily focused on Janie.

"Every time you feel a breeze hit your cheek or see the most beautiful spark at the last second before the sun fully sets, it is us. A rainbow after a storm or butterflies frolicking in the wind gusts, we are there."

Sean nodded, wondering how often he hadn't noticed the signs they had sent his way.

While the two orbs hovered in the middle of the room, Janie said through Evily, "You don't have to be afraid of the night. The white figures you see out are not evil, nor are they ghosts. Sean, throughout your life, you've had many people protecting you. Mikey is one of them."

The blood seemingly drained from Sean's face when he heard his best friend's name.

"Mikey's there?"

"Yes. One of the many people you know. Bernard is so young and mobile now. He is no longer suffering." Janie's voice went quiet.

Evily concentrated with eyes closed.

"She's showing me a glass enclosure with a hint of sunlight. Inside are two rose bushes. One pink and the other white."

Not knowing if it had meaning, she waited to receive confirmation from Sean.

"I planted those at the house after they passed, believing I'd greet them every morning to keep their memory alive. Sadly, it was a constant reminder they were gone."

"The plants died?" Evily questioned, having seen the two rose bushes wilting in front of her, turning brown, withering to dust.

A tremendous amount of guilt poured over Sean upon hearing that.

"It's okay. You needed to let go to continue living, but we have never left you." Evily's voice sounded like Janie's.

He stared at the orbs in bewilderment.

"You feel our presence, don't you? In the house? We visit now and again, but it scares you."

Sean agreed, unable to say a word.

"You must not be fearful," the voice said.

Silence filled the room. Evily shifted slightly on her pillow. Still holding Sean's forearm, she focused on what they were saying.

"Ella wishes to share the details of her departure. Something that's weighed heavily on your heart all these years."

Concerned about what she would reveal, the actor recalled what happened that fateful day. He felt responsible for Ella's death since he tried to calm Janie's fears when she felt something was wrong that morning. She still had five weeks to go. It was too soon. Not heading to the hospital right away, Janie went to lie down, hoping things would improve. Waking in a panic, feeling a lack of movement in her belly, Janie called her doctor's office. They told her to go straight to the emergency department. The look of fear on Janie's face had etched in his memory. Something he never forgot - that and her devastating cries when they told them their baby was gone.

Evily suddenly explained, "Ella says I passed away in the womb. In the Great Book, it said that my life would not go beyond that. A beautiful angel held me safely in her arms when my heart failed. She had long golden hair and delicate features. All dressed in a flowing iridescent gown with intricate wings; the feathers had flecks of gold. She spoke to me without voicing a word and held me close while we stood in the *in-between.*"

"What...What is the *in-between*?" Sean barely verbalized, never having heard the term.

Waiting for Baby Ella's response, she heard her say ominously, "It's a dark place before you fly up. Bad things live there."

His protective instinct surfaced. He felt the overwhelming need to keep his daughter safe from danger, all the while wishing he could have been there for her.

"The angel let me watch you from the other side. You held Mommy so tightly after I was born. The room was silent when they placed my body in her arms. I could feel your love flow through me. Looking up at the angel, she said we were waiting for one more person to join us."

Janie's orb descended to Sean's eye level.

Diverting her attention from baby Ella to Janie, Evily heard her words and explained, "After having Ella, I felt my body wasn't right. It felt weak. Numb. I thought it was the stress of giving birth and losing our baby, but when the headache and numbness got more intense, I knew something was wrong. When they rushed me to the imaging department, I remember my body floating above the gurney. That is when I realized I was not going to make it. Transferred to the MRI machine moments later, I went limp. My body gasped for small breaths of air. Quickly bringing me out of the machine, there was a lot of commotion. They knew I was gone. Hovering above them, I watched the medical staff try and revive me. In my peripheral, I noticed someone standing in the far corner of the room. It was an angel holding Ella. Affixed on our baby's bright eyes, I turned away from my life and reached out. While cuddling her, I heard the doctors in the room call out my time of death. With Ella safe in my arms, the angel took us away. We moved upward through the stars. I felt my connection to you slowly fade, but the love we shared remained strong. Arriving in a world no earthly imagination could ever conjure or describe, we started anew in the afterlife."

With a pause, the orbs floated around the room.

"I am sorry we left you to live life alone. All these years, we've never been far away. We were there when you had your accident and were lying on the road, severely injured and suffering from shock. Unable to remember what had happened, trying to call out for help, you thought it was your time to die. Something that seemed welcomed, almost anticipated, given your state of mind. You had accepted your fate but heard a voice emanating from the sky. That was us, Sean. We watched over you and protected you until help arrived. You were never alone."

The actor nodded, knowing everything she said was true.

"We all make mistakes," Evily explained on Janie's behalf. "The accident that night was a product of evil. Desperation and loneliness caused this error in judgment. You hit rock bottom - the lowest point in your life. A moment of weakness that needed to happen. In the end, you learned life was precious and worthwhile. That experience changed you."

Staying quiet during Janie's communications, he sat on the floor staring at the orb, reliving every detail she shared with much sadness.

Without warning, another frigid breeze wafted through the gap in the door, flinging it open wide. The forceful presence entered the room in the form of thousands of particles flying in unison, swirling about, with a bright white center core.

Shielding their eyes, Evily let go of Sean's arm. Immediately closing her robe tightly to guard against the cold, a shiver rolled down her spine.

The particles quickly formed an orb. The presence had breached the doorway between the two worlds. Not welcome; it was much bigger and brighter than Janie and Ella's souls. Suddenly, it stopped in the middle of the room. Steady and calm, the girls moved aside, visibly willing to let it speak.

The author repeated what she heard. "He says he's glad you didn't become a television puppet? You stayed true to film." Confused, she added, "Does that mean something to you?'

The statement struck a chord with Sean. The emotion that erupted from that one line was overwhelming.

He whispered, "Mikey?"

"He says, Man, you got old."

Recalling his best friend's ability to tell it the way it is unapologetically, Sean nodded his head. "Yeah. Suppose so."

In an attempt to understand what was said, Evily relayed his messages. "He wants to continue with this evening's theme of departures, if that's alright. He says, even if you say no, I'm going to share what I need to, regardless."

The actor recognized the familiar taunts from years past. He whispered to the orb, not holding back, "Did you do it? Did you do what they said?"

Confused, Evily did not know how to make sense of Mikey's response. "He says he took the cup, not the poison."

"Mikey? Just tell me." He was desperate to know the truth and was not in the mood to decipher his classic cryptic messages.

"Those people behind the curtain didn't like my ideologies. My strong convictions deemed me a threat that needed silencing. They knew what I was capable of accomplishing. Fame and conviction is a deadly combination."

"Did you do it, Mikey?"

Upon hearing the next obscure statement, the author didn't know what to make of it. To her knowledge, he was a spiritual entity.

"He says the serpent always wins the souls of the tormented. This doesn't make sense, Sean. His presence is heaven-sent, not demonic. How did the serpent win his soul?"

Sean knew what his friend meant. Years ago, Hollywood stars paid their dues before becoming famous- sometimes in unthinkable ways.

Listening to the strong presence, Evily clarified, "My death was harder for those who witnessed it. I was unaware of what was happening or why - I figured someone had slipped something into my drink. As I fell to the pavement, a bright light appeared. For the first time in years, I felt nothing but peace. I was free from it all. And I felt loved, you know, the purest love, like nothing I'd ever experienced in my lifetime. So many adoring fans, and I never felt anything like this. It was hard to resist, man, so I went. My departure paved the way for others to succeed in my place. Those people kept my spirit alive for a time. That includes you."

"I miss you, brother."

Sean found it hard to contain his emotions.

"I miss you every day," Evily said. "Please don't be afraid of death. I know it terrifies you. On Earth, everyone is simply passing through. Your real home is not there. Life is a test to see who comes out the other side, having learned, fostered, and loved. Live your life, Sean. We will see each other soon. But not too soon."

His orb floated to the ceiling, then over to his girls.

"Mikey thanked them for letting him say his piece," she verbally confirmed.

Disappearing as fast as he arrived, leaving a trail of misty particles lingering in the space, Janie and Ella's souls moved toward Sean. They were now fading, and their energy had visibly lessened.

"They have to go now," Evily voiced quietly. "We'll be back. There is more to say."

Ella's orb came close to Sean. He could see all the sparkles inside it, carrying the essence of his little girl.

"Ella says, don't worry, Daddy. Everything is going to be fine. You've got...Evily now." The author paused halfway through that sentence, wondering what she meant.

The two watched the orbs slide out through the front door. A misty trail followed, dissipating seconds later. Evily stood up and closed it behind them. When she turned around, she saw Sean sitting against the closet, elbows supported by his knees, his hands dangling limply.

"Are you okay?" she asked. "I know this is a lot to take in."

"I, umm, don't know what to say. It feels like what I just witnessed was a dream just now. Was that real?" He stared straight ahead and did not make eye contact with her.

"You weren't dreaming. It was real. Now you see what I've been trying to explain this whole time."

"Yeah..."

Feeling a hint of pessimism from him, Evily questioned, "Why are you angry?"

"I'm not angry." He stopped and thought for a second. "Years ago, I figured I had come to terms with their deaths. The grief never leaves, mind you, but I felt like I was kind of in a place where I accepted it and could try and move on. Now, all of this has dredged up those feelings again." Tears developed in his eyes. "I mean, she called me Daddy. Did you hear that? You know how long I've wanted to hear that word. Never thought I ever would."

Evily needed to comfort him. Ignoring everything, she had a seat on the floor beside the actor. Reaching out, she put her arm around his shoulders, hoping it would help lessen the pain.

Out of the blue, he dried his eyes and said in a monotone voice, "I should get back to my place." Getting up from the cushion, he stood in a zombie-like state. "Not sure if this was a good idea."

Evily also had second thoughts. She figured the agony of his experience tonight had inflicted additional wounds - the unhealable kind.

He slowly walked out the door and continued down the laneway without saying another word. Evily watched the SUV pull up beside him. Getting in, it then drove off into the night.

Troubled by what happened, the author returned to her room and slipped into bed, placing her glasses on the side table. While trying to fall asleep, she could feel his restlessness and sheer grief. His fight or flight was very strong. She was sure he was debating whether or not to return to Los Angeles in the morning. But could not confirm it. All she knew was that their endeavors finished for tonight but were far from over.

Monday, July 29th
Corporation Beach, Massachusetts

There are far, far better things ahead than any we leave behind. ~ *C.S. Lewis*

Bright and early, Evily woke just before eight o'clock to prepare for the day. With hair re-tied in a ponytail and light makeup enhancing her face, she slipped on some workout wear, hoping to take a walk along the beach before the kids got up. The saltiness in the air and the peacefulness of Cape Cod mornings always fueled her soul.

Heading downstairs, rounding the corner to the kitchen, she grabbed a coffee mug from the cupboard before placing a pod in the machine. After pressing the start button, her sights moved to the view out the window. Along the breakwater, she saw a man sitting on the rocks. He was staring out over the ocean, amazed by the forcefulness of the waves. To her surprise, it was Sean.

Happy he had decided to stay and not return to California, she kept a close eye on him. Still unable to read his thoughts, only empathically grasping hints of emotion off him from time to time, Evily needed to see if he was okay. As the coffee machine finished its cycle, she left the steaming cup behind and put on her flip-flops. Wrapping herself in a sweater, the author quickly headed to the shore.

Sean had not moved an inch. Unsure what to do or say, she stood and waited for him to turn and find her there. The last thing she wanted to do was startle him.

Feeling like someone was watching, the handsome man glanced to his left, then right. Spotting a figure lurking, he swung around with a sudden jolt. Relieved that it was Evily, he stared with a blank expression.

"I thought I wouldn't see you this morning," she stated, pulling the chunky knit tightly around her.

"How did you know?" Realizing who he was talking to, he lowered his head and clarified, "The thought had crossed my mind. I was going to leave last night but couldn't. I need to know more despite the pain it's causing."

Understanding his position, knowing this was far from easy, she smiled. "Alright. We can arrange that." Approaching, having a seat on a boulder beside him, she said, "So that you know - they may not return tonight. It takes a lot to manifest themselves. In the past six months, they've returned thirteen times. Given how long you waited for this, I think they'll make another attempt soon, especially because your time here is limited."

"Hope you're right," Sean whispered. "Hey, can I ask you something?"

"Sure. Anything."

"Janie never said if they were there when the doctors told me."

"Told you what?" she asked, needing clarification.

"That she had died too – that I had lost my wife and daughter all in one day."

Those words hit Evily hard while Sean thought about the makings of that slow-moving moment in time.

"I was still in Janie's private room waiting for her to return from the MRI. Standing in front of Ella's tiny body lying in the small bassinet, I studied her features, hoping never to forget what she looked like. They had a cooling mat underneath her, so I wasn't permitted to pick her up."

The waves roared towards the shore. Looking at the clouds floating through the sky above them, Sean described the aftermath of that terrible day.

"The doctor who was supposed to save Janie entered the room and said, *Mr. Bradley? Moments ago, your wife suffered a brain aneurysm. The root cause is a weakened blood vessel that enlarges and fills with blood. As a result, it bulges. Based on the severity, I assume it was sizeable in nature before it burst. I am so sorry. There was nothing we could do. My deepest sympathies for the loss you've endured today.*" Sean sighed as that memory resonated. "You know, right then, I wondered if she was there. If they both were, or if I was alone?" He lowered his head sorrowfully. "On top of it all, that doctor had the nerve to ask if I needed to speak to someone. He wanted to arrange a meeting with a grief counselor. He also asked if he could call a family member on my behalf. If I wanted anyone with me? The only thing I could say was - *I want to see my wife.* The man nodded and said, *please, come with me.* Picking up Ella, I carried her with us to where Janie was. The doctor pulled back the sheet and elevated her head on the gurney." Sean didn't know if he could go on. Sights glued to the horizon, hearing the gulls screeching overhead, he said, "I set Ella in Janie's arms. That is where she needed to be. Resting my hand gently on my wife's forehead, she already felt cold. Leaning down to her ear, I told her I loved her."

Evily cried while hearing the story. She wiped the tears away with her fingertips when they fell, not wishing to interrupt him. She could feel a weight lifted with every word he shared.

"I stayed with them for a few hours. Soon, the doctors came in and said they needed to process their bodies. I didn't want to leave but had no choice. Walking out of the hospital later that day was surreal. I went in with all these hopes and dreams for the future. All of which included a wife and a baby on the way. I left many hours later alone - a broken man. When I reached my vehicle, I got in and started the engine. That is when I lost it. Every part of me exploded with anger. I wanted them back so badly. No money or fame in the world could do that. I don't know how long I stayed there before I drove home. It was all a blur to me from that point on until days after the funeral. It seemed I just went through the motions. Numb. Lifeless. A shell of a person with nothing to live for now." Turning to Evily, finding her emotionally distraught, he said, "From there, you know the rest."

Evily nodded. Reaching out to him, grasping hold of his arm, she said, "I'm so sorry."

"Never told that to anyone. Not one person."

"Thank you for confiding in me," she said.

While scanning the water, he nodded his head. "Wow, I guess I know how to ruin a sunny day."

"You didn't ruin it," she replied hastily. "A big part of this is processing your unresolved feelings, maybe releasing any deeply-rooted resentment. Letting go of the anger. Do you feel lighter having shared that?"

Sean thought a minute. "Suppose so. Nice that it is no longer a dark secret of mine. Talking about it helps a little."

Wanting to shift his mind in a more positive direction, she asked, "Hey, would you like a cup of coffee?"

Turning to her, he solemnly replied, "That would be great."

"Where are the henchmen?" Evily said while standing on the large boulder, not seeing a protection agent anywhere.

Sean shrugged his shoulders. "Don't know. I'm sure they will find me shortly. I kind of snuck away. Needed a break."

The two walked towards the house, the sun shining brightly. When it peeked out from behind the clouds, Evily thought it would be a perfect beach day if the sky ever fully cleared.

Glancing over at him, she could easily see Sean hadn't slept a wink. He seemed withdrawn and distant. "Guess you didn't get any sleep at all?"

"No. It's not like I didn't try. The conversations with Janie, Ella, and Mike kept replaying through my mind. Still can't believe it."

Evily spotted Ivan pulling into her laneway a few yards from them.

"You know, Ella calling me *Daddy* haunted me last night. That has got to be the best word in the world. Wish I could hear it every day."

Arriving back at the house, acknowledging Ivan on the way past the truck, the two offered only a wave to him. Evily opened the front door. Removing her sandy shoes before walking inside, Sean did the same, leaving them on the front porch.

Now bare feet, she said, "Come on in."

Moving through into the kitchen, she pulled a mug from the cupboard. Setting it on the black granite counter, noticing her coffee was now cold, she took it off the machine and placed it in the microwave to warm it up before starting a fresh brew for him.

"All I have is bold. Is that okay?"

"Sure. I need a pick-me-up anyway."

The author placed the pod in the machine, punched the lid over it, and pressed the button. Starting its cycle, she asked, "Cream and sugar?"

"Think I'll decline both this morning. Thanks."

Sean sat on a barstool and looked out over the ocean through the panorama of windows.

"Want to talk about it more, or do you need a break?" Evily questioned, seeing him deep in thought.

Turning to her, he asked, "You already know, don't you?"

His coffee finished brewing. Placing the steaming cup in front of him, Evily contemplated what she should say. "So that you know, I've been cut off from your thoughts since the rainbow incident. I only feel emotion off you now and try to gather what I can from that."

"For sure, no more mind-reading?"

"Nope. No more mind-reading," she confirmed, taking her mug from the microwave.

"That explains a lot."

Evily looked his way, knowing he'd noticed a change. "What do you mean?" she said.

"Saturday morning, when you came to my suite, you were..."

"Unravelling. I know. Apologize for that." Evily was embarrassed by her behavior.

Sean recalled the thoughts that had crossed his mind and the revelation that abounded from that conversation. "No, that's not it. What I mean is, you didn't pick up on what I was thinking."

Not wanting to let on, she'd felt his emotions and made a few assumptions; Evily decided to answer, "No. There was nothing."

While sipping his coffee, she'd sat down on a barstool a few feet away. "Do you think you can handle another visitation?" she wondered, knowing how difficult it was.

He glanced over at her with an abundance of uncertainty. "I'll have to. I can only stay until Wednesday."

"Are you sure you can't extend it?" A part of her wished that he would.

"No, I can't. The premiere is Thursday night. I need to walk the carpet. Contractual obligations, you know."

"Right." Evily realized their time together was dwindling.

"Believe me. I don't feel like putting on a smiley face for the cameras." Sean still seemed defeated in a way. Almost solemn.

"Maybe you should approach it differently. Change your mindset."

Not sure what she was getting at, he asked, "What do you mean?"

"If you think negatively about it, a dark cloud will hang over you that evening. But if you intend to enjoy the event, it won't seem so bad."

Sean smirked, believing she sounded more and more like his agent, Sheri. "You're right. I have to be professional and get the job done. The last thing I want to do is disappoint the fans."

Happy to hear his response, Evily recalled having to do something very similar. She referred to it as *smoke and mirrors*. Expected to attend functions with her husband, Peter, she would style her hair, put on makeup, and get dressed nicely. The epitome of the perfect wife. She always smiled and played the part well. Nobody in her inner circle knew that her life was falling apart. For years, she was the master of disguise. Deciding not to share these private thoughts, she said, "When your star-studded night is over, you can return home, relax, and be proud of what you had to overcome to be there. I promise you will feel a strong sense of accomplishment."

"Good point."

Silence fell upon the two of them. Hitting a lull in the conversation, Sean finished the last of his coffee. Exhausted, hitting the proverbial wall, he felt like he could sleep now.

"Look, I'm going to head back to the house and try and get some rest."

Evily stood up to take their cups to the sink. "I think that is a wise idea. Just FYI, in case you are interested in joining us, the kids and I are going to Mayflower Beach around one o'clock."

"Alright. I'll think about it."

"Text me later, then? We will wait to hear from you."

Sean got up from his chair. "I will. Thank you for the coffee."

"Absolutely. Anytime."

On his way to the front door, Evily followed him outside onto the porch, where he slid on his running shoes.

Before leaving, he said, "Maybe I'll see you guys after then."

"Sounds good."

Nodding, the author watched him walk over to Ivan. The two spoke briefly before Sean slowly walked down the laneway, followed by Ivan in the truck. Seeing the actor turn left on the road while Ivan turned right, Evily quickly went inside. Continuing to the seating area at the back of the house, she kept an eye on Sean while he meandered down the beach to where the guys met him halfway. Not seeing the transformation she anticipated, Evily questioned the whole process.

Maybe I didn't prepare him enough? Or is he too broken?

Feeling it was her fault, she said, "What have I done to this poor man?"

46

Monday, July 29th
Corporation / Mayflower Beach, Massachusetts

At the beach, life is different. Time doesn't move hour to hour but mood to moment. We live by the currents, plan by the tides, and follow the sun. ~ Sandy Gringas

That morning, after Sean left, Evily kept busy. She decided to wash a load of laundry and edit a few chapters of her newest book while the kids slept, but it wasn't easy to concentrate. Sitting in the dining room, her conversation with Sean that morning resonated. She wondered how she could help him through this ordeal.

Why did Janie and Ella want him here in the first place? What did they need to say to him? She couldn't quiet her mind. *There is always a reason why spirits manifest for the living.*

Continuing her work, Evily attempted to stay focused and not sway from the task at hand. She opened her notebooks and began to type, believing she had about an hour before their day officially began.

To her surprise, before eleven o'clock, the author could hear her children rustling about upstairs. Quickly finishing the last chapter, she saved the pages and closed the laptop before heading upstairs to bid them good morning.

Reaching the landing on the second floor, she peeked into Ella's room and found her texting with a friend. With a quick wave of her hand, continuing to type, she said, "Morning, Mom."

"Morning, Sweetie. Sleep well?"

She nodded and giggled while reading another incoming text.

Across the hall, Evan's room was empty. Hearing muffled music, she knew he was already in the shower.

In vacation mode, ready to change into beachy attire, Evily went to her room and selected a navy one-piece. Slipping it on, she added a light, airy white coverup and headed back downstairs to make the kids breakfast.

It wasn't long before Ella and Evan swooped into the kitchen. They could not resist the heavenly aroma of their Mother's famous French toast.

Excited about spending the afternoon by the water, having enjoyed a leisurely start to the morning and an abundance of conversation, the kids helped her clean up before heading out.

Fully expecting to venture over to Mayflower Beach without their Hollywood friend, a part of her was disappointed he wouldn't be joining them. It had been nice to have someone around to talk to when the kids retreated into their own worlds. For once, she wasn't alone.

The teens set their bags in the foyer before going to help their Mother gather the umbrella and towels from the laundry room. Evan also packed a small cooler with drinks and snacks.

Ready to leave, Evily glanced out the front window and noticed a black truck in the lane. Her heart unexpectedly fluttered as her gaze landed on Sean, casually leaning against the vehicle. He looked picture-perfect, dressed in navy board shorts and a crisp white t-shirt, but it was the unexpected accessory on his head that brought about a bright smile.

"Nice hat," she said, thinking the woven straw design was quite stylish.

Sean turned to look at his reflection in the window. "What's wrong? Not the look you were goin' for? Ella said to wear a floppy beach hat. This was all the guys could find at the shop in town."

The teens rolled outside one by one.

"Whoa, Sean. Nice!" Evan pointed, grinning as he adjusted his sunglasses.

"I think it suits him," said Ella, tilting her head to get a better look. "Gives off major chill vibes."

The actor smirked, pushing the brim of the hat slightly lower.

Clearly pleased with her suggestion, Ella beamed, "See? Told you it'd be perfect."

The group began moving toward the vehicles, the energy shifting from playful banter to the eager buzz of anticipation for their day ahead.

"So, what's so special about this beach anyway?" Sean asked Evan.

Ella stepped in, not allowing her brother to respond. "Oh, just wait. You'll see," she stated while presumptuously opening the back tailgate of Ben's SUV. "Hey, can we go with you?"

"Sure, if that's okay with your Mom." The action star turned to her for confirmation.

Evily shrugged her shoulders. "Sure. That's fine."

Carrying the tote and beach umbrella toward the truck, Sean reached out and took both from her.

"Are you doing okay?" she whispered before letting go of the bag.

He nodded with a half-smile. "I'm doing better."

"I'm happy to hear that." Evily was relieved.

Having locked the house, she returned to find her children had already claimed a spot in the third row. She, too, climbed in and found a seat beside Sean in the middle. While Ben pulled away, Evily could silently hear he was concerned about the crowds that afternoon. Being a nice day, chances were, the beaches would be swarming with people. David was with them this time. The other two were back at the vacation rental to rest and prepare for the night shift.

"Only two today?" Evily questioned, happy not to be surrounded by all four.

"Ben is going to scout it out first. If we need the others, he will call them. It's not far, correct?"

"Six minutes, door to door," Ben said studiously from the front seat.

The sun was shining brightly in the sky. Its rays filtered through the windows, feeling warm against their skin. Anticipating the day at the beach, the music on the radio was upbeat, tropical, and catchy. It made them tap their feet and bop their heads to the tunes.

Approaching the Mayflower coastline, Ben pulled into the gravel parking lot. As expected, Dunes Road was busy. Everyone quickly exited the vehicle and grabbed the bags from the back. Ella and Evan immediately ran off, excited to claim their spot along the sand.

As they evaded their sights, Sean and Evily walked up the path. Breaching the hill, they discovered the tide was out. Evily veered left and maneuvered behind a few beachgoers, staying close to the dune line. Sean got a bit nervous at the number of people there.

Tight on the heels of his famous client, Ben whispered something to him before quietly radioing for Ivan and Tim.

"Is everything okay?" Evily asked, having read his mind from afar.

The lead security guard needed to say his piece, knowing what was about to transpire. "Ma'am, I think we need to find a less congested spot."

Sean interjected. "No, Ben. If we walk behind everyone to that area further down, it will be fine. Most of the people are facing the water. Nobody will pay attention to us." He didn't want to ruin the family's plans.

"If you like, we can drive to Chapin Beach. It's just East of here," she suggested.

"No, we're good." Sean was adamant. Moving along, following Evily to the void they had selected, he felt like every other guy carrying the cooler bag and the umbrella.

Ben kept his distance to give his client some space and radioed David to track their location should they need to extract them from a mob of photographers or fans.

"Are you sure this is okay? I just figured nobody would recognize you here."

"Hopefully so. Why? Do I not blend?" he chuckled, wholeheartedly wishing it was that easy.

Evily laughed. "You somewhat blend."

Finding a perfect spot about seventy yards past the sun worshippers scattered along the Mayflower shoreline, Evily turned to him. "How about here? Is this good?"

Happy to see only a few people in the general area, Sean put down her tote. "This is perfect."

Finding the kids, the two waved to their Mother while searching through some tide pools.

"So, how do I do this?" Sean fully opened the beach umbrella, never having secured one in the sand before.

"Just plunge the pole in at an angle. I'll pack the bags around the base."

While he did that, Evily spread out their towels. Once they'd established their spot, she turned to him, her voice light yet inviting. "Do you want to take a walk?"

"Sure," he said, warding off some nervous energy.

Ben watched his client closely as they passed a few sandcastles on their way to the shore. The receding tides rippled the seafloor, creating patterned lines under their feet.

Finally, Sean reached the water and waded in. "Wow, that's cold," he said, shocked by the temperature.

"Yes, I know. It's not exactly bathtub warm, but eventually, you will get used to it."

While strolling through the shallows, the waves rolled gently past their ankles, the salty breeze tangling in their hair. At times, Evily stopped to pick up a shell, her fingers tracing the ridges as she studied its uniqueness.

Sean couldn't help but watch her with silent admiration. Her appreciation for the little things—things so easily overlooked—struck him as profoundly beautiful.

"I have a jar in my bathroom upstairs at the house," she said with a small smile, holding up a delicate shell. "I save the pretty ones and put them there. Each one reminds me of the memorable days we've spent here."

As they walked along, the sand cool beneath their feet, the actor's mind began to drift.

She glanced over at him, sensing his quiet mood. "Penny for your thoughts?"

He didn't answer. She could see the faraway look in his eyes.

"Umm…" Her voice was soft but insistent. "Hello?" Waving her hand in front of his face, he suddenly blinked.

"Sorry, what was that?"

"You seem different today." Given his rough start to the morning, she wasn't surprised.

He forced a smile, but it didn't reach his eyes. "Yeah, I'm just thinking," he replied. With so much gnawing at him, he did not want to burden her.

Desperate to read his thoughts, she stared him down but got nothing. Instead, she felt his heart torn between the past and the present. Catching herself with his sights locked onto hers, she broke away just as Sean did the same.

"Don't worry. Umm, I'm good. There's just a lot to process," he said.

"Well, if you need to talk, feel free."

Unsure what to say to that, he said, "Not yet."

She nodded.

While they moved along, it wasn't hard to see the connection developing between them. About to talk more about the orb experience, he heard Ella's voice.

"Come on, Mom! Over here!" the girl shouted.

Ella and Evan were making their way over with smiles, grinning from ear to ear.

"We're going to explore that tide pool over there," Ella called out.

Raising her hand to shield her eyes from the sun, Evily looked toward the spot her daughter had pointed to. Relieved to see the area was quiet and safe, she nodded. "Sure, let's go."

As they walked side by side, following the kids, Evily and Sean kept up. Their arms brushed at times, making Sean glance over and catch her eye.

Drawn to him, she did the same, with cheeks painted a faint pink.

Both were very much at ease.

Reaching the kids, surprised by how talkative they were, it wasn't long before they peppered Sean with questions.

"So, are you friends with many other celebrities?" Ella asked, her voice bright with curiosity.

"Umm, yes and no," Sean replied, scratching the back of his neck. "Depends on the person."

"What do you mean?" Ella pressed.

"Well, in Hollywood, there are two types of people. More often than not, those around me are acquaintances - those I know and respect in the business but don't regularly associate with. On the flip side, there are a handful of people I trust. Those are the ones I allow into my life outside of work. That group of special people I consider friends. Does that make sense?"

"I think the older we get, the smaller that list of friends becomes, too," Evily added, glancing at Sean meaningfully.

"Yes," he agreed. "I've learned that the hard way."

He caught her eye again, and this time, he quickly looked away.

Evily noticed his aura change. Her brow furrowed, concerned about which direction his thoughts were going, but she didn't push. Instead, she gave him the space he needed, quietly hoping he'd let her in when he was ready.

By the time they reached the tide pool, the mood had lightened. Sean answered Ella's questions about Hollywood but steered clear of the rumor mill while the teens teased their Mother mercilessly, drawing laughter from every angle. He thought her reaction to them was priceless.

Over the next two hours, they soaked in the sun. Counting starfish and hermit crabs, they shared stories and enjoyed their time together.

Ben looked on, happy he didn't have to intervene once. The break from all the paparazzi drama made the experience more relaxing, which their client desperately needed.

Sean found himself smiling more than he had in years, the company of the Andersons filling a void he didn't know he had.

As the tide began creeping closer to the shore, needing to sit, they retreated to their spot along the dunes. Settling back under the shade of the umbrella, Evily liked the warm breeze drifting past her face as she kept her eyes on Ella, who was frolicking in the shallows, chasing the waves and laughing with carefree joy. Nearby, Evan stood a little apart from the water, his posture relaxed yet self-assured as he talked with a group of teens—a mix of boys and girls—who had gathered near him. Their animated gestures and bursts of laughter suggested a lively conversation, and it warmed her heart to see him fitting in so naturally. A soft smile tugged at her lips as she watched the easy way he interacted, noting how one of the girls shyly tucked her hair behind her ear while another boy playfully shoved him, eliciting a wide grin from Evan.

Sean sat beside her, the sand cool beneath the towel he had spread out. Wrestling with a delicate subject burning inside him, he stole a glance at her from the corner of his eye. Her attention was on Ella as her lips curved in a faint smile while her fingers fiddled absently with the edge of her sunhat.

Attuned to the shift in the air, she felt his apprehension before he spoke. It was as if she could sense the question forming in his mind, the quiet hesitation hanging between them. She knew he was about to say something.

That is when, out of the blue, Sean blurted, "Would you mind if I ask a personal question?"

Evily stiffened slightly and kept her sights firmly on her children. "Sure," she said, her voice steady but guarded.

"When we were in Marlborough…" Sean paused, treading carefully. "I noticed you looking at your phone a few times. You seemed…concerned. Who was trying to contact you?"

Her posture remained composed, but her hands trembled as she smoothed the towel over the sand. "It was my ex-husband," she said softly, her tone edged with something Sean couldn't quite place—resentment? Possibly fear? He wasn't sure. The way she fidgeted betrayed her calm exterior.

"What did he want?" he asked gently.

A sharp inhale followed, held for a moment before she let it out in a slow, measured breath. "Nothing new," came the quiet reply, her gaze fixed on Ella. "Just the same old Peter. Checking in. Making demands. He always finds a way to remind me he thinks he still has control."

Jaw tightening upon hearing this, Sean leaned forward slightly and rested his elbows on his knees. "The only reason I ask," came the careful admission, "is because I don't want my affiliation with you to cause trouble. If this is about me…"

A quick shake of her head cut him off. Eyes meeting his, she said firmly, "Peter doesn't need a reason to assert himself. He just does it because he can. Or thinks he can."

Listening intently, he caught the tension in her voice.

"He and I don't speak. We haven't in over six months," she added quietly.

"So the fact he's calling now means…"

Turning to him, she replied, "I'm assuming he's seen the pictures online and doesn't like it."

Thinking things through, Sean felt his protective instincts surface. "Will he act on this?" he asked, his voice low but steady.

She moved her feet through the sand, her gaze drifting back to Ella. "Maybe, maybe not. But he's unpredictable. When he called, I just couldn't…" She let out a heavy sigh.

"What can I do?" he asked, his mind racing with possibilities.

"For now, nothing," she said, her tone soft but firm. "Hopefully, this will just blow over."

The rhythm of the waves and the sound of laughter carried by the wind soon filled the silence. Words hovered, unsaid, as the moment passed. Whatever battle she faced with Peter was hers to fight, but the instinct to be there for her remained—especially if it became unbearable.

While enjoying the warmth of the late afternoon sun, it soon came time to leave. Given instructions from Ben to move in the direction of the caravan awaiting them on Dr. Botero Road, the group gathered their things and followed his advice.

Wandering down the quiet stretch of beach, they soon found the parked SUVs. The group dusted the sand from their feet after handing Tim their bags. Within minutes, they were on their way, relieved the day had passed without having to once deal with photographers and fans. Sean felt like he'd led an average, ordinary life that afternoon. Something that was very few and far between for him.

Wind-logged from all the fresh ocean air, the drive back to the Andersons was calm and quiet. Pulling into the driveway, the teens jumped out and unloaded all the bags and the umbrella. Thanking Sean and the Henchmen, they unlocked the door and went inside, leaving their Mother behind.

"So, any plans for dinner tonight?" the actor wondered.

"Actually, I was going to ask if you wanted to join us at Marshview."

"Marshview? Where's that?"

"A nice restaurant situated along Sesuit Creek. It has delicious food, and the view is nice as well. I make a reservation there each year. I'm sure I can call and add a few extra guests to the table if you like."

"Sounds good, but leave those arrangements to me," he said, happy to accept the invitation. "I'll get the guys to adjust things if that's alright?"

She was unsure what that entailed but went along with it. "Sure, whatever works best for you."

"What time do we need to leave? The guys can drive if you want."

"The reservation I made is for 6:00. It's not far from here. Maybe five minutes away."

"How about a 5:40 pick-up ?" He hoped the time suited her.

"That's perfect. We will see you then."

As Sean climbed into the back seat of the truck, the house glowed warmly in the setting sun, its edges bathed in an ethereal light. Evily stood in the doorway, her silhouette framed in the shadows. Holding the door ajar as she waved, he returned the gesture.

The truck pulled away. Sean rested his elbow on the window ledge and watched Evily disappear inside. He let out a slow breath, the blurred scenery no match for the clarity of the emotions stirring within him. For the first time in years, hope flickered—a fragile yet undeniable spark of something new. But the weight of that hope made his chest tighten. In just a few hours, he'd be sitting with Evily on the foyer floor, waiting for another visit from Janie and Ella. The memory of their presence the night before had dredged up feelings he hadn't fully confronted— feelings of loss, guilt, and the fear of moving forward.

He knew they were gone, but the freedom to live life on his own terms felt more like a burden than a blessing. Letting go of Janie and Ella enough to pursue a life with someone else felt impossible. How could he allow himself to feel something new when the life he'd built with them still lingered so vividly in his heart?

"Are we heading back to the house?" Ben's voice broke the silence, pulling Sean from his thoughts.

"Yes," the actor replied, his tone steady while the setting sun blinded them. Snippets of his day with the Andersons still flashed through his mind. "I could get used to a life like that," he murmured, almost to him-self. Thinking of Evily, of her warmth and her resilience, made him feel like he could take on the world again. Somewhere deep down, he knew he was standing at a crossroads, torn between the life he had eternally loved and the one he might muster the courage to create.

Monday, July 29th
Corporation Beach, Massachusetts

There is something profoundly satisfying about sharing a meal. Eating together breaking bread together,

is one of the oldest and most fundamentally unifying of all human experiences. ~ Barbara Coloroso

While the sun descended toward the horizon, Sean showered away the salt and sand from Mayflower Beach. Because the day had gone so smoothly, he anticipated an uneventful evening with the Andersons. Dressed a little nicer for the much-anticipated dinner out, he looked one last time in the mirror. The famous actor saw a very different reflection. More settled, with a brightness to his eyes, he felt content—something he had not experienced in a long time.

Having contacted Max about the dining arrangements needed that evening, he knew his loyal assistant would handle everything, and there was no need to worry.

Ready to head downstairs, his phone rang. Seeing Sheri's face appear on the screen this time, he answered the call.

"Hi, Sheri. What's up?"

"That is the question," she replied, sounding a bit cranky. "We got more problems, my boy."

"Problems? What do you mean? Nobody bothered us today. There were no fans or paparazzi."

"I'm sending a video your way."

The actor watched for her text.

What more could these people have? He asked himself, quite tired of the drama.

Seconds later, the phone chimed. Quickly clicking on the link, Sean was concerned about what he would find. The video, which featured Evily and him at Mayflower Beach, laughing and talking with the kids, was sold that afternoon to a tabloid news feed. Seeing Ben in the shot, he realized his hovering probably tipped off the person recording the footage.

"What do you want me to do, Sheri?"

"Sean, the producers are extremely concerned about the bad press. They don't want anything negative disrupting this premiere. It could cost them millions."

"What about the article I did on Saturday? Don't you think it will be a strong enough distraction?"

"Yes, of course, it will send a sympathetic message. But, Sean, people are expecting you to be walking the red carpet with Andrea Branti."

"I'm not attending the event with her. I told you that." Frustrated, Sean looked at the time. "Look, I need to go. I'm running late."

"We are in a crisis. Where could you possibly be going?"

Sean smirked, then went dead serious. "The situation I am in right now is not a crisis, Sheri. To me, it is a blessing." Hanging up the phone, he turned off the ringer and slipped it into his pocket before going downstairs.

Finding the guys showered and ready, Sean gathered them together for a quick meeting.

"Just FYI. I got a call from Sheri. A video surfaced this afternoon. It featured the Andersons and me walking along the beach. They know we're here. By tonight, this place could be crawling with photographers. We need to be on alert. Our priority now is keeping the family safe." Pausing a second, receiving another text from Sheri, revealing multiple posts that had erupted on the internet within the past fifteen minutes, he added, "We are supposed to be dining at the Marshview Restaurant tonight. I had Max call ahead and arrange a private dining room to segregate us. I think he sent you the info, Ben?"

"Yes, he did. We are good to go." Never being late, Ben checked the time on his phone. "We need to pick them up in less than five minutes. I suggest we get a move on, gents."

Each of the husky men walked out the door. Tim stayed behind to secure the premises. Assuming anyone could have followed them home this afternoon, Sean figured someone was bound to be snooping around later that night. Aware of this, Tim remained on high alert.

The Henchmen started up both SUVs. Ben was responsible for Sean and the Andersons in his truck while Ivan and David drove point in the other.

Before heading out, the actor made sure he had everything. He sent a quick reply to Max, thanking him for his help. Taking a seat in the vehicle behind Ben, Sean let Evily know they were on their way. Receiving a message in return, he hoped they could get through dinner without any drama.

On route, stressed about searching through his hashtagged name on social media, he wasn't surprised to find countless pictures from the beach that day. Scrolling through the photos and videos, he could identify the professionally taken ones versus those posted by fans. Raising his sights to the view passing by, he wondered how safe it was to have dinner out tonight.

What if it turns into another Starbucks incident or worse? He thought, afraid of subjecting the teens to that.

Needing to address the situation further, Sean said, "Ben, so that you know, the video from today is not the only thing on social right now. We may have to eat and run. If that's the case, we also don't want to compromise the beach house locations. Can you pass that along to the other guys?"

"Roger that," Ben responded, radioing the info to the vehicle in front of them.

David had checked social for updates and was already on it. They knew what they were up against, while Ben relayed their plan.

"We will secure the location and bring all of you inside. Ivan and I agree that there will be no pictures tonight. We will keep everyone off the second floor. Nobody approaches - fans or not. We will inform the owners of this. I will stay with you, and the guys will stand guard at the bottom of the stairs."

"Good," Sean said, content with what he suggested.

Slowly turning into Evily's driveway, Sean noticed the teens scrambling around in the foyer, having seen them pull in. Getting out of the vehicle, he went to gather the troops.

Evan had already opened the door. "Hey, Sean," he said, greeting him in their usual way. "Come on in."

"Hey, my man. Everyone ready to go?"

"Yes, Evan and I are. But Mom is running late," Ella replied, suddenly yelling up the stairs. "Mom! Hurry! Sean and the Henchmen are here!"

The young girl's casual urgency brought a smile to the actor's face.

Watching Evily descend the stairs, dressed in a blue multi-tone, knee-length, belted shirt dress with a notched neckline, she looked like she had walked off a magazine page. With her hair tied in a messy bun, she wore a white cardigan draped across her shoulders. Sean found it hard not to stare. Upon reaching the landing, she bashfully looked away when she saw his eyes glued to hers.

Immediately noticing that Evily and Ella both had pretty dresses, he paused. "You ladies look lovely this evening."

Ella's face brightened. "Thank you," she said, lowering her head shyly.

Her Mother humbly blushed.

"Before we go, can I have your attention for a moment, please?"

Worried by his announcement, everyone stopped in their tracks, unsure what was wrong.

"What? We can't go to dinner?" Ella flashed a look of disappointment.

"No, no. Everything is fine. I just need to share a few things." Sean slid his hands into his pockets, hating to limit their freedom again.

"What is it?" Evily asked, unsure what he was going to say, feeling a level of concern off him.

"Unfortunately, #SeanBradley is getting several hits, and now the pictures aren't from Boston."

"Are you saying the pictures are now from here?" Evily was stunned. Seeing Sean's reaction, she knew. "How did they pick up on us so fast?"

"Mom, the guy is uber-famous. Of course, people are going to spread the word." Evan reminded his Mother, who was not fully aware of the speed of social media.

"So, that said," the actor interjected, "I've arranged for us to go straight to the restaurant's private dining room upstairs. Ben will be with us, and Ivan and David will guard the stairs, so only serving staff will be allowed in the room. Is that okay?"

"I suppose," Evily said, recalling their experiences to date.

The look on her face told him she was reliving the frenzy they had escaped in Boston. "If things get hairy like at Starbucks, we will take the food to go," he said, hoping to reassure her.

"Alright."

Needing to be fully transparent, Sean added, "On top of this, unfortunately, there's the whole situation of being followed home later."

"These photographers could follow us here? Know where the kids and I are staying?" A dire look of concern flashed across her face.

"These people will do anything for a photo." He didn't know what else to say.

"What will we do if that happens?"

"Let's cross that bridge when we get to it. Everything should be fine. The guys will deal with it should something arise. I've always learned to anticipate the worst-case scenario. I want to prepare all of you. Apologize for being so straightforward."

Evily's guard went up. Focusing her energy, she searched through a series of intuitive thoughts for warning signs. Trusting her instincts, she took a deep breath and said, "I feel everything will be okay."

Having faith in her abilities, Sean clapped his hands together. "Good. Shall we get going, then?"

"Sure," she said, still a little frazzled. "We don't want to be late for our reservation."

The teens filed out the door to the waiting SUV.

Sean took Evily aside. "Be honest with me. Would you rather go on your own with the kids? If so, I completely understand. The last thing I want to do is ruin your night out."

"No, absolutely not. It's fine." Evily did not have to think about it. "Let's go. Once we get there, we can always reassess things."

"Alright. If you're sure."

"Yes."

Turning on all the porchlights, Evily locked the house. Sean walked alongside her to the truck and opened the door for her. Settled in their seats seconds later, Ben pulled away and met up with Ivan and David waiting at the road, ready to take the lead.

Leaving Seaside Avenue, turning left on Old King's Highway, they drove alongside the marsh and turned onto Bridge Street. The restaurant was not far - about four hundred yards up on the right.

Ben pulled into the parking lot behind Ivan. "Everybody hang tight a moment," he instructed. "When David gives the okay, we go inside. No stopping."

Evily felt the evening was about to get complicated. Nervous, she clenched her hands together, having sensed a noticeable shift. When the Henchmen went inside, she knew things might not end well if they stayed too long. Images flashed through her mind of people gathering in close quarters—cameras taking pictures and cars arriving in mass, surrounding them from every angle.

Sean recognized the look on her face. "What is it? What's wrong?"

Not turning to look his way, she said the first thing that came to mind. "I think we need to take the food and go."

Trusting her, he asked, "Should we just order, then head to my place to eat?"

"Yes, I believe that would be best."

"Ben, we are going in to place take-out orders." Counting how many cars were in the parking lot, the actor figured they'd find about thirty people inside. "Any requests, man? We'll grab you something, too."

"Just burgers for the guys and me would be great, Mate. Maybe chips with that," he replied.

Ella and Evan heard everything said. They were disappointed at first but knew their Mother was never wrong.

The burly protection agent emerged from the restaurant to wave his clients inside.

One by one, they exited the truck and made their way through the main entrance. All eyes were on them briefly as they passed a few people waiting for a table. The hostess escorted the group upstairs to the private dining room without stopping for autographs or pictures. Once on the second floor, Sean explained their situation to the owner by the name of Mary. He apologized for the inconvenience. But given their current circumstances, he informed her they would not be staying. Understanding their predicament, completely star-struck, she was very accommodating and wanted to help in any way she could.

Since the teens already knew what they wanted, and the Henchmen opted for burgers and fries, their requests got placed first, along with eight clam chowder orders. Evily stuck with her old-time favorite, beet salad with crab cakes on the side, while Sean went with the Seafood bake. Mary orchestrated everything beautifully while attempting to get them out in record time, adding a selection of cheesecake and a flourless chocolate torte for dessert.

Happy to have the special guests dining with them, if only for a short time, Mary offered wine to Evily and Sean and provided sweet teas for the teens. Even appetizers while they waited. Ben remained with the family while Ivan and David watched from below. He could hear the men stopping fans from moving toward the staircase, refusing to confirm Sean Bradley's presence upstairs. It wasn't long before he got word from Ivan that they were creating an unwanted stir. It was time to go.

"Excuse me, Sean." Ben took him aside and quietly spoke to his client.

Seeing this got the Anderson family's attention while gathering around to help Mary box up their appetizers.

Waving the woman over, Sean said with a sheepish grin as she approached. "I'm so sorry for the inconvenience."

The lady chuckled, waving him off. "No trouble at all. Happy to have you dine with us. I hope we will see you again."

Sean smiled. "Hopefully so. Can I settle the bill, please?"

The owner handed him the billfold. After punching in the amount on the point-of-sale terminal, she handed it to Sean. He inserted his card and left a substantial tip before entering his PIN. When the transaction cleared, he handed the machine back to her.

The receipt slowly printed. Finding the gratuity over and above the nominal fee for dinner, she said, "I think you made an error, Sir..."

"No, error," he replied. "Thank you again for accommodating us," the actor said sincerely.

About to rejoin the group, Mary smiled at him. "That was mighty kind of you."

"It's the least I could do after all the commotion we've caused. My guys will wait for our order. Please pass it along to them when it is ready."

"Certainly, I will do that." She handed Evily and Sean the appetizer boxes.

"Have a good evening," he said cordially.

"You as well."

His gaze moved to the Anderson family. "Alright, guys. Let's get a move on."

Within minutes, everyone gathered at the top of the stairs to await further instructions.

The Henchmen communicated back and forth to ensure a smooth exit. Positioning the truck close to the main doors, Ben radioed that he was ready for departure.

Sad to leave so soon, Evily thanked Mary for understanding. Her friend was gracious as always.

Going out the same way they came in, swift and timely, they left the restaurant. Loading into the vehicle, not spotting any paparazzi, Ben pulled away and watched for anyone following them, wondering if they had overreacted, while Ivan and David remained parked outside the restaurant, waiting to receive their food orders from the owner. It wouldn't be long until they would all be enjoying dinner together back at the house.

Zig-zagging multiple side roads to Sean's rental, the lead Henchman made sure they hadn't picked up a tail. Confident that the coast was clear, Ben continued to their final destination. Returning to the seaside cottage, everyone got out when the vehicle stopped.

The teens climbed the stairs to the front door, where Tim was waiting.

"Back so soon," the guy said to them.

Not missing a beat, Ella said, "It's complicated," on the way inside.

The guy chuckled at her straight face. "I bet it was." He immediately went into protection mode and prepared for any unwanted company.

Gathering in the living room, Sean didn't know what to say to the Andersons. He had ruined their dinner.

Picking up on his vibes, Evily said, "Please don't feel bad."

"Sorry, guys," he voiced.

"Don't worry about it, Sean. It's fine." Digging into the appetizers, Evan was unfazed by it all.

"Yeah, it's okay. The food should be here soon." Ella was happily admiring the vacation home's floor plan.

Having the teens' attention, he said, "Well, there's a ping pong table on the top floor and a movie theatre on the lower level if you are interested."

"Want to check it out, Ella?" her brother asked.

Agreeing, she curiously followed him up the stairs, leaving Evily and Sean on their own.

While the Henchmen made the perimeter rounds, Sean walked into the kitchen and asked, "So, red or white?"

"Think I will go with white today." Crossing her arms in front of her, she walked over to the windows overlooking the ocean.

Finding the complimentary bottle in the welcome basket in the fridge, he poured two glasses of wine. "For you," he said, handing her the glass.

"Thank you so much."

"Cheers," he said, raising his to meet hers.

"Cheers."

"Tell me the truth, are you disappointed we had to leave the restaurant?" The whole situation was bothering him.

"If anything, you are the most disappointed, I think. I can tell tonight has caused you a lot of frustration. Please don't be upset. It's okay. We will soon sit down and enjoy the food when it arrives. It doesn't matter where we are. I mean, look at this view. It's stunning."

Sean took another sip of his wine. "For me, missing out is a common occurrence."

The author tilted her head sympathetically. "Don't you ever get tired of it?"

"All the time... But that is my life. The choice I made."

Ivan and David returned to the house. Opening the front door, they had the large food bags in hand. After placing them all on the counter, Evily walked over and opened each one. While distributing everything in an orderly way, she noticed Evan and Ella returning to the main level. The men took their orders outside to guard the front and back decks.

Ben opted to have a seat near the far end of the living room to give the clients their space.

Sitting down with the Andersons at the round dining table, Sean noticed Evily and the kids bow their heads in prayer. But this time, Evily said it aloud. Not saying a word, Sean mimicked what they did and listened to what she expressed. When each ended with an Amen, he, too, whispered the same. Somehow, while eating his meal, it felt different. He could not explain why or how. It just was.

Forever checking their phones, Evan and Ella were distracted while eating their fries at a snail's pace.

"Phones down, please," their Mother instructed. "You know the rules."

"But Mom, this is important," Ella pointed out. "Look."

Taking hold of her phone, not only did Evily find videos and pictures from the beach today, but now, there were photos from the restaurant surfacing. Evily read the captions. A crowd of photographers had gathered minutes ago in mass, hoping to get shots of the Hollywood star and his entourage. She was shocked to see this. Her instinct was right.

Sean looked at the pictures on Ella's device.

"How do you deal with this day in and day out?" Evily wondered.

"Truth?" he asked her.

"Yes, of course," she replied.

"I ignore it all. Never look at the hashtags or search for anything about me. Simple. That way, I don't see anything and, in turn, don't care. Learning that lesson took a long time, but it is the best advice I can give anyone in my situation."

Convinced that she should take the same approach, the group finished their dinner. Evily followed Sean onto the deck overlooking the ocean to watch her teenagers, who went for a walk up the beach. The watercolored sky with colors of yellow, orange, and pink made it look like it was on fire. Offering Evily a seat in an Adirondack chair, they watched the day-ending moment with their wine in hand.

"Have I ruined your summer vacation?" Sean felt guilty given everything that's happened.

"Don't be silly. You haven't ruined it."

He felt otherwise.

"If anything, you've added a bit of excitement." Evily looked at her children playfully running down the beach. "You've made quite an impression on those two."

Not letting an opportunity go to waste, he boldly asked, "And how about you? Have I made the same impression?" Unable to look her way, he was afraid to hear the answer.

Caught off guard, she didn't know what to say. "Hmmm..." she mumbled with a mischievous smile, keeping him in suspense. "Let me just say it's been interesting. Never a dull moment."

Sean smiled. "So, not all bad?"

"No. Not all bad."

Seeing her kids walking toward them, Evily figured it was time to go.

While the brother and sister playfully avoided the waves rolling in, their Mother stood up and said, "We should probably get moving. I'm hoping you will be able to hear more from Janie and Ella later tonight."

Standing beside her, he replied, "Yes. I hope so, too."

The author descended the beach stairs to join the teens waiting for her below.

"Can I walk you guys back?" The actor asked, not sure what Evily would say.

"Are you sure?"

"Yeah, of course. The guys will follow us."

Now dusk, they started down the beach, staying a safe distance from the waves crashing against the shore. The sand had cooled and felt pleasant to the touch. Two of the Henchmen followed them like shadows.

Reaching their house without incident, Sean bid Evan and Ella goodnight before they disappeared inside.

"So, I guess I'll see you later?" Evily confirmed, knowing he would not miss it.

"Yes, for sure. I will be here at 2:30."

"See you in a little while, then."

Sean watched her walk in and lock the door. Standing there for a second, feeling conflicted, he shook from his thoughts and moved toward the Henchmen waiting for him a short distance away. Although almost dark, there was still a hint of color on the horizon.

Arriving back at the house, they climbed the steps to the upper deck. Sean hoped to get a few hours of sleep before meeting with Janie and Ella again. He wondered what message they would have for him tonight. Would they finally reveal why they'd brought him all this way?

48

Early Morning Hours of Tuesday, July 30th
Corporation Beach, Massachusetts

The life of the dead is placed in the memory of the living. ~ Marcus Tullius Cicero

When Sean turned off his phone alarm, it was 1:45 am. He was still feeling pretty tired despite sleeping a solid four hours. Contemplating closing his eyes for fifteen more minutes, he knew he might not wake up and would miss the opportunity to see his girls. Slowly forcing himself to sit on the edge of the bed, his feet soon rested flat on the floor. From there, he tried to keep his momentum moving forward.

Slowly selecting some casual clothes from his suitcase, he slipped on joggers and a T-shirt before grabbing his shoes. Running his hand through his hair while brushing his teeth, Sean searched for a hoodie at the last minute before going downstairs.

When his feet hit the main floor, he found Ben sitting in the living room playing another game of solitaire.

"Ready, Sean?" he asked, knowing he was heading out to the Andersons again.

"Yeah. I'm running a bit late."

Still not questioning what he was doing, Ben allowed his client to go about his business discreetly.

Leaving the house, locking up behind them with Ivan on shift while they were gone, Sean took a seat on the passenger side. It wasn't long before he sensed Ben's curiosity.

When they pulled onto the highway, he needed to clear the air. "So that we understand each other, it's not what you think."

"It's none of my business, Sir."

"Listen, I don't want you to have a bad opinion of her or me. Again, it's not what you think." Sean needed to change the subject. He contemplated asking him this the following day but thought now might be a good time. "Are you happy working where you are?"

"It's good. We are assigned to different people often and never stay with one client long term."

"Well, what if I asked you to come and work for me? Anything tying you to the East Coast?"

"Not a thing. I'm single. No family."

"So, that's a yes?" the actor wanted confirmation.

"Yeah, mate. I'd consider it. Thank you. Appreciate that."

"We'll go through the details later. I was thinking of bringing Ivan on board, too. Thoughts?"

"Ivan's a good guy. He has no ties either and might be interested."

"Good. It's settled, then. I'll also talk to him and have my people get in touch with you. They'll take it from there."

"That's great. Thanks, man."

Ben was about to turn into Evily's laneway. At the last minute, he stopped the vehicle and allowed Sean to get out. Waiting for the porch light to turn on, the protection agent watched his client walk down the road. Once Sean was safely inside the house, he drove to the parking lot to wait.

Sneaking in quietly, hoping not to wake the teens sleeping upstairs, he met Evily.

Quite tired, having just gotten out of bed, Evily's black-framed glasses rested halfway down the bridge of her nose. Reaching up, she tied her hair in a messy bun. This time, she wore a fluffy white robe with a belt knotted at the waist. "Hey. How are you?" she whispered as they got settled.

Prepared for their usual awkwardness, he replied, "Truthfully, I'm exhausted. Think we need to sleep in this morning."

Feeling the same way, Evily left the door open a crack and turned off the lights after lighting the candles. Tossing the cushions on the floor, she turned to him and said, "Ready?"

"Think they will appear tonight?"

Confident, she said, "I believe so. I'm getting a strong feeling."

Sean sat on the cushion and rested his back against the closet door. Evily took her position against the adjacent wall and again desperately tried to ignore the ominous sets of eyes glowing in the darkness across the laneway. Saying her protection prayers, thankfully, they departed. Now, all she could do was wait.

Staying relatively silent, Evily concentrated. "Sean, connect to them. Think about a strong memory and ask a question. Doing this, you draw them in so they can transition."

Quickly closing his eyes, he questioned whether Janie sent him the Missin' You music the other night. Recalling the details of their fight, wishing it would never have happened in the first place, Sean opened his eyes briefly and saw the author sitting on the floor in a calm and peaceful state with her legs crossed. The scene enhanced his feelings. In that moment of weakness, he realized what he was doing and stopped himself, believing he'd just sabotaged the visitation. Refocusing, he frantically thought of Janie, her smile, laugh, and their short but happy marriage.

A few seconds past 2:44, a cool breeze circled through the house, causing Evily to shiver. With those all too familiar signs appearing, she knew they were close. Her sights drifted toward the slightly open door. Sean did the same, following her lead. At that very moment, baby Ella made her grand entrance.

Crazily spiraling about the space in front of them, sparkling like diamonds, the little orb seemed so excited. "Hi, Daddy! Look, I beat Mommy again." Evily smiled while relaying her words to Sean.

"Of course you did. You're so fast," Sean replied, changing his tone to be more playful and fatherly.

Janie slipped through the open gap to join them.

"She says hello, Sean and Evily." The author was surprised to be addressed, too. "We meet again."

The orbs hovered in the middle of the room. There was a moment of silence, and neither Janie nor Ella said anything. Evily thought that was strange. Sean kept glancing over, but the author silently motioned to him, confirming she didn't know what was happening.

Then Janie spoke. Evily caught every word. "She says, we need you to enhance your faith, Sean. When it is time, we want you to join us. As it is now, this may not be possible."

That took him by surprise. It was one of his worst fears.

The orbs got closer to him and brightened.

"Janie said to raise your hand and close your eyes. No matter what happens, do not open them."

Sean was nervous but did what she asked. Placing his hand up in front of him and closing his eyes, he soon felt a tingling in his fingers.

Dense darkness instantly appeared before him, erasing everything. There was no floor, no ceiling, and nothing on either side. He felt like they had transported him somewhere. Afraid, he was about to open his eyes but didn't. He remembered what Janie said.

Breathing erratically, his hands shaking, he noticed a tiny speck of light approaching from his left. One by one, more appeared. Accumulating into orb form, it illuminated a pathway. While walking towards the light, he noticed long golden grass growing beneath his feet. The view slowly brightened, bringing things into focus. Able to see with his eyes closed, he suddenly heard a beautiful humming resonating from the grass. Amidst a vast field with rolling hills, the winds moved the golden blades back and forth in unison, creating majestic patterns for many miles on end. In the distance, a golden city sparkled brightly. However, the centerpiece was an enormous tree towering high into the sky. The base of it was hundreds of yards across. Taller than anyone could imagine. It was translucent, but the leaves and branches shimmered when the winds passed through it. Above that were indescribable beings flying through the air. More beautiful than clouds, he did not have words to describe them. Sean had no idea where he was.

What is this place? He thought. *Where am I? Is this heaven?*

Spotting movement under the tree, a group of children were playing happily. One, in particular, stood out from the rest. Breaking away from the others, maybe six or seven years old, with long, flowing brown hair dressed in white, the young child looked so joyful. Her laughter was carefree and innocent.

While Sean stood on the hill, amazed by this otherworldly place, the angelic child with fair skin and sparkling eyes soon moved in his direction. With her outstretched arms, he tilted his head. The little girl looked familiar. As she got closer, he felt it in his heart. It was Ella.

"Daddy!" she shouted, running and jumping into his arms, expecting to be hoisted high above his head.

He could hear and see her plain and clear. Picking her up, he swung her around. "Ella?" he questioned in disbelief.

"Yes, silly," she giggled.

"You got so big. You're not a baby anymore."

"This is the age you always imagine me to be when I drift through your thoughts, right?"

Lost for words, Sean replied, "Yes, it is. How did you know?"

"I told you. We visit you a lot." Ella got distracted.

Sean turned to see where she was looking. There, a few feet away, was Janie watching from a distance. Approaching, she smiled brightly. Her hair flowed freely in the breeze. As did her white gown.

"Sean, this is our home. It is a peaceful place. We needed to show you, hoping it would strengthen your faith."

Her husband looked around. A waterfall of stars cascaded into a lake flooded with them. Past that was a bridge where animals frolicked and played in the open fields. Above was the blinding light, but it didn't hurt his eyes. Gold flecks rained down over the area where they stood, making him want to stay. There was a disconnect from his old life, causing him to let go. He had no pain, no fear, no worries. His mind was quiet.

"It is not your time, Sean," Janie said, reading his thoughts. "One day, you will join us. We have prepared a place for you. For now, you must return. Do not be afraid to love again. Live a full life with no regrets. I want you to be happy, my Love. To do that, you must move on. We brought you to Boston to meet Evily. Until now, the timing was not right. She is the woman who will love and care for you in our absence. She will foster your faith. You do not need to be alone anymore."

Ella smiled at her dad. Squishing his cheeks between her hands, she looked into the eyes and said, "Remember, you've got Evily now."

Taken off guard, Sean listened.

"I found her years ago when she was expecting her baby. At the same time, most did not know she was suffering through so much hardship and pain. I heard her cries," Janie revealed.

His daughter interjected. "One night, she asked me what she should name her baby girl; I told her Ella was a nice name."

Sean nodded tearfully in agreement. "Yes, it is a beautiful name."

The scene in front of him began to fade. A man waved in the distance.

"Mike sends his love. Knowing we had a short time with you, he didn't want to invade upon it."

Waving to his friend and a group of others who seemed very friendly, Janie and Ella, too, began to wane and become translucent.

"You must go now. We will watch over you." With a loving smile, she added, "Before you go... I'm always missing you, Sean." Janie hugged him tightly, referring to the song on the radio days before.

Ella hugged him and kissed his cheek.

Taking hold of her daughter's hand, the two walked away through the grass to a group waiting for them. Sean's heart ached. Waving one last time, he witnessed that perfect world fade to black.

Instantly feeling a falling sensation, he hit a solid surface with a loud thump. Flailing his arms and legs in a panic, Sean opened his tearful eyes to find Evily cradling his head in her lap.

Able to distinguish where he was, weak and numb, his body weighed a ton. Gradually regaining strength, his breathing normalized to a healthy rhythm.

"Are you alright? What happened? They blocked my thoughts. I could not hear anything they said."

Sean broke down. "It's okay, I did. I could hear them. See them. I saw their home. Felt their happiness there." Blinking his eyes repeatedly, Sean sat up and rested his back against the wall, trying to return to reality.

Evily could see he braved something unexplainable, possibly an experience similar to hers many years prior. She never shared the details of that experience with anyone since the average person could not even fathom such a thing. The author hoped Sean would eventually confide in her and find solace in the knowledge gifted to him. Answers most people only wish they could confirm.

Not saying anything, Sean just sat in silence, processing it all. "What happened here during that time?"

Evily described, "You were sitting on the floor with your hand in the air. Eyes shut. Janie and Ella's orbs touched your hand and your face. You said nothing. I tried to talk to you, but it was like you were gone. I could not hear or see anything from the girls. My mind went blank. Quiet. There was nothing. It was weird. There's never - nothing."

"How long was I gone for?"

"About two, maybe three minutes?" Evily confirmed.

Sean thought it was much longer.

"Without warning, the orbs whisked out the door, and you fell to the floor."

He could barely speak.

"You know what you experienced just now? I have, too."

Unable to put it all into words, Sean turned to her. Suddenly, a fire ignited in his chest and spread this indescribable warmth that caused him to smile. Without a doubt, he could say there was life after death, even though he couldn't explain how or why. He just knew. It's like he had been asleep for so long and now had awakened. The world seemed different.

"If you ever want to share the details, I will listen. If anyone will understand, it's me."

"Okay," he said, still a little dizzy. Mentally exhausted but physically energized, Sean was in limbo. He needed sleep to be able to process his experience with a clear mind, but there was an excitement he could not explain. His body emanated a light, and Evily could see it.

"I think you should go and get some rest despite being wide awake. We will meet up later to discuss everything. The kids and I plan to cycle the rail trail around noon. If you are up to it, you are welcome to join us. Before that, we can talk over breakfast. Maybe around ten or ten-thirty?"

He stared at her blankly, a million thoughts rolling through his mind. Delaying his answer, recalling what Janie and Ella had told him, he calmly responded, "Umm, yeah. Cycling? Breakfast? I can do that."

Helping Sean off the floor, she held him steady while he regained strength. His body still felt strangely unstable. Texting Ben, they soon saw lights pull in front of the house. Able to maneuver out the door on his own, Sean got in the front seat. Holding up a steady hand, he waved, as did she. In that instant, Evily felt a heaviness in her chest - an ominous sign of bad things to come. Praying, she asked for an umbrella of protection for her kids, Sean, the Henchmen, and herself, not knowing who it might affect.

"For every action, there is a consequence," she said, locking the door. Climbing the stairs, she slipped into bed, hoping to get some sleep before their cycling trip.

On the drive back to his place, Sean did not say a word to Ben. He desperately tried to make sense of everything he'd seen. It seemed life had suddenly taken on another meaning. Something utterly profound and unimaginable. It was easy to believe and have faith now. He knew it to be true in his heart.

Arriving in front of the house, the two walked inside. Sean moved straight upstairs to his room. Sitting on the edge of the bed, he fell onto his back. It didn't take long to drift into a deep sleep.

49

Tuesday, July 30th
Corporation Beach, Massachusetts

Some of the most poisonous people come disguised as family and friends. ~ Unknown

Having gotten a few hours of sleep, Evily woke to the sun's rays flooding her room with light. Subtly rolling over in bed, she loved how the house was so quiet and peaceful. Maybe it was the fact she was getting older or appreciated the moments of solitude more; regardless, mornings had become her favorite time of day. Shifting onto her back, she stretched. Hearing the rumble of a vehicle, she assumed the neighbors had arrived to spend the week. It had been so long since she'd seen the Smith family. At least five years.

I should stop by and say hello to Peggy at some point, Evily thought as a car door slammed shut. Alarmed to hear the sound was close, she stopped and listened. Sitting up, she pulled the covers back and slid to the edge of the bed. Gingerly walking towards the hallway, the sound of someone jimmying the front door lock made her heart race. Not knowing what to do, she quickly got her robe and ran to Evan's room to wake him up.

"Evan?" she said quietly, rocking him back and forth. "Evan? Someone is trying to break into the house."

Awakened, he bolted out of bed in seconds.

Inching down the stairs with a baseball bat in hand, something she kept in her room in case they needed it, Evily's chest pounded in fear. Evan immediately took it from her and protectively held her back.

Step by step, the teen descended the stairs, trying to peer around the corner. A figure then appeared and purposefully dropped a brown leather duffle bag loud enough to disturb everyone in the house. Holding up the bat, her son took a deep breath and moved to the landing, ready to fight off the intruder.

"Whoa! Whoa! What do you think you're doing!" the figure shouted with his hands up defensively.

Evan stopped dead in his tracks. His Mother stayed close.

"Dad?" Evan said, "What are you doing here?"

Evily was shocked. "Peter?"

The man responded arrogantly with a mix of sarcasm. "What do you mean? This is my house, isn't it? I thought I'd join in all the fun."

His tone struck a chord, making Evan's body tense. So many times, arguments escalated between them when he spoke like that.

"What do you mean?" Evily knew a fight was about to erupt.

"Come on, Evily." Her ex-husband's eyes were cold and dark. "It seems someone is vacationing with my family, and it's not me."

"Peter, we haven't spent vacations together in years." Evily tried to defuse him.

Raising the bat onto his shoulder, Evan got antsy as the air thickened. "So, where's Jennifer?" he taunted with an abundance of attitude.

His father shot him a look.

Knowing he'd hit a nerve, Evan smirked.

Not skipping a beat, he replied, "She's arriving tomorrow."

Internally grappling, trying to corral enough courage to respond, Evily took a deep breath and said, "The courts say I am legally allowed to be here for these two weeks each year. You get the rest of it to yourself."

"Yes, the courts. Imagine what the courts will say when I tell them you splashed my kids' faces all over social media the past few days. How irresponsible and simple-minded." Peter scanned the rooms within an eyeshot of where he stood. "Where is he, Evily?"

"Where is who?" the author answered.

Peter searched the main floor. "Your movie star, boyfriend."

"Sean?"

"Oh, so you admit it?" Peter said, ducking into the kitchen and laundry room. "You don't think a guy like that will stick around, do you? He's probably got so many women vying for a chance to be with him."

"It's not like that." Evily knew this man would slowly chip away at her self-esteem piece by piece with every word that escaped his mouth. Needing to set an example for Evan, Evily noticed Ella sitting on the stairs, sneakily recording them with her phone.

"Well, tell me. What is it like then, Evily? Because from what I see, things have heated up between the two of you the past week."

His father intimidatingly stepped toward his Mother. That prompted Evan to stand his ground between them.

"First of all, that is no longer your concern. Second, you can't stay here until our two weeks are up." She tried to be brave.

"Oh, my dear, but yes, it is my concern. If it affects my children, then it affects me," he stated concretely with a tilt of the head, his eyes zeroing in on hers. "I can do whatever I please."

Peter noticed Ella sitting on the steps. "Oh, there she is. Aren't you going to say Hello?" He didn't realize his daughter was recording him.

Panic spread through Ella's body from head to toe.

Evan sternly told his sister to stay where she was. Unafraid of the man before him, the growing boy now stood six feet tall and weighed one hundred and eighty pounds. Extending his left hand outwards, he confidently moved his Mother back from the ominous figure, ready to defend them at all costs. His sights bounced back and forth between Ella and their dad.

Feeling his sister's fear, he shouted, "So, ruining our life wasn't enough! What do you want? Why are you here?"

"You don't talk to me that way. I'm your father!" the man shouted.

"Yeah, well, not anymore. You gave up that title when you left!" Evan knew things could get rough.

"Well, you ungrateful little shit! Big man now, aren't you? Think you're the leader of the house, huh?"

"Someone's gotta be." Straightening up to tower over the hateful man, who was now a few inches shorter than him, puffing out his chest, the anger inside the teenager boiled rapidly. "You're not welcome here."

Poor Ella started to cry while sitting on the landing halfway up the stairs, terrified to witness her brother's confrontation with her father.

"Listen here, son. I own this house and its contents. None of this belongs to you or your Mother. I own all of you," his father grinned sinisterly, scanning their faces.

Evan opened the front door and said, "You need to leave, or I'll call the police."

"Do whatever you like. Who do you think they'll believe? You or a high-profile lawyer with connections?" Pausing, he laughed. "The only way to get rid of me is for all of you to leave."

Evily's face went blank.

"That's right. I'm kicking you out of my house." Peter pulled an envelope from his pocket and threw it on the floor at her feet.

Picking it up, she slid the document out to find a court order evicting them from the premises. Peter had listed her maiden name as a tenant. Not his ex-wife.

"You can't do this. I'm not a tenant. It's in our divorce agreement."

He flashed an evil look. "I'll see to it our agreement changes. After all, I am the law, remember?"

Evily knew she could not win this battle. Willing to keep the peace, not wanting to create further drama, she turned to the kids and said, "Evan. Ella. Go and pack your things. We need to go."

"No!" Evan shouted angrily. "No, we are not leaving!" In turning to his dad, Evan pointed his finger in his face. "You owe us this much for all the shit you've put us through!"

"Did your mother not teach you it's not polite to point?" Peter slapped his finger out of his way.

That is when Evan saw red. Without hesitation, he launched at him.

"No, Evan!" his Mother shouted. "No!"

Handily wrestling the man to the floor, Evan punched him repeatedly in the chest and face. His father struggled to defend himself.

"No, Evan! Stop!" his sister cried out.

Evily hovered around the two, trying to find a way to break them up. Shoved backward, brushed with a fist to the face, and forced to the floor, she didn't know what to do.

Out of nowhere, another body flew through the front door and pulled Evan off Peter, who was now bloodied and beaten. Sean had broken up the fight. He'd heard Ella's screams while walking down the laneway.

"Evan, what's going on? Who is this guy?" Sean asked, leaving the nameless man lying there in front of them.

The athlete had a small cut above his eye. He refrained from making introductions.

Sean quickly tended to Evily.

"This is my ex-husband," she said tearfully.

On his feet, blood dripping from his nose, Peter replied, "Yeah. I own this place."

"He has a court order for us to leave." Evily handed Sean the papers.

Glancing at the documents, Sean knew it wasn't legal. The guy was trying to infringe power over his family revengefully.

To keep the upper hand, Peter demanded, "Go and pack your bags, Evily. You need to be out of here by noon."

Evan launched another attack, making Sean grab hold of the teen's shirt to hold him back. The boy stared at his father with hatred in his eyes.

"Evan! Stop!" Sean shouted, knowing it would only worsen the situation. "Go outside and wait there."

Fuming, the hockey player hesitated, then stormed out the door.

Ella sat on the steps, terrified by what had happened.

Seeing her daughter crying hysterically, Evily went to comfort her. Holding the young girl, she whispered calmly, "Ella, go and pack your things, okay."

"But, mom..." she uttered in defeat.

"Please do it for me. Pack up your brother's room, too. I'll be upstairs in a minute."

Ella climbed only two steps, afraid to leave them alone with her dad.

Unfazed by all the blood, continuing to wipe his nose on his shirt, Peter got cocky again. "So, I take it you're the famous Sean Bradley everyone is talking about."

"Listen, this is not in the kids' best interest, and you know it. Why are you doing this?" Sean posed with the document in hand.

"What I decide for my family is none of your concern."

Evily placed her hand on Sean's arm. "It's okay, Sean. We will leave."

He could see the pain the whole situation had inflicted. Without hesitation, he said, "You and the kids are coming with me."

"What? You think you can barge in here and take my family?" the arrogant man stated, looking quite disheveled since Evan roughed him up.

"They don't seem to be yours anymore." Sean motioned for Evily to go upstairs. "You go ahead. I'll wait here."

The celebrity remained in the foyer with the disgruntled man.

Going to gather their things, she grabbed hold of Ella on the way up, removing her from the situation. Once in her bedroom, Evily got the suitcase from the closet and set it on the bed. She didn't care how the bag got packed. Throwing clothes into it, she cleared everything from the drawers and the bathroom, including her jar of treasured shells.

"Why did he come here, Mom?" her daughter asked quietly.

"He must have seen the pictures online. Maybe the entertainment news footage. Who knows. It was probably embarrassing for him to have his family in the public eye."

"But it's not like that. We aren't doing anything wrong."

"I know, baby."

Ella quietly asked, "Can he do this to us?"

"Sadly, he can do whatever he wants." She placed both hands along her daughter's cheeks. "Now, please...go... We don't want to leave anything behind. I'll do another sweep of the rooms before we leave."

Evan paced outside the front door, watching Sean, who stood firm at the bottom of the stairs while Peter stared him down.

"You will never take them from me," the man threatened.

Sean wanted to keep things peaceful. "It's not what you think. We're just friends."

"Yeah, right. I was friends with my secretary, too," Peter sneered.

The Hollywood star flashed a look of disgust his way.

"What? It's not like you haven't dipped your pen in ink many times before, I'm sure."

Sean got angry. "You don't know me."

"Oh, but I do. See, I checked up on you, Sean Bradley. It seems you've had a few paternity suits brought against you. Interesting read."

"Well, you also saw that the courts ruled in my favor, not against me. I didn't even know those women. All they wanted was money."

Ella and Evily came down the stairs with a few bags and two suitcases. Cautiously moving past Peter standing in the hall, they set everything on the front porch. Evily made eye contact with her son to pack them in the truck.

"Sean, can you help Evan with the suitcases? Don't forget his hockey equipment in the garage," she said, quite overwhelmed.

Peter had a smug look on his face.

The actor knew he was up to something. "Are you sure you're going to be alright?" he asked, concerned about leaving her alone in the house.

"Yes, I'm just going to gather everything from the kitchen. It's okay."

Passing by Peter, he walked outside. The first thing he did was text 911 to Ben. Not knowing what this guy was capable of, he figured he might need backup.

The garage door opened when Evily hit the button in the kitchen remotely.

Upstairs, placing her brother's things in a suitcase, Ella soon returned to the main floor and took his bags outside, not once making eye contact with her dad. In minutes, she joined her Mother in the kitchen to help her grab Evan's protein shake canisters and snacks from the cupboard. Stuffing it all in shopping bags, Evily figured the rest of the groceries would probably have to stay.

Peter sat in the chair by the window, enjoying every moment of this horrible encounter, and questioned, "You're really going with him?"

She turned and rested her hands on her hips. "Well, you've given us no choice," she stated firmly. "You know, once again, you've pushed your kids even farther away with your aggressive nature. You will never have a relationship with them."

With a sinister expression, the man demanded, "Ella. Put your bags back in your room. You're staying here with me."

The young girl flashed a look of terror and shook her head.

"Over my dead body." Evily's motherly instincts surfaced. "Ella, go outside. Now."

The girl did as she asked.

"Times' ticking. You'd better hurry," he taunted.

Trying to buy some time, Evily went into the laundry room to take the clothes from the dryer. She believed it would distract her ex-husband enough to calm his anger.

Once outside, Ella saw Evan packing the truck while Sean gathered the hockey equipment in the garage. Her brother immediately knew something was wrong when Ella emerged from the house onto the porch with a shell-shocked, blank stare. Tears erupted. Barely able to speak, she didn't need to explain anything. He knew what had happened. Angered, Evan was sure his father was making threats again. Pacing back and forth, he suddenly stormed inside.

Sean didn't see him go.

Fuming with rage, Evan went straight to the back of the house.

Just as his Mother was about to exit the laundry room, Evan flew past, intent on attacking again. In slow motion, she shouted, "Evan! No! Stop!"

His father smirked and stood up from his chair, ready to confront his son. "You were always a cowardly kid."

The teen stood his ground and stared the man down. "What did you say to her? What did you say to Ella?"

"That does not concern you, boy."

Evily swiftly got in between them.

"This is between him and me!" Peter yelled at her, violently grabbing her face with one hand and shoving her backward. Losing her balance, she fell awkwardly.

Seeing she hit her face on the barstool, Evan shouted, "No! You son of a bitch!" Tackling his father, he pounded his fist into the man repeatedly.

"No! No!" Ella screamed while holding her phone, recording the incident, knowing her father's history of twisting the truth for his gain.

Hearing Ella cry out, Sean raced inside. There, he found Evily bleeding on the floor, with Evan overpowering his father. Suddenly, the man turned the tables and tried to strangle his son. Breaking up the fight, he forcefully released Evan from Peter's deadly grip. The teenager gasped for air and slid backward across the floor to escape the horrid monster. No longer able to control his anger, Sean swung his fists at Peter repeatedly, landing multiple shots to the head and chest, leveling him in seconds.

"Evan, take the truck. Go to my place. Bring your sister with you. I'll protect your Mom."

The teen shook his head and said, "No," while glaring with immense hatred, happy Sean had put his father in his place.

"I promise I will get her out safely," Sean reassured him, offering his hand to lift the teen off the floor. Looking him straight in the eye, he said, "Go! This is no place for you." Focused on Evily, Sean knelt to help her.

The protective teen did what he said and left the room to escort his sister outside. Lugging the last of their bags and throwing them in the back of the SUV, Evan got in the driver's seat while Ella jumped in beside him.

"Evan, wait. We can't leave them." She was distraught.

Pounding the steering wheel with both hands, Evan outwardly agreed with his sister. The two returned inside, not knowing what they would find. Ella was relieved to spot their Mother sitting on a kitchen stool. Sean was applying pressure to the cut on her face. The teens saw their father glaring at them from the corner of the room.

Peter said, "So, what is this then? Are you screwing my wife?"

Not turning to offer a respectful reply, Sean angrily stated, "She is no longer your wife. You don't deserve her, nor do you deserve those two wonderful kids. If I'm not mistaken, you know, I'd think you're a bit jealous there, Pete."

The tone of that comment hit a nerve. Peter clenched his teeth. "How dare you come into my house and tell me what I deserve! You are nothing. Nothing! Wait until the press gets a hold of this. I'll have all of you brought up on charges."

Before taking Evily out of the room, Sean smirked at the man, knowing the damage he could inflict on him with just one phone call.

Ella stepped forward. "No! No, you won't, you monster! I videoed everything you said! Everything you did! From the moment you got here! I have it all! Mom and Evan are going to press charges on you! I've witnessed everything!"

With eyes affixed to his daughter, Peter wiped the drops of blood on his sleeve. "Oh, little Ella. Always so naïve. I'm sure you'll grow to love your new room at my house when your Mom and brother are behind bars."

Laughing in her face, Ella cried, then looked at her Mother. Bringing her sights back to her dad, hurt by all his insults, she said, "My whole life, you never cared about me. But that's okay because I don't care anymore, either. I never want to see you again. Ever!"

"That's fine. You're weak-minded anyway. You'd make a terrible law-yer," he stated ruthlessly, oblivious to how those statements impacted his daughter.

Evan stood behind his sister, who was now psychologically maimed. Peering past her, he had recorded the whole conversation with his phone.

Angered by this, his father said, "What? You actually think that recording will hold up in court? It won't. I'll have it manipulated. It will look like you're to blame."

Sean swiftly guided Evily and Ella toward the front door. Evan helped him.

In a moment of clarity, Evily said in a daze, "Wait…"

The author continued upstairs, leaving Sean with the kids. While scanning each room, she made sure they had everything.

For those few minutes, the foyer was silent. Thankful to hear their Mother returning downstairs, she rounded the corner into the living room and grabbed her manuscript, almost forgetting it. Unplugging her laptop and packing it into its case, she passed it to Ella.

"I just need to clear out the things from the kitchen," she told Sean, who went back with her to get the grocery bags and the pile of unfolded laundry on the counter.

Evily still felt like she'd forgotten something on the way out the door. The four of them walked to the truck. Sean placed the last of their things in the back seat.

"You are all dead to me now! You hear me! Dead to me!" Peter shouted from inside the foyer.

Seeing the Henchman rushing towards them, the actor waved them off and got Evily in the passenger side of her SUV.

"Take the kids!" Sean instructed the men. Sending Ella a reassuring look, he added, "It's okay, Sweetie. Go with Evan and Ben back to the house. We will meet you there. Everything is going to be alright."

Ben guided the brother and sister safely to his vehicle. One by one, the trucks pulled away from the vacation home.

Not looking at her ex-husband standing in the doorway, Evily kept her head down as they left. "I'm so sorry, Sean," she whispered, embarrassed by the whole situation while they drove down the main road.

"That, right there, was not an ounce your fault." Sean reached over and placed his hand on her arm while surveying her face. "Are you okay?"

She broke down upon hearing the sincerity and concern in his voice. She silently mouthed the word no, unable to produce a single sound while shaking her head. Bursting into tears, she covered her swollen face with both hands and cried.

Abruptly stopping the truck at the side of the road, he threw the gear in park. Reaching over, he wrapped his arms around her tightly and pulled her in close. Kissing her forehead, she grabbed hold of him as every ounce of emotion exploded out of her. Chest heaving, tears flowing in an uncontainable flood, she tried to expel it all before having to face the children. Sean did not let go. Whatever she needed, he would give.

"It's okay. It's okay. I got you," he whispered while she trembled. "He won't hurt you anymore. I promise. You're safe with me."

Evily surrendered willingly, feeling secure in his arms. Soon, there was silence. With a few deep breaths, she realized what had happened. Mortified by her outburst, she shamefully lowered her head.

Seeing this, recalling his Mother doing the same years back, Sean said softly, "No, don't lower your head. You must stay strong. That man is evil. Do not let him break you."

She tried to keep her head held high. It was something easier said than done.

Unsure of what to say, Sean shifted the truck in gear and reached over. Gently taking hold of Evily's hand, he lifted it to his lips. Kissing the back, he offered a few gentle squeezes of reassurance. Angrily processing everything that happened, he thought about returning to the Anderson house later that night with the Henchmen to teach that man a lesson and silence him for a while. Knowing they couldn't, he figured he'd deal with it legally once and for all, so the family never had to worry about him ever again. A lawyer or not, Peter wouldn't know what hit him after his legal team finished dragging the guy through the courts. Sean was going to make him pay dearly for what he did today.

"Listen. You are welcome at my place for as long as you need. The guys and I will make sure you are all safe. You don't have to worry. Alright?"

Nodding her head, still sobbing from the encounter, terribly shaken up, Evily thought of Evan and Ella and what they endured. Knowing the damage inflicted would inevitably haunt them for a lifetime, she couldn't get to Sean's fast enough.

50 |

Tuesday, July 30th
Corporation Beach, Massachusetts

The scars you can't see are the hardest to heal. ~ Astrid Alauda

The Henchmen's caravan moved along swiftly through the countryside. Not long after, Sean pulled into the vacation home on Bay View Avenue and parked behind their SUVs. Glancing over at Evily, he caught her staring at her children sitting on the front steps. Evan was comforting his little sister, trying to stay composed. She could tell how noticeably shaken he was. Looking down at herself, Evily realized she was still in her nightclothes.

"Don't worry about that," he said, taking notice of her reaction. "It's fine. You can change inside once you get settled."

Ben, Tim, and Ivan were unpacking the bags and taking them inside the house. Tightly clutching the top of her robe to close it across her chest, she was desperate to comfort her children. Rushing over to them with both arms extended, she reached out with tearful eyes.

"Are you both alright?" she cried solemnly.

"We are okay," Ella confirmed, seeing her Mom's swollen cheek. Clinging to her, she didn't let go.

Evily inspected the condition of Evan's face while he towered over the two of them. Her son reassured her that he was fine, even though, deep down, he wasn't.

To give the family a moment to breathe, Sean kept his distance.

"What happened over there, Mr. Bradley?" David questioned, seeing how distraught the Andersons were.

"Her ex-husband ambushed them. He had an eviction notice." Sean's fists clenched at the thought of the man. "He doesn't know they're here. We need to keep it that way. Make sure nobody hovers around the beach steps."

"Roger that, Sir," the former linebacker confirmed before making his way to the back deck to stand guard.

Evily turned to Sean.

He inched forward and said, "Come on in, everyone. Let's get you settled."

Climbing the stone steps to the front door, still left open by the Henchmen, Sean walked into the foyer.

"There is one bedroom free on this level and two upstairs. You decide what works best. I am on the second floor. The Henchmen are on the lower and upper floors."

Evily instructed the children, "Go ahead upstairs. I will be there in a minute." Not ready to converse with them, she went with Sean, who guided her over to a chair in the living room.

Sitting her down, still in shock, he knelt in front of Evily to survey her face before getting an ice pack.

"Thank you for this," she said quietly, not knowing what to say.

"Don't even give it a second thought." Prepared to clean her wound, he said, "You doing okay?"

She shook her head back and forth and broke down silently in tears. Collapsing into him, she placed her hand over her mouth to muffle her cries. The last thing she wanted was for the kids to see her in such a state. The fear, uncertainty, and hurt were very intense. "This was what my marriage was like," she said. "He made me feel worthless and blamed me for his violent outbursts. It was always my fault. When the kids came along, he'd blame them for things even when they were young. Knowing he had an affair with his secretary gave me grounds to leave him, but he decided that for us both. Evan was always in the middle, forever defending and protecting me. I am so happy he did. He could have easily become like his father. Thankfully, he's the opposite." Evily leaned back in the chair. "Guess you know my deepest, darkest secret now."

"I feel like this happened because of me. If it weren't for you helping me, Peter would have never come to the house, and you would have had a peaceful vacation."

"Things happen for a reason, both good and bad. Only in hindsight will we know why." Evily patted the tears from her face with her sleeve.

Sean stood up and went to find a cloth to wipe her forehead.

Joining him in the kitchen, she said, "Umm, thank you. Thank you for saving us."

His heart sank. Walking over, reaching out, he held her close while she tried to control her sobs.

Calming down, she found the strength to compose herself. Leaning back, Evily looked up at him.

Gently cleaning her face with a wet towel, removing a few streaks of dried blood, he surveyed the small cut along her hairline. It was a surface wound, nothing more. Not saying a word, sweeping a few strands of hair away from her eyes, he knew he loved her. From that day onward, their relationship would be different. Now, there was no turning back.

"I need to go and speak to them," Evily whispered, emotionally drained.

"Take all the time you need. I'm going to grab a couple bags of ice." The actor said softly, releasing her from his embrace. "I'll bring it up in a minute."

"Okay," Evily nodded, running her hand over her cheek. It hurt to the touch.

Once she had left, Sean searched the kitchen for something to hold the cubes. In the process, he stopped. Resting both hands on the edge of the counter, straightening his arms, and leaning forward, he lowered his head. The vivid details of what transpired that morning replayed through his mind. For him, it was like history was repeating itself.

Desperate to hit something, needing to rid himself of the pent-up anger, he took a deep breath and refocused.

"You will pay dearly for this, Pete. Trust me. I am about to make your life a living hell," he whispered, unable to shake the vengeful feeling overtaking him.

One by one, he opened each cabinet in the kitchen. Finally, he found a few boxes of ziplock bags in a drawer. Scooping the ice from the bin in the freezer, partially filling both bags, he sealed them tightly. Moving toward the foyer, he could hear the Andersons talking upstairs. Reaching the upper level, he stood outside the bedroom to the left and listened a minute while Evily did her best to comfort her kids. Ella was sobbing. The sound of it broke his heart. Not wanting to interrupt them, he waited in the hall.

"Guess this means our trip will be ending early?" Evan questioned, looking for clarification.

Ella asked quietly, "Is that true, Mom? Do we need to go home?"

With both of them needing an answer, she paused and exhaled. "I'm so sorry. We have to. There is nowhere to stay here, and if your father is at the house, I don't want to run into him. I hope you understand."

That got Sean thinking. Knocking on the door, interrupting their conversation, he said, "Here you go." He handed one to Evily and the other to Evan. "I'll be downstairs if you need me."

Pressing the cold against her face, Evily said, "Okay, thank you. Give us a few more minutes, and we will join you."

"Take your time. No rush." Sean left the room and went back to the main floor. Grabbing his phone, he headed outside onto the deck overlooking the ocean. Dialing Max, he waited for his assistant to answer.

"Hey, Sean. Everything alright?" he asked.

"I am going to need a favor, Max. It's a big one. Need you to come through for me, and it's gotta be fast."

51

Tuesday, July 30th
Corporation Beach, Massachusetts

Your trauma is not your fault, but your healing is your responsibility. ~ Elizabeth Wirija.

Evily, Evan, and Ella stayed to themselves for the rest of the day and evening. Besides briefly coming downstairs for dinner, when David returned to the house with homemade stone-fired pizzas, Sean continued to give the Andersons their space to deal with the aftermath—something that needed to be private between them.

The Henchmen went about their duties keenly, keeping a tight perimeter around the beach house while Sean remained in his room. Busy making calls, he was excited to reveal the arrangements he'd made through Sheri and Max. He hoped these plans would materialize because he wanted to surprise Evily and the children. If it helped them forget what had happened with their father, all the effort would be well worth it.

While working, Sean heard Evily quietly knock on his bedroom door. When she peeked inside, he noticed her face was not as swollen.

Happy to see her, he said, "Hi. Everything okay?"

Inching into the room, she replied, "Yes. I think we are going to head to bed now. I want to thank you again for letting us stay with you." Evily crossed her arms defensively in front of her. Sadly, she seemed broken.

Sean walked over. "Of course, I wouldn't have it any other way."

Unable to look him straight in the eye, a tear rolled down her cheek.

Instinctively reaching out, he hugged her tightly.

Evily let down her guard. Fully trusting him, her arms found a home around his waist.

Standing in silence, Sean whispered, "You're safe here. Don't worry."

She nodded, not saying a word.

"Try and get some rest, alright."

Parting ways, she replied, "Yes, you too. Goodnight."

"Night, Evily."

As she walked out the door and rounded the corner, Sean ran his hand through his hair.

You gotta tell her, man, he thought to himself. *She needs to know. Or does she already?*

Frustrated with himself, not sure how to express his feelings given the makings of today, he knew the timing wasn't right. Returning to his spot on the couch in front of his laptop, he continued working a while longer. There was so much to do - so many arrangements to make.

Near midnight, Sean turned off the lights and tried sleeping in the dark for the first time in years. To his surprise, the fears that had once haunted him suddenly lifted, filling the space with nothing but peace and serenity. Lying there, anxious about how his plans for tomorrow would go, he hoped the author would be on board and not overthink it. They deserved better. His heart went out to them. Out of all his responsibilities, his main priority now was to get the family far away from here. Fluffing his pillows and resting his head, he wanted nothing more than to be part of their lives. No matter the capacity. From now on, he would be their rock. Their refuge. Their protector. The man they needed to keep them safe from harm. For once, he felt hopeful for the future. After all this time, love was rising from the ashes.

52

Early Hours of Wednesday, July 31st
Corporation Beach, Massachusetts

Faith is moving forward even when things don't make sense. Trusting that, in hindsight, everything will become clear. ~ Mandy Hale

Hours passed while Sean tossed and turned, unable to sleep. His mind raced with a million thoughts. Bothered by what happened yesterday, concerned about how the morning would go, his eyes opened. Sitting up in bed, he leaned against the headboard to check the time. Somehow, it wasn't surprising to see it was two o'clock. Frustrated, he knew this had become his new normal.

The moon hovered brightly over the ocean while he slipped on a T-shirt and opened the door to the balcony. Captivated by the view, Sean found a spot on the red bench. The speckles of light reflecting off the water were mesmerizing. Overwhelmed by the powerful waves crashing against the beach, his gaze moved upward to the makings of a dark, cloudless sky showcasing a universe of stars twinkling above. Thankful for his girls watching over them, it was almost impossible not to dwell on the violent encounter with Peter. Sadly, it would be a day ingrained in the family's memory for a lifetime. Nightmares erupt from horrific experiences like that.

"All in all," he whispered to himself. "It could have been much worse. What if I wasn't there...."

Deep in thought, he heard a door open. To his left, standing in a fluffy white robe, was Evily.

"Hey. Are you okay?"

"Yes, we are fine," she said quietly. "It took some time, but Ella finally drifted off." Pausing a moment, she asked shyly, "Mind if I join you?"

"No, not at all. Please, have a seat." Sean pushed over to give her some room.

Sitting down with an extra blanket, she covered her legs and clutched the collar on her robe to keep it closed. "I can't sleep," she said while looking out over the water.

"Given what happened today, I'm sure your mind is racing. Mine is, too."

They stayed silent, enjoying the calming sounds of the surf. The tide had rolled in, churning the waves along the shore.

"It's about quarter past two. Are you disappointed Janie and Ella are not coming tonight?"

"Part of me is, yes. But somehow, it's okay. You were right. There's this feeling of inner peace. Closure, I suppose. It's hard to describe. I can't put it into words. But, as you said, they wanted to settle my soul. Maybe that's what I feel now. The guilt I've carried seems to have gone."

"I'm so glad to hear that. I told you this experience would be life-changing."

Sitting there, Sean recalled the details of the orb visitation the night before and how his girls asked him to live a life here on Earth without regrets. He knew they were safe and happy in heaven. Knowing that Mikey was watching over them helped, although Sean now understood that someone far more powerful had that job.

"Your face looks much better," Sean said, glancing over sympathetically, which caused tears to develop in her eyes. Seeing her lower her head, he said, "I'm sorry. The last thing I want to do is make you cry."

Evily stared at the moon lofting high above. "Yes, thankfully, it didn't bruise too much. The ice helped a lot," she said with a hint of positivity. "It's been a very emotional day. I am still processing."

Sean did not know what to say.

Taking a deep breath, she added, "But no matter how bad things get, I will always stay strong for my children. I have to. They are all I have, and they need me." She put on a brave face as a chilly ocean gust rolled in, making her shiver. Quickly pulling the blanket to her chin, she huddled under it as best she could.

Knowing she was cold, Sean slid over without having to think twice. Repositioning the blanket, covering them both, he reached one arm up and wrapped it around her shoulders. Pulling her in, he melded their bodies snugly together. In an instant, his throat went bone dry. "Is that better?" he asked.

Evily nodded timidly. Dangerously close to Sean Bradley, her body trembled. Sitting in silence, feeling his warmth and the rhythm of his heart beating rapidly, she didn't need to read his emotions. His actions spoke volumes. Protective and attentive - the perfect man. He embodied the top two qualities she showcased in every male character written in her stories. It was as though one of them had come to life and lept off the page.

Realizing it was now or never, the Hollywood star worked up the nerve to share his feelings, even though he didn't know where to start.

"What is it?" she asked, only feeling apprehension.

Put on the spot, eyes glued to the horizon, he inhaled and held it a second before quietly exhaling to speak. "I can't believe how much my life has changed in less than a week. When we first met, I knew I wasn't the nicest person in the world, and I'm sorry. That day, after spending time with you and the kids, I discovered you weren't the person I had painted you out to be. You welcomed me into your life when you didn't need to and sacrificed so much to give me a chance to communicate with Janie and Ella. For that, I am eternally grateful. Since they passed away, I've been drowning in life. In addition to my work, I suffer greatly from sadness, grief, and guilt. It is so heavy at times it feels like I am suffocating. But in a matter of days, you turned that around and saved me. Suddenly, I've gone from having nothing in life that matters..." he paused, able to see her look at him out of the corner of his eye. "...to having everything I've ever wanted. Now I know why the girls brought me here. It was you, Ev. They wanted me to meet you."

Overwhelmed by what he said, never feeling so appreciated, Evily got emotional and couldn't contain it.

Afraid to look into those beautiful blue eyes, Sean turned, wondering what she would say. Thankfully, he saw tears of joy and happiness staring back at him.

Clutching her tightly, he lovingly whispered, "I am here now, and I'll never leave you."

Almost unable to compose herself, she nodded, knowing he meant every word.

Using the edge of the blanket to dry her tears, he traced her browline with one finger while her hair danced in the breeze. Gently tucking a few strands behind her ear, his touch silenced her troubling thoughts.

With her legs weakening, she tried to take sips of air. Slivers of panic gave way, allowing her to trust him wholeheartedly. She could feel the depth of his love—the kind that lasts a lifetime—a love so profoundly rooted that it intricately blended into the very fabric of her being.

Fragile, treating her with the utmost care, he stayed mindful of the fears cultivated by her past. Slowly, he leaned closer as the space between them seemed to vanish. Never having been loved the way she should have been, his fingers carefully grazed the hollow of her neck and swept in behind her ear. Endearingly moving his thumb along her face, studying every feature, he leaned in and pressed his lips upon her forehead. Leaving them there a moment helped him gather the courage for more. Nuzzling his cheek against hers, eyes falling shut, he tilted his head slightly and let his lips wash over hers, bringing a wave of warmth that helped shield them from the unseasonal chill gradually enveloping the house. Enticing and addictive, they both struggled to part from the soft, gentle kisses. Once their eyes drifted open, a familiar tingle spread into Evily's hands and feet. Simultaneously looking upward, both of them knew they had company.

Safe in her protector's arms, with her heart all aflutter, they noticed hundreds of tiny blinking lights. Amazed, not knowing where the sparkles came from, Sean soon discovered they were fireflies. Lighting up the night sky, creating a magical scene, one flew past just as Evily raised her hand. Landing in her palm, they marveled at the tiny creature bravely entertaining them. Easily counting multiple orbs of many sizes and colors floating in the distance, it seemed the spirit world wanted to celebrate along with them. Incredibly blessed to be gifted such an extraordinary experience, Sean had so many to thank for making it happen. Each person loved him enough to resurrect his life from the ashes. Something he would be eternally grateful for for years to come.

Turning to Evily, Sean offered a smile that melted her heart. Ready to begin this new chapter in life, uncertain of what the future would hold, they stayed strong in their faith, knowing whatever happened next, they had each other.

53

Wednesday, July 31st
Corporation Beach, Massachusetts

Every sunset brings the promise of a new dawn. ~ Ralph Waldo Emerson

Rising early, Sean got up before eight, excited to share his plans with the Anderson family. Anxious for the day to begin, he finished packing. Descending the stairs, leaving his suitcase at the front door, he reminded the Henchmen of their tight schedule. Each swiftly went about their duties to prep for the group's departure in a few short hours.

Hearing the family stirring, Sean went back upstairs to greet them. Standing outside Evily and Ella's room, listening for a moment, he heard them talking. Rapping one knuckle on the door gently, he waited.

Evily opened it an inch.

Sean could only see one side of her black-framed glasses and noticed her hair tied in a messy bun. Sporting a natural glow, she looked beautiful. "Good morning," he said. "Any chance I can talk to all of you? I need to ask you something."

"Sure. One second." Evily shut the door in his face and disappeared.

He could hear the water running in the bathroom. Crossing his arms, he waited patiently in the hallway, thinking about what he would say.

In less than a minute, she opened the door fully, with hair now cascading over her shoulders, no longer wearing her glasses. "Come on in," she said, smiling so brightly it warmed his heart.

Evan was already sitting beside Ella on the bed, their backs resting against the headboard. Unsure of what was happening, their Mother joined them.

Seeing three sets of eyes now looking his way, he stood at the end of the bed and took a deep breath. "As you know, I have to be in LA tomorrow to attend the movie premiere."

Met by variations of disappointment, the family knew their vacation with Sean was about to end.

Unwavering, crossing his arms in front of him, he explained, "So, that said, I don't want to leave you just yet."

"So, you're staying?" Ella questioned.

He squinted one eye and said, "Well, not exactly."

Confused, the young girl lowered her head.

"What I am trying to say is...." He thought he had kept them in suspense long enough. "If it's okay with your mom, I thought maybe all of you would like to come with me."

Needing clarification and believing she had heard him wrong, Ella asked, "Wait? Like, attend your movie premiere?"

"In Los Angeles?" Evan finished his sister's sentence.

"Well, I was hoping you would agree to also walk the red carpet alongside me. Of course, that's if you want to. No pressure."

"What!" Ella screamed. Immediately hugging her Mother, who was in shock, she pleaded, "Oh, Mom! Please, please, please! Can we go? Can we? Please, please!"

Evily didn't know what to say.

Solely based on her delayed response, Evan figured she was about to decline the invitation.

The Hollywood star stared into her eyes. "It would be an honor to have you join me." Sean tilted his head and raised a set of praying hands.

Rationalizing the nature of his request, Evily said, "It's not that we don't want to go. I mean, we would love to, but we didn't bring formal clothes to go anywhere like that."

Sean smiled confidently. "You don't have to worry about a thing? I've got that covered. Trust me."

Nervously fidgeting, Evily scanned every face around her. She didn't know what to say.

Holding her breath, Ella awaited her Mother's decision.

Closing her eyes, Evily fearfully whispered, "I suppose we can go."

"So, that's a yes?" Her daughter crossed her fingers.

"Yes, let's go to California."

"Yeah!" Ella embraced her, tackling her on the bed. "I can't believe it! We are going to LA!"

Quietly celebrating with a fist pump, Evan watched his sister stand and start jumping up and down.

"This is going to be epic!" Ella hugged Sean with utmost excitement. "Thank you for inviting us!"

Never having interacted with a child in that way before, he awkwardly hugged her back. The gravity of the moment was surreal. That is when Sean truly felt like part of the family.

Seasick from her daughter's trampolining, Evily got off the bed and walked over to Sean.

"You're sure you're okay with this? Especially being in the public eye and all?"

A little fearful, she nodded. "I'm scared. But I guess that's to be expected, right?"

"Don't worry. I will be by your side the whole time." Wrapping his arms around her shoulders, he embraced her lovingly.

Witnessing this, the teens looked at each other with raised eyebrows. They knew something was different about the actor and their Mom.

"When do we leave?" Evily asked, needing a timeline.

"Well, let me see." Checking his phone, he said, "In three hours."

"What? Three hours?" Flashing a look of shock and concern, she questioned, "You're serious?"

"Yep," Sean said casually. "All you need to do is go with the flow."

The author went into overdrive and began spouting orders, not waiting another minute. Excited, the teens obeyed without question. Everyone frantically went to shower and get ready for the day. Packing their things and tidying the rooms, they descended the stairs and lined up their bags at the front door within the hour.

Everyone said their goodbyes to Tim and David. For now, only Ben and Ivan were traveling with them. The teens and Evily were sad since the guys had become a part of their family, too.

While making a final sweep of the house and her SUV, Evily double-checked that they had everything. In the process, Tim promised to return her truck to the Boston Airport in their absence while they moved Evan's equipment to Ben's vehicle.

Piling in, with every stitch of luggage in tow, the group got on the road right on schedule. The Andersons settled in for the long haul back to Boston, knowing it was almost a two-hour drive.

"Sean?"

"Yes, Ella," the Hollywood star replied.

Excited, the young girl had so many questions she didn't know where to start. "Umm, where are Mom, Evan, and I staying while we're there?"

Turning to Evily, he said, "I was hoping you would stay with me. The house has eight bedrooms. You guys can pick whatever one you want."

Evily felt like it was an imposition. "I can get a hotel too. Whatever is easier for you?"

"Given what has been happening, it's probably best that you stay with me. That way, the guys will be able to watch out for us. Agreed?"

The Mother of two nodded, forgetting that was the case.

Ella silently celebrated, realizing they'd be staying in Sean's mansion, which Paul McClair had designed. She knew this would be the most amazing trip just because of that.

About to reach the main highway, Evily noticed that Ben had gone the wrong way. Driving underneath the overpass, she figured he would backtrack at some point. Not saying anything, she watched him continue along the county road.

"Can I help you navigate, Ben?" she offered.

"Thank you, but no need, Ma'am. I am good," the main Henchman said.

His client also did not say a thing.

Signaling and turning into a corporate area minutes later, Evily read the sign. "Aerodrome Center? Where are we?"

"Barnstable Airport," Sean revealed.

Confused, Evily asked, "Are we flying out of here?"

Met by a security guard standing at the main gates, he authorized their entrance before Ben went through and turned the corner to the right. Driving beside the large building, the Andersons couldn't believe their eyes. There, sitting on the tarmac, was a silver and platinum grey private jet.

"Wait?" Evily said. "What's going on?"

Loving the look on her face, Sean grinned as they got sight of their first surprise. "Max sent the plane for us."

"Is it yours?" Evan ran his hand through his hair.

Sean nodded casually. "Yep."

Unable to utter a word, Ella's jaw dropped to the floor.

The family was speechless.

Stopping a few feet from the welcome carpet, Ben looked like he had done this many times before.

"Passports, please," Sean politely requested.

Evily handed theirs to him. Getting out, he met with the pilot and airport security. Watching the three gentlemen shake hands, Ella and Evan tapped their Mother on the shoulder, hoping she would moMotherthey could exit the third row. Opening the door, she stood beside the truck and pulled the seat forward for the teens to get out.

Within minutes the Henchmen had transferred their bags onto the plane and cleared out the SUV.

Feeling like she was in a dream, Evily felt apprehension soon set in. *Am I doing the right thing? Sean's world is complicated and so public.* While her instincts sounded the alarm, she thought of Evan and Ella. Her main job was to protect them first and foremost. *What if they get scrutinized on social media for the decisions I make?*

Noticing the author seemed out of her element, Sean walked over, hoping to calm her nerves while he handed their passports back. "So, are you ready?"

With excitement, Ella answered him instead. "Yeah! We're ready!"

Hyped and all smiles, the teens approached the plane.

The handsome actor reached out his hand to her. "Shall we go, Ms. Landy?"

Taking hold of his hand, she climbed the stairs. Following behind her children, they stepped inside the luxurious aircraft. Finding a beautifully decorated, spacious cabin, she soaked in all its grandeur. Ella and Evan quickly claimed their spots near the front. Passing them by, running her hand over the quilted light grey, butter-soft leather seats and platinum accents, Evily loved the burnt red pillows, giving a pop of color to the neutral palette. Sean led the author toward the back. Offering her the window, she sat down before he sat beside her.

Greeted by the stewardess, she handed them mimosas in fluted glasses before supplying the teens with lemonade and soda.

Looking into Evily's eyes, Sean made a toast. "To our adventure in California."

She clinked her glass with his.

Not feeling as much excitement from her, Sean thought something was wrong. "Is everything alright?"

Hesitating, she exhaled, not sure how to explain herself.

"What is it? Please, tell me."

"I am just worried. What if the world hates us being together?" she solemnly questioned.

"Why would you think that?'

"What if your fans hate that we are with you?" The thought visibly shook her.

"They won't." Sean wanted to put her mind at ease. "I'd like to share the details of a recent project of mine."

Not knowing what he meant, she stayed quiet and listened.

"For a few days, I've been finalizing an interview for a notable magazine to address the enigma that is my life. During the interview, I candidly revealed the tragic loss of Ella and Janie and how my life had been so empty since their deaths. Not wanting to fall into a depression, I chose to channel my grief by keeping busy. It was the reason behind my crazy work ethic. I thought not having any time to think was a good outlet for me. Long story short, though, at the end of the article, I said that recently, my life had taken a turn."

"Oh? How so?"

Grasping her hand, giving it a few loving squeezes, he acknowledged, "And that is when I confirmed that I found someone who has made me happy again, asking that everyone respect my privacy during this time."

Her heart skipped a beat.

"Truth be told, I knew it the first day we met," he smiled.

54

Wednesday, July 31st
Barnstable Airport, Massachusetts
Los Angeles, California

Only when we are no longer afraid do we begin to live. ~ Dorothy Thompson

The private plane smoothly glided from coast to coast, floating among the clouds. In addition to watching movies, Sean prepared the family for who they would meet upon arrival and what to expect in the coming days. He intentionally left out a few special arrangements to keep those a surprise.

Hours later, enjoying an uneventful flight, Sean pointed out the window to the majestic Pacific coastline below before circling back towards Van Nuys Airport to prepare for landing. The teenagers gathered their things while Ben and Ivan explained Max's departure plan before the plane descended into the city of Los Angeles.

Touching down in the land of sunny beaches, palm trees, and Hollywood stars, Evily peered out the window while they taxied over to a hanger. A caravan of four shiny black SUVs parked in a straight line awaited them.

"Are they here for us?" Evily asked.

Sean smiled. "Yes. That's Sheri and Max. I can hardly wait for them to meet all of you."

After completing the arrival procedures, the group got permission to exit the plane. Holding Evily's hand tightly, Sean led her down the stairs.

A mature woman with a silver bob, dressed in a dark pantsuit, Pucci-patterned blouse, and red-soled heels, approached with her head held high.

Evily thought she looked so regal.

The action star greeted his agent and happily made the introductions. "Sheri Reade, meet Evily Landy Anderson and her children, Evan and Ella."

All business, the woman wasn't the friendliest person. She looked at the family oddly from head to toe, sizing them up. "Pleasure," she said intimidatingly before addressing the new Henchmen.

Max waited his turn with subdued excitement. Impeccably dressed in a navy-tailored suit, sporting a neatly pressed, brightly-colored silk pocket square, he straightened his flashy tie before stepping forward, wanting to make a good impression. "Evily Landy! I'm so happy to meet my Andersons finally." Embracing the woman who stole his boss's heart, moving on to the teenagers he'd heard so much about, catching them all off guard, his facial expression suddenly went from totally care-free to all business at the drop of a hat. "We have so much to do from now until tomorrow night. It will be a whirlwind, but don't worry; I've got your back."

Sheri, not a fan of children, stood to the side and observed. She was stunned to see how well-behaved they were.

Evily picked up on it right away. Smirking at the agent's thoughts, she heard her silently say they'd be *easy to handle*.

Intent on getting her client out of the public eye, Sheri rounded up the troops militarily by raising a finger above her head and swirling it around in a circle. "Let's go, people! Move out!"

The family of three and Sean all found seats in one vehicle, while Sheri and Max were in another. Boxed in from front to back by security, the doors simultaneously closed before the caravan of trucks left the airport and headed toward the 405.

Ella looked out the window for anything exciting. "Where is the beach? And the ocean? Are you sure we are in California?" she asked, disillusioned by her preconception of the iconic state. She believed she would see lush greenery, palm trees, and surfing, but she seemed disappointed at the concrete jungle surrounding them.

"I promise to give you the whole West Coast experience in the coming days. Let's just get the premiere behind us first," he chuckled, knowing how much they had to do in such a short time.

Ben followed the GPS instructions. While traveling down North Beverly Glen, zigzagging over to Bel Air Road, he turned left onto a narrow roadway. Climbing the hills, taking a few twists and turns, Ella discovered many new builds along the way. Marveling at the beautifully landscaped yards, she noticed some manicured trees sculpted to look like mushrooms. At the top of the hill, the caravan rounded a sharp corner.

Sean leaned forward. "Just move straight ahead to those gates," he pointed out to Ben. "Max will hit the button."

The large steel barrier inched slowly to the right while each vehicle moved into the hidden circular courtyard surrounded by living green walls and the sounds of peaceful waterfalls. The family was amazed by the size of the home. With her face glued to the window, Ella was in awe.

When the group got out of the trucks, Max gathered the Andersons together to offer further instruction while Sheri stood beside her SUV and waited, not saying a word. It wasn't hard to sense the woman wanted to speak privately with Sean. Giving the actor the eye, the talent agent swayed her head in a controlled way to silently signal for him to talk to her.

Evily didn't like that. She thought it to be rude.

Sean got the less-than-subtle hint. "You guys go ahead with Max. I will be there in a moment."

The young man immediately caught on and ushered the group toward the front door. At the top of the steps, Evily wondered what the woman was about to say. Purposefully hanging back, hovering about, discussing the waterfall wall's design and the Aztec-like carvings with Ella, she zeroed in on Sheri's comments. Concerned that he went against her better judgment, thankfully, Sean stood his ground.

"Sheri, there is nothing to discuss. This is a decision I've made. Evily and the children will be a permanent part of my life from now on. End of story."

"Very well." Sheri did not argue with him. She calmly nodded and left the premises in an overly dramatic way, with every security agent jumping at her beckoned call.

As her SUV pulled out of the courtyard, Sean bounded up the steps, excited to welcome the family into his home.

Proudly opening the enormous pivot door embedded within the glass wall, they could see his staff waiting with anticipation to meet them the moment they walked in.

Happily offering a bright smile, Evily met Marianna, Hildy, and Michelle, the ladies of the house. The author desperately wanted to make a good impression, so she gave each of them her undivided attention. They were overjoyed to see that she was so lovely. Not having grandchildren of her own, Hildy was looking forward to hearing some youthful banter within the walls of the otherwise large, lifeless home.

Barely there five minutes, there was no rest for the family just yet.

Max stopped them in their tracks and said, "Okay, everyone. First things first. Evily and Ella, you need to go upstairs with me. We need to get you outfitted for tomorrow night. Sean, you, and Evan head to the lower level and do the same. Everyone is waiting for you."

"Wait?" Evily was so nervous. "What do you mean – everyone?"

Max felt like a real-life fairy godmother. "You'll see."

His eyes focused on hers; Sean waved to Evily. "Have fun, you two," he said joyfully.

Guiding the girls upstairs, Sean's assistant rounded the corner into a room filled with shoes, jewelry, and racks of designer gowns. In the middle sat a large mirror and an elevated pedestal. Ella and her Mother were overwhelmed. The entire experience felt like a Cinderella moment.

In seconds, a group of consultants began showing the ladies their options. Excited, the young girl went first and tried on only two dresses before deciding what she loved the best. The pretty gown made her look and feel like a princess. Her face said it all. She beamed while looking at her reflection. Her mom had never seen her daughter so happy. Soaking it all in, Ella treasured the moment. They were so thankful for the stylists' expertise. Each made her feel confident and beautiful in everything she tried on from head to toe.

Selecting five dresses from the display, Evily finally found one that fit her perfectly. Staring at herself in the mirror, admiring the pretty, wispy blue designer gown flowing all around her, she was less frightened about attending the premiere. However, she was still concerned about her children being in the spotlight.

"Is it too much?" the author questioned, never wearing anything like this before.

Max's face lit up. "Absolutely not, my dear. You're going to be the Belle of the Ball. It certainly reflects that. I think it is perfect."

Humble, Evily smiled. "Okay. I will wear this one."

"Wonderful choice," he said before turning to everyone in the room. "That's a wrap, people."

Upon hearing this, the group immediately began packing all the gowns in bags and placing them on the mobile racks very efficiently.

A woman stepped forward and stood beside Max. "She is just going to see if it needs any alterations."

Nodding, Evily said, "What is your name?"

"My name is Anna, Ma'am,"

"Nice to meet you, Anna. I'm Evily," she replied, always wanting to know the names of those around her.

The woman pulled and tugged on the dress to check its fit and floor length. Anna pinned it in various places, making sure it would not hinder Evily's appearance at the premiere. "Stepping back, happy with everything, she said, "Okay. All done, Ma'am."

"Thank you so much." The author made sure to show appreciation.

Anna, in turn, tilted her head slightly to the side, almost as if she'd never been spoken to so kindly before.

Changing out of the dress, she passed it along to Anna, who left without saying a word. Evily took that personally and feared that the rest of LA would probably treat her the same way. Feeling like an outsider, she compiled a list of pros and cons. In her heart of hearts, she could see that everything would be fine. There didn't seem to be any red flags popping up despite the hesitancy brought about by her protective instinct. At this point, she trusted Sean and knew he would never do anything to put them in harm's way.

This is where blind faith comes in, she thought to herself. *I must have faith in the gift given to us.*

Taking a deep breath, she changed from the robe they supplied her and got dressed. By the time she finished, the entourage had already moved most of the wardrobe racks out of the house. Evily checked on the teens who'd settled in their guest rooms. Finding each immersed in conversations with their friends, giving them their space, she closed their doors and went in search of Sean.

Not seeing him since they arrived, she timidly strolled down the hall and descended the glass-enclosed staircase. Impressed by the beautifully decorated rooms and unique artwork on every wall, still overwhelmed to a degree, the author ventured into the main floor seating area that opened up to the pool deck outside. There, she spotted him sitting on a lounge chair.

Aware of her presence, he smiled and silently waved her over.

He wrapped up his phone call and said, "Hey, you. All settled in?"

"Yes. I think so," she replied, feeling out of sorts.

Shoving over, giving her room to sit beside him on the double chaise chair, she took a seat, astounded by the view of the Los Angeles skyline.

Not sure why she seemed off, he asked, "Are you alright? Did you find something to wear?"

With a bright, nervous smile, Evily leaned back. "Yes, thank you. The gown is stunning - Ella's, too. I can't believe we are in LA. I am just...." she exhaled. "I mean, everything that has happened today has been unbelievable."

Sean knew she was appreciative. "What you've done for me far outweighs anything I could ever offer you. Believe me." Still feeling that there was something she wasn't telling him, he questioned, "What is it?"

"I don't know. I'm just nervous." Evily grabbed her knees and brought them close to her chest, making her compress into a ball on the chair.

"About what?"

"The premiere, of course. All of those people with eyes on us. I don't know if I'm ready for that. Especially all the negative."

Taking her hand in his, Sean looked deep into her eyes. "Please don't worry. You'll all do great. I promise. Just be yourself. Let them see the person I have fallen in love with."

She gasped upon hearing those words.

"I can wholeheartedly say I love you, Evily Landy slash Anderson," he confessed, slipping in a bit of humor.

Not given any choice but to gush over his statement, she humbly beamed. "I love you too, hashtag SeanBradley."

"Really? Truly?" Wrapping her in his arms, he knew it felt right.

All Evily could do was agree. "Yes."

"Excuse me, Mr. Bradley," Marianna interrupted politely. "Chef Stan has dinner prepared when you are ready."

"Thank you, Marianna. We're coming." Sean got up from the chair. Offering his hand and taking hold of hers, he helped her to her feet. Just captivated by Evily's eyes, he leaned in and gently kissed her without reservation, still feeling the newness and excitement of their budding relationship.

When their lips parted, he whispered to her, "I guess we should round up the kids?"

Hand in hand, the two walked back inside.

"I'll go and tell them dinner is ready."

About to let go of Sean's hand, he surprisingly pulled her back.

"Wait. There's no need to do that," Sean said. "I can do it from here." Lifting the receiver on the phone, he pressed a button and said, "Paging the Andersons and the Henchmen. Dinner!"

Evily's eyebrows raised as the announcement echoed through the home. "Well, that is convenient. I need to have this phone installed at my house."

The Henchmen emerged from the lower floor first, unfamiliar with the principal client's plans. Seconds later, they could hear Evan and Ella bounding down the glass-enclosed staircase.

Locating the group in the living room, each of them began talking simultaneously.

"When can we go swimming?" Evan said first, overlapped by Ella asking, "Can we have a tour of the rest of the house?"

"Excuse me," their Mother said sternly. "Mind your manners, please."

The teens toned down their excitement.

Not knowing who to answer, Sean figured ladies should be first. "Yes, Ella. I will give you a tour of the house, and Evan, you can swim whenever you want to." Given the eye from Evily, he added, "Preferably, after dinner."

His Mother nodded. "Yes, we need to eat first."

Addressing Ben and Ivan, noticing they seemed lost, their new boss said, "You guys need to get accustomed to joining us each night. You're part of the family now. That includes sharing meals."

With muted gratitude, thankful for the opportunity to work for their famous client, the group moved to the covered outdoor kitchen where Chef Stan had made a selection of gourmet burgers with a choice of toppings, homemade pizza, salad, and of course, truffle fries on the side. A casual meal perfect for their teenage guests.

Everyone helped themselves from the bistro-like buffet. Chef Stan was so excited to cook for more than just Mr. Bradley. Seeing the teens fawning over the food made him extremely happy.

To conclude their evening dinner, Max had them practice their grand entrance at the premiere. There was a specific protocol that needed to be followed and understood. Each took to it quite well, making him feel more confident about the family's introduction to the world.

As promised, when Max released them from business duties, Sean proudly gave everyone a house tour. Ella was in awe of every design element in the famous architect's creation. She loved the uniquely imagined spaces - every square inch. Her brother's favorite part was the actor's elaborate car collection.

Before bed, Evan immersed himself in the infinity pool. Ella joined him. After swimming for over an hour, racing while doing their laps, the teens finally retired to their rooms, leaving Evily and Sean alone again.

The ladies of the house would nosily walk by periodically and glance outside, so thankful to see the brightness of life the family brought to the home and their boss.

Still sitting poolside, Sean got up. Reaching his hand to her, he said, "Walk with me. I want to show you something."

The two went inside and climbed the stairs before turning right on the second floor. Evily knew he was taking her to the opposite wing of the house. The only space he neglected to show off during the tour. Swinging open the tall double doors, they walked into the primary bedroom. She looked around and paused while Sean remotely turned on the fireplace and kept the lights dimmed.

"This is my favorite room in the house. Mostly because of..." Drawing out the last word, Sean guided her to the far corner by the glass wall. Finishing his sentence, he added, "...this swing. The view from this spot is incredible at night."

With a touch of another button, the Fleetwood doors soon parted and slid along their tracks automatically. Now exposed to open air, with a slight breeze wafting through, they enjoyed the twinkling lights of the Los Angeles skyline.

"Want to sit with me?"

She nodded and said, "Sure."

Holding the swing steady, Sean waited until she was comfortable before he had a seat. All snuggled into the plush chair suspended in mid-air, moving about freely, Sean wrapped her in his arms.

"I can see why this is your favorite spot," she said.

"Sometimes, when I feel down or need time to think, I come here. There is just something about it," the handsome man divulged. "Over the past few years, I've made countless decisions in this swing."

Swaying back and forth repeatedly, Evily asked, "What type of decisions?"

"Some life-altering, some not so much."

Afraid to mention it again, she asked hesitantly, "So, are you certain you want us with you tomorrow night? No second thoughts?"

Sean chuckled before he turned to her, presenting the sincerest of expressions. "There is not a doubt in my mind." Reaching down to raise her legs to cross over his, he embraced her tightly. "I love you," he whispered. Not allowing her to reciprocate, he leaned in and lightly kissed her lips.

Taken by the tender moment, Evily felt a little overwhelmed, and her heart raced. Trembling, She suddenly pulled back and lowered her head. Deep in thought, she found it hard to focus.

Sean trod carefully.

"I...umm...," she replied. "I'm sorry, umm, it's been so long since..."

Being the gentleman he is, he said, "It's okay. I wasn't expecting us to...."

Interrupting him, she said, "No, no. Not that." Blushing, she added, "Well, that too...."

"I don't understand."

"What I meant to say was... It's been so long since I've felt loved."

Sean's heart went out to her.

"To be honest, I don't think anyone has truly ever loved me," she confessed. "All of this is quite foreign. I still feel like I'm dreaming."

"Evily, you deserve to have someone who will give you his whole heart. Not want to live a day without you by his side. You should be loved and protected always. Please, allow me to be that person. The person who gives you all of those things."

The author cried and nodded her head.

"You know, before we met last week, I felt destined to live a lonely life."

"And now?" she quietly whispered with an element of hope, barely able to take a breath.

"You've infused excitement and newness into my life. A world now filled with color. I feel like I am no longer lingering amidst the grey." He paused and said, "I want us to be a family. You, Ella, Evan, and me. I hope you are thinking along the same lines?"

Filled with joy, the author nodded tearfully. "Yes. I can't seem to imagine my life without you in it now."

Sean cupped her face with a gentle touch, his thumb brushing lightly against her cheekbone. His gaze lingered on the eyes that had captivated him from the start, drawing him in with their quiet intensity. Slowly, he leaned in until their lips met in a soft, lingering kiss that left Evily feeling as though she were floating, untethered from the world. Unable to think of him as Hollywood action star Sean Bradley, now, to her, his role had changed. He was now the love of her life.

Parting, Evily quietly asked, "Did we just make our first life-altering decision in this swing?"

With warmth in his heart, he replied, "Yes. I'm sure it will be the first of many."

55

Thursday, August 1st
Los Angeles, California

Sometimes, the dreams that come true are those you never even knew you had. ~ Alice Sebold

Opting to sleep in her appointed guest room, intent on setting a good example for her children, Evily woke the following day to the sounds of a gentle knocking on her bedroom door. Listening intently, not sure what was happening, she heard a voice on the other side, and it wasn't a spirit asking for help.

"Ms. Evily? Ms. Evily?" it whispered.

Out of bed, she wrapped herself in a robe before opening the door a crack. "Max? What is going on?"

"Good morning, Ms. Evily. We must get moving. You and Ella have many appointments to keep."

"Appointments?"

"Yes. You have your final fittings, and then we are off to hair, make-up, and, can't forget, manis and pedis. Chop chop," he announced, clapping his hands twice.

Watching him divert to Ella's room, she knew he wouldn't be well-received so early in the morning.

"Ms. Ella? Oh, Ms. Ella. Rise and shine, my dear."

"Max? Go away," the girl shouted sleepily from the room.

Quickly tossing her hair in a messy bun, Evily moved Max aside and went into Ella's room to wake her. "I've got this, Max," she said.

The assistant gave a single nod and went about his morning routine.

Not long after, both ladies joined Evan and Sean, having breakfast downstairs in the kitchen. The two had already worked out in the well-appointed gym an hour before and were now enjoying their energy-packed smoothies and bowls of healthy oatmeal and berries while talking with Chef Stan.

"Where are you two off to when we are gone?" Evily asked while Ella took a seat at the table.

Max checked the schedule. "They have an appointment for hand massages and gent manicures before moving on to haircuts."

Outwardly objecting, Evan said, "No way. I'm not doin' the nail thing."

Sean laughed. "It's not what you think. They just clean up your hands. Make 'em look good. Come on, man. Don't make me go there by myself."

Seeing the look on the actor's face, Evan conceded. "Fine."

"Maybe we could head to the arena to see if the Kings are practicing afterward?" He knew that would pique the athlete's interest.

"Are you serious?" Evan wasn't sure if he was joking.

"Sure. Why not? We will have time. The ladies won't be back for a while. It'll be just you, me, and the Henchmen. You in?"

"Yeah, for sure."

"Great."

Sean happened to glance at Evily, who had been staring at him throughout the conversation. Nodding, giving off a maternal vibe, he knew she trusted him to spend the afternoon with her son.

"Well, you two have fun then," she said sentimentally, thankful that Evan would have a father figure who wanted to spend time with him. Seeing her children happy, with bright faces and eager eyes, was the greatest gift.

Max looked at his watch. "We had better get a move on, ladies. We can't be late."

Walking out the front door, Max corraled the family, Sean, and the Henchmen to the SUVs waiting in the courtyard, trying to keep their tight schedule. While settling in, Evily could hear the thoughts of each protection agent. Especially Ivan. He was secretly happy to be assigned to Sean and Evan, knowing they'd be attending the King's practice, while Ben had the daunting task of dealing with Sean's high-strung assistant belting orders at him the entire day. Chuckling to herself, Evily was thankful to hear Ben's main priority was keeping her and Ella safe despite having to adhere to Max's every wish. He felt like they were a joy to be around and was certain the ladies wouldn't be afraid to put Max in his place if things got too out of hand.

Assigned to the first SUV, Ben got in on the passenger side once his clients had settled in the second row. Greeting the driver, he said, "Hey, Mate. How are you? I'm Ben. The ladies' security detail for the day."

"Nice to meet you, Ben. I'm Geoffrey," the sharply dressed older gentleman said.

Max reached forward and passed Ben a card with the address of their destination. "We need to be at the hotel in thirty minutes," Sean's assistant instructed.

Passing the card to the driver, the man looked at it and said, "Okay. No problem." Not having to enter their destination in the GPS, Ben sat back, assuming the guy knew the city inside and out.

Their driver put the vehicle in gear, ready to depart, getting the hint from Max, who was tapping his Rolex. Slowly pulling up towards the main gate, it automatically slid to the left.

The guys could hear Ella shouting, "See you guys later!"

"Bye! Have fun, ladies!" Sean shouted back.

The gate opened to a crowd of photographers gathering on the street. The scene made Evily panic and prompted Ella to roll up the window immediately.

"How do all these people know where Sean lives?" Evily asked Max.

"Sadly, word gets around. Once, someone followed him home. It became public knowledge quickly," he replied in a monotone voice.

Inching their way through the crazy commotion, an outside security team handled the mob to allow them to depart for their intended destinations.

Finally, underway, Max introduced the girls to his trusted friend. "Evily and Ella Anderson, meet Geoffrey Williams. He is a long-time friend and trusted member of the Bradley team."

Glancing in the rearview mirror, he said, "Pleased to meet you both."

"Hi, Geoffrey!" the young passenger said with abundant energy, making him jovially laugh.

"Pleased to meet you as well," the author said, offering a pleasant smile.

About to speak, the man hesitated. Evily knew he wanted to share something but figured he shouldn't since Max was in the vehicle. Catching the refined-looking man grinning while driving along, the author decided to hone in on his thoughts. This was not hard to do. He was an open book with a heart of gold. Able to hear him and even see a few images flashing through her mind, she learned something unexpected. The last time he saw his boss was when he departed for Boston. He knew something was very wrong the second Sean had gotten in his truck. It worried him. Knowing he was in a terrible mood, Geoffrey remembered giving his friend some space. He recalled Sean constantly scrolling through his phone and being quite angry by the time they reached the airport.

Their driver glanced back a second time at the author and her daughter. Evily could feel how thankful he was to see life in his boss's eyes again. He felt God had intervened in this situation. Immediately noticing a change in Sean today, there was no doubt in his mind that the Andersons played a massive part in that.

Looking out the window, Evily smiled. She was happy he was accepting of them. It made her wonder if the fans would think the same.

Driving into the heart of Beverly Hills, still awe-struck by everything that had transpired the past few days, Evily fell deep in thought. In a blur, passing by the beautiful shops along Wilshire Boulevard, she felt like she was in a dream. Almost waiting for someone to wake her, she turned to her daughter, who was exuding a great deal of wonderment at the sights around her. Taking everything in, Evily realized this would be Ella's first visit to a spa. It was something they never took the time to do all these years. The thought of spending the day with her daughter was priceless.

When Geoffrey pulled up in front of the hotel, Ben quickly got out of the vehicle and scanned the area before opening the back door to allow Max, Ella, and Evily to depart.

"This way, ladies," Max said, taking the lead. "We are off to dress fittings first. Afterward, I have you scheduled for full premiere prep at the spa."

Timidly taking hold of her daughter's hand, they followed Max inside with Ben right behind them, excited for their day of pampering to begin.

56 |

Thursday, August 1st
Los Angeles, California

You don't find love, it finds you. It's got a little to do with destiny, fate, and what is written in the stars.

~ Anaïs Nin

Parting ways, upon exiting the gate, driver Dimitri headed south, opting to take a separate route into Beverly Hills. Winding around, corner after corner, they soon arrived at Sunset Boulevard. Evan hadn't said much. But he still had a million questions for Sean despite him answering many during their workout session that morning.

While scrolling through his phone, responding to Insta follower requests, he asked, "We are just going to this nail thing and the barbershop, then we get to see the King's practice, right?"

"Yes. That's the plan," Sean replied.

"So, how long will these things take exactly?" Evan wondered, more fixated on getting to the rink.

Sean chuckled. "My man, I think we need to suffer through about ninety minutes, then we'll be free to do whatever we want. Deal?"

"Ninety minutes, huh?" Evan repeated. "Okay. I can do that. It's a small sacrifice to make."

"Yes, it is. It will go by fast."

Arriving at the Noir grooming appointment right on time, Ivan escorted his clients inside while Dimitri waited in the truck for them to return. It wasn't long before they were on to the next appointment at the Beverly Hills Barber Shop. Enjoying all the attention from the people who make Sean look like a star, he posted their experiences on his Insta and was excited to see all his new followers. It was hard to believe how the day was turning out.

Now looking dapper and fresh, the two traveled to the Toyota Sports Performance Center to take in the King's practice. Sean made a few calls along the way.

When Dimitri slowly turned into the famous arena, Evan marveled at the team's signage displayed proudly on the walls of the building. Stopping at the main entrance, Ivan got out of the truck and secured the area before allowing his clients to get out. A gentleman dressed in a King's warm-up suit was waiting to greet them.

Sean reached out his hand to the man. "Hey, it's good to see you, my friend," the actor said.

Evan followed his lead.

Turning to the teen standing behind him, Sean said, Evan Anderson, meet Matt Price. He's the Head Strength and Conditioning coach for the Kings." Sean briefly explained his connection to the man, stating, "Long story short, he was my trainer years back. He helped me prep for a few movies."

Nervous, the teenager firmly shook Mr. Price's hand. "Nice to meet you, Sir."

"I'm sure Evan Anderson will be on your watch list this year. He's a Junior player from Chicago."

"That's awesome, man. Looking forward to seeing you at one of our camps." Matt turned and said, "Let's go inside. The guys just got on the ice."

Walking into the building with all eyes on them was unnerving for the young man. They stopped briefly along the boards to watch the players in the warm-up phase before finding a seat on the wooden benches. The young player's eyes lit up as the NHL team flew across the ice from side to side. He stayed quiet and paid attention, taking note of every pass executed to perfection, and each shot sniped on net. Not only did Sean want to share this experience with Evan, but he had brought him there also to discuss something pretty important. Being the man of the Anderson house, he saw it fitting to include Evily's son in his decision.

In awe of all the activity on the ice, the two commented on the drills executed with great precision. Evan videoed a few plays to study later.

When the head coach called for a water break, Sean asked, "Hey, Evan? Can I talk to you about something?"

"Yeah, sure? Shoot. What is it?"

The Hollywood star rested his elbows upon his knees and leaned forward. Rubbing his hands together in front of him nervously, he said, "So, I know I've only known you, Ella, and your mom a short time. But, I have to say, you have had a profound effect on me."

Evan interjected. "Yeah, this has been the most amazing week, despite the run-in with my dad."

Watching Drew Doughty swing past them, Sean tried to muster some nerve. "So, I am not sure if you know..."

"Know what?" the teenager asked.

"I'm just going to come out and say it."

Evan turned to the famous actor.

"You've probably gathered in the past twenty-four hours that I've developed feelings for your Mom."

Evan's eyebrows raised. "Yeah. Kinda figured."

"So, are you okay with it?"

"Sean, this vacation has been rough, but I have never seen her happier than when she's with you." Evily's son was so sure of that statement.

Bidding a sigh of relief, Sean replied, "I'm glad you think that. There is something else I need to ask."

Already aware of what he was about to say, he decided to help him out. "You want to date her, don't you?"

Surprised he'd picked up on that, Sean replied, "Well, something like that. I wanted to ask your permission first."

"Appreciate it." Evan focused on Sean. "Look, if you promise, you will never leave her. You will love her and care for her. Never hurt her, then I'm good with it. If you do any of those things, I swear, I'll kick your ass, and don't think I won't. Movie star or not, you will have to deal with me."

Sean grinned and nodded his head. "Fair enough, my man. Understood."

The teen stared straight ahead. "You know, given how bad things have been with my father, it will be good to have someone there to keep Mom and Ella safe, especially if I move out next year. It gives me peace of mind knowin' I'm not abandoning them. It'll be nice havin' you around, man."

"Thank you. It means a lot."

Evan gave him a nod and offered a manly handshake, bumping shoulders.

Relieved their conversation went better than expected, the two returned to the action on the ice before being invited to meet the team.

Awestruck, Evan was in his glory when introduced to his idol, Drew Doughty. But the big surprise was talking with Todd McLellan. When the Head Coach told him he was already on his scouting radar, it boosted the young player's confidence. Today, hands down, was the best day of the young athlete's life.

Ivan realized it was getting late. He'd received many reminder texts from Max in the last half hour and reluctantly had to bring the King's visit to an end. Escorting the guys back out front to Dimitri waiting in the SUV, they quickly left the arena and headed northwest toward his house in Bel Air.

Sean caught up on a few texts while Evan updated his social media with his King's practice pictures.

Taking a phone call, the actor said, "Hey, Neil. Is everything good to go? Yeah, that would be great. Can you have it delivered by eight tonight? Yeah, yeah. Perfect. I appreciate it. Thanks."

Evan was too immersed in his social media to notice or listen in.

Just before four o'clock, they threaded through the crowd gathered on the street outside his house. They knew the girls were already there. Unable to see them before the big reveal, the guys had a bite to eat before getting dressed. The premiere was now just hours away.

57

Thursday, August 1st
Los Angeles, California

No matter her age, every girl deserves one happy ending in life - a memorable Cinderella moment.

~ E. A. Stark

Alone in her room, Evily took a deep breath and turned to stand in front of the eight-foot mirror leaning against the wall. Closing the clips on the waist of the beautiful designer gown, not moving an inch, she stared at the woman before her, thrilled by the reflection. Still concerned about their public appearance alongside Sean Bradley, Evily concentrated and shut her eyes. The author focused on the images moving through her mind like a scroll. Nothing negative appeared. She knew they would be fine tonight after seeing only happy moments in the pictures. Nervous, with a stomach full of butterflies, she was thankful to get dressed without the entourage. It would have added to her anxiety if she'd been fawned over by so many. Able to smile, she exhaled and walked over to the bench at the end of the bed, feeling like a modern-day, mature Cinderella. Carefully slipping on the dainty shoes with clear straps and jeweled applique, she believed they resembled glass slippers.

How fitting, she thought.

"Well, Evily Landy. It's time to take a leap of faith," she said, standing tall.

Adding the earrings and necklace supplied to her, almost forgetting the tiny clutch on the dresser, she took one last glance before departing.

Meanwhile, across the hall, with her hair, makeup, and nails professionally done, draped in delicate diamond jewelry, Ella exited her room to find Max standing in the hallway, bursting with anticipation.

"Oh, my dear! You look so lovely," he gushed while the young girl glowed.

Realizing her Mother had yet to emerge, the two waited patiently. Max stayed in the wings, holding a tissue box, prepared for anything.

When Evily's door swung open, Ella's face lit up brightly. "Mom! You look amazing!"

Evily could not speak. On the verge of tears, she reached out to her daughter with open arms, trying to stay composed. "Oh, Ella. You look gorgeous. So grown-up."

She raised her hands to her chin and said with tears in her eyes, "I can't believe it, Mom. This trip has been like a dream, don't you think?"

All Evily could do was nod.

"Ladies, ladies. We must control the waterworks," Max said, converging with urgency, blotting their tears with a tissue in hand, mindful of their makeup. Powdering their faces, Max stepped back.

Evily held out her hand to Ella. "Well? Are we ready to go?"

Her daughter agreed. "Yes, I'm ready."

Downstairs, in the main foyer, Sean paced back and forth at the bottom of the stairs while waiting for the girls to join them. Looking dapper in Tom Ford, he'd opted for a simple black-on-black look, while Evan went with a more colorful and hip jacket. Fidgeting, Sean kept checking his reflection in the mirror.

"So, this kind of thing happens often in your world?" Evan laughed, wondering why anyone would want to put themselves through such stress.

"Don't worry, when you make the NHL, this reveal thing will happen to you every game night. Nerve-wracking, isn't it?"

Hearing Max announcing that the girls were on their way, Evan and Sean stood beside each other.

"Alright. We are ready," Sean bellowed back to the second level.

Holding hands, Ella and Evily proceeded down the hall to where Max stood at the top of the stairs.

"We need to have the big reveal," he said, "Let's give the guys a show, shall we? Ella, you're first, my dear."

Max checked her over quickly. Happy with everything, he offered his hand to her. Leading the vision in soft petal pink down the glass-enclosed staircase, Evan and Sean looked up to find the pretty girl descending in an intricately designed midi Marchesa gown. With her hair tied back with gentle cascading curls framing her face, she smiled nervously as the gentlemen greeted her.

"Wow, sis, you look great." Evan was surprised at the sight of his sister looking so different. It made him feel like she wasn't so little anymore.

Sean approached and offered her his hand. "You look beautiful, Ella."

"Thank you for this lovely dress and shoes. For everything, really."

"You are so welcome." He twirled her around and asked, "Are you excited about the premiere?"

"Yes, but I'm also a little scared."

"Don't worry. We will all stick together tonight. Just be yourself. Everyone will love you."

"Wait until you see Mom," Ella gushed with anticipation.

While quickly checking his phone, Evan did not notice Max beginning to escort his mom down the stairs.

"Evan, put that away! She's coming. Pay attention," his sister prompted sternly.

"What? I'm getting like two hundred new Insta followers an hour. This is awesome." He quickly tucked his phone into his jacket pocket.

Dressed in a long powder blue Prada gown with sparkled beading around the skirt, Max and Evily stopped on the landing so she could have her *moment,* as Max described it. Sean gazed up at her in amazement. She looked angelic. Her hair flowed along her shoulders, with a small section pulled back, beautifully pinned with an abundance of sculpted swirls. A simple hanging teardrop diamond necklace graced the plunging neckline. It was specifically selected not to take away from the essence of the gown.

Met by his bright eyes, she felt uncomfortable, as Sean seemed mesmerized. Always preferring to blend in with the background rather than be the center of attention, Evily knew tonight would challenge her. Gently lifting her skirt with every step, she descended the staircase with grace and poise. Sean approached at the bottom to meet her. Lost for words, he offered her his hand as Evily watched his face light up the room.

"You look stunning," he whispered with her hand in his.

Nervous, she lowered her head upon hearing the compliment. In her lifetime, no one had ever described her in that way. Thankful for her blessings, Evily locked eyes with Sean. "And you look so very hand-some." It made her feel as though she was dreaming.

Ella spied Evan immersed in his phone again. She hit his arm, giving him an unexpected jolt, and motioned for him to say something to their Mother.

Sliding the device into his jacket pocket a second time, he said, "You look really pretty, Mom."

"Thank you, Evan," she replied humbly.

While talking amongst themselves, quite excited, they snapped a few pictures. Soon, the foyer erupted with laughter and anxious banter. It delighted the ladies of the house, who looked on with absolute delight.

Confirming their limo had arrived, intent on keeping the group on schedule, Max grabbed a few things off the front table and shouted over everyone, "Okay, people! Let's move! Everyone outside. The limo is here! Do we have the Henchmen?"

Ben and Ivan joined the others, dressed sharply in all-black suits with no ties. Given their stature, wearing the confining attire was prob-ably bad enough without adding the strangling accessory. Flanking the group, they walked out of the house and down the long walkway, checking their comms.

On their way to the courtyard, Max lifted Evily's dress so it wouldn't drag on the ground. Descending the stairs, he helped her walk to the luxurious, custom Sprinter awaiting them. Boasting a soft, buttery grey leather interior and modern black accents, Ella got inside first and found a seat, mindful of her dress.

"This is crazy! Look at this!" Evan exclaimed while climbing aboard, live-streaming along the way for his friends to see.

The Hollywood star helped Evily inside the vehicle, but Max quickly stepped in to show her how to sit down without wrinkling the fabric. Noticeably hyper, he instructed Ben and Ivan to travel with their group and the other Henchmen to follow in the SUV. The two men sat in the back row behind Evan and Ella, doing what Max asked.

"We are ready!" the assistant bellowed to the driver. "Let's go!"

After giving the signal, the door automatically closed. Opening the gate remotely, the security crew exited first, leading the sprinter van through the mob of photographers along the street.

"This is all because of us?" Ella asked, a little concerned since the crowd had exploded since their departure earlier that morning.

"Yes. Don't worry. It'll be fine," Sean replied, thankful to see over twenty security guards gathering around to help the caravan safely maneuver through.

Quite nervous, Evily was having a hard time reading those around her. It seemed her mind was a muddle. Clasping her fingers together, Sean noticed her anxiousness.

Reaching over, taking hold of her hand, he whispered, "Everyone will love you. I promise."

With an uncertain half-smile, she hoped that to be true.

58

Thursday, August 1st
Los Angeles, California

Your smile is your logo, your personality is your business card, and how you leave others feeling after an experience with you becomes your trademark. ~ Jay Danzie.

On Sunset Boulevard, the teens talked amongst themselves, pointing out beautiful sights along the way. Unlike Evan, who searched for exotic cars and motorcycles, Ella was more interested in the immaculately manicured grounds, well-maintained trees, flowers, and foliage, not to mention unique architecture. Excited to see the iconic streets lined with palm trees finally, the driver changed lanes and turned left to travel along Hollywood Boulevard.

Knowing they were closing in on their final destination, Max gave them a five-minute warning.

Doubling back, taking a detour across Franklin Avenue, and veering south on North Highland, Ella immediately noticed the Hollywood Walk of Fame on the right. There were flocks of people everywhere. "Sean? Do you have a star?" she questioned, unsure of the answer.

Evan heard what she asked and wondered what he would say.

"Sure do. It's coming up in front of the Dolby Theatre," he replied.

"Wow, that's so weird." The young girl flashed a strange expression.

Not sure why she thought that he chuckled and said, "Why?"

"Well, because to me, you're just Sean Bradley, the guy who's been hanging out with us in Boston," she giggled. "Not Hollywood star, Sean Bradley."

"Hey, I'd rather be that guy in Boston more often." He gave Evily's hand a few gentle squeezes.

She smiled.

Approaching his commemorative star, Sean pointed to the area where it was situated. The teens were in disbelief.

"Super cool." Ella was awe-struck.

All eyes were on their vehicles, wondering who was inside. Seeing spotlights swirling upward ahead of them, bringing attention to the event, the driver slowed down and put on his flashers, making the family nervous. There were so many people.

Stopping outside the TCL Chinese Theatre, met by a massive crowd of fans and photographers lining the barriers on either side of the street, security was everywhere. The crowds were screaming from every angle. Evily's heart rate increased, and she started to fidget. Able to see a few yards down the red carpet, booths of reporters were prepped and awaiting their arrival. The author could barely breathe.

"Don't worry." Sean squeezed her hand.

Trying to take a deep breath, she exhaled. Her hands shook.

"What does your gut feeling say?" he asked.

Evily brightened slightly. "That this will be a night like no other."

He laughed. "See, there you go. Never doubt your gut."

She nodded her head, still scared beyond belief.

Max stood up and moved forward to the door when the sprinter van slowly came to a halt. Surrounded by security, he waited for the signal to emerge. Giving final instructions, he said, "Remember, simply step out of the van the way we practiced. Gather outside for your Mom to exit last. Let's see all those pearly whites! Wave to the crowd with a steady hand; don't flop it around like a fish." His last comment was directed humorously at the teenagers to instill some comic relief.

Both gave him a thumbs up, waving the way they'd rehearsed, with an abundance of laughter. It caused the assistant to applaud their ability to follow instructions.

Tickled by the latest entertainment news headlines, the stylish assistant revealed, "All of you look wonderful! Rumor has it the world has dubbed you #TheBradleyBunch, so let's show off just a little, my new Hollywood family! Shall we? And don't forget to have fun!"

Evily turned to Sean, stunned by Max's statement.

Before she could comment, Sean clarified, "He's always over the top - loves theatrics. Take it with a grain of salt."

"Where are my Henchmen?" Max moved aside for Ben and Ivan to exit. "You're first!"

The door slid open right on cue, allowing the men to help secure the area.

Once they were in position, adding to about thirty other security guards working that section, Max turned to Sean. "Ready, my friend? You're up. It's showtime."

"Here we go." Sean took one last look at the Andersons. "I am so proud to have you here with me tonight. Just wanted to thank you for that. I'm excited for everyone to meet you."

Sean surfaced in star-studded fashion, making the crowd erupt the second his feet hit the red carpet. With a steady hand, he confidently waved to his fans and scanned every face surrounding him, moving so the photographers could get the perfect shot.

"Evan! Your turn," Max said militarily.

The athlete stood up and walked toward the door. His Mom held out her hand. He took hold of it on the way by before stepping out the same way Sean did. Remembering what they practiced, the actor rebelliously decided to sway from that formal greeting and replaced the gentlemanly handshake with a friendly dap, to Max's dismay.

Quickly over the boys' stunt, Max alerted, "Ella, my sweet girl. Your turn."

Max checked Ella's hair and her dress. The whole time, she held her Mother's hand.

"Are you okay, Sweetie?"

Without skipping a beat, her little girl said, "Piece of cake, Mom. I got this."

So proud, Evily laughed at the bright spark that ignited inside her.

When she stepped toward the open door, Sean offered his hand. The crowds melted at the scene unfolding.

"Just look at me, Ella," he said confidently. "It's okay." Sean encouraged.

Nodding her head, she let go of her Mom's hand and took Sean's as he helped her step out and join him. Giving her a side hug, the crowd cheered, prompting Ella to wave gracefully, wowing the crowd.

Finally, Max turned to Evily. Bending down, eyes meeting hers, he said, "This is your moment, dear. You look stunning. Now, go and join that handsome man."

Inhaling, trembling like a leaf, Evily could feel her heart racing faster when she stood up.

Double-checking everything, Max smiled. "You are ready."

Giving a silent nod, she took hold of Sean's hand, lifting the hem of her dress stylishly while her feet found the red carpet. The Hollywood star beamed, and everyone on earth could see it. The cheers surrounding them were deafening. Sweetly kissing her on the cheek, hearing welcomed applause, Sean offered her his arm in the most attentive way. Evan followed suit alongside Ella. Focused on every camera lens on the way up the red carpet, the movie star and his guests paused and posed for photos. The entire time, he never left the family's side. Evily and the teens had enamored the fans. Their presence made some cry tears of joy, knowing the lonely Hollywood star had finally found happiness after all this time.

While walking up the red carpet with the family by his side, Sean knew he'd given the world a rare glimpse into his private life. Strategically releasing a feature article with an accredited Magazine to coincide with the premiere, he divulged information on his past and described, most recently, the precious gift he had received. Offered a second chance at love, he proudly inched his way toward a sea of news booths eager to interview him and the now-famous Anderson family. Sheri arranged for the Entertainment News to be their first exclusive interview at the premiere.

Approaching the well-known news anchor, Sean put out his hand to shake hers. "Hello," he said. "How are you?"

"Sean Bradley! I am doing very well. Thank you!" The woman was very upbeat. "Welcome!" Amidst a flood of applause and screams, the famous actor and the family waved before the pretty blonde host asked, "Who do you have accompanying you? Is this the famous Anderson family everyone is talking about?"

"Yes, it is." Pointing to the teens, he said, "I would like to introduce you to Ella, Evan, and their mother, Evily." Slipping his hand around her waist and pulling her in tightly, Sean stood tall as the host greeted each of them.

"So, what's it like being here - walking the carpet? Are you enjoying the limelight?" The camera zoomed in after the host asked the question.

Positioning the microphone in front of them, Evily answered, "Well," she paused. "It's been overwhelming. Please be patient with us. This is outside our norm. When Sean asked us to join him, we couldn't say no. We have had quite a journey, which led us here to meet all of you." Turning to the fans lining the street, she said, "Thank you for warmly embracing us. I'm so grateful."

Her humble response went viral immediately. Max found it trending on Twitter before she even finished her statement. The fans loved them and, more importantly, accepted them as a part of Sean's life. Very few rejected the announcement.

After the pleasantries, explaining who everyone was wearing, the blonde female host asked, "So, Sean Bradley, what's next for you? Any new movies on the horizon?" Switching the microphone in his direction, she assumed he'd introduce his newest project - something he usually did.

"Well, at this point, I have decided to take a little time off," the movie star revealed. "I have a few projects of my own I wish to explore."

Turning to the Anderson family, the popular host looked confused by the actor's statement. She immediately understood what he was hinting at.

"Are you two thinking about getting married? Making it official?"

Sean stayed tight-lipped. "No comment," he said while grinning ear to ear.

Eager to pose a follow-up question, Max decided to cut her off and quickly whisk the family onto the next booth. He was well aware of the reporter's uncanny ability to pull things out of people. The last thing they needed was an unwanted rumor to surface.

Over the next hour, the four gave enlightening interviews, captivating the reporters visiting from across the country. The movie producers were in awe of all the positive publicity—far more than they could have generated with his co-star on his arm.

Upon reaching the theatre entrance, Sean briefly made eye contact with Andrea from a distance. The woman gave a subtle nod, acknowledging their successful night. Not creating a scene, she then disappeared behind her handlers.

The group followed the Henchmen through the narrow halls to where the Sprinter van was to pick them up at the back of the building. After walking the red carpet with Sean Bradley, the teenagers moved swiftly, feeling an adrenaline rush. It all seemed surreal. Their Mother stayed close to Sean while Ivan followed. Scouting the perimeter, Ben arranged for added security around the exit transfer. There were more people in the zone than expected. The Andersons and Sean all stood together and waited for everyone to get organized.

"Is that it?" Ella asked. "Do we not get to see the movie?"

The famous star replied, "A private screening is waiting for us at home. We are all done here. It's too risky to stay past this point. We were supposed to attend an afterparty, but I feel like I want to return home and spend the time with all of you if that's okay."

Not at all disappointed, Evily nodded. She had had enough attention for one day.

Expertly orchestrated down to the second, the Sprinter van moved into position. Right on schedule, Max guided everyone out the door. One by one, the Andersons took their seats in the vehicle while Sean stopped for a photo op and autograph session arranged for a small group of contest winners. Only six feet away, Evily witnessed Sean's connection with his fans. Parched, she took a sip of water.

"Umm, Mom?" Ella said, pointing out the window. "I think Sean wants you."

There, she found him waving her over. Nervous, she looked to Max for advice.

The assistant got flustered but said, "Alright, people! When the fans speak, we listen." Opening the sliding door and making a spectacle of himself, he called out, "Where are my Henchmen!"

Realizing they were already flanking Sean, security helped Evily step out to join the Hollywood star. They kept their eagle eyes on the area the entire time the two of them took photos with the fans.

Amidst the crowd, Ella and Evan also had young admirers. Joining their Mother and Sean, they talked with the lucky group of fans for another twenty minutes. Max witnessed the family's down-to-earth vibe, which he knew was the reason people connected with them so quickly.

"It just comes naturally," the assistant said, seeing how seamlessly the family worked together with his famous friend.

Beginning to fidget, knowing they were now running late, Max was about to have a meltdown. He hated losing control of a situation. To him, as far as he was concerned, #TheBradleyBunch was exaggeratingly sprawled from there to Hollywood Boulevard despite being at arm's length. Checking the time, he knew they needed to draw the line. Finally stepping in, Max announced a formal apology to the fans for breaking up the meet and greet.

Loved by all, the famous actor and the family graciously waved and said goodnight to everyone. Boarding the vehicle, Evily felt like, in a small way, they had an impact on the people who came out to see them. It made her think they could use this platform for the greater good. Given the state of the world, their little light could shine brightly and make a difference in the lives of others.

Once his boss and the Andersons were safe and accounted for, Max was thankful to slide the door shut and finally head home.

Counting, he said, "Okay, I have three Andersons, two Henchmen, and a Bradley." Dramatically collapsing in his seat, Max felt mentally shot. Since the night was not yet over, he pulled out his phone and soldiered through, checking news feeds for how the hashtag was trending. Overjoyed with his findings, he loudly revealed, "Yes! You killed it, Bradleybunch! We just hit number one on X!"

"Do you really have to call us that?" Evan stated, quite put off by the name.

"Look, it's what the world wants. Just run with it. You should check the hashtag on social. The attention it's getting will blow your mind."

The rest laughed at Max's comment, not having a problem with the crazy title.

Briefing the group, he ran through the night's agenda. "So, we now have dinner waiting for all of you back at the house. For the most part, your evening should be fairly low-key, as requested. You also have the option of watching Sean's movie."

"Unless nobody wants to see it. Either way. It doesn't matter to me," Sean joked. He didn't like watching himself on the screen.

"No. I want to see it," Ella chimed in.

"Me too!" Evan said enthusiastically, wanting to find out where the sequel would take them next.

The Sprinter slowly moved along Sunset to the gates of Bel Air.

While climbing the hills and maneuvering the narrow roadways, Evily looked at Sean and said, "Well, we did it. We made it through the night."

Squeezing her hand lovingly, he replied, "I never doubted that for a second. I knew you would."

Soon, they arrived at Sean's beautiful Bel Air home. Inching their way through the crowds of photographers that had grown since they left, Police were on hand to deal with the mayhem. The black steel gate slid open for the Sprinter to thread through. Everyone felt a sense of relief when it closed behind them. Inside the courtyard, the family stood up, more than ready to exit the vehicle.

"Home Sweet Home," Max stated, thankful that the night went off without a hitch.

Ben and Ivan scanned the grounds before allowing their clients to step outside. Escorted through the garage entrance, deciding not to walk along the front of the house, they moved past Sean's luxury car collection.

"Still can't believe these are all yours." Evan went crazy.

Sean glanced over. "Yes. I'm thinking of selling all of them. Maybe keep the G-Wagon. It's the only one that seems practical."

Following Ben through the open door leading to the lower level, passing the bar and TV area, he moved along to the main staircase, accented by stone boulders on the floor and some seemingly suspended in the air.

Ascending to the main level, Sean stopped there. "Does everybody want to change out of these clothes into something more comfortable before having dinner?"

"Wait. No." Evily stopped everyone in their tracks. "Can we get a few pictures together since we're all dressed so nicely?"

"Ahh, Mom," Evan complained. "Can't you just select one from social? I'm sure there are a million to choose from."

"Please... For me," his Mother pleaded.

Evan couldn't say no to her. "Fine."

Max took hold of Evily's phone while she and the teens posed for the camera.

Sean stayed to the side, prompting Evily to say, "Aren't you joining us?"

Hesitating before stepping into the frame, the actor felt privileged to be in the pictures.

Hildy and Michelle looked on, so happy for their boss. Each had a whimsical expression.

"This is just wonderful," Hildy tearfully expressed to Michelle.

Exhaling, Michelle said, "Yes, it's so romantic."

After Evily got the photos she wanted, the teens went upstairs to the second floor separately, leaving Evily and Sean in the foyer.

"Make sure you neatly hang everything up," their Mother bellowed.

"Okay!" They both replied, already out of sight.

Evily turned to Sean and asked, "Are you changing then?"

"Yes. Absolutely."

About to move up the stairs, Sean held Evily's hand a little tighter and playfully pulled her back, swaying her beautifully, practicing a few smooth waltz moves learned years ago for an eighteenth-century film. Elated, she giggled, entirely smitten by the handsome man who stole her heart. He was so happy to see she loved to dance, too.

Stumbling upon the couple while going about their duties, the ladies of the house whispered to themselves before shyly moving along to offer them some privacy.

With her wrapped in his arms, he said, "Thank you for joining me today. Despite all the attention, did you have fun? You did wonderfully, you know."

"Well," she laughed, "I don't know if I would call that fun, but it was nice to get dressed up and greet your fans. Truthfully, I felt like a princess today. I don't know how I could ever thank you for everything you've done for us." Evily choked up.

Lifting her chin with his hand, he said, "No, thank yous required. I would do anything for you, Ella, and Evan." Their eyes met lovingly.

Sean pulled her even closer. Leaning in, he kissed her lips, making her feet seemingly float off the floor. Parting, he happily pointed out, "And just for the record, they are now our fans."

Hearing the kids' voices in the upper hallway, Sean respectfully broke away from Evily. "Guess we should go and change now, too?"

She nodded, still in disbelief of the man standing before her. While climbing the stairs, hand in hand, she lifted the hem of her dress gracefully. At the top, Sean turned right while Evily veered left. With outstretched arms, letting go of each other at the last second, Evily found herself not wanting to be separated from him - ever.

59

Thursday, August 1st
Los Angeles, California

I want to be with you until my last page. ~ A. R. Asher

That evening, everyone gathered at the dining table for dinner. The air above was light with laughter and conversation while the Andersons got to know the ladies of the house, Marianna, Hildy, and Michelle. Sean watched how Evily interacted with them. Able to seamlessly blend in, it was like they'd all been friends for a lifetime. He wondered if she would share her gift with the ladies one day. Especially Hildy. Knowing her husband had passed away many years ago, he'd give anything for her to have the experience he did with Janie.

Sitting quietly at the head of the table, Sean sat back and scanned the faces of each person surrounding him. Thankful not to be eating alone, this was one dinner he wouldn't take for granted. Grateful for his blessings, there was a glimmer of the life he always wanted. His heart felt full, solidifying his decision from the day before.

By eleven-thirty, having had the most magical day from start to finish, the teens said goodnight to everyone and went off to their rooms. Behind the bar, Sean topped up their glasses of red wine before walking over to Evily, who was lounging on the sectional.

Handing it to her, he said, "A toast," raising the glass to meet hers. "To a memorable day..."

"...with many more to come," she interjected.

Their glasses clinked gingerly with a ting. Taking a sip, Evily looked from one side of the house to the other. "Why would you want such a big house for just you?"

He quickly scanned the ample space and said, "I don't know. This place checked many boxes. It has enough square footage to sprawl when I need it. After wrapping a movie, I don't like being in close quarters."

"Good to know," she said.

"I practically live in a hotel room the whole time when I'm not on set." He thought more about what she asked. "This house has enough room for the security and house staff. It helps them out and gives them a roof over their heads. But really, I fell in love with the view. It kind of feels like I'm on top of the world here."

"Yes. It does," she wholeheartedly agreed.

"Speaking of which, care to visit the rooftop terrace? The skyline is pretty clear tonight. The city will look like diamonds, I'm sure."

Sean stood up and offered his hand. Mindful of their wine glasses, he led Evily up the glass staircase to the second floor. At the top, they went left before swinging open a heavy door. Holding it, he prompted her to go first while they ascended the outdoor staircase. Greeted by the wind rustling the leaves in the nearby trees, keeping his sights on her, Sean watched as Evily found something even more beautiful than the city lights shining brightly. All decorated with tall potted trees draped with mini lights twinkling in the breeze, the illuminated slate terrace had lanterns of various sizes grouped in threes, with pillar candles nestled inside to create the most romantic backdrop. Lost for words, she could smell the heavenly aromatic scent from the many bouquets of white lilies, hydrangea, and roses accented by greenery and ivy. Her eyes flashed with wonderment, making him smile while gently guiding her to the glass railing. A champagne bucket stood a few feet away from that spot.

"Sean?" Evily was barely able to speak.

"I hope the right words come to mind. I didn't rehearse what I wanted to say. Figured I would speak from my heart," he revealed while gathering his thoughts. Nervously caressing his thumbs across the tops of her hands, he said, "Evily, the past week has been nothing short of miraculous and life-changing for me. Despite knowing you only a short time, I feel we've grown leaps and bounds. You've continued to captivate me since our eyes met in your hotel lobby. Initially, not be-lieving in your special talents, you persevered and proved me wrong at every turn. Minute by minute, you drew me into a life of faith and gifted me the most extraordinary experience I could ever wish for. You did this selflessly to help a stranger, and I'm so grateful. Because of you, Janie and Ella were able to settle my soul and give me closure. I feel enormous peace and best of all - they brought me you. Through all the ups and downs we've had, I first thought of you as a friend, but now, that has grown into a love we both share. I stand humbly before you - not as Sean Bradley, the famous actor, but as a happy man hopeful for the future. I thought it fitting to say these things under a ceiling of stars tonight - in this place where our world meets the next."

Getting down on one knee, he pulled something from his pocket. In disbelief, he presented Evily with the most brilliant Neil Lane diamond ring sparkling in the dim light. Trembling uncontrollably, she wiped away the blissful tears flowing down her cheeks with her right hand while Sean took hold of her left. Pausing a moment, smiling, with eyes affixed to hers, he asked, "Evily Landy, will you do me the greatest honor of becoming my wife? I do not wish to live another day without you by my side. I promise to be true to you, protect you, and love you forever. I will be a strong fatherly figure for Evan and Ella. No matter their future struggles and successes, I will cheer them on as you have, supporting and protecting them through thick and thin, offering unconditional love. In front of hundreds of witnesses in the heavens above, I hope, and pray, that you say yes."

Tearfully nodding her head, almost unable to speak, Evily was able to whisper the word, "Yes." Filled with emotion, she watched him slip the ring on her finger.

Rising off his knee, they shared an abundance of celebratory kisses under the starry night sky. Out of the blue, a joyous commotion suddenly erupted.

"Woohoo!" Evan and Ella hollered. They had watched and recorded the whole thing from the spiral staircase nearby.

Max, Hildy, Marianna, Michelle, Ben, Ivan, and Chef Stan appeared within seconds. Sean had let them in on the surprise an hour earlier. Gathered silently, hidden from sight, the group had heard everything.

"Congratulations!" they all said, simultaneously converging on the newly engaged couple and embracing them with abundant love.

Max stood with his hands pressed flat together. "Now, I have a wedding to plan. I am so excited!" he said with ideas already parading through his mind.

Sean immediately noticed Ella's enthusiasm and remembered he had yet to give the young girl her gift.

To get her attention, he said, "So, my dear Ella, earlier today, Evan got a special surprise. Now, it's your turn," Sean said. "I have something for you too."

"What? What is it?" She was super excited.

"Well, hmm, let's just say a good friend of mine will be stopping by tomorrow afternoon for a visit. If I'm not mistaken, rumor has it he is your idol, Mr. McClair. I told him all about this talented young architect I found, and he is dying to meet you."

Overwhelmed, Ella teared up. Raising her hands, she covered her mouth and looked at her mom before returning her sights to the Hollywood star. "Really? Truly?" she squeaked.

"Yes. Really, truly. I promised I'd arrange for you to meet him, didn't I?"

Ella nodded and approached with open arms.

Hugging her tightly, he said, "And I keep my promises."

"Thank you," she whispered. "This day has been so special, not just for my Mom, but for all of us."

"Well, I'm glad. It's been pretty special for me, too."

Evan looked on, so happy for his sister.

But Sean wasn't done yet. "And, Mr. Evan, I just got word that you'll have to get up early in the morning...like before eight."

"Why? What's happening?" Evan hung on every word.

"Well, Coach McLellan requested your presence at the team's morning skate. Don't worry, I'll be the guy in the stands offering encouragement and support - from the bench, that is."

"No.... For real?" Evan knew he wasn't joking.

Evily marveled at the man who had mysteriously entered their life not long ago.

Catching her glance his way, he approached with open arms. "Sure you want to be Mrs. Evily Landy slash Bradley?" he asked, holding her tightly.

Evily shook her head, not pleased with the suggestion.

Confused, he did not know what to say. Thinking about it, he boldly made another suggestion. "Mrs. Sean Bradley, then?"

"That is much better," she beamed.

Sean was so honored by that. Looking around, seeing so many joyous faces, he knew it was the beginning of their new life.

60 █

Friday, August 16th
Chicago, Illinois

Still reeling from their whirlwind trip to California, the Anderson family was back in Chicago two weeks later, having to return to reality. Photos of #TheBradleyBunch's magical outing spread quickly. It seemed overnight they'd become a household name. Not wasting a minute, each of them used this new platform for the greater good, compiling an extensive list of charities and organizations they'd be collaborating with for years to come.

Evily got used to all the attention, and eventually, it became part of their new normal. Inspired, she kept up her writing while separated from Sean, who continued to fly back and forth from LA to Chicago, tying up loose ends before entering semi-retirement. He hired David and Tim to protect the family in Chicago, while Ben and Ivan stayed with him during the transition.

The teens' lives changed dramatically from that point forward. Their global popularity fueled a series of social media vlogs geared at bringing awareness to the specific causes near and dear to their hearts. Ella's charities included homeless teens, orphans in foster care, and her fight against animal cruelty. Evan focused on environmental ocean protection and clean-ups, animal shelters, and fostering youth hockey programs. He was thankful for the added attention from the scouts, especially the LA King's affiliate, Ontario Reign. Within a month, he had received countless athletic scholarship opportunities making his dreams of playing NCAA hockey and earning an education well within his grasp.

Ella continued conversing with her idol, Paul McClair, via email and video chat. Impressed by her advanced design capabilities, he offered the straight-A honor student a remote-learning apprenticeship over the next few years until she graduated high school. Years from now, he had every intention of hiring her when she finished university. An opportunity Evily knew her daughter would embrace with all her being.

For the next month, Max was in full-scale wedding planning mode. Evily and Sean were excited to host the event for a few close family and friends at their newly purchased property on Keene Lake in Barrington Hills, Illinois - a picturesque suburb nestled amongst forests and lakes, located an hour outside Chicago. The majestic, gated location would soon become their new home.

61

Friday, August 30th
Chicago, Illinois

When telling the story about your life, don't let anyone else hold the pen. ~ *Rebel Thriver*

A month after the premiere, on a Friday afternoon, sitting in her study with many entities flying fleetingly above her head, Evily finalized the last chapters of her newest book. Printing off the pages, thankful to be finished, she placed the cover design page on the top of the stack. Binding it together with elastics, she got ready to leave. It was an important day.

Scheduled to meet with her literary agent Dani and publicist Angela in the bustling city of Chicago, Evily walked outside to find David waiting adjacent to a chauffeur-driven SUV parked in the driveway. Within minutes, they were on their way into the busy downtown core.

The manuscript stayed on her lap the entire time. She ran her hands over it, recalling the story so near and dear to her heart. Releasing this book was not her idea but Sean's. Every night, Evily recorded their love story as it happened. The good, the bad, and every unfathomable supernatural piece in between. They both agreed that people should know about their experiences and the existence of the afterlife. They hoped it would ignite someone else's faith, maybe settle another's soul. Their story needed to be shared.

Stopping in front of the office building, clutching her new manuscript tightly, Evily walked with David alongside her.

When the elevator opened on the twelfth floor, she immediately spotted Angela waiting for her.

"Hello!" Evily said as the woman approached with open arms.

"Evily Landy! How are you?" Angela looked at her strangely. "Wow. You look different."

"How's that?" she questioned her observation.

"A woman in love always glows brightly. Now let me see that ring," she giggled.

Evily presented her hand as the woman gushed. "It's beautiful, Ev! Congratulations."

"Yes, the past month has been nothing short of a fairy tale."

Angela was aware of all the media attention. "I'm so excited for you and the kids. You deserve all the happiness in the world. Am I on the guest list? I better be," she laughed.

"Yes, of course you are. Thank you for the support, Ang. I really appreciate it."

Nodding and crying joyful tears, Angela let her client lead the way into the literary agent Dani's office.

"Evily Landy!" Dani enthusiastically greeted, liking all the recent press coverage their firm had received. Hugging her most successful author to date and doing the same with Angela, she said, "I see you've been managing all the Bradley Bunch hype quite well."

"Yes, it's been an adjustment, but we are doing fine."

The women had a seat in the large corner office. It didn't take long for Dani to spy the manuscript in Evily's hands. Straight down to business, she asked, "So, what do you have for me?"

The author handed over the fully edited copy with a cover already designed with her new name proudly printed along the bottom.

"Oh... This isn't the title I thought you were bringing me."

"No, but I think you will like it more."

"The Orb's Gift from Heaven by E. Bradley?" Dani read, looking over the professional-looking cover. "You're changing your name?"

"No, just coming out of the shadows," she smiled.

"What's it about?"

"You'll see," Evily said, wanting to leave it at that.

Both she and Angela knew meetings with Dani were always short and sweet.

"Happy Reading," the author said in closing before wistfully walking out the door, leaving the woman in suspense. Glancing back, Evily noticed she had already started reading the first chapter.

Reclining her chair, the woman called out to her secretary, "Louise! Hold all my calls!"

About to leave the downtown core that day, she blended amongst the crowds of people from all walks of life and wondered how many of them truly held on to faith. She'd written the last book for one man, but this new story—this labor of love—was destined to span the globe. It would be a beacon of hope for those who needed it most, just as Sean experienced.

After years of hiding behind the written word, Evily was finally ready to share her gift openly, her heart unburdened. Glancing skyward beyond the towering buildings, she saw a rainbow smile breaking through the clouds. It was another unmistakable sign.

As she stood there, her thoughts turned to Sean, the man who had restored her faith in love. Ready to walk down the aisle and marry him, she thought of Janie and Ella, knowing they would be there to bless their union.

"Thank you," she whispered tearfully, her voice trembling with emotion. The words were seemingly too small for the gratitude swelling inside her, but she spoke them anyway, hoping they were enough.

Light as a feather, Evily finally felt free. Her children were thriving, having stepped into their own spotlights, and she was days away from the joy she had once thought was impossible. After enduring so much pain and suffering, she could finally say that she was truly at peace.

Before slipping into the SUV, her hand instinctively covered her heart, where Janie and Ella's presence was forever etched. Only now did she fully understand—for years, they had never left her side. The two had been with her all along, guiding her through every heartbreak and triumph, leading her to the life she now shared with Sean.

"Will you stay with us?" she whispered, her words carrying upward.

At that moment, as the sunlight brightened and wrapped around her, Evily got her answer. She knew *The Orb's Gift from Heaven* had not only freed her from the past but had guided her to a level of happiness she had always dreamed of. Eternally grateful, she promised to keep Janie and Ella's memories alive and cherish what they had given her by living it with gratitude, purpose, and boundless love.

"Faith is the assurance of things hoped for, the conviction of things not seen."

— Hebrews 11:1

THE END